Longlisted for the 2011 James Tiptree, Jr., Award

A 2011 Best Book of the Year from Fantasy Book Critic,
January Magazine, SF Signal, The Booksmugglers,
The Mad Hatter's Bookshelf, and more

One of Amazon's Best Science Fiction/Fantasy Books
of September 2011

"*All Men of Genius* is utterly charming. A large ensemble cast revolves around the central character, Violet Adams, as smoothly as gears in a precision clock. Like the best steampunk, it feels as though it were written in a much older time. Witty, dashing, and a little bit dangerous." —Mary Robinette Kowal, author of Nebula and Locus Award nominee *Shades of Milk and Honey*

"*All Men of Genius* is filled with a contagious joyful abandon." —Angela Zeman, author of *The Witch and the Borscht Pearl*

"Rosen writes with color and verve, particularly in his descriptions of mechanical marvels, and also offers moments of unexpected poignancy." —*Kirkus Reviews*

"A charming and fast-paced debut . . . Fans of Shakespeare and Wilde will delight in the transformation of the source material into something wholly original." —*RT Book Reviews*

"This tale of cross-dressing, science, romance, and rampaging automatons, complete with a host of quirky professors that may remind readers of those in the Harry Potter series, will delight teen readers, as will the rough-and-tumble descriptions of college life, with the young men's focus on sex and drinking. . . . The romance will appeal to recent teen fans of Gail Carriger's Parasol Protectorate series. . . . A brilliantly fun novel." —*School Library Journal's* Adult Books 4 Teens

"*All Men of Genius* is a true steampunk novel, a romance, a mystery, and a fun romp through an alternative Victorian England . . . a fast-moving, joyful experience that will leave the reader thoroughly satisfied." —*Seattle Post-Intelligencer*

ALL MEN
of
GENIUS

Lev AC Rosen

TOR®

A TOM DOHERTY ASSOCIATES BOOK
New York

ALL MEN OF GENIUS

Copyright © 2011 by Lev AC Rosen

Edited by Liz Gorinsky

A Tor Book
Published by Tom Doherty Associates, LLC
175 Fifth Avenue
New York, NY 10010

www.tor-forge.com

Tor® is a registered trademark of Tom Doherty Associates, LLC.

The Library of Congress has cataloged the hardcover edition as follows:

Rosen, Lev AC.
    All men of genius / Lev AC Rosen.—1st ed.
        p. cm.
    "A Tom Doherty Associates book."
    ISBN 978-0-7653-2794-9
    1. Women science students—Fiction.   2. College students—
Fiction.   3. London (England)—Fiction.   4. Steampunk fiction.
I. Title.
    PS3618.O83149A79 2011
    813'.6—dc22

                                                    2011021544

ISBN 978-0-7653-2795-6 (trade paperback)

First Edition: October 2011
First Trade Paperback Edition: November 2012

Printed in the United States of America

0   9   8   7   6   5   4   3   2   1

Shakespeare, twins, and mad science?

Clearly, it's for Lauren.

Author's Note

THIS novel is a work of fiction. Even though it may contain characters eerily similar to historical figures, who also happen to share their names, it should in no way be read as an actual historical account, and most definitely should not be used for educational purposes.

Additionally, any or all depictions of, or suggestions about, science, or the way anything in the world works on a physical, chemical, biological, astronomical, or atomic level should not be analyzed for accuracy, as I'm sure it would be sorely lacking.

Furthermore, I don't recommend emulating the behavior of any of the characters contained within. They're all quite mad.

The truth is, I have no idea what I'm talking about.

Except about love. We all know a little about that. Or nothing at all. In any case, we're all on equal footing.

I quite agree with Dr. Nordau's assertion that all men of genius are insane, but Dr. Nordau forgets that all sane people are idiots.

—*Oscar Wilde*

ALL MEN
of
GENIUS

PROLOGUE

THE two men sat silently in the carriage. The heat was stifling, but the windows were not open, and the carriage was not moving. The younger man shifted his feet anxiously and risked a glance upward. He could feel sweat dripping down his neck. "That was very kind, sir, what you did for my son."

"It was a triviality," the older man said. His hands clutched the knob of his cane, and he stared at the carriage window, though the curtains were drawn. "Something to distract him and your wife while I took you away for a short while. I haven't used that key in years. It's my fail-safe, in case I forget the others." He looked down at the large bronze ring on his finger and twisted it. The younger man looked at his own hand, adorned with a matching ring. "Those locks have all been changed so many times, I'm not sure it even works any longer."

"He'll enjoy it anyway, sir, I'm sure."

The older man sighed. "He's a smart one. If things . . . It's all ending, Volio. Bonne has returned to his island and vanished. Canterville is dead, probably at Rastail's hands. Voukil hasn't been heard from in years. And Knox . . ." The older man looked up at the drawn window again. "I had to kill Knox myself last night."

"Sir?" Volio gasped.

"Poison in his tea. It looked like a heart attack. He was determined to enact that damned plan. Nothing was in place for it; none of us agreed on it. It would have failed, and failed spectacularly. It would have brought the Queen and her guard down on all of us, on all scientists, and on Illyria. I could not have that."

"I . . . understand," Volio said, looking down.

"It doesn't matter if you understand or not," the older man said.

"It's ending. There are just a handful of us left, and I'm nearly done for, anyway. I'll be gone in a year or two—"

"Sir, no—"

The older man's ferocity flared up. "Don't interrupt." He tapped his cane on the ground. For a moment, the air in the carriage seemed to stir.

"I'll be gone in a year or two, and then my son will take over Illyria. He knows nothing of us. And I want it to remain that way. When I am done, so is our Society. You may attempt to keep together the rags of what is left. Teach your sons, if they're hard enough." The older man coughed, and then looked at his hands. "Mine isn't. But keep it secret. Our goals . . . they are good goals, just, and right." He stared at Volio. "But they must be carried out in secret. Our Society has failed. For now, anyway. Perhaps in the future, someone will get it right."

Volio nodded.

"That is all I have come to say. Leave me now."

Volio gratefully hopped out of the coach and into the warm, fresh air. He mopped the sweat from his brow with a handkerchief and turned to look at the coach. It was a great bronze thing, totally enclosed, with black curtains and tinted glass. On the back was the seal of Illyria: a shield with a gear inside it.

The coach was of the older man's design. It required no horses, just a man in front who shoveled coal into a boiler and turned a wheel to direct the coach's movements. He nodded once at the coalman, who began shoveling, then drove the horseless carriage away amid vents of steam and the sound of aching metal. Volio sighed and went inside to enjoy his son's birthday.

✦◉✦

INSIDE the coach, the man with the cane sank back into the velvet-lined seats. Even though it was hot, he was old, and his bones were always chilly. The coach ran smoothly and quickly back to London, where it stopped in front of Illyria College. He used his cane to climb slowly out of the carriage, but instead of going through the front door, he turned toward the garden and opened a small hidden doorway in the wall of the school. It was a clever door, one he had installed himself to make his comings and goings harder to track. From the outside, the door looked like part of the wall, solid stone, a few ornamental carvings of gears and faces of great inventors. But a simple tug on the nose of the gargoyle with the face of Robert Barron caused the bricks to creak forward.

He crept down the shadowy stairs inside. He wound up in the basement, which smelled of chemicals, metal, and water. He walked the twisting passages without the aid of a torch and came at last to a great underground train station with a small train waiting at the platform. He had designed it all—the station, the train, the labrynthine basement, the college itself. And now he was dying, and there was no one left who knew it as well as he did. Instead, he had torn up his knowledge into a puzzle, giving each person only a piece of it. The assembled picture, he knew, was too much for any one person to handle without feeling like a god. And the time for such man-made gods was over. Aboveground, in the college proper, his son would rule when he passed on, but here, below, this train . . . he hoped his son would never need to know about it.

It was hard work for the old man, but he slowly began disabling the train. He locked the brakes in place so it would not move, and hid the locks. It took hours to finish, and by then, he was tired and dirty, covered in sweat and grease worn like warpaint. No one would be able to enter the tower now, not even members of the Society. That part of him was locked away and safe.

He headed back to the entrance to the basement, and from there, into the lift, which took him back up to the college. The lift was in a corner, out of sight from the rest of the college, but he was careful stepping out, making sure no one could see him. He walked through the bronze halls slowly. It was late by now, and he didn't want to rouse people from their beds.

"Algernon?" came a voice as he headed toward his living quarters. "Algernon, you're filthy." The woman who came forward was younger than he, but not young. She had gray stripes through her dark hair.

"Ada," he said.

"What have you been doing? Where have you been? You missed

supper. Ernest and Cecily were frightened, so I made up a story about you working on something in your lab. . . ."

"I think," Algernon said, "I think I need to go take a bath."

"Well, you certainly do. You're covered in dirt and you smell like oil. What have you been doing?"

"It's not important now," Algernon said. "Just let me take a bath, and leave me in peace."

"Fine," Ada said, crossing her arms, "I'll walk you to your chambers. But you had best tell me everything you've been up to when you're clean."

"I don't answer to you, woman," he said, not kindly.

"No, I suppose you don't. Which is part of your problem. Find your own way to your chambers, then." She walked away from him, down the hall, stomping her feet angrily. He almost called after her, but didn't. Instead, he slowly made his way to his quarters, and, once there, to his private bathroom. He was nearly done.

I.

VIOLET and Ashton's father was leaving for America to help decide where time should begin. It was Violet's duty to retrieve her brother and bring him to the door to say good-bye, but he was not paying her any attention. Instead, he was absorbed in his piano playing. If she had been luckier, she thought, her twin brother would have inherited her father's obsession with time, at least insofar as learning to play the piano with some sense of it.

"Ashton!" she shouted. He ignored her. "Ashton!" she shouted more loudly. She was standing by his shoulder. He could clearly hear her, but was pretending not to.

"If music be the food of love, play on!" Ashton yelled over his rackety playing. Then he attempted to sing the same lines along with the music—to think of it as "in tune with the music" would imply that the music had a tune. Violet, impatient, tapped him on the shoulder with a little force.

Ashton finally stopped playing and turned to look at his sister. "I think I play the piano rather well. Perhaps not technically well . . ."

"Or well at all," Violet said, smiling.

"If I were speaking to someone who was about to do me a very large favor—indeed, who was about to assist me in a most unorthodox scheme—I think perhaps I'd be a little nicer."

Violet narrowed her eyes. She did need his help, so she forced a falsely cheerful smile. "Anyone can play technically well, brother," she said sweetly. "But you play with real feeling."

"Thank you," Ashton said with a large grin. "Your compliments mean ever so much to me."

"Father is about to leave, and we must say good-bye."

"Ah," Ashton said, and closed the piano. He stood, took Violet's arm, and walked with her toward the door. The two of them were as attractive a pair as two seventeen-year-olds of fine English breeding could be. Violet was a lovely specimen of her sex, with dark auburn hair, which always seemed to have the look of having been blown in the breeze for a while. She was fair, with rosy cheeks, and though she was a bit tall, she had a fine, womanly figure. Her strong-jawed oval face showed her great intelligence in both the sparkle of her clear gray eyes and the sharply arching smirk of her bow-shaped lips. She seldom took pains with her appearance, and so possessed a carefree beauty that would not have been out of place in a gothic romance of the sort she loathed. Ashton, also with pale skin and auburn hair, had a more dandyish appearance—as carefully dressed as Violet was careless. He often carried a cane, and wore outlandish bespoke jackets made by a tailor in London.

Their father, Dr. Joseph Cornwall Adams, was one of the leading astronomers in the country, and Violet and Ashton had grown up crawling the winding tower of stairs to the observatory on the top of their manor, where they would stare at the various devices that moved lenses and recorded images of the night sky. But each of the children had learned different things from this. Ashton had focused on the romance of the stars and the night sky, and as he grew, devoted his energies to poetry and the arts, whereas Violet saw the brass instruments her father used and decided she would be the next to design such devices. By the age of eight she had fashioned herself a lab in the basement of the manor, where she taught herself the Great Principles of the Sciences: natural, chemical, and especially mechanical. To deny her genius would be to deny the truth, for she was truly gifted. Since then she had managed to create many marvelous inventions, much to the delight of her brother and the chagrin of Mrs. Wilks, their governess.

Ashton and Violet headed to the entry foyer and watched the servants load their father's coach in the rain. It was difficult for Violet to hold still, as she was anxious for her father to go. It was not that she wanted him gone—in fact, she already missed him, and was sad at his parting—but she had spent the past few weeks orchestrating a great scheme, which would help her to fulfill her dreams, and she could not begin it until her father had left.

"Children," Mrs. Wilks said from behind them, "come away from the door. It's a little drafty, and you'll catch cold." She beamed at them until they moved away. She had been their governess since birth, and their mother's maid and friend before that. She had named the twins after their mother died in childbirth, and had raised them as a foster mother. And though she was filled with love for them, she was also filled with worry. Consequently, the twins often regarded her as they would a maiden aunt who loved them nearly to the point of suffocation and would have preferred they stay safe, probably bundled with many quilts and tied to their beds, where nothing bad would ever happen to them and where she could spoon-feed them her love and possibly also homemade pea soup.

When the carriage was loaded outside, the three of them looked up the stairs as if expecting Mr. Adams to appear with a flourish, bid them all good-bye, leap out the door and into the coach, and drive it away himself. Had that actually happened, however, they all would have fainted from shock, as Mr. Adams was not one for flourish. A moment later, Mr. Adams came carefully down the stairs, holding a bulging briefcase in one hand and a few loose papers in another. He read them as he walked, trusting his feet to find the next step.

"Father, do be careful," Violet said.

"Ah. Violet, Ashton, Mrs. Wilks," he said, as if he were surprised to see them all standing there.

"The coach is ready, sir," Mrs. Wilks said. "If you don't leave soon, you'll miss the airship."

"Ah, well, I have time to say good-bye, don't I?" Mr. Adams asked. Mrs. Wilks nodded.

"Are you excited, Father?" Violet asked, giving him a hug. "America must be wondrous."

"Indeed, I am rather excited. Not just to see America, but also for the conference. All the great minds in the field of astronomy and cartography will be there. It seems a great number of them feel that the proper place to put the First Meridian is in Greenwich. Ha!" And here he laughed a little; a sweet, cheerful, sort of coughing laugh, suitable to a man of his years and his temperament. "It is a good thing that we will have a global meridian, of course, but it was a mistake placing England's in Greenwich. I certainly hope we can fix that by placing it somewhere else for the entire globe." He smiled, making the creases around his eyes wrinkle into deep lines. Violet smiled also, for her father's amusement made her happy. He was a short man, about fifty years of age, with a long, gray, bushy mustache. His shoulders were often thrown back a little too far, and his chin was always a little too high, perhaps stuck that way from constantly gazing up through his telescope. His clothes were usually shabby and too loose, but he knew how to dress himself well if he were going to meet anyone outside the household. His eyes, once a sharp gray like his children's, had become softened and blurry over time, like dissolving clouds. He blinked perhaps more often than is common, and sometimes had to force himself to smile, because in truth, although he loved his children, he always felt a little sad for having lost their mother, whom he had loved more than the stars.

"Will you bring me back an arrowhead?" Ashton asked, also hugging his father.

"One for me as well!" Violet said.

"Oh? Well, yes, if I find any."

"You're going to be there a year. The conference won't take that long, will it?" Violet asked.

"Well, the conference doesn't even start until October of 1884. But there are a series of smaller conferences beforehand, and some ridiculous social meetings of various astronomers. . . ." Mr. Adams looked off distantly, as if dreading interacting with his peers.

"So you can explore! And bring us back arrowheads," Ashton said, satisfied.

"I'll see what I can do. Now, you children must promise to be good, and listen to Mrs. Wilks." Their father smiled, and they smiled back. They needed him to be comfortable and trusting for what they had planned next. Luckily, he *was* comfortable and trusting, and his head was so filled with the night sky that he couldn't see the small deceptions his children would sometimes practice on him.

"Actually, Father, Ashton and I have decided to spend the season in London."

"Well, Mrs. Wilks will go with you, then."

"Oh no, Father. Mrs. Wilks needs to stay here to look after the manor. I'll get a maid more suited to city life. One who knows the most modern hairstyles, and about dresses and hats and things."

"Hats?" her father asked.

"I know about hats," Mrs. Wilks said.

"I hear they're very fashionable. Last time he went to the city, Ashton brought me back a gray top hat with a green ribbon and a white veil. He says all the women were wearing them." Ashton nodded.

"Were they? Well . . . I haven't really noticed."

"Mrs. Wilks knew nothing about it, either. So you can see why I'll need a new lady's maid."

"I know about hats *now*," Mrs. Wilks said, crossing her arms.

"I suppose," Mr. Adams said, a finger on his chin.

"This seems a sudden decision," Mrs. Wilks said, frowning. "Perhaps we could discuss it more thoroughly through the post. The children and I will send you a note explaining why they want to spend the season in town—"

"I want to spend the season in town so that I am ready to come out at the end of the year," Violet said, batting her eyelashes.

"Come out?" Mr. Adams's eyes shone with happiness. Finally, his daughter was going to start behaving like a proper girl, get married, and give him grandchildren, which he secretly desired, because he loved the way babies smelled like flour, and how they would reach out and touch all his astronomical instruments because the stars were still new to them. He had been hinting around the subject for years, afraid to suggest it, in case she was offended. But now, she had decided upon it herself, and he could already imagine the tiny grandbabies in his arms. At that moment, he would do anything for his daughter. He blinked, and planted a kiss on her forehead. "If those are your plans, dear child, then you should enact them. Mrs. Wilks, you shall tend to the household here. Come February, Violet will find a maid in town, and her brother shall take over the sometimes difficult task of guarding her reputation. Doesn't that sound wonderful? You can have a break from them."

"I don't know, sir—," Mrs. Wilks said, raising her hand up as if to stop the conversation from going any further.

"Oh, don't worry so much, Mrs. Wilks. I promise to be very good," Violet said, lowering her eyes. She would need to be in town long before February, but Ashton had a plan for that. "And I will write to you every Sunday so you know we're safe and sound. You should stay here, though, and rest. Think of how hectic the season is in London, and how it would afflict your nerves."

"My nerves are quite fine, I think," Mrs. Wilks said.

"Don't worry, Mrs. Wilks," Mr. Adams said, clapping her on the shoulder. "They'll be quite all right."

"If you say so, sir." Mrs. Wilks looked more anxious than usual. She started to twist a stray brown curl around her finger.

"And I know they will look after each other. You will, won't you? A girl with your sister's beauty is liable to catch the attention of all the rogues in London. You must pay careful mind that she is always on guard."

"I'll watch out for her, Father," Ashton said. Violet held back a snicker at this. "In fact, I was thinking that in order to better acquaint her with how the season works, we could both go down to London as early as October, for the little season."

"Little season?" Mrs. Wilks asked.

"Yes," Ashton said. "It is the season before the season—attended by bankers, civil servants, and small gentlefolk who don't have estates out of town. And, more important, artists, poets, painters, literati, and the like. There will be readings and small exhibitions."

"Will that be appropriate?" Mrs. Wilks asked. "I doubt there will be many ladies among the literati."

"Why, some of the bankers have wives, and the wives of the small gentlefolk and civil servants will be there. Besides, Mrs. Wilks, you speak as though poets don't have wives, or indeed, that poets cannot be ladies."

"A woman poet is hardly a lady," Mrs. Wilks said.

"I think it's a splendid idea," Mr. Adams broke in. "It will be a good example of how ladies in society behave, even those of lesser society. We can't have you talking only about springs and levers during the season, now, can we, dear?" he said, his eyes twinkling.

"Of course not, Father," Violet said sweetly.

"Very well. You may go in October. But, Ashton, mind the art she sees is all . . . decent."

"Of course, Father," Ashton said, grinning at Mrs. Wilks, whose brow was furrowed.

"Have a safe trip, Father," Violet said. "And, if you can remember, make a note of the operating system of the airship—steam powered, I'm sure, but is the steering mechanism spring based or does it use additional tanks of compressed air? And if so, how many? And where are they located on the ship?"

"I will try to remember to find that out," Mr. Adams said, sighing. "Now, come wave good-bye to me as I go."

The three of them walked outside into the rain, which had lightened considerably. The carriage was waiting, loaded up with Mr. Adams's luggage, and pulled by two strong black steeds. Violet thought, not for the first time, how convenient it would be if her father would just buy one of the new, steam-powered coaches which did not require horses, and moved very quickly, but he had thus far denied all her requests for one.

Mr. Adams hopped into the carriage before he could get very wet. With one final look at his children, he rapped the window. The driver took off, pulling the carriage out of the courtyard and down the drive. Violet and Ashton stayed outside, Ashton even waving his handkerchief, until they couldn't see the carriage any longer.

Mrs. Wilks still stood in the doorway, her lower lip wobbling slightly. "So you're goin' to London, are you?" she asked, her eyes widening, as if already seeing the dangers that awaited them.

"Yes, Mrs. Wilks, but not till the season starts in October. So you will have us all summer!" Ashton said with a smile, then bounded forward, kissed her on the cheek, and ran inside to try his hand on the harp, which he insisted he was picking up a real talent for.

Violet tried to slip past the stunned Mrs. Wilks, but she caught her arm. "You'll be a good and proper young lady, won't you?" Mrs.

Wilks asked, putting her other hand on Violet's arm. "Your father is a good man, but he doesn't see how dangerous the city can be to a young girl. You won't do anything that might shame him?" She looked Violet up and down, a pleading look in her eye, her chin jiggling slightly.

"I'm always a good daughter," Violet said with an innocent smile. This did not fool Mrs. Wilks, who had long ago learned that mischief was native to Violet's soul. She knew Violet had a good heart, but also knew Violet was willful and independent, and not in the least bit ordinary. She loved Violet, in her way, but she also feared that one day Violet's forthright nature would land her into the sort of trouble from which Mrs. Wilks could not extricate her. So she stared at Violet a little while longer, hoping to transfer some of her own reserved nature into the girl through eye contact, until Violet smiled again, curtseyed, and left the hall, heading toward her bedroom.

The estate, called Messaline, was one of those large and traditional manses of the gentlemen scientists of the day, just outside of London. Though originally decorated in natural hues which suited the late Mrs. Adams' taste, in recent years, Ashton had made changes to modernize the décor, creating striking contrasts of ivory and ivy, brown and gold.

Though he had often tried to bring his sensibilities to Violet's bedroom, Violet insisted it remain untouched by Ashton's renovations. It was a room unencumbered by the sorts of dolls and pillows that were so often found in young ladies' bedrooms of the time. The only indication that this was in fact Violet's room was the many books piled up on her dressing table, texts by Babbage and Ada Byron, John Snow, and of course, Duke Algernon of Illyria, the great scientific mind of the age. All his books, from his first, *The Mechanics of Biology*, published in 1840, until his last, *Transplantation of Living Organs to Better God's Creatures*, published a few years after his death, lined the shelves where another girl would have kept her powder and sewing supplies. Several large, shabby notebooks were piled on her writing desk, their pages frayed and sticking out from under the worn leather covers.

Violet threw herself on her bed and withdrew a portfolio from under her pillow. She unlaced the ribbons binding it and took out the papers within, to gaze at them again. These were the application papers for Illyria College, where, if her scheme succeeded, she would be spending the coming year. Illyria was currently the best scientific college in the world. While many colleges of the day required letters of reference and banker's notes, Illyria admitted students upon proof of their scientific genius alone, and gave them a completely free education. What it did not do was admit women. Violet found this quite frustrating, as some of Illyria's counterparts, such as Cambridge, had begun accepting women into their classes, even if they could not yet get degrees. Violet had no doubt she was the equal of any male applicant of the day. This seemed so absurd and unjust that the only clear solution was to apply under her brother's name with the intention of disguising herself as him and spending the year in the guise of a man.

She was interrupted from her reverie by her brother's sudden arrival. "And so, dear sister, it begins," he said dramatically.

"Yes. Are you sure it wouldn't be better to abandon the pretense after the interview?" Violet asked, continuing a conversation from the day before. This had been Violet's plan before Ashton convinced her that she would have to stay in character for the entire first year. His variation certainly seemed more daring than hers, and she liked to be daring. However, Violet still had a great fear of bringing shame upon her family and her father's name, and dressing *travesti* was liable to bring plenty of shame with it.

Ashton answered her with a grin. "You surely couldn't shame the family any more than I plan to," he said. She laughed and embraced her brother tightly. It would be risky, but the rewards would be worth it.

"It's going to be a good year, isn't it?" Violet said.

"I certainly hope so." Ashton planned to spend the year at their town house, free to do whatever he liked as Violet wrote letters to Mrs. Wilks, assuring her of their continued good behavior. It was her brother's price for his cooperation in the scheme.

"Don't let Mrs. Wilks catch you looking at that," he said, gesturing towards the application on her bed. Violet nodded, too, and crossed to the bed, sneaking one more look as she put it away. Ashton, seeing her reabsorbed in the papers, laughed and left.

The application required, of course, a name and address, as well as educational history—Violet had written "Private Tutors," for between her father and her books, she felt she was well educated in the sciences, and because of Mrs. Wilks, knew a very little French. There was also an essay on the state of the modern sciences, and detailed plans or formulae for some scientific invention, such as a clockwork automaton, or chemical draught of invisibility, or perhaps an example of a surgery successfully resulting in the creation of a two-headed bird—or, in Violet's case, a most interesting perambulator. All the applicants who made it through the first review were expected to produce the completed product at the interview, but Violet had finished her perambulator a while ago, as a favor for Mrs. Henderson, Mrs. Wilks's sister and a nursemaid who sometimes visited the manor. Violet was still unsure that her essay, on the soon-to-come development of a mechanical aethership that would penetrate the heavens and visit distant planets, was quite up to par. But it felt well reasoned, and she had been on several steam-powered airships in her years, and had thoroughly examined their various mechanisms. She thoughtfully licked her finger and flipped through her essay one more time, though, just to be certain.

When she had finished rereading her application, and found it still met with her approval, Violet went down to the basement to work on her devilish machines. It hadn't been easy to create a laboratory in a basement that was intended to be used as a wine cellar. However, Violet knew from a young age that she would not be able to achieve scientific greatness in her bedroom, and so painstakingly directed the servants in cleaning out and remodeling the basement. There was still a small wine cellar, of course—in fact, it was all one would notice at first, if one were to go down to the basement. But there was also a door, a rather thick door, with heavy bronze hinges. From the crack under the heavy door, one might see lights flickering occasionally, as one is wont to do when staring at the door to a scientific laboratory.

The laboratory within was more cozy than one might have expected. Several candles were set about, and a large bronze potbellied stove flamed cheerfully against a wall. A wide table took up most of the space in the room, and it was strewn with books, papers, sketches, notes, and various bits of machinery and scrap metal. A few stools were set about, and one large brown armchair by the fire in which Violet would read when her hands had tired of tinkering. The whole room smelled of warm stone and heated metal, of wood and paper, and Violet loved it.

Currently, she was working on a toy. Normally, she wouldn't have bothered with such things, but she wanted to be prepared at her Illyria interview to demonstrate that she could create not only great works of mechanical genius, but also the simpler affectations of the playful scientist, clockwork dancers and the like, which would impress the soft-minded among the nobility. She had worked out all the basic principles, and created the basic constructs: a large clockwork mother duck and several rolling ducklings that would follow her path without any attachments, due to magnetized pieces that the mother duck left in a trail as she moved along on the power of her springs. However, since this was a toy, she needed to make it ornate, and so planned to spend the rest of the day doing careful metalwork and affixing glass gemstones she had pried out of the costume jewelry that Mrs. Wilks had given her as a child. The mother duck was mostly done, with sparkling green eyes and carefully engraved feathers, and even a gold-gilded beak. But the ducklings were giving her more trouble: they felt unfinished. She sat down at the table and stared at the line of unembellished ducklings. Their bodies were cast out of brass, and had only the basic shape of ducklings, supported on strong brass wheels. The mother duck's head swung back and forth as it rolled, thanks to a simple clockwork mechanism, but the ducklings were too small for that sort of effect. Violet's eyes widened as she realized that she *could* give them thin wings that flapped slightly as they rolled. She instantly opened a large sketch pad and worked out the basic structure of the wings. She could even make them out of real feathers, with simple brass wing bones. She rang the bell that hung near the door to the lab. A moment or so later, one of the younger servants came down. Violet suspected that it was only the servants who were in trouble with Mrs. Wilks who were sent down to her, as a sort of punishment. This one was a boy, a few years younger than Violet, who probably worked in the kitchens. Violet looked up at him briefly. He held his shaking hands together, and his knees were bent as though he were preparing to run.

"I need feathers," Violet said, looking back at her metal ducklings. "At least four dozen of them. By the day after tomorrow. Strong ones, not the downy sort. Preferably from a duck, but as long as they look like they're from a duck, it doesn't matter.."

The nervous serving boy nodded and left the laboratory quickly. Violet stoked the fire and got out her tools to begin fashioning the bronze wing bones.

There was little that satisfied Violet more than the feel of metal in her hand. She enjoyed conceiving of new inventions, yes, but to actually put them together and feel each cog and spring click into place, to feel her designs living and working in her hands, was what pleased her most. She had one of those rare minds that could pick out from a dozen seemingly identical springs which was strongest, which had the most flexibility, which was the most likely to break. By glancing at an inferior invention, she could tell you what was wrong with it, and how it could be repaired. She worked for a few hours, crafting three pairs of beautiful skeletal wings and attaching them to each duckling. Testing each duck, she rolled them forward and back, happy to see their little naked wings flap up and down as though they were trying to take flight.

The clock on the wall, which had kept perfect time ever since Violet designed and made it by hand at age nine, chimed seven o'clock, and Violet quickly ran upstairs and washed her hands before heading into the dining room. Mrs. Wilks served supper promptly, and became more nervous the later someone got. Violet and Ashton ate their soup with a quiet contentedness while Mrs. Wilks sat at the far end of the table, knitting with what Violet felt sure were unnecessarily long needles.

"Ashton," Violet said when her soup was half-finished, "I am going into town tomorrow, and I was wondering if you would escort me. I have visited the town house on only a few occasions, and never lived there, so I think it would be best to inspect it and see what I need to bring from home." Violet tried to sound as casual as possible. Really, she just needed an excuse to go into London without Mrs. Wilks so that she could deliver her application in person. She longed to look upon towering Illyria College, and though she doubted they would let her through the gate, she hoped that she could at least glance inside as they opened the door to take the application.

"I'll go with you," Mrs. Wilks said, not looking up from her knitting. She was not a foolish woman. There was probably some deeper scheme behind this trip, and such schemes were invariably trouble. Trouble was a great fear of Mrs. Wilks's.

"Oh no, Mrs. Wilks," Violet said sweetly, "I couldn't ask you to do that. You have so much to do here. And besides, I was hoping you would go to the dressmaker and ask for samples of various colors. I will need new dresses, after all. At least six, I would think: three for the evening, and three for daytime. Or do you think I will need more? I am so unversed in these things. I don't even know what colors look right on me, which is why I so hoped you would bring me some, so I may hold them up to my face in the mirror and decide if they suit my complexion."

Ashton snorted into his soup, trying to cover his laughter.

"We can stop by a dressmaker in London, then," Mrs. Wilks countered. "I'm sure they have plenty of fabrics in all the latest styles."

"Oh, don't be silly," Violet answered. "London dresses are so much more expensive, and we have been ordering my dresses from Mrs. Capshaw since I was a child. It would be cruel to go to someone else now, when the dresses will finally be seen by people outside the household. If you feel uncomfortable going to Mrs. Capshaw alone, Mrs. Wilks, then we can both go the day after tomorrow."

"I don't feel uncomfortable going to Mrs. Capshaw alone," Mrs. Wilks said, blinking rapidly. She could sense Violet trying to manipulate her. Like many things, this made her anxious. "Why don't you and I go into London tomorrow, and then to Mrs. Capshaw the day after?"

"Oh, Mrs. Wilks," Ashton said, grinning, "I couldn't tear you away from your duties here. I shall gladly escort my sister into town tomorrow. I was hoping to buy a new cigarette case, anyway."

"You don't smoke," Mrs. Wilks said slowly, turning her head to Ashton.

"No, but I plan to start," Ashton replied. Mrs. Wilks sighed. Against the both of them, what could she do? She would have thrown her arms up in exasperation, but such large gestures at the dinner table invariably knocked things over.

"Very well," Mrs. Wilks said. "Violet, you and I will go to Mrs. Capshaw together the day after tomorrow, and spend all day looking through her drawings and fabrics. I won't have you going to your first season in London dressed like a country girl."

"Oh, of course, Mrs. Wilks," Violet said, looking as kindly as she could, in order to soothe Mrs. Wilks's nerves. Her expression also contained some of the joy that was radiating within her at the chance to see Illyria tomorrow. It was well worth a day of being prodded by Mrs. Capshaw and inspecting seven shades of pink fabric that all seemed the same to her. She was looking forward to tomorrow, and to October, when she felt quite sure she would begin life as a student at Illyria College . . . and, incidentally, as a man.

II.

THE next morning, Violet was awake before the maid came in to rouse her. The maid, a young girl from a nearby farmhouse, was startled to find her mistress pacing in her closet. Violet almost always enjoyed sleeping in, and almost never went into her closet.

"I don't know what dress matches the top hat my brother bought for me," Violet said to the maid with a sigh. The maid, who was unused to Violet speaking to her, wasn't sure if she should answer, so instead she went about the motions of making the bed and starting up the fire in the fireplace.

"Do you know which dress should be worn with a top hat?"

Now Violet was asking her directly. She felt like a trapped animal, too frightened to speak, and not sure how to escape. She was new, but had already heard stories of Miss Violet Adams and her sinister inventions. The older maids said that they'd heard clanging at all hours of the night from the basement, and that Violet had crafted a serving man entirely of bronze, which she used to kill those servants she didn't like and for other unladylike purposes, the thought of which made the maid blush.

Violet stared at the maid, holding a top hat in one hand and tapping her foot. "Do you know which of my dresses I should wear with this?" Violet asked again.

The maid shook her head and left the room quickly. Finding Mrs. Wilks down the hall, she tugged frantically at her sleeve and told her that Miss Adams was behaving most strangely.

Mrs. Wilks's eyes widened in concern, and she took off down the hall. When she burst into Violet's room to find Violet holding the top hat and looking confused but unharmed, she breathed a deep sigh of relief.

"Oh, Mrs. Wilks, thank goodness. Could you tell me which dress I ought to wear with this hat that Ashton got for me?"

"I think that hat would be a little hot, miss, in August. Perhaps a summer hat would be more appropriate?"

"Oh, I had rather hoped to wear this hat, though, because Ashton bought it for me in London—do you really think it will be too hot?"

Mrs. Wilks was confused by Violet's apparent earnestness. Violet had not asked Mrs. Wilks her opinion on anything since childhood. She smiled and reached out for the hat. Violet gave it to her, and Mrs. Wilks rubbed the felt in between her fingers. She could tell Violet wanted to wear it, that this hat would somehow be a comfort to her, and she hated to deprive Violet of comfort.

"It will be a little hot, but this felt is thin. You should wear the green coat over the gray riding outfit with it."

"Oh, thank you, Mrs. Wilks," Violet said, and turned back to her closet. "Where are they?" Sighing again, Mrs. Wilks helped Violet dress herself, and even arranged her hair in front of the vanity, Violet rudely tapping her foot all the while. But when Mrs. Wilks's work was complete, and they gazed in the mirror at Violet's reflection, it was a pleasure to see. Violet seldom dressed up so nicely, and when she did, she appeared a real, sophisticated woman instead of some awkwardly large girl with too-fierce eyes. Violet put the hat on and studied herself in the mirror. "This is splendid," she said, and she meant it, for while she had never cared about her appearance beyond looking decent, and while she knew nothing of fabric, all ladies—in fact, all people—enjoy the look of themselves in well-tailored clothing. Mrs. Wilks was also happy to see Violet so grown up and elegant. Perhaps she hadn't let Mr. Adams down in attempting to make his little girl into a woman of whom Mrs. Adams would be proud.

"Come down to breakfast, then," Mrs. Wilks said, "and take off the hat until you are outside." Violet obeyed, excited about the day.

Her brother was already seated at the table, having helped himself to eggs, toast, and kidneys. Today he had on a fine blue suit and white shirt, with a white rose tucked into his lapel. When his sister first entered, he almost didn't recognize her, and stood up, assuming a guest had come to call. Then, looking fully at her face, he burst out in joyous laughter.

"Do I look ridiculous? Mrs. Wilks, are you playing a trick on me, dressing me like a clown?" asked Violet anxiously.

"No, sister, you look splendid, but it is quite alien to me, seeing you dressed so elegantly."

"I wanted to wear the hat you gave me," Violet said, sitting down, "and truth be told, the clothes are not uncomfortable. The corset is a little tighter than usual, yes, but it makes my back stay perfectly straight. And the bustle isn't nearly so bad as it looks." Ashton smiled and sat down again.

"You will be the toast of London," he said. Violet stuck her tongue out at him in response. "Well, I suppose we can dress you as a lady. The behavior, however, will take some teaching."

Too excited to really eat, Violet nibbled on a little bit of bread and butter, not paying much attention to it. How could Ashton take so long at breakfast, knowing what excitement she must feel? She kicked him under the table.

"All right," he said, glaring at her. "Let's call the carriage, and we'll head into town." Violet popped up from her chair like a loose spring and headed for her room to collect her things. She carefully folded her application and put it in her handbag, covering it with some money and a scarf, so no one would see it. Then she ran back downstairs, where Ashton was finishing up a cup of tea. She groaned and headed to the courtyard to meet the carriage.

The weather was much more pleasant today: the sun shining brightly over the pastorally rolling hills and trees. Mrs. Adams's garden sparkled brightly in green and purple. When the carriage drew around, it was still muddy from taking Mr. Adams to town yesterday, but the horses looked well rested, and the carriage driver, a handsome youth named Antony, looked ready for the journey.

"We're going to London, today, Antony," Violet said, hopping up into the carriage excitedly.

"I know, miss. I'm takin' you there," Antony said, and nodded.

Ashton came out of the house a moment later, strolling in far too leisurely a manner for Violet's tastes. He winked at Antony as he climbed into the carriage himself, and then, finally, they were off.

It was a long ride, a little more than an hour to London. Though she was excited, Violet was a smart enough girl to at least make an attempt at patience, even if she didn't really feel it. She spent much of the ride staring out the carriage windows, for though she did not possess her brother's poetic sensibilities, she was not immune to the romance of the natural world. She admired the great sweeping trees and the long winding brooks that babbled so peacefully, and she enjoyed the wildflowers and the green hills they passed through.

"How will you spend the day?" she asked her brother. He was gazing out the window, probably composing odes to the fields, or to the field hands.

"I will go to the town house and find out if there is anything in particular we need for the season, since you said you would be doing that. Then I may grab a pint with a few friends I have who are still in the city."

"That sounds lovely. I don't have much else to do besides deliver my application, so I may ask Antony to drive me around London a little, so I can get a feel for it."

"If you want a feel for London, then you'd do better to walk. A carriage ride through the park is all very well, but to truly know London, you should spend a little time on foot, explore the small alleyways and crannies, perhaps take the underground railway."

"I long to see the functionality of the trains beneath the city. It's rumored that the Duke of Illyria put a train station of his own design beneath the college when he built it, powered in some mysterious fashion."

"That sounds ridiculous," Ashton said.

"It may sound it, but it is quite possible, in theory."

"You scientists have created a great deal that seems as though it shouldn't work in theory. Didn't your hero, Illyria, manage to successfully create an elephant the size of a house cat?"

"Yes," Violet said, proudly.

"And Babbage's analytical engines can predict patterns the human eye cannot see?"

"Well, yes, but only if the person using the engine is a skilled reckoner. You can't just ask the engine how many people will be born in Cambridge next year. You need to know what you're doing. And Illyria's elephant actually *was* a house cat. He just took the skin of an elephant and transplanted it onto the cat, along with a trunk and large ears. It still behaved quite like a cat, jumping around and rubbing its head against things. It never once trumpeted its horn. Science has its limits."

"That sounds positively ghastly. Don't tell me stories like that anymore."

"I've never been particularly interested in the Biological Sciences, but by all accounts, the cat seemed quite happy. It loved playing with its long nose as though it were a piece of string." Ashton shuddered, but Violet continued anyway. "And it wasn't as though it were just some house cat. It was a cat that had been badly burned and lost much of its skin already. A great many biological scientists aren't so generous."

"I prefer the mechanical songbirds you can buy on street corners."

"If you want a mechanical songbird, let me make one for you. Anything you buy on a street corner will be broken within a fortnight, I'm sure," Violet said with a sigh. The carriage had reached the outskirts of London, and she could see the looming, powerful buildings, and smell the smoke in the air.

"So, the duke just had elephant skin lying around in case his cat should explode?"

"He was experimenting with using it to heal factory workers who were badly burned—he felt it was close to human skin, but tougher, more durable, and so would protect the workers better. At the time of the cat incident, though, he wasn't really ready to try the procedure yet."

"That doesn't explain giving the cat an elephant head."

"That was the suggestion of his student, Erasmus Valentine. He thought that it would be more attractive that way."

"So, did anything come of these elephant skin bandage experiments?"

"The duke died before he could try it on human subjects. No one carried on the research." Violet slumped her shoulders and looked down at the floor of the carriage.

"Well, I'm happy you're the scientist in the family. I'll stick to poetry and art, and all that nonsense."

They had entered the city. Outside were more carriages and people walking in front of them. The place smelled like smoke, sweat, and manure, but Violet didn't mind. She was closer to Illyria now. She could feel the mechanics of the place vibrating through the cobblestones and dirt to the wheels of her carriage and up through the soles of her feet, which were tapping impatiently.

"Our house isn't on the fashionable side of the park," Ashton said, "but it's not on the unfashionable side, either. It's the right sort of place, because no one is watching you, but you have a view of everyone else."

"I won't be spending very much time there, if all goes according to plan," Violet said.

Outside on the street corner was one of the mechanical bird merchants. He propped a long stick over his shoulder, carrying cages filled with little brass birds, all fluttering and singing in a repeating pattern.

"Ah," said Ashton, following her gaze, "now that you see one, you want one. Should I hop out and buy you a bird?"

"No," Violet said, still looking at the birds, frowning. She could hear the inferior quality of the birds' mechanisms. Poorly made inventions always made her unhappy.

Their carriage rolled along gradually, through the less dignified parts of town and eventually into the more dignified parts—though, according to Ashton, just because the houses were better kept didn't mean the denizens of them were.

"Lady Daphne Bertram, since the death of her husband, has been having a most obvious affair with Sir Haberdash," he said as they passed Lady Bertram's house. This was the fifth house they had passed where Ashton claimed to know intimate details of the occupants' lives.

"How do you know all this?"

"I have friends in the city, so even if I don't usually spend the whole season here, I know the gossip. It's the reason I don't spend the season here: What's the point when I already know everything? And, of course, I would hate to be away from you, dear sister." He patted her knee to demonstrate fraternal affection; Violet rolled her eyes. A few more houses, a few more scandals, and the carriage came to a stop in front of their home. She had been to the town house several times before, and it was as she remembered it. Elegant, white, a bit plain. She understood why her parents had never spent much time here; stars and flowers were far more interesting than anything these whitewashed walls could offer. The city had its charms, to be sure, but Violet preferred working in a small, dark underground laboratory in the country to working in a small, dark, underground laboratory in the city because in the country, no one—aside from the easily ignored Mrs. Wilks—would force her to dress up, do her hair, and go to dances where the people spun about like the gears and springs she wished she was working on at home. Except, of course, for Mrs. Wilks.

Antony hopped down to open the door for them, but Ashton held up a finger, and Antony turned away politely to give the twins a moment alone.

"Now, Violet," Ashton said, taking Violet's wrist. "I'm afraid I must be serious for a moment."

"Pray, don't," Violet sighed. Her brother would occasionally use this statement to preface a dreary lecture on the dangers of the world, as though he were an elder brother, and not a twin, as though she were a child who knew nothing of the world. And though she conceded that she knew little of the world, and he knew more, she did not appreciate such lectures. Normally she would half listen, supposing his dreariness to be an extension of the poetic mind, forever seeing the dark shadows of life. So she looked at the ground and prepared herself for the depressing condescension that was to come.

"Before I step out of this coach," Ashton said, "before you go and turn in that false application, you must understand something." Violet felt her brother's eyes on her, staring at her, asking her to raise her eyes to meet his. She kept her head down. He squeezed her wrist, but continued. "If you do this thing, enact this scheme, and if you are caught, it will not just mean humiliation for you and father. Dressing in a man's clothing is illegal."

"Just a misdemeanor," Violet said defensively.

"Yes. But if the current duke is embarrassed by the scandal you cause him, he can also issue charges of fraud and impersonation. Father may be a gentleman, but he is no duke. If the duke wishes, he could probably have your head."

"I'd be executed?"

"It is the worst possible outcome, yes. More likely, you would just be sent to prison for upwards of twenty years. Father would go bankrupt trying to free you, and of course, this would ruin his reputation. And that is just if the duke finds you out. I hope I need not dwell on the . . . unpleasantness that can befall a young lady surrounded by men. I just read of a Beth Kindly, who, when we were children, tried to disguise herself as a man and enter Oxford."

"I know," Violet said quietly. She had read of her as well. There had been an article in the paper two nights ago, following her release from prison.

"Her roommate discovered her and took gross advantage—"

"I know," Violet said louder, and looked up at Ashton. Her eyes were wet. "Why are you trying to frighten me so? This was your idea."

"It was an idea for a play. And it was fun to come up with it. But I need to know you understand, Violet, that if you make this idea a reality, the stakes are high. Twenty years in prison, unable to work on your inventions, Father and I selling off Messaline, you losing your youth, most of your life, or worse. Is all that worth it for one year at Illyria? Think before you answer, dear sister. I will go along with it if it is."

Violet stared down at the carriage floor. The carriage was pulled by two horses, and Violet could think of twenty better designs, better even than the horseless ones that drove about, spewing smoke and whistling. But she could not make them on her own, and even if she could, no one would ever hear about her work.

"It is worth it," she said, raising her eyes to meet her brother's.

His gray eyes stared back, cool as iron. "All right," he said, dropping her hand. "Then best of luck to us both."

She smiled. "Thank you."

Ashton opened the door to the carriage and hopped out, then looked back up at his sister. "And, Violet?"

"Yes?"

"Keep in mind also, that even if your plan succeeds, you'll be revealing yourself at the end of the year, and then some of what I have just mentioned will apply again. Think it over during the carriage ride. If you choose not to get out when you reach Illyria's gates, I will not think any less of you or your brilliance. It would be a shame to nurture your mind if in the end, it lost you your head."

Violet swallowed and nodded, unable to say anything.

"Antony," Ashton said to the coachman, "drive slowly."

"Where to, sir?" Antony asked.

"My brilliant sister," Ashton said with a pleased look, "wishes to visit Illyria, and perhaps drop off a letter there. You know where it is?"

"Yes, sir," Antony said.

"Thank you," Violet said. "And it would mean ever so much to me if you didn't mention this little side trip to Mrs. Wilks. It's perfectly innocent, I promise, I just want to see if they'll let me see the astronomy tower. I want to plan a surprise for when Father comes home, but Mrs. Wilks will think it ever so scandalous and begin to fret. Even if they don't let me through the door, which they probably won't," Violet said.

"Are you sure you don't want to come in for some tea before going out again?" Ashton asked, looking up at his sister, who was still sitting in the carriage.

"No," Violet said sternly, "I want to go see the college. It's what

I'm here for. I'm sure it won't be long. You'll still be here when I return, most likely."

"Provided you don't spend hours just gazing through the gates."

"I shan't promise anything," Violet said, and closed the carriage door. She waved to her brother from the window.

·**:❁:**·

ILLYRIA College was on the Thames, near Charing Bridge and just a little north of and across the river from the Houses of Parliament. It had been designed by Illyria himself, working with the American architect Le Baron Jenney, who devised the metal frame of the building, and with the engineer Elisha Otis, who built the mechanical lifts. The building itself was six stories high, with an astronomy dome and two large clock towers at the top. It was built directly on the river, with a huge waterwheel of Illyria's design used to power most of the laboratories in the building, as well as the elevators, the water pumps, and much of the lighting. The book Violet had read, *The Building of Illyria College*, by Caleb Leeds, had dashed through all the interesting parts about how the building worked, focusing more on its history and how the Duke of Illyria and Le Baron Jenney had gotten on, as well as people who visited it and come out saying what a lovely building it was. He also spent a few chapters on the rumors of secret meetings of brilliant scientists at Illyria, rumors that Violet found ridiculous—why would scientists need to meet in secret, after all? Violet suspected that in fact Mr. Leeds had never actually been inside the building, but it was one of only a few texts on the college, and so she had read it cover to cover, several times.

She had passed by the college in the carriage a few times, since her father loved to drive along the Thames. She had often pushed herself against the window during such rides, straining to see the complexities of the tall, polished-stone building that rose up against the water, or make out the figures on the ornate clock towers. The clocks—designed by Aaron Lufkin Dennison—were supposedly marvelous things up close, with life-sized human and animal automata that moved and sang differently according to the hour. The simpler of the clocks told the time, but the other traced the paths of the celestial world, constellations and planets all ticking along at their own pace. And each constellation had been modeled into a complex automaton by the duke, so that each corresponded to a great thinker. Leo was Leonardo da Vinci, and Capricorn was John Snow. Violet didn't know which ten other lucky minds had been chosen to adorn the heavens, but she wanted to go up to the clock towers and walk among them—a statue garden devoted to Reason and Sensibility.

Violet gazed out at London and swallowed. Her brother's warning had not been lost on her. She was smart enough to know that her plan was risky in ways she could not forsee. But she also knew she had to try. To stay locked away in the basement, working alone on her inventions, seemed too small for her now. If she ended up in prison . . . or dead . . . she could at least know she tried, and that she had been a woman worthy of Illyria. She did not want to think about what else could happen to her if she were discovered by a group of men, and so she swallowed, dabbed her brow with a hand-kerchief, and stared intently at the water, imagining gears beneath it, turning each ripple and wave. Her hands shook despite her efforts to clasp them in her lap.

The carriage stopped, and Violet stared out of the window at the gate of the college. Antony opened the door for her and helped her out. She paused to gather her bravery. The hot August sun beat down on her, and she felt that perhaps she should have listened to Mrs. Wilks and not worn the top hat. In fact, she would have pre-ferred not to wear any hat, let alone her gloves or the small jacket or the dress. She would have much preferred one of her simple white dresses that she wore in the heat of her laboratory.

"I shouldn't be long, Antony," Violet said, and set her jaw. The gates to the grounds were slightly ajar, so she pulled them aside and let herself in. It was probably a bit undignified, she thought, going alone toward this great tower, but she didn't care very much. No one of any importance was there to see her, as it was August, and besides, what would they say if they did? That she was taking in the gardens at a college? She could hear the steady, heavy sound of the water-wheel now, the half-groan of gears not sure they could handle the

stress—but they could, Violet could tell by listening—and the sound
of water, pouring over itself and splashing again into the river. It was
a steady, comforting sound, and she matched her footsteps with it,
feeling as though she belonged.

She came to the door and breathed in with awe. She was close
enough to touch the building now, to admire the careful carving
around the huge stone doorway: interlocking gears and springs
mingled with flowers and stars, blending science and nature. She
admired the building for a while before reaching out and laying her
hand on it. The stone felt cool and strong through her glove, and she
could even feel the building pulsing under her hand. She yearned
to enter, but knew that would have to wait awhile longer. Women
were forbidden within the building itself, and being discovered
within would not reflect well on her—her brother's—application.
So, she balled her hand into a small fist, grabbed at the large door
knocker shaped like a great hand holding out a gear, and knocked
as loudly as she could. She could hear it reverberating through the
halls, and then the sound of a bell ringing. It was probably a clever
device built on the vibrations of the door knocker on the other side,
Violet thought with excitement. After waiting what seemed like
forever, she raised her fist to knock again, when she heard a voice
behind her.

"I'm afraid everyone is out right now. The school is on break, so
there's very little staff, and the professors are away for the summer.
Is there something you needed help with?"

Violet turned, raising her chin, as she assumed she was being addressed by a servant. But the man behind her did not seem to be a
servant at all. Certainly, he wasn't dressed like one, in a fine gray
suit, golden tie, and a shirt of soft blue. He wasn't styled like a servant either, with rich brown hair parted neatly on one side and swept
back with oil. His eyes bespoke great intelligence and also, she half
thought, gentleness.

"I am dropping off an application for my brother," Violet said
after she realized she had let the silence hang for too long. "He is
applying to the college for next semester."

The stranger held out a hand, and Violet reached into the purse to produce her application.

"I'm Ernest," the man said. "I'm the headmaster here."

"Oh," said Violet, surprised, and extended her gloved hand for him to take. "I'm Violet Adams, Your Grace. I am a great admirer of your father and, of course, your fine institution."

She bowed her head slightly. She had read of the current duke. He was said to be a great thinker and headmaster, but he had never published a paper or produced a single noted invention. Some said he was just not his father, and knew it, and so left off inventing altogether, while others said he was the sort who could never pull his thoughts together enough to finish a project. Some simply said he was the spoiled child of a brilliant man, without an original idea of his own, but looking at him, Violet thought that maybe there was a touch of his father in him, around the eyes and chin. His mouth, though thinner than his father's, had the same half-soulful expression that she had seen in all the photographs and sketches of the late duke, but with less intensity. This duke, Ernest, was perhaps thirty, and tall, with a fair complexion and hazel eyes.

He bowed slightly over Violet's hand, then smiled at her.

"It is always a pleasure to meet an admirer of my father," he said softly.

"Well, then you must nearly always be in a state of pleasure," Violet responded, taking back her hand. It was inappropriate, she thought, to be in the company of a young gentleman without an escort. She glanced over the duke's shoulder, out past the gate and at her carriage, to see that Antony was still there, and felt a little safer when she saw him leaning against the carriage, facing them.

The duke laughed at her joke and nodded. "Yes, I often meet admirers of my father," he said, and looked down for a moment, "but seldom are they young ladies. You are dropping off your brother's application, you said?"

"Yes," Violet said, taking it out of her purse. "I told him I would do it, as he thought it might be bad luck to come here himself."

"Well, I shall bring it inside for you, as I am afraid I cannot let you in. But if you'd like, I can give you a tour of the gardens," he said, offering her his arm. Violet raised an eyebrow. A tour of the gardens would be lovely, and it would give her a chance to observe the building more closely, but she did not know this young duke, apart from his lack of reputation and various theories about him in scientific journals. While he may have had some of his father's characteristics, he might be a brute in scientist's clothing. But Violet was never one to shy away from something new, especially if it could give her some advantage, and certainly being kind to the duke would make him look favorably on her—her brother's—application.

So she took his arm, and said, "That sounds quite nice, though not as nice as seeing the inside of the college."

"You're not the first lady to say so, but I'm afraid I can't let you in. My father decreed that, like the King of Navarre, the students were to have no female companionship within."

"And there are no exceptions?" Violet asked sweetly.

The duke smiled, but looked away. "Well, my apartments are in the building itself," he said, "and my ward lives in my apartments, as does her governess. And sometimes my godmother, the Countess Lovelace—Lady Byron—comes to visit."

Violet was shocked, but tried not to let it show. She was instantly jealous of his ward, whoever she was, and even jealous of the governess, for being able to walk the hallowed halls to which she so desperately sought entry. She could not envy the Countess Lovelace though. She was one of the greatest scientific minds of the century, and deserved to be there far more than Violet did. "I am a great admirer of Lady Byron's," Violet said. "It must be an honor to have her as a godmother."

"Ah, yes. She and my father became close after he saved her life with an experimental surgery he pioneered. A few years later, I was born, and my parents thought Aunt Ada would be a good godmother."

"To have grown up surrounded by such brilliant thinkers must have been wonderful." The duke stared out at the river, then nodded slowly. They had walked to the edge of the gardens, where the river lapped against the walls of the college. The huge waterwheel turned, the water rushing over and under it. Violet stared at it awhile, studying its artful craftsmanship, the way each paddle bent at exactly the right angle, the way the wheel itself was low enough in the water to feel the full force of the river's current.

"Do you like gardens?" the duke asked, "or did you just want to see the wheel up close?"

"I confess," Violet said, "I had a keen interest in the wheel. I hoped that by seeing it, I could understand better how it works. But it seems to me that it's just a waterwheel of brilliant design. I cannot see how it powers the whole building."

The duke smiled at her, and Violet smiled back, feeling a little embarrassed.

"I did not mean I meant to take advantage of your kindness," Violet said.

"I did not think that you had. And I will tell you how the waterwheel powers the building: with gears. Interlocking ones. Everywhere. The inside of the building is constantly clanking with the sound of gears, like living inside a giant mechanical contraption. Which I suppose it is."

"Fascinating," Violet said, still staring at the waterwheel.

"But let me show you some of the gardens," the duke said. "I hope you have an interest in them?"

"My mother was the gardener, and while I appreciate the chemical extracts taken from flowers, I know only the most rudimentary horticulture." Violet nodded as politely as she could. She did not like being thought of as the sort of young lady who was interested in nothing but flowers.

"But do you enjoy the way they look, and smell?"

"Well, yes," Violet said, surprised at the question.

"Then that is all you need to enjoy them."

Violet blinked at this, a bit thrown, but let the cheerful duke lead her around the gardens. He showed her hydrangeas, which looked to her like clockwork made of delicate petals. She said so, and the duke smiled broadly, showing a row of fine white teeth.

"I'd never thought of it that way, but you're quite correct. Nature can be very mechanical, and all the more beautiful for it."

"If I recall, the petals themselves grow in a sort of mathematical formula," Violet said.

"I thought you said you knew only the most rudimentary horticulture."

"Math isn't horticulture."

"I suppose that is true. Tell me, does knowing that the petals grow in a pattern dictated by mathematics make you appreciate them all the more?"

"Yes," Violet answered simply.

"Why?"

"Because I can see that both Mother Nature and I have something in common: a love of numbers." She laughed, and the duke laughed, too, in time with the sound of water rushing over the great wheel.

"You are a very clever girl. If your brother is anything like you, I'm sure he'll make a fine student."

"My brother and I are twins. Identical in nearly every way."

"Excellent," the duke said. "I look forward to meeting him. Now, let me show you the snapdragons." The duke took her, arm in arm, around the garden. At times, Violet nearly forgot that she walked in the great shadow of Illyria and its forbidden halls. The duke seldom spoke of science, though when she brought it up, he responded intelligently. Instead he spoke of the color of the flowers and their stems. While Violet found this sweet, after he had shown her the snapdragons, the asters, and the nasturtium, she began to think that he spoke of the flowers' beauty not because he didn't know about the sciences, but because he felt the sciences were inappropriate to discuss with a woman.

"Have you studied much of the science of flowers, or only their loveliness?" she asked him when they came to the dahlias.

"To talk of how a flower grows seems to me a tedious subject when outside the classroom," he said, his voice a little hurt sounding. "We are not scientists, you and I, nor are we gardeners."

"I am a scientist," Violet said, pulling her arm gently out of his.

"Yes," he said, "I mean, when we walk through the gardens, we are not scientists. We are merely enjoying the gardens."

Violet pursed her lips. She felt she was being condescended to by a man whose most notable claim of intelligence was having a brilliant father, and she was tired of it. "Thank you, Your Grace, for this lovely tour," she said, "but I've been here too long already. I hope you will accept my brother's application. He is quite brilliant."

"I hope that we accept him as well," the duke said, his brow furrowed. "Let me walk you to your carriage."

"That's quite all right," Violet said. "I know the way." She turned quickly and left the confused duke standing alone with the dahlias, their huge pink starburst blooms drooping slightly out of pity for him. For the duke was quite taken with Violet. He admired her wit, and that she had not fawned over him simply for being a duke. He did not entertain any romantic notions, for he had only just met her, but he had enjoyed her company, and was sad that she had so suddenly abandoned him when he thought they had been enjoying sweet conversation and beautiful flowers. He rubbed the spot on his wrist where her hand had lain moments ago, looked down at the sagging dahlias, and nodded slowly, thanking them for their understanding.

Violet, did not feel particularly understood as she left the garden and got into her carriage, which had grown stuffy in the heat. The duke, and the unexpected encounter with him, had taken her quite by surprise. She thought she had maintained her dignity, but when they stopped over the hydrangeas and their careful, mathematically arranged petals, she realized that perhaps the duke was just entertaining himself. A woman with an interest in the sciences, she imagined him thinking. How unique; how amusing. I shall show her the flowers and see what she says, as it is summer, and I am quite bored.

Violet sighed. Perhaps he did not think that. But she could think of no other reason for his showing her the gardens, and for his clever talk, or his open smiles. She had had a few male friends in her time but none had made her feel quite like the duke had. Being inexperienced in romantic feeling, Violet had assumed what she was feeling was his disdain. She leaned into the carriage seat and took off her top hat. Stray wisps of her dark hair clung to her wet brow, and she pulled them away, annoyed. She didn't hate the duke, she knew, but she rather wanted to. It was then and there that she decided that it wasn't just to Illyria-the-school that she would show her uncanny brilliance, but also Illyria-the-duke.

III.

VIOLET arrived at the town house just in time to find a young man leaving. He smiled at her, his blond, dandyish curls dancing over his forehead, his blue eyes sparkling at some secret. Her brother was just inside, looking quite content.

"Who was that?" Violet asked.

"You've taken off your hat," Ashton said, disappointed.

"It was warm," Violet explained. "Who was that young gentleman?"

"It was Ronny Findlay. His family has a town house just a few streets down."

"I wish you'd introduced me," Violet said sweetly.

Ashton glared at her. "Next time."

Violet had long known about her brother's inversion, but didn't particularly care about it. She'd always thought that people were like gears: one could spin alone and accomplish something minor, but when two gears fit together perfectly, and rotated in time, they could do so much more. And gears did not have genders. They simply fit or they didn't. Ashton had tried aligning himself with many other gears. Thus far, none had fit quite right, but Violet was sure that one would eventually. As for herself, she imagined that one day, after she was recognized as a scientific master, she would find another scientist, and they would collaborate on so many inventions and projects together that after a while they would marry out of habit and mutual respect. But that, she thought, was probably a long way off. She would be the sort who married later in life. A spinster. Spinsterhood didn't matter much to her; she was already married to science.

"Did you already go out and have a drink?" Violet asked. She was eager to go home. She longed to work in her laboratory again, to feel the solid reassurance of metal in her hands. To burn off the scent of the hydrangeas, which she could still smell on her fingertips.

"I did," Ashton said. "You were gone quite a while. Did you try scaling the walls and breaking in?"

"I did not," Violet said. "I made the acquaintance of the Duke of Illyria, actually."

"Oh," Ashton said, his eyes widening. "That's not very good, is it?"

Violet sighed and sat down on one of the nearby chairs. "I don't know," she said. "He seemed perfectly nice."

"But won't he recognize you? When you go back for an interview?"

Violet looked up. She hadn't thought of that. "No," she said, "I'm sure your disguise for me will be quite clever. And, besides, he didn't seem very bright." She stuck her chin out, asserting her superior intellect.

"Let us hope," Ashton said.

"So, are you ready to go? I'm getting a bit hungry, actually. I would love to change from this dress and have some scones."

"Or muffins," he added. "Yes, let's be off, then. Once I've thought of muffins, I can't be satisfied until I have some."

Outside, Antony was watering the horses. The whole city shimmered in the orange heat, and smelled of horse manure and stale alcohol. Violet understood why anyone who could left London in the summer. Inside the carriage, Ashton produced a bottle of white wine and two glasses with a devilish look.

"We have a cellar in the city, too. And since we're hardly ever here, it's well stocked," he explained. He managed to pour the wine without it being upset by the bumping of the horses, which made Violet wonder how many times he'd drunk in a carriage. She rarely drank, but the wine was exactly what she needed. She could feel herself cool off as she sipped it.

The sun had by now begun its descent, and between the wine and the breezes that wafted in as they approached the outskirts of the city, Violet was feeling quite comfortable again by the time the carriage bumped off the cobblestones and onto the dirt road leading away from town.

"I have figured out how to costume you," Ashton said, looking at the fading city. "We shall go to my tailor and tell him that you and I are dressing as each other for a costume ball, and have him take your measurements and make you a suit."

"I suspect I shall need more than a single suit once I am a student at Illyria," Violet said.

"I know. I have figured that out, as well. I shall take the measurements from the tailor and bring them to Whiteleys, in the city, and say I am buying suits for a friend. People seldom ask too many questions at department stores, as long as you buy. And as I shall be picking out your clothes, you will be the most well dressed scientist in London."

"I have never been to Whiteleys," Violet said. "Perhaps I should go with you?" She was not lying, but also was worried to let Ashton buy her suits alone. While she did not doubt that he had fine taste, she was afraid he might pick ridiculous dandy's clothes with frills and buttons, which she would be quite unable to work in.

Ashton knew what she was thinking the moment he looked at her. "I will ensure that your shirts are as light and comfortable as that shift you wear when you're working. But you know you'll have to . . . restrain evidence of your femininity, so clothing may be the least of your worries, in terms of comfort."

"I hadn't thought of that," Violet admitted. "I must also embellish certain areas, I suppose?"

"A rolled-up stocking will do the trick," Ashton said.

"And I'll have to cut my hair off, won't I?" she said, touching the carefully wound bun Mrs. Wilks had made that morning.

"Some, yes, although some men wear it to their shoulders these days."

Violet let her head roll back and stared at the carriage ceiling with a sigh. "This is going to be more difficult than I had originally imagined. I thought I would simply need to know science better than the rest of them, which I do. But to learn how to look, and behave, like a man? I am sacrificing more than I had originally planned upon."

"You can always cancel your plans," Ashton offered, filling his

glass for the fourth time, "write them and tell them you have decided to be a country gentleman, or that you'd prefer Oxford."

"No," Violet said, and tilted her head back to stare at Ashton,
her eyes filled with resolution. "No, it must be Illyria, and I will do
whatever it takes. Hair grows back, and what little physical discomfort this disguise will cause me is surely less than the pain I'm feeling
right now in this corset." She swallowed, thinking of the sacrifice to
her safety she was also making. Physical discomfort wasn't the worst
that could be in store for her.

"I thought you liked the corset."

"For about a half an hour, I liked the corset. Then I didn't."

"Is that Jack?" Ashton asked, looking out the window. Violet followed his gaze. There was a figure walking along the side of the road,
but he was walking toward the sun, and so he was just a silhouette
to Violet. "Jack!" Ashton called out the window. The figure turned,
and Ashton rapped on the carriage wall so Antony would stop. As
Antony brought the carriage up alongside the figure, Violet could
tell that it was indeed John Feste, Jr., whom everyone called Jack. Jack
was their estate manager's son. Being the same age as Violet and
Ashton, he and they had grown up together, playing together as children, catching frogs and making small toy omnibuses to carry their
reptilian captives about. Child's play. But when they were around
ten or so, Jack was sent off to boarding school, while Ashton and
Violet were tutored at home. Now they saw less of him, except during
the summer and holidays.

Jack waved up at them through the window. He had a large mouth,
filled with what seemed to be too many teeth.

Ashton opened the door to the carriage and held out a hand.
"Come on, old boy, ride with us," he said. "We haven't seen you yet
this summer—we must catch up."

Jack grinned and hopped into the carriage with them. Over the
years, he had grown from small child to gawky teenager and had
finally settled into a handsome young man. True, he was a little
ruddy, his blond hair was a little thin, and his lips a little pink, but
he had a good pointed chin and fine strong shoulders that he held
with the easy confidence of the jokester he had always been. It was,

after all, Jack's idea to drive the omnibus filled with frogs into the maids' sleeping quarters.

"Where are you coming from?" Ashton asked Jack, giving him his still mostly full glass of wine.

Jack accepted the glass with one of his boyish grins and downed it in one go. "Thanks," he said. "Needed that. I'm coming from London. I was dropping off my application to Illyria College," he said, looking proud.

"Why, so were we!" Ashton exclaimed.

Jack raised his eyebrows and looked to Ashton, whom he knew to have no real interest in science, and then to Violet, who was a brilliant scientist, but wouldn't be allowed in Illyria. Then, remembering a trick he had convinced the twins to play when they were children, he smiled. "Like the time we convinced Mrs. Wilks that Ashton was Violet and got her to brush his hair a hundred times on each side," he said, then slapped his knee and laughed.

"You won't tell, will you?" Violet asked.

"Of course not, Vi. If anyone deserves to go to Illyria—besides me, I mean—it's you! This will be a great trick. How are you going to decieve your father, though, and Mrs. Wilks? Is Ashton going to stay up here dressed as you the whole time? And what if you're caught?"

"Father has gone to America for a conference and plans to stay there a year, for sightseeing," Violet said, with a mischievous look. "And I don't plan on being caught."

"Violet convinced Father to let us spend the season in town, in preparation for her coming out," Ashton said before bursting into laughter.

"I could come out if I wanted," Violet said indignantly. "I'm sure I would be quite the toast of the town."

"Of course you would," Ashton said, struggling not to laugh.

"And Mrs. Wilks?" Jack asked.

"I told her I wanted to hire a lady's maid more familiar with the current trends." Violet snickered. "I'm going to name her Laetitia."

"Laetitia. She sounds charming," Jack said.

"She's a bit stern, actually," Violet said, "but she knows over two dozen hairstyles."

They all burst out laughing again. They had been like the Three Musketeers in their youth, and found that this sudden chance meeting, and possibly also the wine, had brought them back to that same state. They were a group of too-clever children, the kind people love to watch, provided they are not their own. For the rest of the ride home, they told stories of the past few years: Violet described her recent inventions, Ashton his poems and scandalous encounters in the city, and Jack spoke of school, and the various ways he had managed to humiliate the headmaster but still graduate Head Boy.

"I hope we both end up at Illyria," Violet said as they approached the estate. "It will be nice to have someone I can be honest with, and a familiar face among all the strangers."

"I'm sure we both will," Jack said.

"You must," Violet said, "after how you attached bat wings to a ferret and taught it to fly, they must let you in. Few scientists successfully accomplish anything like that until they are well into their fifties."

"As long as they don't ask me to produce the actual ferret," Jack said. "It flew away."

"Flew away?" Ashton asked.

"I released it into the rooms of one of the girls from the town who had refused to kiss me. As I understand it, her father thought it was a bat and beat it with a broom until it took off into the night."

"Oh dear," Ashton said.

"So there's a wild winged ferret roaming the countryside?" Violet asked.

"I'm afraid so. His name is Bill, if you see him."

"Does he respond to his name?" Violet asked.

"Well . . . no. But I always called him Bill."

Outside, the light was fading, and the fields and trees were lavender and peach. Jack's father's home was off through the fields a ways, but Ashton and Violet, sensing he was about to ask to be let out, preemptively invited him to supper.

By the time the carriage pulled up to the door of the manor, the sun was halfway down the horizon, and the air had become stuffy with summer heat. Mrs. Wilks was waiting in the doorway for them, twisting a stray curl of her brown hair around her finger, wondering what had gone wrong for those few hours they were out of her sight. She blushed when Jack got out of the carriage with them. She had always considered him a naughty young man, ever since he had figured out how to herd ants so they would spell out "I Love You Mrs. Wilks" in the courtyard.

Mr. Wilks had been somewhat naughty as well. When he was still alive, they had both worked hard around Messaline, but still made time for the occasional romantic dalliance in the stables, or the pantry, or even the wine cellar. Jack reminded her of Mr. Wilks slightly, and this reminder sometimes made Mrs. Wilks uncomfortable.

"Mrs. Wilks—dear, dear Mrs. Wilks," Ashton said, "do we have any muffins?"

Jack and Violet burst out laughing.

Mrs. Wilks looked at them, confused, but nodded. "I'm sure we have some muffins left over from breakfast. Will Mr. Feste be staying for supper?"

"Yes. We found him walking back from London. He's finished school and is applying to Illyria College, in London. Isn't that wonderful?" Violet said, "We might spend the season together!"

"I'm sure if Mr. Feste finds himself a student, he shall spend his time studying, like a good lad, and not dallying about with the two of you," Mrs. Wilks said, and turned to go inside and tell the cook that there would be another for supper, and to put muffins out on the table.

"You must tell me more of this deviant plan," Jack said.

"Let me get the muffins," Ashton said.

"We'll meet you in the garden, at Mother's bench," Violet said, and Ashton nodded. Violet walked off into the gardens. Mother's bench, as she and Ashton had always called it, was a simple wooden bench, well worn, which sat under a cluster of ash trees, surrounded by violets, looking out on one of the ponds. Their father had said it was her favorite spot.

Violet sat down on the bench, Jack beside her. The light was nearly gone, but a storm of summer fireflies was out. Occasionally, a fish would jump out of the pond and grab a firefly in its mouth, snuffing it out with a small splash.

"Fireflies are curious," Jack said after a moment. "I wonder if whatever makes them glow could be applied to other creatures. Glowing ferrets, maybe."

"I think you should try working with a more docile animal than the ferret," Violet said.

"Probably. But they amuse me."

Violet smiled. Jack was like another brother to her, and she found herself relieved to find that he could be her ally at Illyria.

"You'll have to become used to calling me Ashton," Violet said.

"That shouldn't be too hard," Jack replied. "It really is a brilliant plan. But you'd best learn to behave like a man, and you'll need a great disguise."

"The disguise will be simple," Ashton said, coming up behind the bench, eating a muffin, and holding a basket filled with more. "And I shall spend the summer teaching her how to behave."

"I'm not sure if you're the best example of manliness," Jack said, reaching for a muffin.

Ashton pulled the basket away. "No muffins for you. You question my manliness. While I may appear a dandy, I assure you that that does not take away from my masculinity. And besides, who has spent more time admiring the virtues of men than I?"

"A fair point," Jack conceded.

"Good," Ashton said, holding the basket of muffins out for Jack again, "but you can certainly help, if you'd like."

"Sounds like an excellent joke," Jack said.

"It's not just a joke," Violet said. "I want to prove that I am smarter than half the men in that school already. And I want to learn, even if only for a year."

"A year?"

"After that, Father will return, and the jig will be up. I plan to reveal myself at the faire at the end of the school year."

"You could say you've invented a device that changes men to women," Jack said.

"I think that would offend, rather than impress, most of the scientists who will be there," Violet said. "No. I shall have to come up with something truly brilliant. Something that outshines even the displays of the older students, even those of the professors. I just don't know what."

They all went silent, the pond making small splashing notes and the dusk humming into night.

"This is going to be an excellent summer," Violet said, taking a muffin and breaking off crumbs to throw to the fish.

"I hope so," Ashton said.

"I promise to make it so," Jack said, then turned to Violet. "First, we make you a man. Then, we are interviewed, probably in a month, and then, in October, we begin school. The labs of Illyria are said to be wondrous. I can't wait to see their supplies and spaces. And they can acquire any animals students ask for. And I hear they have a resurrectionist, as well."

"You surely don't plan to experiment with human flesh?" Violet asked. Ashton shuddered.

"I've been thinking," Jack said, sounding more serious than usual, "of trying to transfer hearts from monkeys into men. If the men need them, I mean. If their heart gives out. We could take the heart of another creature, and maybe with only a very little tweaking, put it into the dying man. We could save lives." Jack pushed his blond hair back from his face, and Violet felt proud to see his eyes glow with a passionate determination she hoped she could match.

"Come now, gentlemen," Violet said, rising. "I'm sure supper is nearly ready, and if I don't wash up before we eat, Mrs. Wilks will tut at me all through supper, and it will take all my energy to keep from laughing." Each man held out an arm for her. She took them both, walking between them through the garden back to the house. Behind them, in the darkness, the fireflies twinkled over the pond, creating a galaxy of shooting stars, above and below.

IV.

ERNEST, the Duke of Illyria, considered the dahlia, and its repulsive effect on women. It had been nearly a month since they had driven away Miss Adams, and now he had a vase of them in the study, and his cousin and ward, Cecily, hadn't come to see him all day, even though she had only just arrived back the day before last after spending the summer with Aunt Ada.

He knew that it wasn't really the dahlia's fault. He had sent Cecily off to enjoy nature as a girl, hair in braids, and she had returned, inexplicably, a young woman. Before, having Cecily in the college seemed fine, for while she was technically female, she was still a child, and that made her genderless in principle. But in those short months, a sixteen-year-old child had become a sixteen-year-old woman. It probably hadn't all happened while she was in the country. The duke was far too clever a man to think that the blooming roses had resulted in Cecily's blooming. No, more likely it was just that he hadn't seen it until he sent her away, and when she had come back it had struck him dumb: suddenly he had a woman in his care, and women were often distracting to young scientists. And so he had politely suggested to her last night at supper that perhaps she should go away to school in the coming year, causing her to become quite upset with him for even suggesting the idea. She had run off to her room without even staying for pudding, and hadn't come to see him since.

Women, he thought, sitting at his desk, were difficult. Cecily was especially difficult, as she was so many things: a cousin and a sister, for she had been put into his father's care eight years prior, following the death of her mother and the disappearance of her father, a renowned explorer who had vanished searching for the lost world of

Lemuria. And now, Cecily was like a daughter, as he had taken over her care when his father passed away two years later.

But still, the dahlias. He had nearly finished sorting through the applications for the incoming class, well over a hundred this year. When he got to Ashton Adams's file, he had, without thinking, looked up at the vase of dahlias. It was clear that young Adams was brilliant and deserved an interview, but the duke wondered if he was as peculiar, as fickle, as his mysterious sister. The duke had thought of Violet in the past month or so, remembered the green ribbon around her hat, and the deep silver of her eyes. He was not one to spend hours daydreaming about a young woman, but he wondered about her, and her sudden departure. He was intrigued. She was like a machine that seems to be in perfect working order but suddenly stops. Had he knocked against it? How could he repair whatever damage he had done? It was a puzzle.

He looked at the clock on the wall. Nearly supper time. With a sigh, he stood up and pulled the cord that summoned his footman. The footman, like most of his staff, had first worked for the duke's father. The duke often felt that he held him in a sort of contempt, that he was not as great as his father. But the duke could never dismiss him, either, because he secretly suspected that he was correct, and it would set a poor precedent to get rid of people just because they were right.

"Please go and bring Mrs. Isaacs, and tell her I'd like a word with her before supper?" he asked the footman, who nodded, and possibly sneered, then vanished from view. Miriam Isaacs was Cecily's governess, and the duke could consult her on the problem of letting Cecily stay at Illyria. She would know best.

Mrs. Isaacs appeared quickly and silently, her hands clasped in front of her. Though she was younger than the duke—in her mid-twenties, perhaps; she had an ageless quality about her, and he had never asked—she intimidated him.

She was a Jewess born in Persia. Her family had moved to Paris when she was young, and then to London when she was sixteen. She had married, and been widowed, before she was nineteen, and both her parents had died as well. And yet she stood strong and steady, with a certain foreign dignity the duke found far more serious than any local, English dignity. She always wore what seemed to be the same black dress, though it was never dirty, with a high collar and long sleeves, and her thick black hair was always pulled back in a bun. She was thin and dark, with large almond eyes, so she wasn't what anyone would call fashionably pretty, but she possessed a certain sense of restrained exoticness, and she spoke English—and French, and German, and Persian, not to mention reading Hebrew and Latin—with a lilting, musical tone. She was clever, she had seen the world, and she had loved and lost. For all these reasons, he had hired her. She was also an excellent governess, always calm and serious, but still affectionate toward Cecily. The duke found her to be reassuring, and thought of her as the mother figure he could consult on the rearing of young women, especially when Cecily seemed to hate him.

"You asked for me, Your Grace?" Mrs. Isaacs said, stepping into the room.

"Will you convince Cecily to join me at supper tonight?"

"She is most upset with your talk of sending her away, Your Grace. I'm not sure she can be convinced to attend." Mrs. Isaacs paused, waiting for the duke's resigned sigh, which came a moment later. "Should I bring her supper in her room or would you prefer to let her come and eat what is left when you are finished?"

"I would prefer she eat with me, so I can discuss this matter with her. Do you think it is inappropriate for me to send her away to school?"

"Speaking frankly, sir, I think sending her away from the world's finest educational institution to go to school seems backwards."

The duke nodded and put his hand to his chin, scratching below his lip. "But she's a young woman now. Surely it isn't appropriate for her to spend all her time in an institution filled entirely with young men?"

"I think, sir, that as long as she is chaperoned, that time around young men is normal and healthy. You wouldn't have her shut up in a nunnery, would you?"

"Well, no. But won't she be a distraction to the students?"

"Sir, she has been a distraction to the students for the past two years, when she first started becoming a young woman. You notice it now only because she has begun wearing her hair up, instead of in braids."

The duke nodded again. "I suppose you are right."

"Sir, you must do what you think is best for both Cecily and Il-lyria. If you choose for her to remain here, I assure you I shall keep guard over her virtue and instruct her in proper behavior. If any of the students try to take inappropriate liberties with her, I will report them to you immediately."

"Yes, of course. I trust you, Mrs. Isaacs."

"You honor me, Your Grace," Miriam said with a small curtsey. "And may I also point out that Cecily is approaching the age where suitors are not uncommon. Would it be such a terrible thing if her suitors were among the most brilliant scientists in the world?"

"No, I suppose it wouldn't . . . ," the duke said.

"Your Grace hasn't noticed any decline in the aptitude of the students these past years, have you?"

"No."

"And yet Cecily has received over a dozen love letters last year alone," Miriam said with an arched eyebrow.

The duke started up in his chair, leaning forward with shock. "Really?"

"Yes. And may I suggest that perhaps an optional poetry class be offered? Some of the letters are really quite droll."

The duke smiled. Miriam found the whole thing amusing, he could tell, and that made it all seem like harmless children's games. The students were young, after all: the eldest was twenty-one. Let them woo Cecily. If their grades declined, he would expel them.

"Thank you, Mrs. Isaacs. You may bring a tray up to Cecily if she does not feel like coming down for supper."

"Of course, Your Grace," Miriam said. She bowed, then turned to leave.

"Oh, and Mrs. Isaacs . . . ," the duke called after her.

She spun back around, her hands still clasped in front of her. "Yes, Your Grace?"

"Do women find the dahlia to be a particularly repulsive flower?" he asked.

Miriam stared at him for a moment. "I wouldn't know, Your Grace," she said, and walked back into the shadows beyond his door. The duke looked back at the dahlias in the vase, glowing pink and yellow in the light of the gas lamps. He took one out and put it in his buttonhole before heading down to supper.

V.

VIOLET had a suit, and it fit her quite well, but she still couldn't speak like a man. This was a problem, since she interviewing at Illyria tomorrow. She was so excited to finally enter those golden halls that she could barely focus on her brother's talk of pitch and timbre. She wondered how they would look: Would they be hung with portraits of famous inventors? Would there be a test of her mechanical mettle right there in the chamber in which she was to be interviewed in front of all the professors?

"Your o's must be heavier," Ashton said. "They are a bag with *stones in them.*"

"Stones in them," Violet repeated, slowly and deeply.

"Not bad," Jack said. They were sitting at Mother's bench, with books in hand, to make Mrs. Wilks think they were performing parts of a play for themselves.

"It is bad," Ashton said. "It is terrible. You have already met the duke. You must prevent him from recognizing you. And while I admit that with the suit we have for you, and the false sideburns, you look like a boy slowly breaking into the halls of manhood, and you do rather have the walk down—"

"I just think of slow-moving gears," Violet said. Jack smirked.

"—your voice is still quite feminine," Ashton finished.

"So maybe it hasn't changed yet," Violet said, her hands on her hips.

"At seventeen?" Ashton asked. "That would be a scientific discovery in itself. Now, come on, try it again."

"Stones in me' pockets, stones that weigh me down," Violet said.

"Better," Ashton said, "but there's no need to adopt a lower-class accent."

"I wonder what the inside of the building will look like," Violet said, still in her masculine voice.

"A man opened the door when I turned in my application," Jack said. "I didn't see much behind him, but it looked like high, vaulted ceilings in gold and bronze, and I could hear this clicking noise."

"The entire school is powered by the waterwheel, with gears to repeat its effort," Violet said, "or so the duke told me."

"Slower, speak slower," Ashton said. "You sound too mincing."

"*You* don't speak slowly," Violet said.

"I am a man. I don't need to pretend to be one."

"Maybe I'm your sort of man, then," Violet said. "It would make sense—we're twins. Were I a man, I would be quite like you, I think."

"No, you must be a boring man," Ashton said. "Average, plain, so that no one will think you are a woman."

"Won't being dull just draw more attention to my feminine eccentricities?" Violet asked. "Shouldn't I hide everything in plain sight? Be a feminine dandy? Then they would just think I was a man who acted like a woman."

"No," Ashton said. "Scientists are rarely dandies, and not very good dandies when they are."

"I beg your pardon," Jack said. "I could be a bit of a dandy."

"You are a jokester, a jester, a comedian," Ashton said, "which are all very much like a dandy, but not actually a dandy."

"I think I'm a bit more than all that," Jack said sulkily.

"Of course you are. We all are more than what society calls us, but if society is to call us something—and it will—we may as well choose what. And you, dear brother Violet, must be the sort of man society calls plain. Brilliant, to be sure, but average in all other respects. The sort who will marry and have children named Mary and John—"

"I beg your pardon," said Jack again.

"—and while he may be noted as a brilliant mind, will never be seated next to the host at dinner parties, because his conversation is always quite predictable."

"I don't think I want to be that sort of man," Violet said. "I think I much prefer being a woman to that, Illyria or no."

"Well, then, at least speak like a plain man. Then you may act however you wish."

"All right," Violet said, again in her manly voice. "I am Ashton Adams, and I speak as though I am the most boring man on the globe. Which I'm sure you find very comforting, as those who speak as though they are boring are inevitably the ones trying to cover up some scandal, and those who speak as though their life is naught but excitement usually are quite dull, and know it."

"Quite good," Ashton said. "Good enough for the interview, I think. It will be hard to maintain it for a whole year, but it's really just the first few weeks that matter. After that, no one will suspect anything, because to do so will mean they were tricked in the beginning."

"What invention did you submit for the interview?" Jack asked.

"My perambulator," Violet said. Jack had seen her begin building it last summer.

"Ah, quite good. Though perhaps a bit practical for some of the professors."

"I know. Which is why I have also devised a row of clockwork ducks that follow each other without strings."

"Did you? Can I see them?"

"Of course. They're in the laboratory. I used real feathers."

"How extraordinary."

"Shall we all take a trip to my laboratory right now?"

"Let's," Ashton said, and headed back toward the house. "Mrs. Wilks can't stare at us from a window down there." Ashton smiled and waved once at Mrs. Wilks, who had taken to watching them from the windows even more frequently than usual.

Violet was excited and happy as she walked back toward the manor. Her suit was more comfortable than she had expected. Her perambulator was in perfect condition, and the magnetic ducklings were finished and worked beautifully. And she felt quite sure that tomorrow, at her interview, she would gain entry to Illyria.

Ashton, meanwhile, was looking forward to a season in London as a bachelor. There were shows he wanted to see, and pubs in the bad parts of town he wanted to try. And of course, dinner parties and affairs and small scandals that, if he could not take part, at least he could watch from afar. Ashton, like any dandy worth the title, enjoyed a good scandal, if only because he enjoyed watching his elders run around with shocked expressions. He was still at the age where shocked expressions meant that he had somehow made a difference in someone's life, not yet realizing that a tiny smile can signal a much more significant impact.

They went to the laboratory and played with Violet's mechanical ducks, and soon thereafter ate and went to bed. But Violet found it nearly impossible to sleep. Instead she turned about in her bed, staring at the ceiling and thinking of what little she had seen of Illyria. When she fell asleep, she dreamed that the duke was giving her a tour of the college proper, and not just the gardens.

❖

IN the carriage the next day, Violet clung to her handbag and practiced for her interview.

"The mechanics of space travel," she recited in a low and husky voice, "are within our reach, though they would require significant funding, and much experimentation. But the principles are all well established."

"Good," Ashton said, "you sound quite right. Now, try not to move your mouth so prettily, or pout. Keep your lips thin and your jaw stern."

Violet raised her eyebrows, for she had never thought of her mouth as having pretty movements before. Much to her own surprise, she had awoken nervous about the interview. Her confidence, so often overwhelming to those around her, had wavered and deflated at the time she needed it most. What if this disguise was ridiculous and she ended up looking like a clown in front of the most brilliant minds in the world? Or, worse, what if they did believe she was a man, but simply not good enough for Illyria? That would be the crushing blow. If that happened, she secretly vowed, she would give up inventing altogether, start dressing like the pretty mindless thing Mrs. Wilks wanted her to be, and marry some dull, respectable member of Parliament within the year. If she didn't die of grief first.

"Try it again," Ashton said. Violet looked up from her worries and tried to put on a brave face. But Ashton could see through such faces. "You're worried, aren't you?" Violet nodded. "Well, I don't know why you should be. I'm sure my opinion counts for very little in terms of science, but Jack is quite brilliant and says the flame of his genius is but a candle next to your bonfire."

Violet smiled. "Jack is modest," she said. "He is much cleverer than I. I could never make a flying ferret."

"And he could never make a handbag as useful as the one you're now holding. You each have your own strengths. And you're quite passable as a man, if I do say so myself. An odd sort of man, but in an endearing way. You'll do fine, and I'm sure you'll be walking through those halls come October."

"Thank you," Violet said, and laid her hand on his. They rode like that until Antony stopped in front of their town house and opened the door for them. They stepped out into the cooling early autumn air, tinged with the smell of smoke and dying leaves.

"Now, Antony," Ashton said, "we're about to do something quite shocking. It is vital you tell no one about it, especially not Mrs. Wilks. You will do that for me, won't you?" Ashton laid his hand on Antony's shoulder. He had often suspected that the young carriage driver had a particular affection for him. He had even wanted to indulge it on occasion, but was unsure if that would be improper. To make love to someone else's help seemed perfectly acceptable, but to make love to your own help seemed a mite graceless, as though you couldn't find lovers outside your immediate household. But his smile had the desired effect on Antony, who nodded, wide eyed and faithful, as Ashton and Violet went inside to transform Violet into her twin brother.

Violet had mastered the art of dressing herself by now, binding and stuffing as she would have to do as a student. Her hair she tied back and tucked into her shirt collar so it appeared much shorter, and her sideburns she applied carefully. She looked at herself in the mirror again and found the image quite striking, if only because she saw a man holding a handbag, which seemed rather odd. There was no helping it now, though. She opened the door to her closet for Ashton to come in and look her over.

"You look quite the gentleman," he said. "Let's put you in the carriage before I lose my nerve."

※◎※

ANTONY had always thought himself a regular fellow. True, he had begun to have an unexpected curiosity lately in regards to young Mr. Adams, but he knew that at heart he was a common coachman. One day, he would settle down and have children. One day he would look back on his days as a coachman for an eccentric family of scientists as an adventure. His life would not be a grand one, but it would be a pleasant one, without surprises. So when he saw Violet emerge from the townhouse, looking for all the world like a small, genteel man, he did not at first recognize her. When he did, though, his shock was evident. His mouth dropped open, and his eyes bulged.

"Don't look so surprised, Antony," Violet said as she got into the carriage. "I plan to be a student at Illyria, and I deserve that, don't I? Then this is the only way." Ashton winked at Antony, who quickly closed his mouth and looked downward, not just because of the wink, but also because of the incredible plot to which he was now a party.

"Take him to Illyria," Ashton said. "Call him by my name. I promise your discretion will be appreciated."

With a deep breath, Antony took his seat on the carriage again. As he drove toward Illyria, he did his best to keep his eyes forward and his mind on the work, but he could not help but consider this scheme over and over. Certainly, he knew of Violet's scientific proclivities, and certainly he wished her the best, but this sort of behavior was surely inappropriate for a young lady. And if she were unmasked, and he were revealed to have known . . . No, Ashton and Violet would never implicate him, and he could always feign ignorance. He was in no danger. And who was he, a common coachman, to question the games of the aristocracy? The extra pocket money they'd give him would surely be nice to have. And of course, there was always Ashton's gratitude to consider. . . . Antony shook his head again and concentrated on the pull of the horses and the cobblestones. Best not to think at all while working. Best to work and then go home later and enjoy a good brew with some of the lads.

The coach pulled to a stop in front of Illyria. Violet hopped out and nodded at Antony, who bowed slightly. The gates were open already, as various young men had been coming and going all week to interview for the five coveted spots in the incoming class. Violet bravely steadied her shoulders, thrust them back, and walked forward with a slow and masculine gait. She took no notice of the gardens as she walked through them, sensing that lingering over the dahlias might bring about some feminine feeling, which she would just have to repress. She focused instead on the door ahead, and the servant who stood outside, wearing a top hat and coat and holding a piece of parchment.

As Violet approached, the servant looked her over. She tensed, but his expression revealed nothing but boredom. "Your name?" he asked.

"Ashton Adams," Violet said.

The man looked over the list, nodded, and pulled open the great door for her. "Wait until your name is called," he said.

The room immediately inside was small, but with a high, vaulted ceiling in the Gothic revival style, done in dark brass and gold, so that upon her stepping inside, Violet's fair skin instantly took on a golden luster as it reflected the yellowed light from the room. The ceilings were ornately carved with what looked like scales and springs, and with images of gears and beakers and stars and elephants and all sorts of scientific symbols along the bottom, where it met the paneled dark wood and golden papered walls. The effect would have been gaudy if it weren't so dark, but a little light crept in through the high windows, which made the place seem cathedral-like and eerie, as if everything should be whispered.

"Ashton!" Violet heard Jack call. She was confused for a moment—was Ashton there?—then remembered that he was talking to her. She looked across the room. There, sitting among a few other prospective students on low, dark wooden benches was Jack, grinning from ear to ear at the ruse.

"I thought you weren't interviewing until next week," Violet said, walking toward Jack. The other students were clearly thrown off by their friendship, and eyed the pair warily.

"I lied," Jack confessed, shaking Violet's hand before anyone could tell she held it out palm down, like a woman. "I wanted to surprise you, thought it might ease your nervousness a bit. And the look on your face has certainly taken away a bit of mine."

Violet smirked. "Well, thank you," she said, sitting down next to him. At his feet lay a small covered cage. "Did you find your ferret?" she asked, gesturing toward the box.

"Alas, no," he said. "Bill is still roaming the countryside, a free-flying ferret." One of the nearby applicants stared at Jack, his eyes wide. "Yes," Jack said to the young man, "I made a ferret who could fly. What did you do?"

"I bred a purple frog," the man said nervously.

"May I see it?" Jack asked excitedly.

"It died," the student confessed, "but I have testimonials of those who saw it."

"Well, I'm sure that will be splendid, then," Jack said, and turned back to Violet. "No," he continued, "Bill is still missing, so I made another. This one is female. I named her Sheila. She's sleeping now, though, and doesn't seem quite comfortable with her wings yet. I hope she still impresses the panel."

Violet nodded. The panel would consist of all five professors and the duke himself. She swallowed, her mouth dry. Would the duke recognize her? If he did, would he expose her? What sort of an impression had she made on him? Would he remember her favorably?

"Relax," Jack said, "you're shivering like a woman."

Violet narrowed her eyes at him, and he grinned widely. "How did you know I would be nervous, anyway?" Violet asked.

"You're a confident . . . fellow," Jack said, catching himself before he said girl, "but I knew you as a child. All those moments before you tested an invention for the first time, you would bite your nails and twitch and fret as much as Mrs. Wilks. I assumed today would be similar."

"Well," Violet said affectionately, "thank you for knowing me so well."

Violet and Jack waited impatiently as the sands of time seemed to become muddy, moving both too slowly and too quickly. Other potential students marched into the room beyond two large doors as their names were called out by a footman, then tramped out again a few minutes later, some happy, some with their heads hanging low, and a few actually sniffling. They made small talk, Jack amusing himself by trying to throw Violet off her guard and trick her into some sort of innocent mistake. Violet enjoyed the challenge, but their hearts were not really in it. Rather, their hearts were beating in time to the large clock that hung on the wall, with its visible twirling gears, and the heaving mechanical sound that echoed through the building.

"John Feste, Jr." the footman called suddenly. Jack's eyes widened slightly. Violet wanted to squeeze his hand to reassure him, but knew that this was a feminine inclination, so she patted him heartily on the back instead.

"Good luck," she said in a heavy voice.

"Thanks," Jack squeaked, for he was now overcome with nervousness. He almost forgot his second flying ferret and had to come back for it after taking a few steps. The door slammed behind him, and Violet stared after, offering a silent prayer for his success.

But a minute later it seemed that he didn't need it, for much shrieking laughter and clapping came from within. Relieved, Violet focused her attention on the sounds of the building. She could hear the large echo of the waterwheel and a thousand clicks and grinds of gears elsewhere in the building, though what they were operating, Violet couldn't tell. The sounds composed a sort of music for Violet as they moved in time, grinding along, with the occasional twang of springs like a violin floating over it all. Were these the gears that powered the entire college? Violet bit her lower lip, trying to imagine all the machines the college must have: Babbage's analytical engines, of course—several of them, she imagined—a lift, a forge, and loads more.

Violet realized that biting her lower lip was probably a rather feminine gesture, so she released it, just as Jack emerged from the hall. He looked a bit flustered but quite cheerful, his face red but smiling, his hair tousled and stuck to his forehead with sweat. His green eyes twinkled with repressed laughter. The cage in his hand shook, and small squeaking noises escaped from it.

"I let Sheila out, to prove she could fly," he explained. "She could, but catching her was a bit of an adventure."

Before Violet could inquire as to how Jack retrieved the ferret, the footman said, "Prospective students who have already interviewed must leave the premises," and gave them a pointed look. Jack shrugged, then made a face at the footman when he turned away.

"Good luck, mate," Jack said, slapping Violet on the back. "I'll see you tonight." Violet nodded and continued waiting. A few more young scientists were called into the room and came back out again, all of them looking exhausted afterwards.

"Ashton Adams," the footman intoned. Violet swallowed, her throat suddenly dry. Then she steeled herself, picked up her handbag, and went through the doors.

The hall Violet entered was over two stories high, again with tall vaulted ceilings of bronze and gold, and paneled wood walls. There were windows, plenty of them, and though some light did make it to the floor in small patches, much of it was eaten or tinged with bronze. In the center of the hall was a platform holding six large chairs, a man in each of them. Violet recognized the duke immediately, and the others vaguely, since they were all famous in their fields and she had seen their portraits before. But she was so distracted by the wall behind them that she paid little attention to them at first.

This wall was obviously the other side of the wall with the waterwheel, and at last she understood how it powered the school. In the center of the wall was one giant gear, rotating in time with the waterwheel. This gear was beautiful: gilded, with gemstones set into it, and the school's motto—ARS GLORIA HOMINI EST, "Invention Is the Greatness of Man"—engraved on it in large, beautiful letters. This gear alone was a work of art worthy of admiration, but what truly earned the sigh of joy that escaped Violet's lips was what it was attached to: hundreds of thousands of other gears, all connected, all of which would turn for as long as the Thames kept flowing. They coated the wall, breaking only for windows, and rose high into the ceiling. Violet reasoned that they must keep going beyond it, to the other floors, and other parts of the college, a wall of constantly turning gears, energy perpetually on tap for any inventor anxious to use it. On either side of the great gear were smaller gears with large gaps that showed two large stained glass windows, depicting John Snow and Charles Babbage. They projected a dim, warm light onto the floor.

"It's a clever idea, isn't it?" the duke said. "It was my father's, of course. It extends to the top of the building, and down into the basements, too. It powers our analytical engines, some of the machines in the kitchen, mechanical room, and student lounge. The gears are all fitted so that you can attach extensions to them to power any invention of your own. For testing, really. A machine that has to be fit into the school for a power supply isn't all that impressive."

Violet marveled at the wall, lost in the complex pattern of gears reaching forever higher and out of sight.

"You're Ashton Adams," the duke said.

Violet nodded, and tried to focus on the duke and his companions.

"Please, have a seat." The duke indicated a small chair that stood in front of the platform, so that the panel of judges could gaze down upon the applicant.

Violet sat, and discovered it to be most unnerving to be watched thus.

"I met your sister," the duke said.

Violet inclined her head. "She mentioned that she had the honor of meeting Your Grace," she said, "and that you showed her the gardens. That was most generous. She was touched."

"Was she?" the duke asked. "She left in such a hurry."

"Yes! She wished to apologize for that," Violet said, thinking quickly as she could. "She suddenly remembered a promise to Mrs. Wilks—that's our housemaid—that she would be home for a dress fitting by five."

A man at the end of the platform laughed in what Violet thought was a most undignified manner. He was heavy, and his black curls were receding in a rather frantic way. His skin was puffy and had the blotchy appearance of illness, and his eyes seemed to be bulging from his skull. "Women and their dresses," he said. "She was rude to a duke because of a dress!" Here he laughed again, a horrid barking sound. Violet tried not to stare.

"This is Professor Bracknell," the duke said, "he is our Astronomy professor. Professor Cardew, our usual Astronomy professor, has left for America, to help decide how to standardize global time," the duke said. "Professor Bracknell is his substitute. Are you familiar with Dr. Cardew?"

"Yes. My father is J. C. Adams. He's at the same conference."

"'E used to be the head astronomer at Cambridge, right?" Bracknell said, his eyes narrowing. "I hear 'e's a bit of a loony. Wants to start time in London?"

Violet bit her tongue to keep from defending her father, but luckily the duke stepped in. "Now, now, Professor Bracknell. I've read Dr. Adams's work. He is a brilliant man with reasons for his decisions. And we certainly shan't refer to him as a loony again, particularly in front of his son." The duke looked over at Bracknell as he said this, and Bracknell mumbled some meek agreement. "Let me introduce the rest of the faculty," the duke said to Violet. "Next to Professor Bracknell is Professor Curio, who teaches the chemical arts." The man sitting next to Bracknell was tall and lean, with a prominent chin and eyes that seemed to be of two different colors. He nodded at Violet, and then nodded again—or perhaps he twitched; Violet couldn't be sure. "And next to him is Professor Prism, who teaches reckoning." Professor Prism, Violet thought, seemed like the sort of man who could be someone's grandfather—he had a white beard and mustache and a puff of misty white hair on his head. He also wore a pair of glasses with several lenses attached to them on hinges, so that they could be flipped in front of his eyes as necessary. He currently he had two lenses—one clear and one red—in front of his left eye, and four lenses—two clear, one green, and one blue—in front of his right eye, and there were many more of them flipped up, like little antennae. The effect was quite strange. Professor Prism smiled broadly and cocked his head at Violet, making him seem like a large, hungry bug, and Violet nodded back, trying not to look terrified. "To my right is Professor Valentine." Violet had seen many portraits and photographs of Valentine, who seemed to love having his image captured. He had chin-length blond curls, a rather pointed nose, and was constantly pinching his face as though he had smelled too much ether. In person, Violet thought, he looked as though he wore rouge—and if that were not odd enough, he wore it more heavily than any woman—and while the other professors all wore plain suits, Valentine wore what looked like a blue smoking jacket. He took a handkerchief from his pocket and waved it happily at Violet, grinning. Violet nodded. "Valentine teaches biological science, as I think you know. And to his right is Professor Bunburry, who teaches mechanical science." Violet had read about Professor Bunburry, and his numerous unfortunate accidents with his machines. He was a tall, broad man, with very little hair and an extremely erect posture, probably owing to the giant metal brace around his neck, which stretched from just under his chin to over his shoulders, like a funnel. One of his hands had been replaced with a clockwork appendage that he had designed himself, and he walked with a limp from the weight of his metal foot. He wore a pair of tiny spectacles, which looked quite fragile balanced on his nose. He looked at Violet but made no motion, so Violet simply bowed her head low. The man was a mechanical genius, to be sure, but it was hard to tell where he ended and the mechanical began.

"Now that you have been introduced, let's go over your application. I'm the only one who has read it, so I will tell all of you that young Ashton here wrote a quite brilliant essay on the possibilities of space travel"—Bracknell snorted, but all the other professors ignored him, and Violet thought it best to follow their example—"and the plans for a rather clever handbag which he made."

"A handbag?" Professor Bracknell sneered.

"Is that it?" the duke asked, nodding to the handbag that Violet was still clutching with nervous palms.

"Yes," Violet said.

"Why don't you show my colleagues what it does?"

Violet took a deep breath and stood, taking the toy ducks out of the handbag and placing them on the floor before demonstrating. The handbag was simple enough, not very stylish, but not ugly. Plain and simple. Violet held it up for the professors to see, then opened it. On the handle of the bag was a switch, which she flipped. The bag trembled slightly in her grasp as the gears inside it set to work. Quickly, but with a clean motion, the handbag unfurled itself, cloth stretching out where it had been tucked, bars unfolding, wheels emerging, all from their little hiding holes within the handbag. Within a moment, Violet's hand lay on the handle of a full-sized perambulator, its wheels resting on the ground. For show, Violet gave the perambulator a push, and it rolled forward a few feet.

"Extraordinary," the duke said.

"Very smooth," Professor Bunburry said, his voice harsh and croaking.

"It's a purse that turns into a baby carriage?" Bracknell asked. Violet nodded.

"It's quite clever," Professor Prism said, "and it was a pleasure to watch unfold. Where did you come by the idea?"

"Our housemaid, Mrs. Wilks, whom I mentioned. Her sister, who was a nursemaid in the city, often complained of how difficult it was to manuver the perambulator about. So I created one for her that could easily be stowed. This is actually the second I've made. The handbag is functional, too. Anything inside it during transformation ends up in this side pocket, here." Violet pointed. "And it changes back just as easily." Violet flicked the switch back on her handle, and the perambulator curled itself inward, stowing its bars and wheels until Violet was left holding the handle of the handbag again.

"What prevents the perambulator from folding up while there's still a baby in it?" Bracknell asked. "What if the lady accidentally flips the switch?"

"There is a safety mechanism in place: if anything weighing more than a pound and a half—about the weight of a three-volume novel—is in the carriage of the perambulator, it will not transform."

"And what if the lady is using it as a purse in a crowded place and accidentally flips the switch to make it unfold?" Bracknell prodded.

"There is a lock to prevent that," Violet said.

"You think that'll stop some dumb woman?" Bracknell asked, and began his irritating laugh again, clapping Curio on the back fiercely. Curio's eye twitched, but he didn't seem to react otherwise. Violet bit her tongue holding back a retort.

"It's quite ingenious," the duke said.

"It's a cleverly built, useful invention," Bunburry croaked out. "Very impressive, Mr. Adams." He then descended into a fit of coughing.

"Thank you, sir," Violet said.

"Yes," Valentine said with a wave of his lace-covered hand, "it's very *practical*. And for what it does, it does it beautifully. But do you have anything more . . . artistic?"

"I think that's quite a piece of artistry," Bunburry said to Valentine. "Just because it's not a ferret with wings—"

"Of course," Valentine said, "what I meant was, something more frivolous. Something that perhaps has less function and more beauty?"

"I brought these, sir," Violet said, turning around and retrieving her ducks. "They're just a child's toy, but they might be what you're looking for."

"Well, show us, then," Valentine said. Violet set the ducks down in a row, passing her hand between each of the ducks to demonstrate that there were no wires. Then she wound up the mother duck and let it go. The ducklings all followed, feathers bobbing merrily in a row.

Valentine clapped his hands excitedly. "No wires!" he exclaimed. "However did you do it?"

"Magnets, sir," Violet said.

"Very clever," Valentine said. "Fetch them. I want to see them up close." Violet ran to where the ducks were still rolling and stopped them.

"A nice trick," Bunburry coughed, "but not as clever as your handbag."

Violet nodded at this, then delivered the ducks into Valentine's outstretched hands.

He looked the ducks over with a series of hmmms and ah-has and the occasional oh my before giving them back. "You have a good eye, young man," Valentine said. "I'm glad that you have not weighed your intelligence down with practicality."

At this, Bunburry glared at Valentine, who didn't seem to notice. Violet, unsure whether or not it was a compliment, simply bowed her head.

"Do you have anything else you want to say?" the duke asked her.

"Only that I have always dreamed of going to Illyria, and will work harder than any other student."

The duke smiled, and a few of the other professors smirked. "Then thank you for your time," the duke said. "We'll let you know if you've been accepted as soon as we have met with all the applicants."

"Thank you, sirs," Violet said, bowing, then collected her ducks and handbag and left. Outside, she took a deep breath and looked once more at the golden interior of the college, fearing that it might be the last chance she had to take it in. She let her hand glide along the walls as she walked out, and stared at the ornate carvings, and listened to the gears turning throughout the building. She didn't want to leave, but the footman was staring at her, and she knew she was overstaying her welcome. With a resigned sigh, she left, reassuring herself that she would be back in October.

VI.

A LETTER can sometimes take many days to reach its destination. First it must be written, of course, then signed and sealed, and then given to a page to take to the post office. From there, it must be sorted, handed off to an officer of the post, who will deliver it the next time he is on the correct route. And if the letter one is waiting for is instead delivered to one's twin, who decides to hold onto it for as long as possible for his own amusement, then it may take even longer.

Every day, starting just five days after her interview, Violet would go to Ashton's bedroom before breakfast and knock gently on the door. Then, if he didn't respond, she would knock louder, and if there was still no response, she would burst in in a flurry of white cotton and auburn hair. Then, shyly, with poorly suppressed anxiety, she would ask if he had perhaps received a letter from Illyria? The ninth night after the interview, he began locking his door. After the fifteenth, Violet had devised a machine to open it without the key. And on the eighteenth day, when he received her acceptance, steamed it open, read it, and resealed it, he decided that as revenge, he would keep it to himself for a while. Ashton was not cruel. Only after he confirmed that his sister had been accepted did he decide to hold on to the letter in secret. To keep failure from her would be mean-spirited, he reasoned, and would take the fun out of the prank, but to delay her success was a good joke.

Jack received his acceptance on the nineteenth day after their interviews, and came by the house to tell the Adamses and have a celebratory drink with them. This is when Violet first became suspicious. Ashton could see her suspicions right away, of course. The way she narrowed her eyes at him when Jack showed them the letter from Illyria; the way her sweetness toward him became saccharine and insincere, instead of pleading.

"How funny it is," Violet said to Jack, looking at Ashton as she did so, "that your letter has already arrived. I suppose that since my letter is late in coming, I must not have been accepted."

"I doubt that," Jack said, drinking thirstily. "If I got in, you can get in. You impressed that Bunburry fellow, an' if his eyes hadn't been open, and he hadn't coughed a few times, I would have thought he was asleep all through my interview."

Ashton had heard all about both their interviews. Violet's seemed promising, especially given the duke's compliments, and Jack's had been exciting, if nothing else. His new winged ferret had yawned when the cage was opened, and stretched before poking her head out the door. Soon after that she had bounded out, curiously sniffing the floor. Valentine said it was quite adorable but wondered if it really could fly, so Jack gave the professor a bit of bacon to hold out to the ferret. The ferret, smelling it, leapt into the air and flew straight at the bacon, snatching it from Valentine's hands and retiring to the ceiling to eat. This is what had caused the outburst of laughter and clapping from both Valentine and the duke. Then they summoned a footman, who, with the aid of a butterfly net—Valentine had one in his office, as he often, if unsuccessfully, hunted butterflies in an attempt to grow their wings and attach them to canaries—on a very long stick, managed to catch the ferret and bring it back down to earth.

When they picnicked on the twenty-first day, Violet spent most of the day sighing and bemoaning her fate; without Illyria's acceptance, she must, after all, marry and give up her life of invention. Jack was taken in by this and argued that her mind should not go to waste, but Ashton recognized her ruse and agreed that she should marry. "I think," he said, grinning, "you ought to marry Jack here. Then at least you can keep on inventing. I'm sure all your genius will be attributed to him, what with you being a woman and all, but at least you'll still be able to work." Jack burst out laughing at this, and then blushed.

Violet crossed her arms. "I know you have the letter," she said finally.

Ashton poured himself a glass of wine from the basket and bit into a cucumber sandwich. "What letter?"

"The letter! The letter from Illyria. You've got it, and you won't give it to me. And that is a very cruel thing, brother."

"Of course," Jack said, nodding, "the letter would be sent to you, Ashton. You probably do have it. You're a dog, Ashton. What a prank. What if she isn't accepted at all? Then you'll feel horrid."

"You think there's a chance I won't be accepted?" Violet asked, jumping up from the picnic blanket.

"No, no," Jack said, his hands held defensively in front of him, "I only meant that I agree with you. Ashton must have the letter. And it's really a very cruel prank."

Violet crossed her arms and walked away from the pair of them, annoyed.

"You have it, then?" Jack asked. Ashton nodded and sipped his wine. "Have you opened it?" Ashton nodded again. "Did she get in?"

"Of course she did. I wouldn't be having so much fun if she didn't," Ashton said, and the two of them began laughing, causing Violet to glare at them from over her shoulder.

"You must let her have it, though," Jack said, "or else she will kill you in your sleep."

"I'll give it to her before it goes that far," Ashton said, "but she woke me before ten every day for a week. This is my revenge."

On the morning of the twenty-third day, Violet strode into Ashton's bedroom without even a knock, which gave Antony precious little time to gather the sheets around his naked body or hide in the closet. Violet stood over the pair of them, apparently only a little surprised to find her brother naked in bed with the coachman, even though Ashton had worked so hard to be discreet for the past week. Violet raised an eyebrow, appraising them. Antony cowered.

"Oh, all right," Ashton said, and reached under his pillow and pulled out the letter from Illyria. "Congratulations. Now, leave my bedroom and keep your mouth shut." Violet grinned, kissed her brother on the cheek, and left, opening the letter and reading as she walked. Ashton sighed and leaned back in his bed.

"What was that all about?" Antony asked. What he really meant was *Will she tell anyone what she saw?*

"Nothing of import, my dear boy," Ashton said. "There's nothing to worry that beautiful head about." Ashton leaned over Antony and smiled reassuringly. Antony, reassured, smiled back.

❊◈❊

THE duke was not reassured as he took the lift down to Illyria's basement to hunt for monsters. This was one yearly tradition that he dreaded. It began the year after his father's death, his first year running the college, when he had been roused from bed one night by a frantic knocking on his door.

The servant there, a young maid, was pale and shaking. "There's a monster, sir, in the cellar."

After dressing and going down to the cellar to straighten things out, he couldn't disagree with the maid. The thing that had crawled up through the corridors of the basement could be described in no other way than "monster." The maid had found it while retrieving flour from one of the storerooms. She had opened the door, and there it was, anxiously licking up a spilled bag of sugar. If it resembled anything, the duke thought, it was a squid—dark and dragging a score of tentacles behind it—but with two disturbingly human arms reaching out of its loglike torso. Huge alien eyes stared out from above the tentacles, and a large toothed mouth crowned its head. It lay on the floor, about as long as the duke was tall, and moved by pulling itself forward on its human arms, crawling like a man dying of thirst. It was covered in water and mold and dirt, as though it had come through long tunnels to get there. It had finished the bag of sugar, and was gorging itself instead on the flour the maid had been sent for. Upon sensing the duke's entry, the thing turned at him and opened its mouth wide, showing a circle of sharp fangs and emitting a loud hiss. The duke took a good long look at it; then, with one motion, unholstered his pistol and shot the thing three times in its head. It slumped down dead into the bag of sugar, and then rolled over the floor a few times, landing by the duke's boots. The duke had swallowed, managed not to vomit, and then, with the help of some of the male servants, he had wrapped the creature up and burned it in the garden. He then locked up that storeroom and forbade anyone to use it again. He sent some additional servants to search the rest of the cellar. They found nothing else, though the duke suspected they hadn't looked very thoroughly. It was a huge basement—so huge, the duke had no idea of its scope or where the creature could have come from within it, so when nothing else followed the creature up in the next few days, he felt it had probably come alone.

The duke's father had had many secrets, the duke knew. And this creature could have been one of them. It could also have just been a castoff from former experiments by the students or professors, a random mutation from chemicals consumed by an animal thought dead. But to the duke, it was more a physical representation of his father's secrets, rising up through the cellar to try to take back Illyria. And the duke knew his father had had more than just the one secret. So from then on, in case others welled up, every year before classes began, he had taken a trip to the basement to make a personal tour, lantern in one hand, pistol in the other.

The lift shook as it hit the basement floor, and the duke stepped out. He stood at the entrance of a series of dimly lit halls, like a maze, all grime-covered stone and gas lamps that had gone out years before. In the time since that first encounter, the duke found nothing else to warrant the use of his pistol, and he had begun to feel as though he probably never would—that when he shot the grasping creature, he had killed the last of his father's secrets. But several years back, the students began using the basement as a place to initiate the first-year students, and so the duke wanted to be sure it was as safe as he could make it.

He generally explored only the area around the lift—that was where the storage rooms were, and where the students went for initiation. Beyond that, to the areas where the walls curved and twisted in unpredictable ways, where the air seemed damper and faint mechanical screeches crept around corners, he did not go.

Tonight's explorations were the same as in every year previous. The basement was dark and smelled of rust. Things that he could not see brushed up against him, and he had to clench his jaw at times and reassure himself that it was only a basement, and that he was the Duke of Illyria. There was nothing to fear down here, he told himself.

Not one part of him believed it.

No one knew the reason behind his annual forays. If asked, he said he was taking inventory. Once, he told a serving girl he had been close with about his real reason for coming down here. She called the trip "monster hunting" and insisted on coming down with him. They found nothing, but he had made love to her pressed against the dirty walls, her red hair a candle flame in the dark. He smiled as he stalked the halls, remembering that night. He wondered if there were other women who would go monster hunting with him. Women with fierce gray eyes like those of Miss Adams.

He was nearly done exploring. So far, he had found nothing, to his relief, when he heard footsteps behind him, and turned with lantern and pistol both outstretched.

"S-s-sir!" said a frightened-looking Professor Curio.

"Curio," the duke said, relaxing the arm that held the pistol, "you startled me."

"S-s-sorry, s-sir. Are y-you d-d-doing your annual t-tour of in-in-inventory?"

"Yes. And I've found nothing out of order."

"G-g-good."

"What are you doing down here?" the duke asked, tilting his head slightly.

"J-just pre-preparing for the y-y-year," Curio said, not meeting the duke's gaze. The duke paused, but didn't press further. Curio twitched suddenly in the darkness.

"Good, then," the duke said. "I suppose I'd best get to bed. Let me know if you find any monsters down here."

"A-any o-o-other monsters," Curio said, nodding.

"Good night, Curio," the duke said, and walked off toward the lift. He was anxious to shower off the grime of the basement and go to sleep.

"G-g-good night s-sir," Curio said, standing alone in the darkness as the duke's swinging lantern bobbed out of sight. In the shadows, the sound of footsteps echoed through the basement. Then those faded, too, and there was only the sound of the winding gears.

VII.

IN the last week of September, all the servants of Messaline gathered to see the young master and mistress leave for the city. When they had heard that the Adams twins were going to London, nearly all had been shocked. The young master, certainly, seemed an urbane sort of fellow, but the young mistress? Surely her going to London would cause great trouble, most of it for London. The serving girls told stories of horrible automata that would soon be roaming the city streets, and the stable boys wondered if she would go out at night, testing her strange experiments on the beggars. But all were agreed on one thing: they were relieved to see her go.

Ashton, Violet, and Jack waved at the gathered staff as they stepped into the coach. They were all quite flattered that so many of the servants had come to see them off—assuming, of course, that it was a gesture of love, and not merely them wanting to confirm that Violet was really and truly going. Antony tied their luggage to the top of the carriage. It was mostly filled with dresses made in the latest fashions by Mrs. Capshaw, one of which Violet wore.

"I wonder where Mrs. Capshaw gets her feathers," Violet wondered, sitting down. Antony closed the door after them.

Jack looked at the hat. "Pheasant," he said. "A large one, I'd guess."

"Is everything planned out?" Ashton asked softly. He was clearly anxious for the scheme to go off perfectly. Jack and Violet would go to the school tomorrow, to enroll and begin the semester. Ashton had already bought several suits and shirts in Violet's size, and Violet had mastered her own costume. Sharing rooms was required for the first- and second-year students, so Jack and Violet had both written to the duke requesting they be roomed together, and the duke had granted this request.

"We'll be fine, brother," Violet said with a sigh. They'd been over the plan countless times. She wanted to focus on the joy she would have as a student, not the stress of keeping up her disguise.

"We'll meet you at the house every Sunday," Jack recited, sensing Ashton's nervousness. "Violet will have a letter for Mrs. Wilks, and you'll mail it. This will keep her from coming to town unexpectedly. Although, hullo—I've just thought of something. When we go home for breaks, won't Mrs. Wilks expect Violet to bring her new lady's maid with her?"

"I'll just tell her I sent her home for the holidays," Violet said.

"That may work for Christmas," Ashton said anxiously, "but not for always. This is a problem." He began fussing with his vest.

Violet hated this particular nervous habit of his. She put her mind to the task. "We'll hire an actress," she said. "Explain the situation and have her pretend to be my lady's maid. We'll pay her well, and she'll stay in a nice house in the country. All she'll have to do is be able to put up hair. Most actresses have to do much worse."

"Some actresses," Ashton huffed, "are more than just streetwalkers on a stage."

"I hope so," Violet said, "because she'll have to fool Mrs. Wilks. But, in any case, we don't need to worry about that just yet."

"No," Ashton said, "not when there are so many other things to worry about." Violet sighed and leaned back into the chair. For the entire trip to London, Ashton made them go over the plot: the rules they must follow, the ways they would communicate, the ways of behaving like a man that Violet had yet to master, and what to do if someone discovered her secret, which usually amounted to bribery. Violet and Jack listened and half responded, thinking more of what they would feel in Illyria.

※💮※

WALKING into the college as an accepted student was, for some reason, more terrifying than walking in as a potential student.

Perhaps it was the feeling that she was now being judged, or that what was once just a ridiculous idea had blossomed into the actual fruit of a plot dangling heavily on the branch, likely to fall down any moment, leaving only shattered rind, pulp, and juices.

She swallowed.

"No helping it now," Jack said, grabbing her by the arm and steering her through the garden and into the college. Other students were rushing past them or standing off to the side, admiring the flora before going in. Each was dressed in his best suit, with tie and hair firmly in place. Behind them, in a busy dance, porters and servants took luggage from the students' carriages and brought it into the college.

The Great Hall, where the students assembled, was set up as it had been for the interviews, but now Violet and Jack took more time to admire it. It was at least two stories high, with doors from the lobby and a few pairs of doors to the side as well. The entrance they used brought them in facing the great turning wheel and the wall of gears. A story or so above them, a bridge with a marble railing stretched from one wall to the other. There didn't seem to be a way up to the bridge from inside the Great Hall. It seemed instead to lean over the hall, from one part of the school to the other. There were fifteen chairs set up in front of the raised stage, each with a name on it. Jack and Violet found theirs in the front row and picked up the sheets of paper attached to them.

"Our schedules," Jack said, flipping through his packet. "A map of the building, and book lists, and when lectures are going to be. Ah, and room keys," he said, pulling a thin key out from the sheaf of papers. Violet glanced at her schedule. It was surprisingly simple: a class from nine to noon every day of the week except Saturday and Sunday, and then she was expected to work in one of the labs independently, under a professor's supervision, from one to six. On Saturdays there was a lecture by the headmaster or a special guest in place of class, and then more independent time in the labs. Sundays were free—to worship, Violet supposed. The class schedule would change every trimester. It seemed simple to Violet, and gave her plenty of time to use the school's resources to work on her own projects. She smiled. She flipped to the map and began studying it, trying to memorize the location of each lab. The Great Hall was flanked by the dining hall and kitchens, through the halls to the side, and the duke's private apartments, which the map clearly stated were off-limits without an invitation. In the basement was the mechanical laboratory and the chemical laboratory. Above the kitchens were the professors' offices, and above that, the—

"Sit down," Jack whispered. Violet looked up. The chairs were all full and everyone was seated. Violet quickly sat down just as the side door flew open. In marched the duke, followed by the professors and, to Violet's surprise—and not just hers, she wagered by the sudden intakes of breath around her—the Countess Lovelace, Ada Byron. She remembered that the countess was the duke's godmother, but hadn't expected to see her on the first day.

The professors and the countess walked onto the stage and took their seats; then the duke stepped forward to a podium and addressed the students. "Welcome," he said, "to a new year at Illyria. My father founded Illyria with the intention of creating a place where the greatest scientific minds could come together to learn from one another, and where the most promising students of the sciences, regardless of class or station, can come together and learn. The returning students know this already. You are here to learn, and to work hard to use that knowledge. Fail me in this, fail my father in this, fail yourself in this, and you fail the world. You were brought here to fulfill your promise. Your promise, and my father's promise. Don't disappoint us."

The students and professors all applauded the opening statements. "Returning students, you should know what to do. Go find your rooms and move in, and meet the rest of us in the dining hall for lunch at noon." Everyone behind the front row got up and left quietly, leaving only Violet, Jack, and the three other new students in the hall. "New students. Please stand."

Violet and Jack stood. The professors gazed down on them silently. Violet felt her hands sweating. What sort of initiation would they have to endure?

"What I have said goes doubly for all of you. The returning

students have proved themselves as men of intelligence and good breeding, worthy of another year. You have yet to do that. Follow the rules. They are outlined in the papers you have—I recommend memorizing them, as 'not knowing the rules' is not an excuse for breaking them. After supper, you have free time to use as you wish. I recommend you spend that time in the student lounge studying. The wall behind you, as I'm sure most of you have gathered, can be used to power various inventions, and this wall extends to the student lounge. However, I do not like to be awakened at three in the morning to fend off some large clockwork automaton that has gone mad, so be careful. The making of weapons is forbidden within these halls. Out in the real world, use your skills as you wish, but here, no weapons. Anyone violating this rule will be instantly expelled. I'm sure you've all heard rumors about experiments gone awry that still lurk in the lower basements of the college. They are all false, I assure you. That said, students are forbidden from going into any of the lower basements. They are mainly used for storage, but they are labyrinthine, and it is easy to get lost, and I don't like having to take professors away from teaching to form search parties. Now, our honored guest, Countess Lovelace, would like to inspect all of you. She is a fine judge of character, and I hope you will listen to any advice she has."

Countess Lovelace rose and slowly descended from the platform to stand in front of the students. She was a small, pale woman with flashing dark eyes. She was sixty-seven, a widow, and dressed in deep navy, which seemed to bring out her careful, knowing smile. Her hair was pulled into a high bun on top of her head, and was almost entirely gray, but for a few streaks of black. She smelled faintly of brandy and smoke, and leaned heavily on a bronze and wood cane, peering at each of the new students in turn. "They look as though they'll do," she called over to the duke.

"I'm glad you approve, madam."

She walked past the line of students and stopped in front of Violet, who could feel the woman's breath on her. She kept her eyes fixed on the floor and tried not to look into Ada Byron's dark, fiery gaze. "What's your name?" Ada asked after a moment.

"Ashton Adams, ma'am," Violet answered, keeping her head down.

"You may walk me to the dining room," Ada said, offering an arm.

Violet nodded. She could feel the other students' jealous gazes on her. To be favored by the great Ada Byron, the first Reckoner, to be picked out by her, to touch her. Looking forward, but not at the countess herself, Violet took her by the arm and escorted her out of the room.

Once in the hallway, Ada stopped and released her arm from Violet's.

"The dining hall is this way, I believe, madam," Violet said, still not daring to look Ada in the eyes.

"When you nodded to me back in the hall, you almost curtsied. You'll have to work on that," Ada said.

Violet looked up into Ada's mischievous eyes and tried not to let her shock and chagrin show. "Ma'am, I—"

"Don't treat me like an idiot, girl. Any fool can see you're a woman. Luckily, this is a school full of geniuses, so I don't think you'll have too much trouble. Unless you keep curtsying. I'd improve your walk, and don't look down all the time. And your voice sounds too deep, like a child pretending to be a man."

"Countess, I didn't mean to—"

"Of course you meant to. You're here, and they all think you're a man, and it's really very clever, if you can pull it off. Now, take my arm again; the rest of them are coming." Violet did so, as the huge bronze doors opened and the students walked out into the hall. Seeing Lady Byron, they all kept their faces somber and their voices low, parting around her like a stream and heading to the dining hall, while Ada and Violet ambled slowly along after them. Finally, the last of the students was in the dining hall, and Ada released Violet's arm again.

"Countess, I—"

"I can't help you, you realize. You're on your own if you get caught. I'm around the school only a few times a year, and I can't show you too much favor or it will draw more attention to you, and more attention isn't what you need. So stop dressing like a dandy. It only highlights your femininity. Honestly, girl, who dressed you?"

"My brother."

"Well, get the help of someone else. Is your roommate in on your little hoax?"

"Yes, ma'am."

"Good, it might be unseemly otherwise. Have him help you. But don't let him abuse you. Some men might be prone to take advantage of this situation."

"I trust him."

"Good for you. Now, be a good boy, and take me to the dining hall." Violet took the countess's arm once more and led her, much more quickly now, to the dining hall. Violet opened the door for her; then the countess left her to sit to the right of the duke, while Violet found a seat next to Jack.

"Already the favorite," Jack whispered to her.

"She recognized my gender," Violet replied. Jack's eyes widened. "She gave me advice."

"Well," Jack said, "that's something."

Ernest led the students in grace, and the meal was served: eggs, porridge, toast, kippers, tomatoes, various cheeses, bacon, and ham, which smelled heavenly to everyone. At the duke's table, the duke leaned in to the countess and spoke softly. "What was that about, Ada? I've never seen you favor a student so blatantly."

"I'm growing old, Ernest, and I find myself enjoying the company of young men more and more." The duke laughed at this. "Will there be cards after supper tonight?"

"Of course, Countess. What is a day with you without gambling?"

"And cigars," the countess added, and smiled happily.

The dining hall was larger than the Great Hall, which made it quite large for the fewer than thirty people eating. The professors and the duke ate on a raised platform at the end of the hall, but the students chose their own seats from among the small tables placed on the main level. There was a balcony with a twisting marble stairwell coming down from it on the side of the room from which they had entered. On the balcony was an archway, which Violet assumed led out to the bridge she had spotted stretching over the Great Hall.

Jack took out the map from his sheaf of papers. "That archway, there," he said to Violet, pointing to the balcony, "must lead to the bridge, which goes to the duke's private apartments. That's his personal entrance."

"I suppose so," Violet said. She was staring at the other three men at their table, who were staring back, nervous. Jack looked up. He had apparently forgotten all about the other students he was sitting with, all first-years, like himself and Violet. No one spoke. They just ate, sometimes staring at one another. At the other tables, conversation hummed.

"So," Jack said, "I guess we're all going to be in our classes together. I'm Jack Feste. This is Ashton Adams. Who are you lot?"

The three young men stared back piggishly. The most handsome of them spoke first. "I'm Roger Fairfax, Earl of Cheshireford," he said, proudly sticking his chin out in a way that no longer made him look the handsomest.

Then the tallest extended his hand to Jack's to shake it. "I'm James Lane," he said.

Finally, the shortest one eagerly stuck out his hand and introduced himself. "Humphrey Merriman," he said with a faint Irish accent. They all shook hands and then settled into silence.

Violet looked at the men across from her, and around the room, and was pleased to note that she didn't feel any sort of romantic feeling for any of them, even the most attractive, and so wouldn't be distracted by flowery emotions.

Violet was luckier than the other students in this regard, for at that moment, Cecily Worthing, the duke's cousin and ward, appeared in the archway at which Jack had just been pointing and began to descend the winding stairs to join her cousin at the table. The conversation hushed slightly as the students noticed her one by one and stared. The returning students, of course, had seen her before. Most went quickly back to their eating, not wanting to attract the duke's wrath, though they all secretly wished to invite her to sit with them.

Of course, as Cecily was the one young lady permitted to roam the halls of the college, it was only natural that the students would all find her attentions something to be sought after, as many young men enjoy the attentions of young women. However, even if Cecily were but one of hundreds of young ladies set free to roam the halls of Illyria as they pleased, she would still be the most sought after for companionship.

She was charming. A little short, but with a comely figure, long golden hair, and clear fair skin that glowed in the bronze hallways. Her smile and laugh were the sort that would make everyone around her smile and laugh as well, not just because of the fine pink color of her lips, or her perfect set of teeth, but because when she was happy, she seemed like a fresh country breeze that has somehow snuck into the heavy coal-stained air of the city.

Jack, who had not been prone to romance before this moment, fell immediately in love. He had known his share of women in school, the village girls who grinned openly and had an unrefined charm. And he had known Violet, of course, though she was more of a sister. Going through London, he had often seen the aristocratic ladies with their huge hats and slim waists, but he had never seen anything like Cecily. She walked through the rows of tables like a swan floated on the river. She kissed the duke on the cheek with the lightness of a hummingbird, and swept her loose hair back behind her ear with a simple gesture, like a dove taking flight. In that moment, Jack knew that he could live and study for a thousand years and never be able to create anything as beautiful as her. "Who is that?" he asked.

"That must be Cecily," Violet said, eyeing the girl. She felt strangely jealous, probably because the girl had been raised here, whereas Violet had to hide herself to gain entry. "She is the duke's cousin and ward."

"Oh," Jack said, staring after her.

"Don't stare too hard, now," said a large student who had come up from one of the other tables. "The duke is mighty protective of her, and he has views on how women are distracting to us student types." The man placed his hand on his belly and chortled. He had brought with him another student, thin and terribly pale, who laughed as well. "I'm Toby, and this is Drew. We're upperclassmen, so it's our job to welcome you newlings and show you the ropes today. So, who are all of you?"

No one spoke immediately. Violet studied Toby, who was scratching his stomach and looking unimpressed. Drew stood behind him, occasionally looking toward the duke's table and then snapping his attention back to Toby. "Ashton Adams," Violet said, extending her hand. "This is Jack Feste, James Lane, Roger Fairfax—"

"Earl of Cheshireford," Roger interrupted.

"Yes. And Humphrey Merriman," Violet finished.

"Okay," Toby said, "that's a start, anyway. I saw you escorting the countess in, Adams. Never seen that happen before. Usually the duke brings her in."

"She asked me to escort her. She wanted to have a word with me about my wardrobe."

"You do look like a bit of a git," Toby said.

"My . . . sister dressed me. I normally don't pay attention to clothes, but it was a special occasion, so—"

"Ha!" Toby barked. "Can't dress yourself." He slapped Violet on the back. "I'm just joking with you, mate. I don't know how to dress myself either. Let Mother buy all my suits. Well, it was a pleasure meeting all you fine first-years. I imagine I'll be seeing more of you tonight. I wouldn't sleep in your nightshirts tonight. You never know when you'll be doing a lot of running." Toby smirked and walked back to his table, Drew following.

"Sounds like an initiation," Jack said, grinning widely at Violet. "We'd better prepare." The other first-years all seemed frightened, except Fairfax, who didn't seem to be paying attention to anything.

"I'm sure it won't be that bad," Violet said, "but it probably wouldn't hurt to sleep in our trousers and have some tricks in our pockets."

"I didn't bring any tricks," Lane said.

"Then we'll make some," Jack said. "The entire college is open for exploration today. I'm sure we can nick some stuff from the labs."

Violet nodded. The others looked scared, but Jack and Violet didn't. They were excited for an adventure, and eager to prove themselves. They happily finished their meal and waited for the duke to dismiss them.

❈❀❈

THE duke, meanwhile, was talking with his godmother and the other professors. "I think it will be a good year," the duke said to Ada. Cecily also leaned forward, which made him flinch slightly. He wasn't sure if it was appropriate to discuss the virtues of the young men, even in the abstract, in her presence.

"It's certainly a promising-looking group," Ada said, "though none of them seem to have much range."

"Is it so bad to be an expert in one's field?" the duke asked.

"Your father was a master in every field," Ada said, "and so are you, though you're oddly loath to admit it."

"Your eyes are clouded with the affection you bear me."

"In any case, master of one area is a fine thing, a great thing, more than most men will achieve. But this is Illyria, the place for scientific greatness. You should be breeding geniuses of every craft."

"We only take the best."

"Perhaps if you took students who seemed to do well in all fields instead of mastering one of them, you could make that student a master of all the sciences. Think what such a genius could accomplish."

"I quite agree with Auntie Ada," Cecily said. "A student who shows great skill in all fields is one worthy of Illyria, if not its ideal." The duke nodded into his food but didn't look up. He didn't like Cecily disagreeing with him on matters scientific, particularly in front of the professors, who he could feel were all grinning.

"I'll take it under consideration," he said. "I think that mealtime has gone on long enough, though, hasn't it?" He stood and clapped his hands to get the attention of the students. He looked out over their faces, young, clever, full of ambition. This was a good group, he thought.

"Go. Unpack, get your books, settle in to your rooms, explore the college. Tomorrow, your classes begin. Today is your last day of holiday. Spend it wisely."

The students all stood and filed out quietly, the air around the first-years trembling visibly with exhilaration. After a moment, the professors left, too, for their lounge on the second floor, or for their offices, or to prepare for their first lectures tomorrow. Only Ada and Cecily stayed with the duke as the servants came in to clear away the dirty dishes.

"I'm going to go lie down for a while," Ada said. "Cecily, would you escort me to the lounge in your apartments?"

"Of course, Auntie Ada."

"I'll see you at supper, Ernest," Ada said, walking with Cecily toward the stairs to their private apartments. He would suggest she use the lift out in the hall, but he knew Ada would be insulted by any insinuation that she was frail. Instead, he watched Cecily support her as they slowly climbed the twisted marble stairs and headed out through the archway, toward home. The servants danced around the dining hall, cleaning and scrubbing the floors till they gleamed.

The duke sighed and rested his head in his hands. It wasn't sadness that caused this gesture, for he was a man content with the luxuries life had afforded him. If one were to ask what caused him to sigh, he would have no answer, for he was not conscious of the malaise that troubled him. All he knew was that he had felt as though he had had something in his grasp, and that it was now slipping away again. But he had work to do, and would not let himself indulge in his emotions. Instead he would head for the labs to inspect everything, then look in on the dormitory and demonstrate to the new students that he could drop by at any moment to make sure they were behaving.

And then there was the first lecture he would be giving on Saturday, for which he had to prepare. It would be on the possibilities of space travel, the duke had decided. The idea had stuck with him since he'd read Ashton Adams's essay. There were strong ideas there, which warranted exploration for the entire student body. The Adams twins were a striking pair. Even young Ashton, with his gentle face, struck the duke as a handsome lad, filled with promise. In fact, the duke had thought of both the Adamses a lot in the past month, though only in passing. He thought he would like to meet their father. They were a remarkable family, clearly.

The duke looked up at the clock on the wall. It was time to visit the labs.

⋯⋯⊙⋯⋯

VIOLET was herself visiting the labs. It hadn't taken long for her and Jack to settle into their room, though they'd had a small argument about whether or not to hang a sheet across the room for modesty's sake, so Jack couldn't see Violet sleeping. Violet had insisted that it was quite unnecessary, and suspicious to boot. Besides, she wasn't the sort of girl who was modest. She could change in the water closet—each of the rooms had one—and her nightshirt wasn't revealing in any way. On the other hand, Jack wanted it because he was afraid of Violet seeing his naked legs and making judgments. Violet promised not to make any judgments whatsoever, and so no sheet was hung.

The rooms were pleasant, if small, with green rugs and wood floors. They all opened onto a hall, at the end of which was the student lounge, with its constantly moving wall of gears, and several tables to work on. Many of the returning students were already hard at work in the lounge, catching up on their work or chatting with friends while showing off various inventions they had perfected over the summer. Violet saw a clockwork automaton in the shape of a large insect that seemed able to sense walls and avoid them, and odd potions that put people to sleep right away—the latter demonstrated on Merriman, who seemed eager to get on well with the older students. But as exciting as these were, what she and Jack wanted to see most were the labs.

The chemical laboratory smelled of strange toxins and smoke, and the once-golden walls had rusted into a deep brown in places, giving them a mottled look. Professor Curio walked around the room, sometimes mumbling to himself as he rearranged the potions on the cabinets, then placing them back in their original order, then rearranging them again. The microscopes that lay at one end of the room were large and shone expectantly, as though they had missed being used all summer. When Curio spotted the students, he stared at them silently until they left.

The reckoning laboratory was tall and contained six huge analytical engines, looming towers twice as tall as Violet. They had huge slots in the middle for the reckoning programs, and another slot where the parchment printed with results came out. They hummed silently in the dark, ominous. In the center of the room were a group of tables for punching out the reckoning programs. Violet and Jack walked through the room silently, Violet pausing to touch the machines, gently caressing the long levers, but after a little while, the quiet humming under the cranking of the gears became a bit disarming, and they left.

The astronomy lab at the top of the college seemed to Violet less sophisticated, if rather larger, than her father's lab back at the manor. But the two clock towers outside the glass dome were of particular fascination to them both. The door out to the landing was locked, but through the glass they could see life-sized statues that danced at the striking of each hour.

"I think we should pick the lock and go ride the statue of the lion," Jack said, pointing. "You still have that lock-picking tool you made?"

"It's down in our room," Violet said, "but I'd rather not get into trouble before classes have started. Besides, the lion already has Leonardo da Vinci riding it. I don't know that there'd be room for you."

"I'm sure Leo wouldn't mind," Jack said. They both stared at the clocks awhile longer, and then descended back into the college.

The biology and natural science lab smelled like embalming fluid, but Jack was soon clearly quite enamored with it. Despite Violet's objections, he started going through the cabinets, picking up pickled mice and various bottles of strange glowing fluids and cooing excitedly over each one: "These are liquefied jellyfish!" "Strips of preserved hog hide!" "An empty armadillo shell!" And so on. After a few minutes of this, Violet said she was going to continue with the tour. Jack waved her on, barely looking up as he said he would catch up with her later. Violet headed down to the basement, where the mechanical lab was located.

She tried to restrain herself at first, images of Jack going wild in the empty biology lab still fresh in her mind, but she couldn't resist for long, and was soon at one of the large tables, hands sticky with oil and grease and the beginnings of a small invention lying in front of her. She was so taken by the endless supplies of gears and springs and the huge wall of clanking, forever-turning wheels that she didn't notice how much time was passing.

"Getting started early?"

Violet looked up. Standing in the door was a shadowy figure of a man, looking as if he'd been there for a while. Violet raised her hand above her eyes, hoping to make out a face, though she had already begun to suspect who it was and started blushing.

"Don't do that now," the duke said, striding into the lab. "You'll get grease on your face." He reached Violet's table and grabbed at her wrist to keep her hand from her face. "Too late!" he said. "Make sure you wash that before you go to bed." He grinned down at her.

"Oh," Violet said, standing. "Sorry, sir."

"No need to apologize, Mr. Adams," the duke said. "It's admirable that you're already working. May I ask what it is?"

"I don't quite know yet, sir," Violet confessed. "I was just so energized by the supplies and tools and space that I started toying about. I can take it apart and put all the pieces back."

"Don't be silly. There are cubbies over on that wall that you can keep your small inventions in. Larger things, you can just push to the side. This place gets crowded by the end of the year. Now, let's see what you've got."

The duke leaned over Violet, placing his hand on her shoulder with a feeling of camaraderie. But Violet couldn't help but notice that the duke's breath on her neck was far warmer than the flames of her own lab, back home.

"Well, at home, I designed a device that could pick locks," Violet said, trying to focus on the gears and knobs in front of her. "I used it to terrorize my bro—sister. Jack was just talking about it earlier.

And some of the elder students said at lunch that we might have some sort of initiation tonight. So I guess I was thinking I could make some sort of attachment to the lock-picking—"

"You brought it here?"

"What?"

"The lockpick? You thought you'd need a lockpick?"

Violet pursed her lips, and the duke couldn't help but notice that young Mr. Adams's lips were remarkably smooth, and how long and attractive his neck was. Still, he had brought a lockpick to school. That implied a mischievous streak. Although, truthfully, the duke was torn—he also wanted to see the lockpick. It sounded clever.

"I brought most of my small inventions. I didn't really know what I'd need."

"Well, don't go breaking into my apartments with it."

"Oh, of course not, sir!" Violet said, blushing.

"So, what were you thinking this attachment could do to assist you in your initiation this evening?"

"You know about the initiation?" Violet asked.

"It's the same every year," the duke said, "but that's all I'll tell you."

"Well, I don't know what it could be, but the basic mechanism of the lockpick is adaptable, so I thought that I could create an attachment that could make it multipurpose . . . a few different tools, a small electrical torch, maybe—that's what this part is. I used Volta's theories and some ideas from a young scientist named Tesla. It generates a constant electrically generated light if I keep squeezing this trigger, here . . ."

"May I see?" the duke asked, placing his hand over Violet's on the trigger and squeezing. The device whirred slightly and then projected a beam of light, before the whirring slowed down and the beam faded. The laboratory was dark, and Violet and the duke were both suddenly aware, in the darkness, of the touching of their hands.

"Impressive," the duke said, taking his hand off the device.

"It'll be easier to use attached to the lockpick," Violet said. "The lockpick generates more energy with a pull, so the beam will stay on longer."

"Very impressive, Mr. Adams," the duke said, "and I'm sure it will come in quite handy tonight. Mind that you sleep with it in your pockets, though. Won't do any good in your room."

"Thanks," Violet said, smiling.

"You look quite like your sister, when you smile," the duke said. Then he turned around and walked out of the lab, leaving Violet biting her lip in the dark.

The duke walked down the corridor and up the stairs, stopping by the students' lounge and walking the dormitory hall, where the students all went quiet as he nodded at them. It was nearly supper time. He and the other professors and Ada would be eating in the professors' lounge tonight, and gambling, and drinking, and—as Ada was there—smoking cigars. He had left the lab quickly because socializing too much with any one student could be seen as favoritism, and also because he had found himself oddly drawn to Ashton Adams, not just intellectually, but physically. This was a new feeling for him: he was a man of learning, and felt that to judge a man on his actions in the bedroom was a ridiculous standard, but he had never considered himself to have inverted tendencies. Yet, he also found Ashton Adams's skin to be of a lovely hue. That thought, creeping into his mind, seemed out of place and confusing. Perhaps it was a side effect of seeing the boy's inventions. Or perhaps it was just that Ashton bore a remarkable resemblance to his sister, Violet, whom the duke remembered fondly. That must be it. Perhaps it was Violet who had drawn out these feelings in him, and Ashton was merely a memory of them walking the halls. In any case, the duke decided, it would be best to avoid any undue intimacy with Ashton, and not to think on the matter any longer. To dwell on the desires of one's heart was to spend time in a world of fantasy, when he belonged in a world of reason.

"Ah-ha!" Ada said as the duke came into the lounge. "I knew you'd show up once I lit the first cigar. Say what you will about bad habits, but I don't believe a word of it. Sometimes I suspect you have me over just as an excuse to inhale the smoke of the cigars I light."

The duke coughed. The smell of cigar smoke and freshly lit matches was spiraling around the lounge. A bottle of brandy was open as well, and everyone had a full glass. "Am I that late?" the duke asked.

"Not too terribly late," Valentine said, "but we're all rather impatient where brandy and cigars are involved."

The professors' lounge was a cozy place that the duke's father had designed with his scientific colleagues at the time. It had a deep brown and gold rug on the floor and a large golden fireplace. Ada sat at the far end of the table, with the professors—save for Bracknell, who was, the duke noted with some relief, absent—gathered around her, craning their necks toward her like daises to the sun—except for Professor Bunburry, who, given the large metal funnel around his neck, could not crane it, so he merely listed slightly in her direction. The duke smiled and sat down in his armchair at the head of the table. Across from him, Ada reclined in her chair, her cigar smoke haloing around her.

"They're sending Welsh rarebit for supper tonight," the duke said. "Pass me the brandy."

Valentine grinned and slid the bottle of brandy down the table to the duke.

"We were just dis-dis-dis-cussing the new students," Curio said.

"The countess has asked us which of the students we think will prove most surprising in this coming year," Valentine said.

"And what do you mean by 'surprising'?" the duke asked his god-mother.

"That's just what we were asking," Prism said.

"I just mean," Ada said, blowing smoke into the air, "the student most likely to do things that are . . . unexpected."

"That's very vague, madam," Valentine said, leering.

"I feel quite sure, though, that by the end of the year, you'll all agree on one student."

"That sounds like a ch-ch-challenge," Curio said.

"Take it as you will."

"You're challenging us to a wager, it seems," Valentine said. Ada's love of gambling was well known among the professors. "But we have yet to hear whom you'll place your money on."

"I'd bet a hundred pounds at least on Mr. Adams," Ada said.

The duke frowned. He didn't like gambling that involved the students. "I hope you're not asking my professors to engage in a bet where punishing a student could work to their advantage," he said.

"Of course not, Ernest. That's why the terms are vague. 'Surprising' could mean any number of things."

"I still feel uncomfortable with this," the duke said. The bell beside the dumbwaiter rang and he rose to open it. Inside, several steaming platters rested on a silver tray. He removed them and placed them on the table before the professors. Normally, a servant would do this, but the duke didn't like having servants in the lounge. He felt it made some of the professors ill at ease, as though they needed to constantly impress the servants with their great skill. And besides, he liked placing the food in front of the professors himself, so as to remind them where it came from.

"Then maybe you will engage my wager, if the professors won't," Ada said, lifting the cover off one of the platters. Steam rose into her face, wavering the wisps of loose hair at her forehead and then blending with the smoke of the room. Her platter held steamed spinach and lemon, and the smell filled the room. "But, instead of money, I will bet something else, whatever you'd like."

"And what will I bet?" the duke asked, aware that if he backed down, he would lose face in front of the professors. They all liked him, but he was younger than they, and everyone knew his position was inherited, not earned. Keeping their respect and docility was a constant struggle.

"If I win," Ada said, the professors looking at her, "then I may pick one student for next year's class. It will give me a chance to bring in a student whom you might not normally recognize as having the potential for true brilliance, such as we were discussing at lunch."

"That seems a small prize for you, Countess," the duke said.

"Perhaps. But perhaps I'll bring in someone unique—someone without all the politeness you always seem to expect from your students."

"Politeness?" Prism asked.

"Your scientists are often statesmen," Ada said, placing some spinach on her plate. "They're all such gentlemen, so refined."

"That's quite untrue," the duke said. The other professors were lifting the lids off the plates and serving themselves. "One of our students this year is the son of a gardener."

"Really?" Valentine asked. "How horrid."

"That may be so," Ada said. "But none of your students are ever rough. They are always charming and polite, even if not always of good birth. Where's the rough-and-tumble son of a fisherman who swears like a sailor and mixes salt water with wormwood to create an elixir?"

"To be a proper scientist these days," Prism said, flipping down a lens of his glasses to look over the food, "you need funding, patronage. And for that, you need charm."

"So teach the charm the way you teach science," Ada said.

"I don't know about the others, but I do teach charm," Valentine said. "By example, anyway."

"You've made your point," the duke said. "You can choose a student if you win. But what if I win?"

"What do you want?" Ada asked.

"You to come work for me," the duke said, smiling. "For one year."

Professor Prism looked up sadly at the duke through his many lenses.

"Don't worry, Prism, I don't plan on replacing you. The countess would become my assistant of sorts. She would sit in on all the classes and offer her years of experience to the students. She would perform lectures when I couldn't. She would be a constant font of wisdom from which the students could drink."

Ada cocked an eyebrow across the table. "Accepted," she said.

Valentine applauded, but no one joined in.

"So, if Mr. Adams proves most surprising," the duke said, "you may choose a student for next year's class. But if any of the other new students proves more shocking, then you will come work here. These are the terms?"

"Yes."

"Very well. Then it is a bet."

"Excellent," said Ada. "Now let's finish supper and play some cards. And this time, do try to win at least a little, gentlemen. I find myself growing bored."

The duke and his godmother and the professors feasted and drank and chatted about their plans and expectations for the coming year. The mood dimmed considerably when Bracknell appeared, just in time for dessert, but he seemed so afraid of the countess that, to everyone's delight, she merely had to glare at him to make him stop speaking. After supper, they smoked more cigars, drank more brandy, and played several hands of bridge. The countess won the majority.

VIII.

LATER that night in the hall of student rooms, the third-year Toby Belch and the second-year Drew Pale were waiting. The initiation of the freshmen had always been run exclusively by the third-years, but Toby was the loudest and most enthusiastic of them, and Drew was his closest friend, so no one minded that Drew was coming along. The other seniors were still unpacking or studying in the lounge, waiting for a signal from Toby that it was time for the festivities to begin. That signal would come when Toby was sure that all the freshmen were asleep.

Toby and Drew spent most of their time in the chemical lab— Toby working on the perfect hangover cure and Drew just enjoying the fumes—so they had turned to Gregory Cheek, the third-year mechanical specialist, for help fashioning a device that would allow them to listen through the dormitory walls to determine when all the first-years were asleep. Gregory had done so happily, and given it to them and explained how to use it hours ago. It looked like a sturdy brass mug with a coil of wire where the handle should be and a small hole in the bottom. It was really a rather lovely piece of work, simple but effective, using the basic properties of sound and enhancing them with a touch of mechanical ingenuity. However, in the past few hours, Toby and Drew had forgotten how to use it.

"You put this end against the wall, and you put your ear against the other end," Drew said, clanging the device against the wall.

"That's backwards," Toby said, taking the device from Drew and reversing it. He pressed his ear against the small tube and the large end against the wall of one of the first-years' rooms. He heard nothing, and narrowed his eyes. Did this mean the students were asleep, or that he was using the device incorrectly?

"So?" Drew asked.

"I don't hear anything," Toby said.

"So they're asleep," Drew said, pleased. "Let's check on the other rooms."

In the next room, Toby heard snoring through the small tube, and was satisfied that he was using it correctly. Pleased with himself, and gracious, he let Drew listen, as well.

"Which ones are in this room?" Drew asked.

"The little one and the tall one," Toby answered. Which meant that the last room was the first-year who had somehow managed to reserve himself a private chamber. The private rooms were supposed to be for third-years only. Usually a first- and second-year ended up living together due to the odd number of students in each year, but this year the duke had sent letters to all the third-years asking if they wouldn't mind sharing with a second year. Toby had written back to say that it wouldn't be a problem as long as he could share a room with Drew. He didn't mind, if it got him in the duke's good graces, but when he found out that it was for some self-important first-year who had refused to share a room, he practically threw the brat's luggage out the window into the Thames.

Drew pushed his ear against the wall of the final first-year room, not using the device. "I can't hear anything," he said. "This is where His Highness is staying, is it?"

"Yes," Toby said, pressing the device against the wall, and hearing nothing. "He's out like a little lamb, he is. I hope he changed into his nightshirt before bed." He snickered.

"Let's wake the others, then," he said.

The four other third-years had all been relaxing and catching up with their classmates in the lounge at the end of the dormitory hall, having quickly settled back into university life. When Toby and Drew walked in, a small bronze sparrow flew by their heads, nearly hitting them.

"It's been flying for over ten minutes," Alexander said, though the device was clearly not his, as he spent most of his time working with the analytical engines. Gregory, who Toby felt sure had created the sparrow that, even at that moment, seemed to be diving for his head, smiled sheepishly. Toby dodged the mechanical bird again, but Drew was not so lucky. It hit him full on the side of the head.

"Oh dear," Tim said from his seat by the window.

"Where's Ivan?" Drew asked.

"Probably in his room, moping," Alexander said. Ivan was from the East, Russia specifically, and consequently had no sense of humor. Toby was glad to be rid of him. In fact, he could have done without the rest of the students, too: Gregory never spoke, and when he did, was impossible to understand through his Welsh accent. Tim had a perpetually glazed look in his eyes and was so tall and thin he made Toby uneasy. He could have kept Alex, he supposed, though Alex had a tendency to be overwhelmingly optimistic at times, and was constantly feeling sorry for everyone. Even now he was frowning and dabbing at the cut on Drew's head with a handkerchief. Drew did not look entirely comfortable.

"Let's go on without him, then," Toby said.

"Are they asleep?" Alex asked.

"Yes," Toby said, grinning. "Remember, when you burst in, be as scary as possible, grab 'em, and throw them out into the hall. Drew here'll blindfold them all, and then we can take them downstairs." Gregory nodded. Alex bit his lip but nodded as well. Toby suspected that Alex would let the first-years grab whatever they'd like if they asked nicely enough. He'd send him into the room with the fat one, who looked like he could use some sympathy.

"Great," Toby said. "Then let's go."

Toby had been correct in assuming Alex would have pity on the first-years. He shook them quietly awake, with whispers of "Up now, up now, it's time to prove yourselves!" and let Merriman put on his glasses before leaving his room. Lane and Merriman had heeded Toby's warning and slept in their pants, shirts, and shoes, but hadn't thought to actually bring anything.

Toby was pleased to find Roger Fairfax, Earl of Cheshireford, the ponce who felt he was too good for a roommate, soundly asleep in his nightshirt, stocking feet, and even a pointed sleeping hat. With all his energy, he screamed Roger awake and then pushed him, still groggy-eyed and confused, out into the hall, where Drew quickly snapped a black cloth around his eyes.

"What is going on?" Fairfax shrieked.

"Oh, relax," Jack said as Drew tightened the blindfold over his eyes. He and Violet hadn't been asleep at all, but had happily hopped out of bed fully dressed when Tim and Gregory had come into the room, their pockets overflowing with tools they thought might be useful. Gregory and Tim hadn't said anything, just pointed at the open door, which, Jack had thought, was a good deal more frightening than screaming and shouting.

With pleasure, Toby poked and prodded the blindfolded first-years, leading them down the halls with which they were not yet familiar and into the mechanical lift, then pulling the lever and letting it fall perhaps too quickly to the lower basement. There, Toby and the others led the first-years to a large dimly lit room with four archways leading off it and gave each of them a good spin.

No one was really sure why there was a labyrinth in the basement of Illyria. Toby and Drew had explored parts of it and suspected it was a safety measure, a way of keeping the more dangerous inventions from being stumbled upon by a layman who might accidentally destroy London with them. Toby and Drew hadn't found anything down here that they thought could destroy London, but they suspected that was only because they hadn't looked hard enough.

With a wave of Toby's hand, the third-years quietly dispersed, leaving the first-years alone in the darkness.

❧⊚❧

VIOLET had no idea where they were, but was terribly excited. Still blindfolded and dizzy, she walked forward a few paces to see if anyone would stop her. Her footsteps were stiff on the stone beneath them.

"Anyone there?" she called.

"Hullo, Ashton," came Jack's friendly reply. Violet took off her blindfold. The room they were in was dark, with one small gas lamp flickering on the wall. Lane, Merriman, and Fairfax all stood there, shivering in the dark. Violet smirked to see Fairfax in a long shapeless white nightshirt.

Jack was already exploring the walls. "There are four passages out," he said, "near as I can tell." He looked over at the other three students. "Haven't you lot taken your blindfolds off yet? Come on, I don't want to waste too much time on this. I'd like to be well rested for class tomorrow." Nervously, the other three took off their blindfolds and stared around them, blinking vapidly.

"Where is this?" Merriman asked.

"Basement," Violet said. "Probably lower basement. We dropped far down in the lift, but we didn't really walk that far, so it has to be the lower basement. I'd wager we just have to find the lift again, and we can go back to bed."

"How do we do that?" Lane asked.

"With our incredible scientific ability, of course," Jack said, skipping back to the group. With a flourish he produced a large jar from one of his jacket pockets. Inside was a thick fluid that glowed white green in the darkness.

"What is that?" Fairfax asked with obvious disgust, lifting his feet off the sticky ground one by one. His stockings were filthy, Violet noted with a smile.

"It's from jellyfish," Jack said. "There was a whole jar of them in the bio lab. I knew most of them could glow in the dark, so I extracted some of their fluorescent proteins and put them in a jar. We can paint it on the walls as we travel, so we know where we've been."

"Very clever," Violet said with some pride.

"Thank you," Jack said with a bow.

"I didn't bring anything," Merriman said, looking nearly ready to cry in the soft green glow of the jellyfish jar.

"I didn't either," said Lane.

Violet tried not to roll her eyes. They had been warned, after all.

"This is an outrage," Fairfax said. "I doubt it's even safe down here. Why, who knows what odd chemical horrors have come together in the wastes of this place? There could be all sorts of dreadful creations stored here."

"I'm sure it's only a little dangerous," Violet said. "The duke said they'd been doing this initiation for years."

"The duke?" Fairfax asked.

"You spoke to the duke about this?" Jack asked, cocking an eyebrow and staring at Violet.

"Well, he came down to the lab, and I was showing him an invention, so I only mentioned . . . that is, I mentioned that some of the third-years had hinted at it, and he said, 'Oh yes, that's been happening for quite some time,' or something like that." Violet shut her mouth before she could stammer further. She could feel herself blushing, and hoped that it didn't show in the green light. She didn't even know why she was stammering like an idiot under Jack's gaze, but she suddenly felt as though she should have kept her private moment with the duke a secret. "Look!" she said, remembering the device that had prompted the conversation. She held it up and pulled the trigger, causing a bright beam of light to shoot forth.

"Most excellent!" Jack exclaimed.

"Amazing," Merriman said.

"It's really not that impressive," Violet said, knowing her modesty was false. Finally, she was among other bright young minds, and they were impressed with her inventions!

"I couldn't do anything like that," Lane said.

"Maybe it's just not your field," Jack said. "Ashton here is a mechanical genius."

"I do feel more at home with chemical experimentation," Lane confessed. "I synthesized a formula that, though it started as a small amount of paste, would gradually evaporate into breathable air. That's how I got in."

"That's marvelous," Violet said. "Why, you could use that to breathe underwater."

"I suppose," Lane said.

"Why didn't you bring it?" Violet asked.

"Do you think we'll be going underwater?" Lane asked. But before Violet could reply, Fairfax let out a horrid screech. She quickly shot a beam of light at him, but could see nothing the matter.

"What is it?" Jack asked.

"Something brushed against me," Fairfax replied.

"There wasn't anything there," Violet said. "There's nothing around."

"Probably one of the cats," Merriman said.

"What?" Jack asked.

"My father works for a family whose son was a student here a while back, when the school first opened. The son said that the chemical professor back then was working on an invisibility potion, and fed it to some cats and kittens to test it. Apparently it worked on most of them—but then he couldn't find them to change them back, so now invisible cats roam the college."

"How marvelous!" Jack said.

"Your father is a servant?" Fairfax asked with palpable condescension in his voice.

"He's a gardener," Merriman said softly. Fairfax scoffed. Jack clenched his jaw.

"I think it's best we try to get out of here, rather than stand about talking," Violet said before Jack could hit Fairfax. "Fairfax, you can stay here if you don't feel dignified traveling with a gardener's son or, for that matter, an estate manager's son. We'll send someone down for you if we remember." Fairfax sneered, but followed as Violet started walking, Jack painting the walls with jellyfish protein as they went. She didn't care where they went, as long as they went somewhere.

They walked in silence for a while, the group following Violet, who chose which twists and turns to follow at random, not pausing to let anyone else speak for fear it would result in an argument. The labyrinthine basement seemed to be used mainly for storage. Blank, unassuming doors lined some of the walls. Violet used her skeleton key device on a few of them, but after only finding boxes of salt and jars of ether, decided they were all dead ends.

"They just leave the doors open?" Fairfax said, his arms crossed.

"I used this to open them," Violet explained. "It's a mechanical skeleton key."

"I didn't realize Illyria trained thieves and servants. Perhaps I should have gone to Oxford after all."

"I'm sure that would have made all of us very happy," Jack said. Violet laughed and heard others chuckling in the darkness as well.

She stopped walking and held up her hand. "I don't think we're alone."

"Another cat?" Jack asked hopefully. He clearly wanted to study them, or was thinking of various pranks to pull with them. He reached into his pocket and took out Sheila. She woke from a peaceful sleep to look around at her new surroundings.

"You brought the ferret?" Violet asked, seeing it in the darkness.

"They have a great sense of smell," Jack said. "Maybe she can catch one of the cats!"

"Cats are twice the size of ferrets," Violet pointed out.

"I'm sure Sheila can hold her own," Jack said.

"Anyway, I don't think it's cats. . . . I think there are people somewhere around."

"Oh, yes," said Jack. "Looked like the older students who warned us about the initiation. I spotted them a while ago. I assume they're just keeping watch on us to make sure we don't get into too much trouble so they don't get blamed if we do."

"Ah, well, if that's the game, then that's all right." Violet said, and went back to pondering which direction to go next.

"My year, we were already safe in our beds by now," Toby said, stepping out of the darkness, Drew right behind him. Violet raised an eyebrow at his coming out of hiding. "Well, if you know we're here, no point us stumbling around in the shadows, is there? May as well just walk along with you."

"Why don't you just show us the way out?" Fairfax snarled.

"That wouldn't be much fun, now, would it?" Toby said.

"This isn't fun," Fairfax responded.

"I didn't mean fun for you." Toby grinned. Drew chuckled.

"Well, I'm having a good time," Violet said, "and I bet Jack is, too."

"I am," Jack said, "though I wish it had been an invisible cat you heard."

"Well then, first-years," Toby said with a wave of his hand, "lead on."

In truth, Toby was a bit worried. This was a part of the basement he had never explored before. In previous years, one of the students had always had a compass on him, and it had never taken long for them to reason that the elevator must be on the great gear wall, so they just had to head toward the river to find the lift. This group seemed like it contained nothing but geniuses with no forethought for little things and people who didn't take initiations seriously. He hoped it wouldn't land them in too much trouble. Just a little while longer, he thought; then he'd take out his own compass.

At the end of one of the corridors there was a door that was very different from the others. The others had been simple wooden affairs with brass knobs and locks. This door was tall—it nearly reached the ceiling—and made entirely of brass. More curiously, there was no knob, handle, or visible way of opening it. But most striking of all wasn't so much the door as the various figures lying around the wall in front of it.

"Skeletons?" Drew asked in a high-pitched voice. Violet swallowed. It seemed the older students hadn't come this way before, and the shadows ahead did indeed look like skeletons.

"Possibly for research," Jack said in a weaker voice than usual, "in the biology laboratory." Violet nodded and shot her light at them, half-wondering if they would come to life. However, the light reflected back not white bone, but brass mechanics.

"They're automata," Violet said with wonder. "But why are they all just lying here?" Indeed, some of them had fallen from their leaning positions and lay in a heap at the end of the corridor. Violet, curious about their design, stepped forward and touched the first one. It was a thin figure, with long bonelike limbs that had at first made it look like a skeleton. But where the rib cage would have been was a large centerpiece with a clockwork key sticking out of it. And where a skull would have been was a smooth, featureless head without eyes or mouth. It seemed oddly familiar to Violet, but she couldn't figure out what she thought she recognized.

It was when she headed past the first figure to examine the second that the first came to life. She gasped, watching as its head straightened itself on its thin slumped neck and its thick heavy feet steadied themselves on the ground. Each movement made a squeal of metal. The thing's hands, which had seemed simple three-pronged claws, stretched out, revealing sharp razors under their outer layer. The razors popped forward with the sound of knives being sharpened, and suddenly the hands were frightening talons that were reaching out for Violet's neck.

Violet stood frozen in horror for a moment. A scream rose in her throat, but wouldn't release. Her body was both cold and hot. Her brain shouted so many things at once that she couldn't listen to any of them. All she could do was keep her eyes focused on the sharp glinting blades that were about to rend her head from her body. How sad it was, she thought, that she would never actually get to attend a class at Illyria.

Suddenly, Jack jumped forward, put his arm around Violet's waist, and pulled her back out of the automaton's reach. The other students had begun running as soon as the thing had come to life. Now Violet and Jack followed them, not looking back to see if the automaton pursued.

They caught up with the other students a few yards ahead. They were all panting from fright and the sudden exercise. Violet listened for any clanking to indicate that the creature was still chasing them, but heard nothing.

"Thanks," Violet said to Jack.

He grinned, his face a little pink from the running. "Not a problem."

"Okay," Toby said. His panting was heavier than the others', probably due to his general lack of physical fitness. "That's enough fun for one night. Let's get out of here."

"No, wait," Violet said, standing up straight and catching her breath, which her chest bindings made quite difficult. "We can do this without help."

"I dropped the jellyfish jar when I grabbed you," Jack said. "We won't know where we've been anymore."

But Violet wasn't listening. She was gazing through a nearby archway. A dim light came through it, which Violet thought shone on something very interesting. Slowly and carefully, she walked up to the archway, and then stepped through it. The room beyond was huge, nearly as large as the Great Hall, but lit only by two dim gas lamps.

"It's real," she said softly. The rest of the students had followed her. They all stood on a large platform, staring at a small train car and a dark openmouthed tunnel in front of it. They could hear the sound of rushing water from the tunnel.

"Where does it go?" asked Drew.

"I don't know," Toby said, staring, "and it's quite the find. But tonight is not the night to figure it out. I'm exhausted, and you may have noticed that we were attacked by skeletal automata. So unless it takes us back to our beds, which I very much doubt, I don't see the point of riding it."

Violet bit her lip and nodded. "You're right," she said, resigned. "Let's go back. I think it's this way," she said, pointing down a corridor outside the archway, her shoulders slumped.

Toby took a compass off his belt and consulted it.

"I have a compass, too!" Lane said, seeing Toby looking at his.

Violet stared at Lane. "I thought you said you didn't have anything."

"Well, it's just a compass. Not a mechanical torch or a jellyfish jar."

The rest of the group sighed. "Oh, right, it's just a compass. Which was created to show direction, help lost people, that sort of thing," Jack said. "The Thames is to the west, I believe. The elevator will be that way, too." He led the way, laughing long and loudly in the darkness.

IX.

PROFESSOR Erasmus Valentine did not like teaching the first-years on their first day of classes. Always so tired from whatever little adventure they had had in the cellar, they chose to sleep in rather than wake up early enough to bathe, so they not only were tired, red-eyed, and lethargic, but they also stank.

Valentine sighed dramatically to get the attention of the five bleary young men before him, then began his annual opening lecture. It was a brilliant lecture, which is why he had never bothered to change it in all his years teaching at Illyria. It was about man's role as improvers of God's original art, and how all the pieces of nature that they used were put there for them to combine into more beautiful works. He cited numerous examples of beauty, from the poetry of the ancient Greeks to Romantic poets to his own creations, the most notable of which was Isabella, the dove-sized peacock that sang like a nightingale. At this point, he took Isabella out of her huge gilded cage and let the students wonder at her. After a while, he continued, explaining in stirring rhetoric that it was now the students' turn to perfect God's creations. Valentine felt that this was not blasphemy, as one of the students had said last year, but the very purpose of mankind. He ended it with a plea, his eyes dewy with feeling, for the students to cooperate with him and one another, and for them to have patience with themselves. After all, they couldn't expect to create their own Isabella on their first day. It was a beautiful lecture, Valentine thought, and modest, since it took only two and a half hours, which left another generous hour and a half to go over the rules of the lab, answer questions, and begin their first assignments.

Violet, staring at Isabella in her cage, found her to be rather sad.

Her feathers drooped and seemed too heavy for her body, and her eyes were covered with the misty film she'd seen only in old people and dogs. But Jack seemed impressed with her, especially the cooing noise she made if one stroked her gullet, so Violet supposed that the miniature singing peacock must be an accomplishment.

In all fairness to Isabella, it was rather difficult for Violet to keep her eyes open. They had spent more time in the basement last night than she'd thought. It seemed that she had only closed her eyes when the small clock on the wall started ringing seven o'clock, and she barely had time to put on her suit and eat breakfast before running to the biology lab. Jack, on the other hand, seemed quite energetic. Violet wondered if he had some trick for getting more rest than she, or if he was merely excited because this lab was to be his second home and the dandy with the too-rouged cheeks, who was currently explaining the proper way to clean a scalpel, was to be his new mentor.

"Now," Valentine said after showing the students the proper place for each tool and object—knives here, feathers there, bottles of blood on the shelf over the box of spare bones—"any questions?" Merriman raised his hand. Valentine pursed his lips and nodded. The young man was short and roundish, the sort Valentine would prefer not to talk to if he could help it.

"Will we be working with plants, sir?" Merriman asked.

"Plants?" Valentine said, and put a finger to his chin. "Well, most assignments will be from the fauna of the world, not the flora, and when you're more advanced, cellular work, but if you'd like to try combining the two . . . why, a dove with rose petals instead of feathers could be quite lovely. That would probably be above your level right now, of course, but it's certainly something to aspire to."

"Begging your pardon, sir," Merriman continued, "but I meant *just* plants. Growing corn with shorter stalks, for example, so it doesn't fall over as quickly. It's only, my father is a gardener, so I was wond'ring—"

"No," Valentine interrupted, his nostrils flaring, "we won't be doing anything like that. Leave crossbreeding of beans to the monks. We are scientists."

"Of course, sir," Merriman mumbled, looking at the table.

"What about bodies?" Jack asked without raising his hand.

"Human bodies?" Valentine asked. Jack nodded. "Well, we do have a resurrectionist on call if you seek to work with the human animal, but personally, I've always found touching corpses to be a bit . . . distasteful. So that would have to be on your own time." Jack nodded again.

After that, Valentine explained that their first assignment was to gild a lab rat with snakeskin. "It's really a poetic assignment," Valentine said. "The prey becomes one with the predator." Valentine set a cage full of squealing white rats on one of the tables and a pile of snakeskin next to it. The rats, smelling the skin of their predators, began to panic and headed for the end of the cage farthest from the skins, rocking it slightly toward the edge of the table. "Use as many rats and as much snakeskin as you need," Valentine said. "I'll be observing your work, but if you want detailed instructions, you'll find them on page thirty of your text *Divine Enhancements*, by myself, Erasmus Valentine."

Jack finished the task in less than ten minutes, with Valentine watching him the whole time. When he was done, only the rat's nose, eyes, claws, and the inside of its ears and mouth retained their mammalian looks.

"Most excellent, Mr. Feste," Valentine said, patting Jack on the back. "Students, look. See how Mr. Feste cut the snakeskin not into simple rectangles, but thought out the curves of the rat itself so that the snakeskin fit securely around its body. Note also how he chose snakeskin in complementary, though not matching, colors. See how the rat begins with reddish yellow fur at the nose—which matches the nose that Mr. Feste didn't cover; quite clever, really—and gradually fades to bright green at the hindquarters. A real work of art, Mr. Feste."

"Thank you, sir," Jack said, smiling.

"Now let's see how it likes its new skin," Valentine said, and put it in a nearby empty cage. "It's beginning to wake up."

The students crowded around to watch the rat groggily raise its head, flinch at the soreness of its new stitches, then cautiously get to its feet. Cautiously, it peered around at the giant looming faces of the students and backed away from them. When the last of the ether wore off, it began to sniff the air, its tail stiff and eyes wide, clearly smelling itself. It looked around, but seeing only the faces of the students, merely cowered in the corner, having no place to run. After a moment, it carefully tried to nibble at its leg and noticed its newly scaled coat for the first time. It started to gnaw at its own skin in terror, and after a few moments of frantic struggling, fell to the ground, motionless.

"That happens," Valentine said with a sigh. "Their hearts give out, poor things—they don't realize that the snakeskin is theirs now, just think it's another snake that they can't escape from. Once I saw one tear its own tail off. Anyway, it's no fault of yours, Mr. Feste. Some rats just can't seem to realize the gift you're giving them." Valentine tutted, took a handkerchief out of his sleeve, gathered the dead rat in it, and threw it down the incinerator.

Jack frowned. He should have been able to predict the results of his assignment, but was so caught up in pleasing Valentine that he hadn't thought it through all the way. He hated losing creatures, hated being responsible for their deaths. He wanted to help them, not hurt them, after all. If he had thought ahead, he could have conceived of a chemical that would have stripped the snakeskin of its scent, and the rat could have gone on to live a happy, armored life.

"Mr. Feste," Valentine said, "you are free to go, if you'd like, or you can stay and assist your friends, or even work on something else."

"Thank you, sir."

"Everyone else, back to work. You have only this class to finish the project. If you can't manage by then, you'll have to come back during your independent study time."

The rest of the students hurried back to their own drugged rats. Jack took the time to explore the lab, peeking through microscopes and looking at the supplies, which included skins of all sorts of creatures, eyeballs drifting in preserving fluids, and many smaller animals resting quietly in their cages.

Lane finished his rat next, Valentine declaring it "acceptable but mediocre work," citing the way the skin bunched around the rat's neck and dragged back the ears. Violet finished next, her rat being "well done, but with no taste to the interaction of the coloring of the scales—it looks mottled, Mr. Adams. Mottled and sickly." Fairfax, who followed the instructions in the text word for word, finished next with a rat that was "pristinely done, but lacks any creative spirit. The book is a guide, but you must also bring part of yourself to these things. It is art, after all."

Merriman finished at the very last minute with Jack's help, but was pleasantly surprised to hear that his rat was "nicely done. Some of the stitching is poor, but it has a scruffy character I find suits it well. It is a rat, after all."

By the time lunchtime came around, all the rats but Merriman's had died and been sent down the incinerator chute. Merriman's rat, a runt that he had named Tiny, was nervously exploring its cage, and sometimes licking its paws. When the bell tolled, Valentine dismissed them with a flourish of his hands, calling after them that they had best read chapters one through eight in *Divine Enhancements* by next week.

Jack and Violet had assumed they would sit with the other first-years, so they were surprised when they entered the dining hall and Toby and Drew waved them over. Toby was already eating and had a full mug of tea in front of him. Drew was looking at his food, fidgeting with it, tapping his finger on his nose, then looking at his food again.

"Hey, you lot. Jack and Ash, right?" Toby called. Jack nodded. "Sit with us today. We're going to decide if you're the sort of folks we can stand to be sociable with." Violet looked over at the other first-years, but as Lane and Merriman seemed to be chatting happily, and Fairfax had found a small table that he could have to himself, she didn't feel like she was abandoning anyone by sitting down next to Toby. Drew, though he had seen Jack and Violet approach, seemed startled, and jumped slightly in his seat when they sat down.

"You had time to shave?" Toby asked Violet.

"Pardon?" Violet said.

"You don't have a hair on your chin. After a night like that, I figured you'd sleep in a bit rather than take the time to do your toilette."

"Oh," Violet said, suddenly nervous. "Ah, well. I had remembered Valentine as being a dandy, so I thought it would be best if I looked as well groomed as I could."

"Poof is more like it," Toby said, sawing through some of the meat on his plate, "but that was good thinking. Valentine doesn't care much for me, but it doesn't matter at this point. Did he give you his lecture on improving on God's works?"

Violet and Jack nodded.

"I fell asleep," Drew confessed, tapping his fork on the plate, "but then Freddy started arguing with him, and that woke me up."

"Freddy?" Jack asked.

"Freddy Chausable," Toby said. "He's a second-year, like Drew, here. Very religious. Thinks God talks to him through the analytical engines."

Violet blinked.

"This school is full of bloody loonies," Toby said.

"Are you a loony?" Jack asked.

Toby barked out a laugh. "I like you, Jack," he said. "Yeah, I might be a bit loony. I *have* come back to this place every year, now, haven't I? And Drew, here, he's mad as a hatter."

"No, I ain't," Drew said.

"Excuse his poor grammar," Toby said. "His family is new to society."

"No, we're not," Drew said. "My grandpa, he's the one who started the parfumerie, and that was nearly forty years ago."

"Wait," Jack said, "you're Pale, as in Pale Perfumes."

"Yeah," Drew said, nodding.

"I once made love to a girl who was passionate for your rose soap," Jack said. "I used to buy it for her once a week."

"The rose is popular," Drew said, nodding. Violet studied her food, trying not to blush. She was also fond of the Pale Perfumes rose soap, and once had received some from Jack as a Christmas gift.

"How about you, Ashton? Ever try to loosen a girl's corset with something Drew's family made?"

Violet bit her lip, then bravely looked up. "I've never really needed any assistance. I can loosen a corset with my own two hands."

Jack snickered, and Toby burst out laughing. "Confident, for such

a scrawny-looking lad," he said. "I like you both, so far. We'll see if
you're really chums. Why don't you meet us in the entryway just
outside the Great Hall tonight, after supper. Most of the lads go
upstairs to study, but Drew and I enjoy indulging in the various delights that the fair city of London has to offer."

"Toby's a baron, so 'e has a little pull about town," Drew said con-
spiratorially.

"So you're Sir Toby?" Violet asked.

"Only if it's a scuffer asking," Toby said with a grin. "Otherwise,
I don't like to talk about it much. Half the nutters in the place have
aristocratic blood. It's bragging about it that makes you look crazy."

"We won't tell, and we promise not to care, either," Jack said.

"Good," Toby said, finishing the meat in front of him and chug-
ging down a large mug of cold tea. "Anyway, I'm off to the chemical
lab. Always looking to perfect the cure." He burped loudly, then
walked out of the dining hall, leaving Violet and Jack alone with
Drew, who was carefully slicing the crust off his bread.

"He's working on a cure?" Violet asked.

Drew nodded.

"For what?"

"Hangover," Drew responded. "I better get going, too. I have a lot
of work to do."

"What are you working on?" Violet asked.

"It's a perfume that will remain subtle until the person wearing it
begins to sweat more," Drew said, his shoulders bobbing slightly.
"Then the scent will compensate by increasing as well. That way,
you never have to worry about smelling foul again!"

"I'd use that," Jack said. "Long as it didn't become too strong.
Wouldn't want to smell like a woman." Violet nodded in agreement,
trying to keep her face stiff and masculine.

"That is one of the problems," Drew said, tapping his nose a few
times, then running a hand through his hair. "When it works, the
moment a person sweats, they smell like a bed of lavender. And it
doesn't always work. It has something to do with the chemical content of sweat. So I need to collect more sweat. Luckily, I sweat a lot,"
he said. Then he smiled and took off, leaving his dirty plate next to

Toby's. A servant, seeing the mess, came over and cleared their things away, leaving half the table empty.

"This is the lot we've thrown ourselves in with?" Violet asked.

"Come now, they seem like good lads. Good for a bit of fun, anyway. We'll see what they want to do tonight, right?"

Violet sighed.

"It's the sort of thing a man would do," Jack said pointedly.

"Very well," Violet conceded. "But if it's a bore, or vulgar, we'll seek company elsewhere."

"Fair enough, but only if it's very vulgar. A little vulgarity is to be expected. It *is* London."

Violet smirked despite herself. She was wary of becoming too friendly with other students for various reasons, the first being that she was, after all, here to study. She didn't want to distract herself too much. But Jack seemed to want companionship beyond hers, which seemed fair. Her other fear was that they would uncover her secret, and troubles would ensue: exposure, blackmail, or some other horror from the various gothic novels Mrs. Wilks was always reading. Finally—and this was a fear she was loath to admit to herself, but logically, she must accept the possibility—that becoming friendly with men could cause her to be attracted to them, which would be both distracting and reveal her sex.

"All right," Jack said, finishing his meal. He took a long drink of water and stood. "I'd best be off to the biology lab. I'm not quite sure what I should work on for the end-of-year faire yet, but I'm thinking something with organ transplanting. Maybe a four-eyed ferret?" He went on to explain how figuring out how to do that could help him give new eyes to the blind. Very impressive, either way.

Violet raised her eyebrows and looked down at her own meal, only half-eaten. How had they eaten so quickly? Perhaps she was still being too dainty and feminine. She nodded at Jack and stood up as well, following him out of the dining hall. This was her first real chance to work in the mechanical lab; she was too wound up to be hungry. True, she had worked there the day before, but the lights hadn't really been on, and Professor Bunburry hadn't been tinkering away at his desk, ready to offer advice and counsel.

He was, however, there today. There were just two other students in the lab, neither from her year, and they were already busy with work. Violet set herself down at a nearby desk and took out some of her drawing paper, wondering what to build. If she wanted to create a true marvel for the end of the year, she had better start now, but the question was, what? The blank paper before her seemed limitless, but so was the pressure to create a wondrous device. Every idea she had seemed too small, or too inelegant. What would be both beautiful and necessary? What would show both intelligence and artistry?

As if to answer these questions, Cecily came into the room. Violet did not notice at first, but after a second without the sounds of the other two students' work, Violet looked up to see what had caused the silence. Cecily was standing in the doorway to the lab, the warm air rushing out past her, causing her hair to stir slightly. She was wearing a dress of dark pink silk with matching plaid underskirts, and carrying what seemed to be a life-sized golden rabbit. She carefully stepped into the room, and Miriam Isaacs followed silently behind her, a thin, lurking shadow. Violet had never seen Miriam before, and though her purpose was clear—who else would dress in a high-collared black dress but a governess?—Violet was curious what sort of woman would seek employment in this chapel of science. Her dark skin, thin face, and large dark eyes did nothing to hide her cleverness. She looked rapidly about the room, taking in the faces of each of the students and evaluating them. Miriam's gaze reached Violet, and plunged into her like a surgeon's hands, looking about and then exiting quickly again, having found no immediate threat to Cecily within.

"Mr. Bunburry?" Cecily asked, approaching the professor. Bunburry made an awkward set of stiff, uncomfortable motions indicating that he was about to rise and bow, but Cecily waved him down. "I don't mean to bother you. It's only that Shakespeare has stopped working. Perhaps one of the students could repair him for me? I'm sure it won't take long. I opened him up and tried to find the problem yesterday, but I was unsuccessful. I'm not as good with gears and springs as I am with beakers and potions."

Violet raised an eyebrow. So, Cecily did have some scientific hunger. She was not just a spectator to the college.

"Of course, my dear," Bunburry said in his rasping voice. "Go ask our new first-year, Mr. Adams, there." He looked in Violet's direction and tilted his head slightly.

"Thank you," Cecily said, and turned to Violet, gliding toward her. Violet felt strange at once. She could see Cecily appraising her as a man, and at the same time, Violet felt an instant camaraderie with Cecily: another woman of science—another woman of intelligence. But Cecily was allowed to be herself, to wear dresses and speak softly, and of that, Violet was jealous. She stretched her back, feeling the tight cloth wrapped over her bosom. And yet . . . how nice it would be to have a friend, another young lady with whom she could discuss science.

"Mr. Adams?" Cecily asked.

"Ashton," Violet said, nodding.

"I imagine you heard me talking to Mr. Bunburry just now. I know the basics of mechanical sciences, but the truth is I've never taken to them, so I was hoping you could help me." She set the golden rabbit down in front of Violet, who looked it over more closely. It was a clockwork rabbit of ingenious artistry and design. The fur was carefully molded and looked soft to the touch, and the seams where the various body parts came together were barely noticeable. It wore a gold collar attached to a long, thin, golden chain, which was wrapped around Cecily's hand. "This is Shakespeare. Cousin Ernest made him for me when I was little, and I've kept him ever since. Usually when he stops working, it's just that a spring has worn out—he is quite old, after all—but I can't find the problem this time. Would you help me?"

Violet nodded. This was made by the duke? Curiosity was overtaking her. She had never seen anything that he had made before, never heard of any great inventions of his. But now, here in front of her, was a creation of his. A sample of his mind. Violet was excited to look at it.

"It pops open like this," Cecily said, reaching behind the rabbit's ear and pushing down what looked like a bit of fur. Shakespeare's torso sprang open, revealing a complex mess of gears and springs inside.

"Could you—? That is, to know how to fix it, it would help to know what it does," Violet said.

"Oh, of course," Cecily said. "How silly of me. It's just a toy. He hops after me, in whatever direction I pull the chain. And because of the pulling on the chain, he never needs winding. I know, it's just a silly thing. I'm sorry to waste your time with it."

"It's an honor, really," Violet said. Cecily turned slightly pink at this comment, but Violet did not notice, as she was already hunched over and examining Shakespeare's parts. Miriam, however, did notice, and stepped closer, hovering just behind Cecily's shoulder.

"Ah," Violet said. "One of the gears has gotten loose. Which wouldn't be a problem, normally, except that it's thrown the chain off a bit, so it stays slack and can't wind itself. It's really quite a brilliant creation. Would you like me to fix it for you?" Violet looked up and smiled at Cecily.

"If you wouldn't mind," Cecily said, smiling back.

"Of course not," Violet said. To repair a work of the duke's, to join her mind with his, would give her a pleasure she had no name for. But this she did not say aloud. Instead, she went to the boxes of parts at the side of the room, picked out a gear of the right size, and brought it back to repair Shakespeare.

Cecily, as a girl of sixteen, had never felt the warm affections of romantic love. Like so many young girls—and though they likely wouldn't admit it, young boys as well—she had often heard of love, and had even supposed herself to have experienced it once or twice, but the flower of love was still growing in her, and had not yet bloomed. When such a flower does bloom within the bosom of youth, the youth often finds him- or herself so unused to the effect that even the smallest amount of pollen from the newly opened flower can overwhelm the heart. And so it was with Cecily when Violet—who Cecily thought was Ashton—first smiled at her. Cecily saw Ashton's fair skin, his long eyelashes, and his wet, pink lips, and her body and soul bloomed in response. What might be interpreted by an older soul as affection or infatuation instantly seemed to Cecily to be love.

Violet carefully closed Shakespeare's body back up and held him out for Cecily. "He should work fine now," Violet said.

"Thank you so much," Cecily said, taking back the golden clockwork rabbit and leading him on a few experimental hops. She sighed, partially happy that Shakespeare was fixed, but also because sighing was something she knew people did when they were in love.

"My pleasure," Violet said.

Cecily hovered a moment longer, staring at Violet in silence.

"Perhaps we should head to the chemical lab," Miriam said from behind her. "I'm sure Professor Curio has the dried willow sap you asked for by now."

Cecily nodded, still looking at Violet. "I'm trying to create a powdered substance that will dry to the hardness of steel when water is added," Cecily explained. "Then we could make gears and the like without having to forge them with heat."

"That sounds brilliant," Violet said, impressed.

"We should go," Miriam said.

Cecily nodded, and smiled again at Violet. "Good-bye," she said, turned around, and walked off, Shakespeare hopping along behind her.

"Bye," Violet said, and watched Cecily turn the corner before looking back at her own work.

"You shouldn't be so friendly with her," said a voice by Violet's ear.

"Pardon?" she asked, looking up. One of the other students was standing at the edge of her table, glowering at her. With his pale skin, black straight hair, and high cheekbones, he might have been handsome in a dark way, if it weren't for the acid in his expression. His eyes were a flashing black, like the nebulae her father used to show her in the telescope.

"The duke doesn't like people becoming too friendly with her. And you shouldn't think her friendliness means anything. She's just naturally sweet."

"I don't think we've met," Violet said, choosing to ignore the stranger's rather rude way of presenting himself.

"I am Malcolm Volio. I am a second-year."

"I'm Ashton Adams," Violet said, extending her hand. "So nice to meet you." She curled her lips in a way that she hoped made it clear she actually found their meeting distasteful.

Malcolm looked at her hand and crossed his arms. "Stay away from Cecily," he said, and stalked back to his table, which was covered with long, thin curved parts of metal, connected by gears. He looked up, saw her staring, and glared, which made Violet turn back to her own work.

At his desk, Bunburry coughed hoarsely and fidgeted with a great mass of gears and poles. In the back of the room, the third student, Gregory Cheek, whom Violet knew only by reputation, was pounding a long sheet of bronze into a wide, curved tube.

The clockwork intricacy of the rabbit had been inspiring to Violet, but that inspiration still refused to take tangible shape. The image of the interlocking gears—like careful puzzle pieces—came back to Violet, and she stared at the towering wall of constantly turning gears behind the forge. These gears were powered by the waters of the Thames, but what if they didn't need to be? A clockwork engine normally required constant turning, but if the gears could be made to turn not just with one another but also back on one another, then a device could run for months, maybe years or decades, with just a few turns of the key. It shouldn't be a difficult thing to do; after all, the escapement method had been used to keep clocks and watches ticking for centuries. It was just a matter of tweaking the idea slightly: instead of locked and unlocked, tick and tock, this engine wouldn't just mete out the energy from the pendulum, but expand on it. It would push the pendulum back when it began to lag.

Quickly, Violet started a sketch. The engine could be quite small, she reasoned, no bigger than a slightly oversized pocket watch, but that might change, depending on what the engine had to power. And what should it power? she wondered. Making an engine was all very well and good, but it would need to demonstrate its perpetual energy in some grand display to attract the attention she wanted.

Violet stopped her sketching and crossed her arms. She had the basic principles of the engine in mind, but she would have to decide on its shell before she could go much further.

Then she heard a soft ringing noise from the other table. Violet looked over to see Malcolm with a small bell in his hands. On the table, the bronze curves had been connected to a sphere and were currently moving about, flopping like a fish on land. Malcolm rang the bell again, and the flopping instantly subsided. He looked up to see Violet staring at the invention and smirked at her, arrogance in his eyes.

Violet blushed and turned back to her sketching. A device controlled by sound? She was going to have to prove herself a genius among geniuses if she wanted to make any sort of impression at the end of the year. She could feel her brow growing damp as she realized for the first time that to really stand out among this crowd would take every ounce of talent she had.

The clock on the wall chimed a deep low note. Hours had passed, between her work on Shakespeare and sketching out her ideas. She heard a soft wheezing behind her, and when she turned, found Professor Bunburry investigating her finished and discarded sketches. His back was bent over the table at a right angle, since he couldn't simply bend his encased neck to look down.

"You can pick them up if that's easier, sir," Violet said, curious as to why he was examining her work.

He lifted the sketch he was examining up to the light. "A clockwork engine that doesn't need winding!" He coughed. "Very clever. You'll need to account for the wear on the gears, though, fashion it out of something that won't wear easily, and won't need regular oiling. If it needs regular oiling, that sort of defeats the principle of the thing, doesn't it?" Violet nodded as Bunburry coughed viciously for a moment. "And while the engine itself would be quite an accomplishment, if you hope to make a real impression among the nobility at the faire, and achieve funding for future projects, you'll need some sort of visual display. Perhaps a dancing girl who can keep dancing for eternity. The upper classes tend to like that sort of thing."

Violet pursed her lips and frowned. "I had just hoped to do something more original," she said.

"The engine will be original," Bunburry said. "You must focus your energies." Violet nodded, and Bunburry patted her on the back, a fatherly gesture. "Such narrow shoulders," he said, and then walked off, limping past Malcolm to Gregory. Malcolm watched as Bunburry ignored him, and then saw Violet noticing as well. Color rose in Malcolm's face, and he quickly turned back to his work to conceal it. Violet smiled slightly to see that Malcolm had made himself so generally unpleasant that the professor avoided giving him advice.

While she waited for further inspiration, Violet worked on a design for a dancing clockwork girl. Violet was sure it would be lovely, but not particularly striking—already she could picture the mustached gentlemen in top hats scoffing at it. Another dancing clockwork girl, they'd say, and keep walking. As she finished the sketch she was working on, she noticed that it was almost time for supper.

"Don't leave your stations messy," Bunburry hacked out before leaving for the dining hall himself.

Her shoulders slumping, Violet put down her pencil and began to roll up the sketches for the dancing clockwork girl. She frowned to herself, thinking on it—what else were women supposed to do other than dancing and bearing children? She and this potential clockwork dancing girl were the same. Not much else had ever been expected from her, but here she was, painfully binding her gender and trying to prove that she deserved an equal hand in the scientific world. If only a dancing girl could prove something like that. Perhaps she could make it a clockwork dancing boy—no, that would just be ridiculous. But there must be something. . . .

For a moment, she felt as though she could break out of this redundant creation, could shatter the dancing girl and reassemble it as something new, but the moment passed as her stomach growled. She finished cleaning up her space and headed up to the dining hall. Only Malcolm stayed behind, gathering his work together in a pile on the table. In the dim lights, he looked sinister and hulking.

X.

JACK was already seated when Violet found him. Toby, Drew, Lane, and Merriman were sitting around him, listening to him talk.

"When I was finished," Jack was saying, "I had a snake with three tails. It looked quite disturbed by the whole thing, really."

Toby burst out laughing, and Drew chuckled manically. Lane and Merriman just looked stunned.

"Telling stories?" Violet asked, sitting down.

"Just telling everyone what I did with my independent study time today," Jack said. "I made a three-tailed snake. Valentine said it was courageous, but lacked subtlety. What did you get up to down in the mechanical lab?"

"Nothing much," Violet admitted, staring down at her food. "I spent the first part of my time fixing a toy for Cecily."

"For Cecily?" Jack asked. Violet nodded.

"She spoke to you?" asked Drew. Violet nodded again. Everyone around the table was looking at her, wide eyed, waiting for more of the story.

"It was a clockwork rabbit the duke made for her," Violet continued slowly. "It was really an ingenious design—the leash, when tugged, pulled the spring so it would hop after her—"

"What was she like?" Jack asked.

"The rabbit? I think it was a he. Cecily called it Shakespeare. It was beautifully made. The duke is really quite—"

"No," Drew interrupted, "what was Cecily like?"

"Well, she was very friendly," Violet said, confused.

"She's so beautiful," Merriman sighed. Lane nodded in agreement.

"You're lucky she spoke ta you," Drew said. "She's never even noticed me."

"Did you mention me?" Jack asked.

"Are you all so in love with her?" Violet asked. All but Toby nodded.

"I have a woman already," Toby said with a satisfied smile, "and she pays plenty of attention to me."

"I can't see other women since I've met her," Jack said.

Violet glared at him. "You first saw her yesterday, and there haven't been any other women to see since then."

Jack gave Violet a pointed look, and she realized that of course, there was her. She felt her cheeks warm, and hurriedly took a bite of the mash on her plate.

"She's the most beautiful, sweet, darling girl in the world," Drew said.

"You're all fools," Violet said. "You should focus on your studies, not your . . . your . . ."

"Pricks?" Toby offered.

Violet felt herself blush again.

"Too much of a gentleman to use that sort of language?" Toby asked, noticing Violet's shock.

"Ashton's got a delicate soul," Jack said, goading Violet.

Violet narrowed her eyes at him. "Bugger off, shite-for-brains," Violet said. Jack looked shocked, but then laughed. Violet felt proud for a moment, then guilty. She didn't mind working in her lab late at night, but she had always felt the use of foul language was somehow below her, as a woman. The boys around her were laughing at her outburst, and Jack clapped her on the back. This was apparently how young men talked, no matter their rank. She would have to get used to it. "Any closer to your hangover cure?" Violet asked Toby, once the laughter had died down. She was happy to be blending in, but didn't want attention to linger on her for too long.

"Perhaps. I won't know for sure until tomorrow," he said with a grin. "Speaking of," he said, taking a pocket watch out of his jacket, "I'm going to go upstairs and change into something a bit more presentable. Have a nice night, lads." He nodded and left the table.

"I should probably be going, too," Drew said, looking around nervously. "I'm done with my food, anyway." Everyone stared at him for a few seconds, and he nodded and left as well. Violet waved them good-bye. They were an odd pair. Merriman and Lane soon excused themselves, wanting to study for Bunburry's class tomorrow.

"Should we make ourselves presentable?" Violet asked Jack across the table when she had finished eating. "I'm not sure where we're going tonight."

"We should probably wash up, in case there are ladies," Jack said, amused.

"I thought you didn't notice any ladies but dear Cecily any longer," Violet said.

"Well, had I noted you as an exception, I think there might have been some trouble for you." He wiggled his eyebrows. Violet grinned, despite herself. Jack was seldom flirtatious with her, but she enjoyed his attention anyway, especially when she felt so odd and not like herself in these tight men's clothes. Becoming a man, it seemed, had made her long to be a woman again, though when she was a woman, she had been all too anxious to become a man. Perhaps she was never going to be really satisfied.

"Let's go wash up, then," Violet said, rising.

Upstairs, Violet rinsed her face with cool water from the sink and washed her hands thoroughly with a soap that smelled like pine—from Pale Perfumes, she noticed. Perhaps Drew's family supplied the school with soap. She chose what Ashton had said was the best of her suits and, with a grunt of pain, tightened the bindings around her chest till she ached. She put on the suit and a clean shirt and gazed at her reflection in the looking glass. It had been only two days, and already she wanted to shed these ridiculous clothes and slip into the simple comfort of a dress. She wanted to feel the long curls of her hair falling over the nape of her neck again. She wanted to recognize the person in the mirror.

She set her jaw and furrowed her brow. Only two days! She would have to toughen up if she was going to prove herself. If she were to abandon the plan before its success, she would not just be letting herself down, but, in the most melodramatic sense, all the women of the world. The truth would come out sooner or later; she just needed to make sure it was later, after she had made her genius so clear that the world could no longer scorn or punish her for what lay between her legs. That was the only way to avoid humiliation, or worse. She swallowed, thinking of her brother's lecture in the carriage, and sucked her lips in. She needed to focus on her strength, she knew, not her vulnerability. Build a machine around the strongest parts—the firmest pistons, the hardest steel—and it would last and work. Build it around a flimsy spring, and it would fall to pieces. She needed to be an iron rod.

"Are you ready, or are you going to keep staring at yourself in the mirror?" Jack asked. "You make a pretty boy, to be sure, but I always pictured you more interested in the kind of man who had intelligence in his eyes."

Violet folded her arms and turned to glare at Jack, who grinned back. "Bloody jackass," she said.

"You're getting pretty good at the foul language," Jack said, "and I suspect an evening with the lads in London will further perfect your skills. So let's go to it, shall we?"

Jack cocked his head toward the door, Violet nodded, and the two walked out together. There were some students in the lounge, but they ignored them as they headed for the stairs and out into the entry foyer, where they had waited for their interviews. Drew and Toby were there already, not looking very different, though perhaps smelling better. Drew seemed to be doused in lavender, and Violet wondered if he was testing a new version of his perfume on himself.

"Good," Toby said, heading for the lift. "Let's go. I don't want to keep my lady friend waiting."

"Lady friend?" Jack asked.

"Where are we headed?" Violet asked as they all got in the lift.

"Special way out," Toby said. "No one watches it. Good for leaving and returning past curfew."

"Lady friend?" Jack repeated.

"It's not Cecily," Violet said, rolling her eyes. She was growing tired of Jack's obsession with Cecily and his ridiculous hopes of somehow spending time with her. The lift descended to the basement, and Drew exited, making a sharp right, away from the labyrinth they had wandered through the previous evening. He pulled on what looked like a darkened gas lamp, and a door swung open, revealing a stairway and the smell of the river.

"Found it my first year," Toby said proudly, and headed up the stairs. Everyone followed, and they came out quite near the river, in the garden, not far from where she and the duke had stood together months before. In the early evening, the Thames shone blue black through the fog, and the smell of coal and smoke was cut through by the smell of running water. The sound of the great waterwheel clanked loudly.

"Did he tell you he found it his first year?" asked a low female voice. Violet and Jack turned. There was a woman waiting for them under a tree, her gray cloak loosely open around her shoulders, revealing a low-cut green dress underneath. Her face and the mass of curls around it were still in shadow. "I found it, years ago. I just showed it to him his first year."

The woman stepped out of the shadows and Violet stared at her. "This is Jack Feste and Ashton Adams," Toby said to the woman. Violet knew she recognized her, but could not place her.

"Pleasure, Mr. Feste," the woman said, "and good to see you again, Mr. Adams."

"Nice to meet you, too," Jack said.

"This is Miri," Toby said, and Violet couldn't help but gasp. She saw it now: This was Miriam Isaacs, Cecily's governess. With her hair down, and in something other than her high-collared black dress, she looked completely different. Her dark skin glowed against the narrow green dress, and though her features were still oddly exotic and her frame still unfashionably boyish, she possessed a sort of wild beauty that Violet found herself envying. And she stood differently, too. She still seemed strong, Violet thought, but whereas as a governess she was docile, a support beam, now she was almost gaudy, like a statue of the Magdalen. In fact, she seemed to have a bit of the demimondaine about her, with her loose cloak, her slim dress, her dark eyes, and easy smile. And what was she doing sneaking out at night with the students?

"You're . . . courting her?" Violet asked.

Toby laughed, and Miriam smiled forgivingly. "I hope you won't tell anyone," Miriam said, "but I am a widow, without family, and I do not think it particularly improper for me to socialize with the young men of the school, as long as it does not interfere with their studies. I know how it must look, but I assure you, I am an honorable woman, in my own way."

Violet bit her lower lip. She couldn't blame Miriam for taking such freedoms, as Violet had taken more than a few herself. She nodded. "We won't tell anyone," she said.

"Thank you," Miriam said. She took Toby's arm and they walked off through the garden in the dull moonlight. The rest of them followed after. At the edge of the garden, far from the school itself, was a small gate that Toby unhooked and led Miriam through.

At the corner beyond, waiting in the dim gaslight, was a cab. The driver raised his hat at them, and Toby grinned back at Violet and Jack. "As you can see, we do this sort of thing rather frequently."

They boarded the cab, and though it was tight, they all fit.

"Where are we going?" Jack asked.

"A surprise, lads," Toby said with a grin. Miriam let out a deep murmur of laughter, and lay her head on Toby's shoulder as the cab took off.

The smells and sounds of London at night came pouring in through the windows. Human musk, ale, smoke, and dirt, the sounds of cackling laughter and pea-pod men calling out their wares and clanging their pots, and the occasional moments of song, all things that Violet hadn't experienced before. She gazed out the window, her eyes wide at the display of people: in rags or suits, tumbling drunk on the street or cowering in an alleyway. London at night was no place for a lady, she could hear Mrs. Wilks saying. Far too dangerous. The cab stopped deep within the city, a part of it she didn't know, next to a pub with a wooden sign hanging above it, which showed a large-bosomed woman with an easy smile holding out a roast pig. Inside, the lights were bright and Violet could hear laughter and music.

"Well, get out, then," Toby said from behind Violet. She opened the door and stepped down onto the street. For a moment, she was happy to have trousers on, and boots to tuck them into, as the hems of her skirt would surely get filthy walking through the ankle-high muck of the streets. When Miriam descended, she merely lifted up her skirts, apparently unconcerned that a man in rags could see her ankles, and even her shins, and was whistling at her. Toby held the door to the pub open for her and then followed her in, leaving the others to open the door themselves and see what awaited them.

"What have we gotten into?" Violet whispered at Jack.

"Don't worry," Jack whispered back. "I'm sure it's just a bit of merrymaking."

"If we end up in a whorehouse, I shall leave straightaway," Violet said.

"Right . . . ," Jack said, opening the door to the pub, "me too."

Inside the pub, it was warmer than Violet had expected. There was a huge fire in the hearth, and the windows were closed to keep the heat in. The barkeep was roasting bangers over the fire, and the room smelled of fat and meat. At one end, a man played the piano and sang a song whose lyrics Violet couldn't quite make out, and some men and women danced near him. At the other end, Toby, Drew, and Miriam were sitting down at a table, waving at Violet and Jack to join them.

"What, never been out?" Toby asked as they sat. "This is the Well-Seasoned Pig: finest ale in the district, and good bangers and mash as well. Lot better than the slop you get back at Illyria." Miriam leaned against Toby in a way Violet felt was probably not appropriate public behavior, even between a married man and woman. But looking around the room, Violet saw many other couples behaving in much the same way. In fact, it turned out that Miriam was dressed quite modestly for the establishment. "Sit down, Ash," Toby said, "and stop gawking. You're worse than Drew here, and he has to stay distracted or he falls asleep."

"S'true," Drew said, staring at a particularly well-endowed barmaid strolling past, "gotta stay distracted."

"Well, this is a good place for it," Jack said, also eyeing the barmaid.

"You fall asleep?" Violet asked.

"Yeah," Drew said. "If I'm bored. Just happens."

"Doesn't that happen to everyone?" Jack asked.

"Happens more ta me," Drew said. The barmaid returned and placed a frothy mug in front of Violet, who eyed it suspiciously, and one in front of Jack, who quickly started drinking it.

"Drink up," Toby said. "My treat for being such good fellows about Miriam's keeping less-respectable company."

"If a lady goes out drinking with men she's not married to, it's she who is less respectable, not the men she drinks with," Miriam said.

Violet closed her eyes and took a swig. The ale was bitter, but curiously refreshing, and felt warm splashing down inside her.

"I suppose that's true," Toby said. "Well, then, it's for being forgiving of my associating with less respectable company."

"You really are quite the flatterer," Miriam said, leaning away from Toby.

"I met the other biology students today," Jack said to Violet as Miriam and Toby murmured to each other. Violet watched Toby's fingers trace up and down Miriam's bare arm and wondered what it felt like to be touched in such a way.

"Oh?" Violet asked, turning to Jack.

"Quite the pair. A redheaded Scot, who doesn't seem to do much besides brush the fur of his cats while telling them they're pretty, and an anti-social Russian, obsessed with figuring out how best to attach elephant tusks to a mastiff."

"That sounds frightening," Violet said passively. Her eyes went back to Toby's hand on Miriam's arm—back and forth it went, like a pendulum.

"Except that Valentine kept tellin' him it wasn't allowed, because it would be a weapon. So instead he seethed silently, then worked on fusing boar skin to a cat, at which point the Scot, Leslie, rushed forward and told him he was being cruel."

"Les is my year," Drew said. Apparently he had been listening in. "He thinks cats is smarter than people. Doesn't really do much to them. He says he waits for the cats to ask him to do somethin' first. Last year, for the faire, he made a cat that could walk upright. He dressed 'im up, too, in a little suit. He said the cat loved it. If ya ask me, the cat was none too happy about it. Kept wobbling around, looking like it was afraid it would fall down."

"That sounds absolutely marvelous," Jack said, grinning. "Perhaps I've underestimated this Leslie chap."

"Good evenin', gents," said a woman, sidling up next to Jack. "I noticed some of you are lackin' company, so me and my friends thought per'aps you'd care ta buy us some drinks?" Violet looked up at the woman. She was at least fifty, probably older, and had caked her face in thick makeup. Her dress seemed off somehow: too tight, too old, perhaps out of fashion—she couldn't be sure without asking Ashton. The woman laid her hand on Jack's. Two other women, one large and certainly not younger than sixty, and the other quite thin, with huge eyes that didn't look capable of blinking, stood behind her.

Jack grinned. "My heart belongs to another," he said. "But if the other lads—"

"No!" Violet said quickly. "My heart . . . um, also . . . yes. Just no. No thank you." Violet looked down at her drink and then took a long swig of it.

"I doubt I'd be very interesting to you," Drew said. "I tend ta fall asleep."

"Oh, do you?" said the woman, her voice syrupy with concern. "Well, I'll have to make sure I don't bore you, then." She circled the table and put her arms around Drew's neck, then sat down next to him, still clinging. The other two women she had been with drifted away toward other men in the bar. "So, will you buy me a drink?" the woman asked Drew. Drew nodded. The woman adjusted herself on her seat and brought the barmaid scurrying over with a gesture. "Champagne, the best you 'ave." The barmaid disappeared, and the woman sighed happily and began stroking Drew's hand, much as Miriam was stroking Toby's. Soon, Violet noticed, they seemed to have settled into a pattern, Miriam's hand up on Toby's shoulder while the woman's hand was down on Drew's wrist, and then they switched back again.

Violet sighed and turned to Jack, who was drinking his ale and smiling. "I'm surprised you turned away companionship," she said tartly.

"Ah, since I've seen Cecily, no other will do."

"Is this really how men behave?" Violet hissed under her breath.

Jack nodded. "And you, I suppose, are still pining over Gwendolyn?" Jack said, perhaps a little louder than necessary.

Toby and Miriam glanced over. "Does Ashton have a girl back home?" Toby asked with a grin.

"Ah, no," Violet said. "Jack is just teasing."

"Well, who is Gwendolyn, then?" Miriam asked, her eyes narrowed. "I promise not to tell Cecily."

"I certainly don't care if you tell Cecily or not, because it's of no concern. Gwendolyn, is . . . uh . . ."

"The maid," Jack said, pursing his lips. "And Ashton has yet to tell her how he feels, because he thinks it improper, and that he would be taking advantage."

Toby roared with laughter and pounded the table with his palm. The strange woman, who was by now sipping her champagne while halfheartedly patting Drew's hand, glared at him.

"Well, come on, lad, take advantage," Toby said.

"I really . . . Jack is exaggerating," Violet said, feeling a sudden urge to hit him.

"Hmmm," Miriam said, leaning back into her chair and looking at Violet intensely.

"What do you think, Mir?"

"I think maybe he doesn't want to reveal the details of his love life to new friends. Give him time, and I'm sure he'll tell us all about how Gwendolyn broke his heart."

Toby guffawed again. "I guess that's woman's intuition for you," he said, and laid his arm around Miriam's shoulder. Violet looked down at her mug and took another drink. It was less bitter this time, and more refreshing, so she kept drinking.

"Whoa, now," Jack said, putting an arm on Violet's shoulder.

"I guess we've stirred up some memories that need to be drowned, eh?" Toby said. Violet licked her lips and put down the nearly empty mug.

On the other side of the pub, the man went back to singing at the piano, and the group turned to watch. Pianos, Violet thought, were remarkable inventions. Their mechanisms had an elegance that suited the idea of music. As the man played and sang, she could hear, over the din of the pub and the conversation that resumed among Jack, Miriam, and Toby, the small wooden sounds of the moving pieces. It seemed to Violet that the piano was playing itself, or should be, not in the inelegant way that the popular mechanical pianos did, but with a sort of intelligence, able to sense its own tones and respond to them. After all, the notes of the music were just vibrating strings, and vibrations fall at different lengths. It wouldn't be hard, she reckoned, finishing her ale, to create a piano that responded to its own vibrations, building on them. You could press one key, and the piano would then compose a random variation of harmony, based entirely on its own sound. Violet smiled as she thought of it, and then tilted her head, a memory suddenly skirting around the edges of her mind.

"Do you enjoy music?" Miriam asked.

Violet turned to Miriam, suddenly realizing that she was being addressed. Drew was asleep on the table, his companion having abandoned him. "I like the piano," Violet said. "My bro—" Jack elbowed her in the side. "—er, my cousin plays it quite often. He enjoys them. I enjoy the mechanics of them. I thought of building one once, but decided the price of ivory was too high for something I would never really perfect." Violet swallowed. She had nearly slipped up. She had to be careful.

"Cecily plays the pianoforte. Perhaps Jack should ask her to play it for him sometime," Miriam said with a grin. Toby smirked.

"Do you think she would?" Jack asked.

"I think the duke would box your ears," Toby said, "so that if she did, it would hurt to listen to it."

"Ah," Jack said.

"She enjoys music," Miriam said. "She once spent three months trying to create a music box that sang like a chorus of birds, but with no success."

"I doubt strings and metal could reproduce an adequate birdsong," Violet said.

"Hm," Jack said, nodding.

It had grown quite late—far past the school's curfew—and the pub was emptying out. Drew snored softly into his arm.

"Well, it's been a lovely night," Miriam said, stroking Toby's shoulder, "but you all have class in the morning, and it would be a great injustice to your new friends to keep them out so late that they suffered and were scorned by their professors."

"I suppose," Toby said, grunting. He leaned over and poked Drew in the ribs, causing him to bolt upright like a puppet.

"Oh?" Drew said. "Did I miss anything?"

"No more than usual, lad," Toby said. "We're heading back."

"Right," Drew said, taking out some money and handing it to Toby. Toby rose and everyone followed suit, Drew stretching a little. Toby gave money to the barkeep, and they all went out onto the street. The cobblestones felt particularly rough under Violet's shoes, and the smell of smoke was heavier than she remembered. She envied the way Miriam lifted her skirts, oblivious of the catcalls of nearby drunks, and walked elegantly forward, toward the end of the street, where a tall electric light stood, buzzing. A group of cabs was waiting, and she climbed into the first one, Toby just behind her. Violet hoisted herself up next, and soon they were all crammed into the carriage. Violet found herself smiling as they took off over the bumpy streets. These were now her friends, it seemed, and she was warm and content. How nice it must be to be a man, she thought, and to always be able to acquire this feeling. Jack threw his arm around her shoulder and brought her head close to his with a fraternal squeeze.

⋆⟡⋆

AFTER the short trip home, they stumbled out of the carriage—well past midnight—and back to the secret door into the school, softly hushing each others chuckles.

"It's been a fine night," Jack said to Violet, and she nodded. Drew shushed them. "Look at the stars, and the river and the moon," Jack continued. "This is our life, these our inspirations. I feel this is going to be a very good year."

"I do, too," Violet said happily.

"I'm sure it will be very, very good," Miriam said, creeping down the stairs into the college basement, "but we can talk about that another time. For now, we must be quiet, or else we'll all get into some trouble." She paused on the stairs, and Toby, who was walking behind her, nearly crashed into her. "That doesn't sound right, does it? Some trouble. Some . . . *grave punition* . . . grave trouble? No. Hm." She put her chin down and they continued walking down the steps, and then back up the lift to the ground floor, where they all got out and headed to the stairs.

Miriam smiled to herself. She felt that lightness of foot from being just the right amount of drunk. She had made new friends, the year was beginning again, so she would see more of Toby, and the London fog had been light tonight, more like a soft rain. Miriam loved the rain.

"It has been a lovely evening—*une belle nuit*," Miriam continued. "Such a pleasure meeting you both, but I must retire to my own room now."

"You slut," came a harsh whisper from up the stairs. Everyone stopped and held their breath, looking into the shadows. Slowly, Malcolm Volio descended, his eyes glowing with a dark fire and a sneer playing on his thin lips. He wore a grease-stained jacket and shirt, and his hands were dirty.

Miriam's blood chilled. She had been discovered. But she pushed her shoulders back in defiance. She'd been called worse than slut in her time, but Volio radiated such arrogance, she had to hold her wrist to keep from slapping him.

"Volio!" Toby half shouted. "You're barely worthy of wearing the dirt on your hands. Now, go back to bed."

"I don't think I will," Volio said. He had finished walking down the stairs and now stood smirking at them in the small foyer. "I thought it odd to hear a woman's voice in the basement tonight, so I came round the corner. And what should I see, but you, dear Mrs. Isaacs, the woman entrusted with our lovely Cecily's upbringing, cavorting with—" He gestured at Toby. "I don't think the duke would approve of such behavior."

Miriam felt her chest go cold and her mouth weak. He was right, of course: The duke would not approve. Her eyes burned with a hatred as hard as iron. She loved her secret life, loved being outside society. It gave her freedom. As long as she crept along the lines between class and race, no one paid her any attention; she was dark-skinned, so no one minded her being unaccompanied at rougher drinking houses. She was educated, so she could be a governess. She was a widow, so she belonged to no man, and wasn't waiting to be given to one. The only group who had tried to claim her had been her late husband's family, but they hadn't protested when she walked away one night and didn't come back. All this gave her the freedom to do as she pleased, provided she was careful. She inhaled slowly.

"You won't tell him," Toby said to Volio. "And even if you did, we'd all say you were crazy. Right, lads?" Toby turned to look at the others. Drew nodded quickly, and after a moment, so did Jack and Violet. The room was dark in the dim electric light, and shadows edged around the bronze, long and engulfing.

"I will tell him," Volio rasped, "and he will believe me. Or, at the very least, he will put Mrs. Isaacs under careful watch. But I think he'd be more likely to end her employment, just in case. He's a careful man, the duke. He'd probably tell anyone else who tried to hire you afterwards, as well. If anyone else were willing to hire an Arab Jewess for a governess."

Miriam could see her freedom slipping away from her. All her life she'd been told what to do—by family, by husband. She hadn't really been free until she was the only one left, and even then she had been terribly alone until she realized that freedom meant she could go out at night, could associate with brilliant and funny young men like Toby, could fall in love, and no one would really care, as long as she was careful. With all that gone, all she would have would be solitude. A life as a woman in a high-collared black dress, looking after other people's children, an outsider and a shadow. She fell to her knees.

Violet felt herself gasp in sympathy, for she could see the tears welling up in Miriam's eyes and knew what she felt. She wanted to go to Miriam and place her arms around her neck, as a sister would, and tell her that it would be fine, that no one was going to lock her up or throw her out. She could still be herself, and free. But Violet was a man now, and such a gesture was not allowed.

"Please . . . ," Miriam said. Toby approached Volio and threw a fist at him. But Volio, not having spent the night drinking, quickly sidestepped it and approached Miriam.

"Don't worry," Volio said, "I won't say a thing. Not about your loose morals, your drinking, your pleasures, your inappropriate associations with students . . . It will all be a secret."

"For what?" Miriam asked, her mouth tight.

"Just give this note to dear Cecily." He produced a note from his pocket and handed it down to her. Miriam glared up at him. He hadn't just heard a woman's voice. He had been waiting for her. He had been prepared. He had known for some time about her sneaking out.

"What is it?"

"It's a love note."

"The duke will not approve." Miriam stared at the paper and sniffed.

"Then we won't tell him, will we? I do hope I get some sort of response, and soon. Otherwise I will suspect you have not done me this favor."

"I cannot make her write to you!" Miriam said, throwing the letter to the floor. "What if she doesn't care for you?"

"Then you will tell her of my great virtues," Volio hissed.

"I cannot make her love you," Miriam said softly.

"I trust you will do your best," Volio said, leaning in toward her. Their eyes locked. Violet, watching from the side, thought that at any moment, one of them would strike the other. Instead, Miriam lowered her eyes and Volio walked away triumphantly, back up the stairs. "Good night," he called behind him.

"Bastard," Toby said. "Bastard!" he repeated before slamming his fist into the wall, which made a soft metal ringing.

"Toby, stop," Miriam said, standing up from the ground. "I'll do what he says as best I can. Or I'll . . ." She shook her head. "To bed. All of us."

Drew headed into the lift. Jack followed Drew and pulled Violet along with him, but Violet couldn't stop staring at Miriam, standing alone in the glowing brass room, suddenly vulnerable, looking as if she were staring down a great wave that would undoubtedly sweep her away. As the lift rose, she watched as Toby went to Miriam and wrapped his arms around her. Then the lift was on the second floor and she saw no more.

They silently padded down the hall to their rooms, waving good night to Drew when they parted. Inside the room, Violet let out a long breath, almost a wail, and fell onto her bed. "I hate him," she said.

"You're not alone there," Jack said.

"The way he talked to her—the way she's being treated—is horrible. And unfair." Jack nodded in the dim light, taking off this shoes. Violet sighed.

"Vi," Jack said, not looking up.

"Yeah?"

"It's your situation, too." He let that hang there for a moment, then took his socks off and lay back on the bed. "I just mean . . . maybe this isn't the best idea. You can still drop out. With people like him wandering the halls . . . if he found out, you'd be ruined. He could try to take advantage of you. . . . I mean, I wouldn't let him, if I could, but I'm just one bloke, and . . ." He stared down at his hands in his lap.

Violet smiled softly. "You're sweet to worry about me," she said, sounding braver than she felt. She knew he was right. She felt unsafe, as though the walls could collapse on her at any moment.

"Not just you," Jack said, sitting up and looking at her. "Your father. He's been good to my family; he's like an uncle. And your brother . . . Well, in his circles, it would probably improve his reputation, actually. But your mother—"

"No," Violet said, cutting him off. "If she were here, she would support me completely. I know it in my heart." Jack stayed silent. "I just won't be caught, then," she said finally, standing up and going into the water closet. There, she removed her various vestiges of masculinity, unbuttoning her shirt and trousers and letting them fall in a pile on the floor before beginning the process of unwrap-

ping the tight bindings around her chest. With each circle she unwrapped, she could feel the air come into her lungs a little easier,
until, by the time she was unbound, she was taking heavy, ragged
breaths. She let the bindings fall to the ground as well, and slipped
a man's long nightshirt on. She looked at herself in the glass over
the sink. Her eyes and skin were red, so she splashed some water on
her face before heading back out into the bedroom.

Jack had dimmed the small electric sconce on the wall. "Sorry,"
he said from his bed.

"For what?" she asked, slipping under the covers of her bed. She
reached up and turned the sconce the rest of the way off.

"I just wish there were some way we could get back at him," he
said. "But I suppose that at this point, any of my pranks would just
land us in more trouble."

"Only if he knew it was us doing it," Violet said. The sounds of
the wall of gears ground outside the room as neither of them spoke.

"Maybe Miriam should just quit," Jack said.

"And let that man determine her fate?"

"She wouldn't be working here much longer, anyway." Jack said
confidently, "I doubt she'll even be working here next year, one way
or another."

"Oh?"

"Toby will marry her. He loves her."

Violet bit her lower lip, but her laughing was audible anyway.
"I didn't take you for such a romantic," she said.

"What?"

"He loves her?"

"Well, he does."

"You can tell from one night?"

"I could tell from one minute. I know love."

"You sound like my brother."

"Some poetry might do you some good, you know. You have
a distinct lack of feminine feeling within your heart."

"You seem to have enough for both of us."

Jack snorted in the darkness, and Violet snickered. "Good night,
then," she said, closing her eyes.

"Good night," he said.

They lay in silence awhile, the sound of the grinding gears swallowing up their humor. Eventually, Violet fell asleep. She dreamed that Volio had discovered her secret, and made her crawl on hands and knees through sharp scraps of brass before he tore off her clothes and began to laugh.

XI.

VIOLET had dark nightmares that night, and woke up blearly and upset in a way she couldn't express. Jack, however, woke up with a plan.

"It would be just like any other prank," Jack said when Violet came out of the water closet.

"What will?" she asked.

"Faking love notes to Volio. We take the notes from Volio, write back claiming to be Cecily, and all is well. Plus we'd get to read his love notes, which I'm sure will be funny."

"And how does it end?" Violet asked.

"What?" Jack asked, putting on a tie.

"How does it end? Volio is here another year after this one. Do you really expect such a ruse to last that long? And what if he speaks to Cecily and she doesn't know what he's talking about?"

Jack finished tying his tie and they headed down to the dining hall for breakfast. "We write back—as Cecily—and tell him we can't speak to him about it in public as long as he's a student. And I doubt Miriam will be here next year, so it won't have to last for long."

"You assume Miriam will be gone soon because of your theory that Toby plans to marry her? What if she says no, or wants to continue to work? It seems wrong to force a time frame on a woman's life based on your sense of romance," Violet said crossly.

"It will be fun," he told Violet as they chose kidneys and eggs from the buffet. "The ultimate prank, really. Long, yes, but enjoyable. A lot like your own little ruse."

"My ruse," Violet said, "is for the betterment of women everywhere."

"And mine will save one particular woman from losing her employment and security."

"If it works."

"Same could be said of yours."

Violet sighed and shrugged, which meant she would give in and play along, though she might occasionally complain about it. Jack grinned and they walked over to the table at which Toby and Drew were already eating.

"Listen," Toby said in a low voice, leaning in after they had sat down, "Mir and I came up with a plan after you guys went to bed. We're going to answer the note ourselves, pretending to be Cecily."

Violet groaned and Jack laughed. "I had the same idea myself," Jack said. "Ashton here is less than enthused."

"I just think it doesn't have an end in sight," Violet replied. "You can't keep him strung along forever. When he graduates, the truth will come out, and then what will happen?"

"I doubt it'll be of much concern by then," Toby said, leaning back into his chair. "The problem," Toby continued, "is getting someone who can write a proper love letter. Miri says she doesn't want to do it alone. It makes her feel . . . unhappy."

"Ashton can!" Jack said, surely thinking of the actual Ashton, and not Violet. Violet glared at him. Realizing his mistake, Jack's eyes widened in embarrassment.

"You?" Toby asked, looking at Violet. "No offense, mate, but you don't seem to be possessed of much romantic feeling. We need something that sounds like it was written by a girl."

"Jack means my cousin," Violet said after some quick thinking. "His name is also Ashton. It is a family name." She stopped to see if Toby and Drew found this peculiar. They didn't seem to, so she continued. "He is a poet, and lives in town. We are supposed to see him on Sunday."

"A poet?" Toby asked. "That could work right well."

"We'll ask him if he'll help. I'm sure he will. He shares Jack's fondness for . . . mischief."

"It isn't mischief," Toby said. "It's taking care of Miri. She'd do the same for us. I know you lads just met her, but she's real loyal, and she likes you. Please?"

"Of course," Violet said, feeling suddenly ashamed.

"Well, we should go," Jack said, rising. "First mechanics class. If we're late, Ashton won't be able to finish both his and my work before class is over."

Toby guffawed and nodded. "We'd best be off to see the new astronomy professor. I hear he's a real brute. Let us know whether Bunburry lights himself on fire or breaks his nose this time."

Violet nodded and strode out of the dining hall with Jack. She had forgotten they were going to mechanics. A whole day in her environment doing what she loved best. She grinned and nearly skipped as her step became lighter.

Jack put his hand on her shoulder. "You're starting to walk a bit like a woman," he whispered as they passed a second-year student, "which is impressive, as you never really did that before."

Violet narrowed her eyes. She was going to say something rude, but they were suddenly at the mechanics lab, and she felt quite content.

❄❁❄

HERBERT Bunburry was sitting at his large desk off to the side of the room. He smiled at Jack and Ashton as they entered the lab. He always began every year liking the first-years. By the end of the year, he would still like some of them, but some he would find terrifying, and others he wouldn't like at all. He wondered what accidents the coming year would bring. Bunburry had long ago given up on supposing there might not be an accident each year. He had worked at Illyria only seven years, and so far had lost his eyebrows when an engine burst into flames, broken his leg and foot after a short-statured but particularly fearsome device had barreled into him at high speed, and broken his forearm after an innocently constructed mechanical singing bird plummeted into him and revealed itself to have a shockingly sharp beak. There had also been the year that Curio's new oil substitute had exploded and turned him dark as a

Moor for several months, and last year, when Cecily's new chemical adhesive had resulted in his not being able to unclench his left hand from a fist for eight weeks. And of course, there was the first accident: an attempt by a student to make a automatic smithy—a giant forge with arms and legs. That had burned his neck and broken it, making it as fragile as a dried blade of grass.

But he didn't mind, in the end. It was all for science; and, besides, he had fixed himself up. The mechanical kneecap prototype he had put into himself had since helped many others. The metal plate on his shoulder doubled as a small cabinet in which he kept vital tools, so he was never without them; and while the neck brace did make certain aspects of life—looking down, or up, or, really, anywhere but right in front of him—difficult, it was also oddly soothing, having the cool metal around his neck all day. He was quite willing to suffer for science. All the same, he hoped this year's accident was innocuous. Perhaps he would just have the rest of his hair singed off—he didn't have much left, after all—or lose a fingernail. That would be nice.

Bunburry knew that many of the other professors had set first lessons, a way of ranking the students' skill in that particular science, but Bunburry tried to make a new first lesson every year. Always something simple and fun, of course, but something that explored the students' knack for creativity, as well. This year, he was especially pleased with his lesson. It wasn't very complicated: He would simply ask them to make a toy. Bunburry knew that this would show him not only his students' skill levels, but also their personalities. What, after all, is more personal than a toy? He was concerned that some students might spend too long attempting to come up with an idea, but he had brought a large book of popular toys to show them for inspiration. He had gotten it from a lady friend of his who worked as a shopgirl at Whiteleys Department Store. He loved department stores, with their huge halls and many floors smelling of wax and leather and metal. He often went to the toy department on Saturdays just to sit and relax and watch his shopgirl, who always treated him very nicely and brought him lemonade in the summer.

The students had all arrived while Bunburry was daydreaming, and were sitting at various tables, looking at him anxiously. He slowly rose to his feet and walked to the center of the room. "The texts for this class," he said, the act of speaking making his narrow throat scratch and wheeze, "are *Advanced Mechanical Science* by John Horrshmann and *The Workings of Things* by the late Duke of Illyria. If you do not have those texts, see me after class. But for today, if you need them, borrow from a classmate." Bunburry stopped to take a deep breath, as his throat could say only so much before it clenched, making breathing difficult. He coughed for a moment, then continued, "Today, there will be no lesson. I want to see what you can do. So your assignment is simply this: Make a toy." Realizing he had left his book of toys on his table, Bunburry limped back to it, still speaking. "I have a book for inspiration, if you can't come up with an idea. You may use anything in the room that doesn't belong to another student, and you have the entire period. I recommend you sketch your design first and let me look it over."

The best part of this assignment, Bunburry reasoned, as another coughing fit hit him, is that he wouldn't have to talk much longer. He reached his desk, collected the large book of toys, and held it aloft. "Use this book, if you have no ideas. You may begin whenever you'd like." The students hurriedly began to work.

Violet sighed and took out a piece of parchment. A toy? She knew that this was the basic class, almost introductory, but she had already designed a toy this year, and it seemed silly to waste her time on another. Still, she may as well get it over with. Perhaps a variation on the magnet techniques she had used for the ducklings?

"Must it be a toy for children?" Jack asked, grinning impishly. He was thinking of a clockwork toy he had seen in an exclusive shop, which used its gears to animate impressively lifelike—though somewhat disproportionate—characters in a rather unchildlike manner.

Bunburry gave him a long look. "I think in your case, Mr. Feste, it would be best if it were, yes."

It didn't take Violet much time to come up with a sketch: she would make a windup juggler. The clockwork would keep the arms moving in time, and the placement of magnets and the magnets in the juggler's balls would keep the arc steady. She showed her drawing to Professor Bunburry, who glanced at it, smiled, attempted to nod, and then simply said yes.

Violet completed the skeleton of her juggler quickly. By then, the others were finishing up their sketches. Fairfax created plans for what Bunburry thought was a thoroughly unoriginal dancing girl, though he was too polite to say so. Merriman produced sketches for a flower bud that would ideally open in a most lovely manner when it was wound up. Lane made a design for a marching toy soldier.

Jack, however, had difficulty conceiving of an idea. "You must help me," he said to Violet, who was carefully hammering softened bronze into a clown-like shape.

"I cannot come up with an idea for you," Violet said, "but once you have one, I'll help you execute it."

"I lack creativity when surrounded by so much metal," Jack said glumly, resting his chin in his hands. "Though I suppose I could just create my usual mischief."

"Good," Violet said.

"Perhaps something to aid a child's strength, so that they could lift chairs and other things too heavy for them to lift otherwise. They could convince their parents the house is infested with spirits."

"Or so they could help around the house," Violet said.

"Well, then it wouldn't be a toy, would it?"

"Hm," Violet said.

"I'm not sure how I would go about making such a thing, though."

"It wouldn't be very hard," Violet said, finishing up her clown. She placed a ball in each of his hands and began winding the key on his back. "You'd want to extend the child's reach and strength, so you'd have to make some sort of harness, with some springs and pulleys. The really hard part would be producing sufficient energy. It'll take quite a few turns of the crank and a fairly large spring." She stopped winding and placed the clown on the table. It began tossing the balls in the air and catching them again, and continued doing so for a few moments as everyone paused to look at it. Then, with a flourish, Violet tossed the last ball at the clown, and as if by magic, it fell into the arc with the other two. The clown continued juggling all three as though it had always been doing so. Merriman applauded. Violet put her hands on her hips, pleased.

"Nicely done, Mr. Adams," Professor Bunburry said. "You may now work on your own project or assist your classmates, whichever you'd prefer. It's really a lovely piece. You could probably sell it to a toy maker."

Violet tilted her head and regarded the clown. She hadn't worked very hard on the visual details, so his grin seemed false, his skull a little misshapen. She shook her head. "Oh no, sir, I would never feel right submitting something I had only made in a day and not spent time perfecting."

"Of course," Bunburry said in an approving tone. "Just put it on the shelf next to the other finished pieces. Sometimes the other teachers like to come in and look around." Violet did as she was told and returned to Jack, who by now had doodled an innocent little girl standing in front of a shocked mother and father, who stared aghast at a pile of furniture in the corner of their parlor.

"I don't think that will help much," Violet said.

"Well, it's all I've got."

"Here." Violet took the pen and paper from Jack and began sketching a design. "The harness needs longer arms and a pump that fits in back to power them. You could make it steam powered, so it wouldn't need any winding, but then it wouldn't be good for children. Next, the child fastens these metal arms over his arms, you put in a clamp or such so he can control the grasp, and there you are. Two long, powerful arms. But as I said, to keep it going for even a few minutes, he'd need to wind it nearly a hundred times."

"You make it look easy."

"It is. Simple mechanics. Now, go ask Bunburry to approve it, and start making it, or you'll be in here during your independent time."

"And you wouldn't enjoy my company?" Jack asked with large, hurt eyes.

Violet glared. "You'd prevent me from getting anything done."

"I *am* quite distracting," he said. "It's because I'm so terribly good-looking."

Violet looked about to see if anyone had heard that last comment, but no one had. Rolling her eyes, she walked to her cubbyhole, took out the plans from yesterday, and laid them down at the table, while Jack went to ask Bunburry's approval for his faux-poltergeist machine.

Violet rolled out her notes from the previous night and sighed. Here were her sketches for the engine—clever, to be sure, and elegant—and here were the sketches of what it was to power: another dancing girl. But this one was cursed more than most, for it would keep dancing for eternity, if her engine worked. No—she could not bring herself to make it. With a growl, Violet crumpled the sheet of parchment covered with sketches of dancing girls into a ball in her fist.

"Angry?" Jack asked, returning from his talk with Bunburry.

"Did he like your plans?" Violet asked, ignoring the question.

"He did, though he says that in future it would be best if you were to let me design my own schematics so that I can better learn the art of mechanical science."

"Ah." Violet looked at Jack's sketches, and his clever drawing of the innocent girl.

"Why did you make it a girl, Jack?"

"What?"

"In your drawing, your child, the one who pulls the prank, is a girl."

"Oh. I suppose a dress is easier to draw than trousers, is all."

"It's not because a girl is weaker than a boy, and so, would have more difficulty lifting something heavy?" Violet could feel that ticking in her brain again, as though someone had finally wound her gears back and the spring was about to release.

"No, that's not what I meant," Jack protested.

"But it is," Violet said, "and I understand why. Women are, on the whole, physically weaker, which is one reason we—" Jack coughed loudly. "—*they* have so long been delegated to second-class status. They're considered fragile." Violet crossed her arms and looked anything but fragile.

Jack shook his head anxiously. "That's really not what I meant by it. Look," he said, drawing on a piece of paper, "a dress is just a tri-angle, like this, but trousers mean you have to show the knee, so its one rectangle over the other, but they need to taper, and—"

"I know, I know. I'm not mad at you," Violet said. "In fact, you've given me an idea."

"Oh, good. So you'll help me build my poltergeist machine?"

"Yes, but you'll have to do most of the work. Professor Bunburry keeps looking over here."

"That's all right," Jack said. "Just tell me what to do."

Violet sighed. "Well, first find a spring."

"Right," Jack said, and went off to the shelf of supplies. Violet un-crumpled the wad of paper still in her hand and smoothed it out on the table, lovingly. Women are not all meant to dance, she thought. Some are meant to do quite different things. She stared long and hard at the paper, and a smile crept onto her lips.

"I have springs," Jack said, holding out two springs of slightly different sizes. "I think the larger one will work better, but I don't want the contraption to be so large, it causes the child to fall backwards and be unable to right himself, like a turtle. What do you think?"

Violet stared at the springs. She had an idea. A very good idea.

"I think you're probably right," she said. And they began to work.

By the end of the class, everyone had produced at least satisfactory toys, and Violet was wearing Jack's contraption and using it to pat him on the head. Lane and Merriman were watching and laughing. But, truly, Violet's mind was elsewhere. An idea had stirred, and now all she wanted was to work.

Lunch flew by. Toby and Drew and Jack discussed possible ways of tormenting Volio with the letters, but Violet didn't pay much attention. In her mind, she was building a marvelous machine. Not just a machine, but a dress. A dress for men and women alike, with marvelous long arms that stretched out farther than Violet was tall. A dress that would give anyone who wore it the same strength, strength enough to build carriages, regardless of gender or age. She imagined swarms of these dresses at the docks, run by women, as-sembling a ship with the ease of knitting a scarf. She saw women going to work each day with their male counterparts, being spoken to with respect, and then, all of them dancing together after work if they chose, as enjoyment, not as purpose.

But, most important, it would look like a woman. Her machine would be more beautiful than the loveliest mechanical dancing girl, but its purpose would be more beautiful, too. It would make women into a symbol of strength. And when Violet revealed herself as the inventor, she would make women into a symbol of intelligence. All notions of women as weak or dumb or made only to run households and give birth would be just memories. She would show the world—or at least the scientific world—that women were men's equals in every sense.

Violet made herself eat because she knew she would need her energy in the lab that afternoon, and probably that evening, too. This project would be vast. She would have to work hard to finish it in time. And she needed to find a metal to make her engine out of that would degrade slowly, if at all, so that the incredible amounts of power her creation required would not destroy its power source. No shoveling of coal—that would make it nearly unusable. She needed constant energy, and that meant she needed her engine to work without degradation.

"I don't think we can get him to kill someone," Jack was saying. "And, besides, who would we want him to kill?"

Violet narrowed her eyes and refocused on the conversation. They were discussing what they hoped to put in the fake love notes to Volio. "No killing," she said definitively. "Little things. Start small. Have him wear his hair a certain way. You must make him believe it's Cecily. Otherwise Miriam will be in great trouble, and none of us wants that."

"He's right," Toby said, leaning back in his chair, "though it was fun to think about."

"I'm going to the lab," Violet said, rising. "I'll see you all at supper."

The next few days were a blur. Violet threw herself into her project, building the shell of the machine out of curves of metal and wire, and paid little attention to anything else except class. She listened to Curio's kindhearted words on the origins of modern chemistry, his loving description of new forays into cellular chemistry, and then his screams of rage at students who handled chemicals without gloves. She suffered Prism's condescending stare through his multitude of lenses as he gave a monotone lecture on Babbage, his great machine, and the best way to use it. During meals, she half listened as the others plotted against Volio, engaging them only when she was not herself engaged in fantasies about her work. On Thursday night, Jack persuaded her to sneak out with them again. At the bar she watched Miriam glide her arm up and down Toby's back, analyzed the way it turned and moved, and wondered how she could replicate that.

"Are you all right?" Miriam asked. Violet blinked and roused herself from her thoughts. She stared down at the untouched mug of ale in front of her. Toby and Drew were loudly and frantically explaining the concept behind Toby's latest hangover cure formula. Drew was actually bouncing in his seat. "It's just, you don't seem very involved tonight."

"I have an idea," Violet said, "for my final project. It's possessing me. I'm sorry if I'm being rude."

"Oh, it's not that. Everyone here is rude. I just like to make sure my boys are all right."

"Your boys?"

"Well, Toby's boys. Toby's and mine. But Toby wouldn't know a thing about caretaking, so, really, my boys. He just finds them for me."

"Like Drew?"

"Drew, yes, though there's little I can do for him. Last year, there was a senior, too—Daniel. Very smart and a little shy—like you— but Toby took a great liking to him right away. Toby can always spot the clever ones. I mean, in that place, they're all clever, but the *really* clever ones."

"I'm not shy," Violet said, taking a drink.

"No?" Miriam asked, smiling slightly and bringing a mug of ale to her lips.

"No. I'm just preoccupied."

"With your project."

"Yes."

"And what is this project?"

"It's a machine. Like an automaton, but not. One wears it, and it enables great strength."

"The duke forbids the making of weapons, you know."

"Oh, no, it wouldn't be a weapon; it would be a tool. For construction, I think."

"You'd best be careful, nonetheless. There was another student years ago—my first year working for the duke—who built automata with working pistols for hands. The duke was so furious, he tried to expel the boy, but it was near the end of the year, and the Minister of Defense heard about the situation. So he stepped in, confiscated the automata, and convinced the duke to let the student finish the year and graduate. No one really knew all the details, so it didn't look bad to the outside world, but the duke was humiliated. He'll talk of expulsion if your creation seems even slightly like a weapon."

"Well . . . it won't. But I'll keep it in pieces as long as possible then, so he won't know what it is. Thank you for the advice."

"The duke inspects all the labs most nights after supper. You should hide anything that looks too dangerous by then."

"I will. I suppose it might all be for naught, anyway."

"Why?"

"I need a new substance for the engine. Something strong that won't wear away over time. It needs to be slippery."

Miriam laughed.

"What's so funny?"

"Cecily told you what she was working on, didn't she?"

"A substance that would harden in molds?"

"Yes. And be both light and very durable. You should speak to her. She's nearly got it, I think."

Violet pursed her lips and took a drink of her ale, then regarded Miriam. "Does it ever bother you?" Violet asked.

"What?"

"That Cecily has full access to the school, the labs, and the education and you don't? That she can be both woman and scientist, a right that's denied to you?"

Miriam looked down and then up again. She was smiling. "I'm

not a scientist," she said. "I have some interest in the sciences, but I don't have the patience to attack them as you, all of you, do. Cecily does. She is *une fille futée*—very smart—and I think her having access to Illyria is for the betterment of everyone, regardless as to whether or not she inherited that right. After all, her being a woman in Illyria isn't what prevents other women from entering."

"I suppose not," Violet said, looking down at her ale.

"So, no, I don't envy her. I respect her, though she does still often act like a girl of sixteen. She is very taken with you, you know."

"She is?" Violet asked, worried.

"Most of the students would be flattered."

"I try not to get distracted by such things."

"Ah," Miriam said, and drank more of her ale, looking sidelong at Violet. They sat in silence. "Well," Miriam said, "just be careful of your creation and its potential for weaponry. You don't want to end up like Ralph Volio, depending on the Minister of Defense to come to your rescue."

"*Ralph* Volio?"

"Yes, the student I mentioned. Malcolm Volio's elder brother, Ralph."

"Ralph Volio—why else does that name sound familiar?"

"He works for the Ministry of Defense now. Very high up, as I understand it, designing weapons. Meets directly with the Queen. It was the oddest thing: The duke caught him making just part of one of his automata—the rifle. But then, less than a month later, after the minister had convinced the duke to let Ralph graduate, he marched two dozen of them out to the Crystal Palace for the Science Faire. No one knows where he was keeping them all. It infuriated the duke, which was probably Ralph's intention."

"Hm," Violet said. She shook her head. Perhaps Ralph had worked in the basement, and he'd just left the automata that he didn't care for there as he marched the others out. But that wouldn't explain the nagging familiarity the head of the one skeleton possessed, as though she had seen it somewhere before.

"Thinking of your machine again?"

"No. Something else."

"Well, I'll leave you to it, then. And thank you, Ashton. *Toda.*
Merci. Toby says your cousin will help us to pull this trick on Volio.
I don't care much about what the return letter says, as long as I am
not caught. I like my job. I like my life. I'd just rather not have it
taken away by that sodding child."

"Of course," Violet said. "How could I not help? He is a villain.
I shall be happy to help you defeat him."

"You talk like a hero. You really are just Cecily's type."

"I very much doubt that," Violet said, and took a long swig of
her ale to hide her laughter.

XII.

THE next morning after breakfast, Jack, Violet, and the other first-years took the long winding stairs to the astronomy tower on top of Illyria. All the first-years were exhausted from the excitement of their first long week.

The astronomy tower was a large dome made of spotless glass plates and thick bronze beams. There were glass doors out onto the balcony surrounding it, which was punctuated by the moving statues on the clocks. Inside the dome were boards hung with star maps and tables covered with various astronomical tools that Violet recognized from her father's lab. Idly, she picked one up and began to toy with it as she did when she was a child, flipping a lens this way, a switch that way. Bracknell was nowhere to be seen. The students stood about, confused as to what to do next.

"If he doesn't show up," said Lane, "what do we do?"

"Well, I'd imagine we get the day off," Jack said

"But this is the one class I'd be good at!" Merriman said. "I don't want to have the day off."

At that moment, the loud clang of the door closing at the bottom of stairs echoed, followed by Bracknell's muttering and heavy footfalls. "Fucking lift. It wouldn't have been hard to have it go all the fucking way up here, would it? No, the buggers want me to walk." Bracknell's head emerged at the opening of the stairwell, red and sweaty. For a moment, he looked surprised to see the students all standing about, but quickly covered that surprise with annoyance. "Adams! Put that down."

Violet swallowed and laid the instrument back on the table.

"Honestly, I'd think you of all people would know better. Isn't your father that bigwig astronomer nutter? Doesn't he teach you how to respect the tools of the trade? Or is he too busy trying to prove life on the moon?"

"Actually, sir, many scholars think that lunar life might be possi—"

"Do I look like I bloody well care?" Bracknell screamed, spit flying from his mouth. "You don't touch anything in the room until I tell you you can, understood?" Violet nodded. "You'd best be careful, Adams, or you'll bring shame down on your father and family. Though, considering the state of your father, I don't know how much more shame is really possible. Everyone, sit down!"

Violet felt her face go hot, but sat down anyway. Jack gave her a pat on the back, probably trying to ease her anger. She clenched her fists. Her father was perhaps thought of as being a little odd, but most people also agreed he was brilliant. Everyone discussed his papers. Even the Queen had written him a letter. She closed her eyes and took a deep breath. She turned her focus from her anger, and thought instead of her invention, and how it would change the world.

"I don't know why they insist on having this class during the day," Bracknell said. "Seems a waste of time. But I'm to teach you the basic theory, and then you're required to come up after sundown at least once a week to do your various assignments. I'm supposed to be here each night, too, but they don't pay me for that, so I'll just leave the door open and you can all come up and do your work and leave the place nice and tidy. If anything is amiss in the morning, I'll have Curio up here to check for fingerprints, and then I'll see to it that whichever of you is too good to clean up after yourself is expelled." He glared pointedly at Violet. "Now. The lesson. Who can tell me which celestial bodies we should expect to see tonight, and at what times?" Merriman's hand shot up. Everyone else stayed quiet. Violet tried to calculate the answer in her head—it was fall, so the stars would show Libra. Or was it Virgo? And what about the planets? "Only the fat one? Nothing from Adams-whose-father-is-a-famous-astronomer-so-he-can-handle-whatever-he-likes-in-the-tower? Fine, Fatty, your answer?"

The lesson went on like that for some time, as Bracknell posed a series of questions, mocked Violet for not automatically knowing the answers, and then called on Merriman, whom he persisted in calling Fatty. By the end of the class, none of the students felt like they had learned anything, and even Merriman felt uncomfortable. "Do you want to sit by me next time?" he asked Violet as they walked down the stairwell. "I can tell you some of the answers. I don't mind not being the one he always calls on. It might make him get my name right."

"That's all right, Humphrey. Thank you, though," Violet said, smiling as much as she could.

"Surely we could report him for something," Jack said. "Abuse of students, maybe?"

"I don't think anyone would care," Lane said. "Curio has called me far worse during his bad spells. I think it's supposed to toughen us up."

"He's a brute," Jack said. "I'm glad he's just here for a year."

"Maybe he'll fall off the tower," Fairfax offered in an unexpected moment of solidarity, which made them all uncomfortable. They walked in silence down to the lift and rode it to the dining hall. Violet felt hot and cold at the same time, angry and embarrassed, and most of all, annoyed that of all the people to make her worry about her venture again, it was Bracknell.

"You okay?" Jack whispered as they got off the lift. She nodded, and bit her lip. "Your father will never be ashamed of you," he said, "no matter what you do." She nodded again. She couldn't let Bracknell break her. If he pushed her to a point of rage, she might give herself away, and that would be unimaginably horrible. Not just because Bracknell would surely expose her, but for what he might do to her before that. She shivered as she thought of him finding out her secret, of his hands grabbing and squeezing her sides and prodding at her body with a hungry, wicked grin on his face.

"Well, well!" called Toby, waving as they walked into the dining hall and approached the table. "I've had a breakthrough! At least, I think I have," Toby continued in a lower voice. "We'll have to go out tonight and get very very drunk so I can test it in the morning."

"Sounds good to me," Jack said, "you?"

"Fine," Violet said, too busy trying to shake off the unbidden images in her mind to listen. She tried to focus on what she was going to do during her lab time, and she half succeeded. By the end of lunch, she was conversing with Drew about the most flattering scents to add to his perfume, and she could smile. But she felt dreary, and during her free time in the lab, she worked sluggishly.

She was fastening together a series of gears to go on the bottom of the machine and enable it to move more easily, when a shadow fell over her work. Cecily had walked in.

"Hullo, Ashton," Cecily said when Violet looked up. Cecily was fluttering her eyelashes and wearing a high-collared blue dress with a long line of buttons cascading down it.

Why did Violet notice the beauty of dresses only now that she could not wear them? It's probably uncomfortable, she told herself, binding at the waist, and limiting to the stride. But Cecily looked quite content in it.

"Good afternoon, Cecily," Violet said. "How are your experiments going?"

"Very well, thanks." She stood there silently for a while. "I'm letting the most recent batch harden right now. I think I have the formula down. If it works, it could revolutionize the way things are made. Machines with gears made of my . . . I don't know what to call it—paste? clay?—could be lighter, and run more smoothly."

"It sounds wonderful," Violet said. "In fact, that may be just what I need for my own machine. If you would assist me?"

Cecily lit up, then turned pink. "Well, of course," she said. "I would be glad to help you in any way I can."

"I need to find a substance that will not wear away. If yours is as hard and light as you say, then the gears shouldn't wear as quickly." Violet pulled out the sketches of her engine. "You see?"

Cecily walked around the table to stand next to Violet and looked over the plans, her body hovering close to Violet's. "Yes," Cecily said, "I see—a few turns of the key and it could power something for ages. This could be revolutionary."

"If your . . . clay works, yes," Violet said. The sadness she felt moments before had faded. She looked at Cecily's face, the way she studied the plans and furrowed her brow when thinking. Here, finally, was a sister scientist.

"Then I shall make sure it does," Cecily said. "What is your engine powering?"

Violet met Cecily's gaze, but paused. She hadn't shown anyone the plans for her machine yet. She had told Miriam the basic idea, but the specifics, the look of it, were secret so far, and she enjoyed keeping that secret. In fact, she feared that if anyone were to look at her plans and see the form of the machine—its feminine shape, the drapes of metal—that they might be able to see her own secret. She looked Cecily over, from top to bottom, wondering if she could trust her. The girl was no fool, certainly, but she was much more of a girl than Violet herself had ever been, and Violet wondered if she was the sort who giggled and gossiped about things that delighted her.

Cecily looked surprised by the delay, and opened her mouth as if to retract her request, but Violet spoke first. "If I show you," Violet said, "will you keep them secret? Even from your cousin?"

Cecily pursed her lips. "Of course," she said, "if you ask me to."

"I do," Violet said, pulling out the plans. "I want it to be a surprise." She unrolled the plans and showed them to Cecily, watching her face. Cecily's eyes sharpened and focused on the sketches and notes, taking everything in a bit at a time.

"Why . . . this is genius," Cecily whispered. "With this device, well, anyone could do difficult jobs. Old men could work well past the age they normally could."

"And women would be able to work as men do."

"Yes. That's why it looks like . . . that's very clever. And so thoughtful, to come up with an idea like this. So sensitive to the gentle sex, that you wish to give us the opportunities this will provide. You're a very generous man," she said, gazing at Violet in a way that made her uncomfortable. Especially when paired with the word man.

Violet stroked her own neck, swallowing. She wanted to reveal the truth, but knew she could not. "Thank you," she said, instead.

"If you sketch me the exact gears you need, with specific measurements, I can make the molds for them," Cecily said.

"Thank you, that's very kind."

"It would be a pleasure. And it will assist me in testing this formula." Cecily looked up at the doorway of the lab, where Miriam stood in the frame, shadowy. "I'd best be going to check on the clay now," she continued. You'll get those sketches ready for me? I can collect them on Monday?"

"Certainly."

"Good," Cecily said, heading toward the door of the lab.

As Cecily walked out of the room, she had to restrain herself from skipping. How good she felt! How nice it was to stand so close to Ashton and look over his designs. And to find that what she knew in her heart—that he was a good, generous man, worthy of her love—was true. She clasped her hands to her chest and walked out into the hallway, smiling. Miriam nodded at her and followed her, walking a step behind, like a shadow.

"Isn't he a wonderful man?" Cecily asked.

"I couldn't really say," Miriam said. How sad Miriam was, Cecily thought, to have lost her love so young and become a widow, without the ability to see the beauty in men such as Ashton, or to fall in love with them.

Cecily boarded the lift and pulled the crank with some force, sending it up a floor, and then pulled the crank again to stop it. It was possible that Ashton had some sort of love outside of Illyria. But Cecily didn't think so. She would know. Ashton didn't have that droopy-eyed look Cecily knew from so many other young men at Illyria. That look of pining, and wandering thoughts. So many young men in the school were in love with someone. She thought maybe a handful were in love with her, and she rather enjoyed that sort of flattery, but it must be insufferable for the others: having to focus their minds on their work while their hearts longed to be far from school, gazing at the object of their affections. How lucky Cecily was that her love should come to Illyria so that she needn't go out and seek him.

As they walked past the door to the biological lab, a rat came bolting out of it. Cecily shrieked and stepped back a pace. She would not faint, though. She wasn't that sort of girl.

"Sorry! I am so, so sorry, Miss Cecily," said a young man who chased out after the rat and grabbed it up in his hands. Cecily nodded, and noticed that it wasn't actually a rat, but a weasel of some sort, with a long, wiggling body and bright black eyes that regarded her happily.

"I thought it was a rat," Cecily said.

"Oh no," said the young man, "it's a ferret. His name is Dorian. Would you like to pet him?" Cecily looked the ferret in the eye as it wiggled about in the young man's hands. It had a charm to it.

"Certainly," she said, stepping forward to stroke the creature's head.

"I'm Jack, by the way," said the young man. Cecily looked up at him, and he smiled. He wasn't a bad-looking young man, she thought. His features lacked Ashton's gentle refinement, but he had sweet bright green eyes and a goodly shaped face, and his blond hair looked soft to the touch.

She smiled back. "I'm Cecily," she said.

"Oh, I know, miss," Jack said. He was sweating now.

"Am I so famous?"

"Yes," Jack said, looking uncomfortable. "You're so lovely. How could anyone not—?"

"Oh," Cecily said. This was one of the handful who was in love with her. Why did they always focus on her beauty? Could they not tell her she was clever, or at least focus on something more specific, like how her eyes shone with intelligence, or her lips curled so nicely? Ashton would tell her those things, she was sure.

"Oh?" Jack asked.

"I'm sorry. It's just that it's very easy to call me lovely when you see no other women during the day but Miriam, who shrouds herself in black."

"Well, I've never had the chance to speak to you before, so I could not judge your wit, or really anything other than the beauty that I've seen from afar."

Cecily raised an eyebrow. "And now?" she asked. "Can you judge my wit now?"

Jack swallowed. "I think I would need more time with you," he said.

Cecily laughed. "You're certainly cheeky," she said. Jack grinned.

"And your ferret is quite cute. What experiments do you plan to enact on him?"

"I want to teach him to sing," Jack said, and looked down at the animal. "Like a bird."

Cecily reached out to stroke the creature's head again. By now it had given up on squirming free. Cecily's hand brushed Jack's as she petted the ferret, and she quickly pulled it back. "Well, that will be quite an accomplishment, if you are successful."

"If I am successful, may I show you?"

"You may show anyone you like, I'd imagine," Cecily said, sounding perhaps a little crueler than she meant. "And next time, if you wish to flatter me, I'd suggest doing so more succinctly. Beauty is such a broad term, as though you're not really sure why you find me beautiful." And with that, she continued down the hall, Miriam trailing after her.

"There are many reasons," Jack called after her. "I shall name them for you, if you let me."

Cecily smiled to herself, but she didn't turn back, so Jack couldn't see her expression as he watched her vanish down the hall.

Nonetheless, Jack felt elated. He had spoken with Cecily. She had spoken back, and proved to be clever and smart. Her hand had grazed his. She really was the most beautiful creature in the world. He clutched Dorian to his chest and sighed as he reentered the lab, then put Dorian in his cage, where he began to leap around wildly, mimicking Jack's heart.

Now, he realized, he needed to make the ferret sing. He hadn't really planned on doing that—he had been thinking about giving it two sets of bat wings, so that it would be able to bounce in the air as it did on land, but that had not seemed like the right answer to give to Cecily. So he would make the ferret sing, evidence of the romance of his soul. Dorian danced about as if on fire.

Jack worked for the next few hours, performing extensive surgery on both Dorian and a pigeon named Albert under Valentine's watchful eye. By suppertime, the pigeon had died and Dorian would occasionally make an uncomfortable sound—half coo, half cough—then begin bouncing around as if shocked and unable to tell where the sound had come from.

"Well, it was a good try," Valentine said, patting Jack lightly on the shoulder, "but I think you should study up on the voice box a little more before you attempt anything like it again. You'll find it in chapter forty-six of my book."

Jack nodded. He needed a drink.

✦❀✦

AT supper, everyone was glum. Jack had killed a pigeon and felt terrible about it, Toby and Drew had had unproductive days in the lab, and Violet felt guilty for even being there, but couldn't talk to anyone about it.

"It's a good thing we're going drinking tonight," Toby said, playing with his food. "And we can still test my formula in the morning, right? Just 'cause it made the rats vomit and faint doesn't mean it'll have the same effect on us." Jack and Violet exchanged a glance. Drew nodded. A peculiar smell drifted off him, like roses and camphor. It did not help anyone's appetite.

"Let's go," Toby said after a minute. "I need a drink before I can eat." The others stood, scooted back their chairs in silence, and followed Toby out.

From the professors' table, Miriam watched them go and wondered when she might be free enough to join them. She missed Toby's arms, and his odd smell—warm ale and chemicals. When they had first met out at the pub, she hadn't thought much of him: large, loud, drunk, not an uncommon man. His being a student at Illyria made him slightly more interesting, and his laughter at her when she asked him not to tell anyone about her going out at night was, if not charming, then endearing. Younger, yes, but full of merriment and generosity. He wouldn't persecute her, he said, just for wanting a drink. He was handsome, too, with soft skin and large smiling eyes, though he hid it under all that bluster and sweat.

"And so," Cecily was telling her cousin, "Ashton said that if my formula works out as I plan, he would like to use it in his own invention!" She was pleased with herself.

174   **Lev AC Rosen**

"I'm not sure, Cecily, that I like you being so intimate with the students," the duke said, casting a glance at Miriam. Miriam met his eyes but said nothing.

"Oh, don't worry, Cousin Ernest," Cecily said. "Ashton is a sweet boy, with a gentle soul, but I wouldn't want to distract him from his studies." She put a particular, wicked emphasis on the word distract. "I'm just going to help him. He's quite clever. He showed me the plans for his engine."

"Will it work?" the duke asked.

"Oh yes, if I can get my parts to work."

"Perhaps I shall go down and see these plans myself, then."

"All right, but don't be so stuffy, and don't tell him not to be friends with me. I may be friends with whoever I'd like."

"As long as his marks keep up," the duke said, frowning slightly, then biting into a piece of bread. What is it about Ashton Adams that is so alluring to everyone around him? First Aunt Ada bets that he will be the most surprising, and then Cecily goes out of her way to befriend him and even assist him in his work. And, the duke had to confess, he felt a strange sort of attraction to the young man himself. It would be best, he decided, to investigate, to drop in on him often, and see how his work went. Maybe Cecily was right after all, and he was simply a genius of such high caliber that he impressed everyone around him. And if that were the case, the duke might enjoy exchanging ideas with him. Which of course, was what an education at Illyria was all about. He would take the young man under his wing, perhaps, and foster his various talents.

Miriam cleared her throat. "Sir?" she asked, and he nodded. Supper was done, and she was free to go for the evening. He never asked where she took herself on her free weekends. He assumed she went to her house of worship, somewhere in the city, but didn't know where it was, and thought it rude to ask.

"Are you going?" Cecily asked Miriam. "Isn't it a little early?"

"Would you like me to stay longer?" Miriam asked.

"No, it's all right," Cecily said with a sigh. "I just always miss you when you go."

"I miss you, too," Miriam said, smiling. She kissed Cecily on the forehead and stood. "But you're a young lady now. Soon you'll have no need of a governess."

"Then I shall make you my lady's maid. I think you will be with me forever and ever."

"I shall be your friend forever, if nothing else," Miriam said, and patted Cecily on the head. "Sweet dreams. I shall see you in the morning." Cecily nodded and turned back to her empty plate. Miriam took the stairs to the high bridge, which stretched across the Great Hall and to the duke's apartments. She had a small room next to Cecily's, with a bed and a wardrobe. Leaving on the weekends was always difficult, as she didn't want the duke or Cecily to see her in any of her more lascivious gowns. But it was cool enough now that she could throw a cloak over her red silk dress, and let her hair down later. She didn't mind these little inconveniences. They were worth her freedom. Keeping that freedom was becoming more difficult to maintain with Volio making demands on her.

She nodded at the doorman as she left the college, and hailed a parked hansom cab. In the cab, she took her hair out of the large bun at the back of her head, let it fall over her neck, and loosed her cloak, showing the low neckline of her dress. She wished for a moment that she had more to show, like Cecily—ten years her junior, and far more voluptuous—but smiled again, thinking of how Toby had once told her he loved the litheness of her body.

Her freedom came in part from her outsider status. She had learned she was an outsider when she was still a child in Persia. She had learned how to *use* being an outsider in Paris, where her family had moved when she was six. At school, she would tell her headmistress she needed to leave for religious reasons. The headmistress, not knowing better, would nod, and Miriam would spend her day on the Seine. Adults would walk by her and assume she was working because her dark skin relegated her in their minds to servant status. Only her family and the Jewish community kept a tight grip on her, and when she came to London at sixteen to be married, that grip slipped. When she was widowed, it let go altogether.

Miriam's late husband was named Joshua, but there wasn't much to say about him beyond that. It was an arranged marriage. She had

moved with her father from Paris to London when she was sixteen
so she could be married. Her mother had died a year before that.
Joshua was a sweet, wiry man, with thick curly hair and perpetual
stubble, no matter how often he shaved. On their wedding night, he
had been sweet to her, but quiet. They had never learned to talk to
one another, beyond simple pleasantries. Then the army had moved
him around for a few months, and Miriam was left alone to make
their new home. Her father died, and Joshua came home and told
her he would take care of her, and Miriam almost believed him. He
had been the sort of man she could have seen herself falling in love
with, given enough time. She also could have grown to hate him,
but he had gentle eyes, and long eyelashes, so she preferred to think
it would have been the former.

And then, nine months into the marriage, he died. Fell off a
horse and was trampled. At the funeral, she didn't cry; afterwards,
her in-laws had tried to take her in, make her family, but she had just
walked away. She remembered that as she walked away from the funeral, from the East End, from the mere outline of a life she had
there, that it had begun to rain, and she had walked through London
in a wet and torn black dress, with a black handkerchief in her hand,
and had felt her chest open like wings.

She discovered that very day that no one in London minded a
Persian—or Arab, or whatever they thought she was—woman
drinking with men at a low-class pub. They assumed she was a pros-
titute. And if anyone knew her as something else—a governess, a
widow—they would never realize that the Miriam Issacs they knew
and that dark-skinned woman at the bar were the same. No one paid
that much attention to dark-skinned women at the bar, after all. Or
anywhere else.

As long as she was clever, she was free to do what she pleased.
And she did. She made love to Toby in hotel rooms on Saturday
night, and wandered the streets of London alone. She let the rain
fall on her face.

Volio could take all this away from her. He needed to be stopped.
Could she trust Toby and the others to handle this for her? She
wasn't sure. Their idea of false notes exchanged with Volio seemed

clever, but how long could they keep it up? And was Volio really so conceited that he could believe that any real note from Cecily would include anything but a polite rejection of his advances? Miriam tilted her head and looked out at passing London. He probably was. Maybe the idea would work. And if it didn't, she would figure something out. She usually did. She wasn't a genius, like the people who surrounded her—Cecily had long ago become more of a teacher than a student in all her lessons but French—but she was smart. She knew how to come back from disaster and form a life, a good life, for herself. And she could certainly do it again, if she was required to. Perhaps she could move back to France, this time. Or Greece.

The cab came to a stop outside the Well-Seasoned Pig, and Miriam was helped out by the cabdriver, whom she paid, and who smiled at her lecherously. She restrained herself from kicking him in the shin and went into the bar. Her group was sitting in a corner, eating and drinking. Toby and Drew seemed to be in good spirits again, Toby chewing perhaps too vigorously on a banger and Drew shifting about in his seat in time to the music coming from the old piano in the corner. She had a certain affection for Drew. He reminded her of a puppy: always eager to play until refused, and then he'd fall asleep at your feet. And he was a good young man, too. A little bit of a follower to Toby's leader, but she imagined he'd grow out of that once Toby graduated. He would have to run his family business one day, after all. And he wasn't stupid; he just fell asleep more easily than most.

And the newcomers. She liked them, too. They were fine additions to their little group. She sat down with them.

"We took off early," Toby said to her, and reached under the table to clasp her hand firmly in his. "We all had rotten days."

"I'm sorry to hear that," Miriam said. They had all clearly had quite a bit to drink already, and were probably determined to become very drunk, and test Toby's elixir in the morning. She slid Toby's glass away from him and took a swig from it. She loved Toby, and his hand in hers made her heart float lazily on a river within her.

"I killed a pigeon," Jack said with a frown.

"Part of your singing ferret experiment, for Cecily?"

"Yes," Jack said wistfully, perking up at the thought of Cecily, and then frowning again. "But it's nowhere near ready yet. Don't tell her I killed a pigeon."

"I can't even tell her that I see you outside of Illyria," Miriam said. "Thank you, both of you," she said, including Ashton, "for not mentioning that to Cecily."

"You saw Cecily today, too?" Jack asked.

"Yes," Ashton said, "she came down to see me. And actually, if all goes well, she can help me."

"Help you?" Jack asked, stricken.

"With my machine. With the engine, really. If her clay works out, then we can mold the parts from it, so they don't wear down as fast. It would be brilliant if it worked."

"What are you upset about?" Miriam asked Ashton.

"He got picked on by Bracknell," Jack said, "just 'cause his dad's an astronomer."

"Bracknell *est un con*," Miriam said. "He pinched my bottom once as he passed me in the hall."

"He what?" Toby roared.

"Calm down," Miriam said. "I forbid you to get yourself in trouble defending my honor."

"Oh," Toby said, and slumped down.

"Do I smell funny?" Drew asked.

Everyone was silent until Ashton said, "Yes, but it's fading."

Jack laughed, then told Ashton, "I can't believe you didn't tell me she visited you." Miriam narrowed her eyes. She expected jealousy, maybe competition, but Jack was acting as though Ashton's befriending of Cecily somehow benefited him. "Did you talk to her about me?"

"No," Ashton said, "we spoke only of science."

"Oh," Jack said, disappointed. "Well, next time, tell her what a great fellow I am, will you?"

"Sure," Ashton said.

"We have to figure out how to help Miriam," Toby announced suddenly.

"I thought we were going to Ashton's cousin Ashton," Drew said, snickering.

"I can't believe you didn't think to tell her how great I was today," Jack said to Ashton.

"It didn't cross my mind," Ashton said. "I'm sorry."

"Yes," Toby continued, "we will ask Ashton's cousin Ashton to write the notes, but we should tell him what he has to say."

"Well, clearly, the notes have to say that Cecily can't speak to him in public," Miriam said.

"Yeah," Drew said, " 'cause otherwise the duke might see, 'n' get real mad."

"Good," Toby said, slapping Drew on the back.

"And we could make him do loads of crazy shit," Drew continued, "like wear ugly yellow trousers. Backwards!" He burst out laughing at this thought and slapped the table loudly.

"I don't think we should do anything too odd," Miriam said, "or he might catch on."

"Right," Toby said, "we just have to keep leading him on: 'I think you're a fine chap, Volio. It's only that I can't ever pretend to know you in public or speak two words to you. You understand, right?' That sort of thing."

"I think Ashton's cousin Ashton could handle that," Jack said, smirking. "Quite well, in fact." Ashton nodded.

"Well, good, then," Toby said.

"There's something that bothers me," Ashton said, looking at Miriam.

"What?" Miriam asked.

"Well, you said Volio's elder brother made weapons—automata with pistols for hands—and led them out of the school without anyone knowing where they came from."

"Yes," Miriam said.

"And Volio somehow found us that night when we came in through the basement. He couldn't have just been dawdling about in the lobby."

"I thought so as well," Miriam said.

"And then when we were initiated—when we explored the

basement, we found these peculiar skeleton automata. And a locked door," Ashton said, looking at Miriam. Miriam watched as his eyes unfocused and then refocused. "I'm sorry," he said. "I don't know what I'm trying to say."

"I think you are suggesting that Volio's elder brother had knowledge of the basement which he shared with his brother." Miriam said, "Secret knowledge. Perhaps a special room—though how they would have access, I don't know."

"We should go back!" Drew said, standing up suddenly. Everyone looked at him. "Yeah, we should go, and find those automata again, and give 'em a good smashin'. Then, we can break down the door, and see if it's Volio hiding there."

"Yeah," Jack said, looking amused. "That could be right fun."

"And it would keep me stimulated," Drew said.

Miriam inwardly groaned. This was not how she wanted to spend her evening. She appealed to Toby. "Wouldn't you rather just stay here?" she asked as sweetly as possible, "drinking with me?"

"You'll come with us," Toby said. "Besides, this is for you. If it *is* Volio, and he's making some sort of weapons like his brother, then we can blackmail him back, and then you don't have to play his soddin' game at all."

Miriam smiled. He was really very sweet. Not quite a knight in shining armor, but almost. She sighed, rose from the table, and downed what was left in Toby's glass. The rest of them stood as well, and headed for the door.

Outside, it had turned completely dark, and the streetlamps glowed yellow. Down here, in the less fashionable parts of London, the streetlamps were still gas, and they made a hissing noise, as if fighting back the darkness of night by scolding it.

They piled into a cab and headed back to Illyria, where they sneaked through the garden and into the secret basement entrance. The others were stumbling. Ashton in particular seemed to be having trouble walking, but Jack took his arm and propped him up.

"Is this his first time drunk, you think?" Miriam asked Toby, nodding at Ashton.

"Nah," Toby said. "Us lads start getting drunk before we're ten.

It's you ladies who don't experience the bliss of sheer inebriation until later in life."

Miriam snorted. "You've clearly never been to a French seder," she said.

"What?" He looked confused. Miriam just shook her head and stepped carefully down into the basement.

"Where was it?" Drew said, peering around the basement. The floors were thick with greasy dust, and only a few electric lights flickered dimly. No one spoke.

Miriam realized what a bad idea this was: hunting through a labrythine basement with a group of drunken students for weapons that were liable to attack them. She cleared her throat. "Maybe we should try this another evening."

"We're doing this for you, love," Toby replied, and held her hand tight in the darkness. There was nothing she could say to that.

"It was this way!" Jack said.

"Wait a sec," Ashton said, fussing with his jacket pocket. "I always bring it with me . . . just in . . . in case," he mumbled, pulling something out of the pocket. In a moment, a beam of light shot out from his hand. Miriam was impressed. She'd seen many marvelous inventions over the years in Illyria, but nothing so practical.

They headed forward into the darkness, Miriam tracing her finger through the grime on the walls, so they could find their way back easily. She was concerned, but not overly frightened. She had heard of the various initiations over the years, and knew that the first-years' minds could play tricks on them. Most likely, they'd find a suit of rusty display armor, or something to that effect. And yet, she had also heard stories while sitting at the professors' table. None of the current professors had been around when the building was constructed, and few of them went down there regularly, but when they did, they found the place eerie, and imagined hearing noises. The duke was always curiously mute on the subject, never mentioning anything about the basement, or its construction. Probably just tricks of the mind, as Prism said, though, Prism had those ridiculous glasses, which made it much easier to trick his mind. She told herself it was perfectly safe down here, despite the occasional feeling of something brushing up against her skirts when she could see nothing, or the soft creaking and sighing noises that came from the darkness. It had to be. The duke couldn't keep a cellar full of monsters a secret, could he?

"It was up here, I think," Drew said, pointing down a dark corridor. Slowly, they advanced down the hall.

Jack saw them first and gasped, causing everyone to stop. Slowly, Ashton raised his beam of light and pointed it at the mound of metal at the end of the hall. They were right, Miriam thought: It did look like a bunch of metal skeletons. And all different metals, too: copper and iron, and maybe even silver and gold, though why anyone would gild so complex a machine, she didn't know.

They stepped closer, and the closest skeletons seemed to sense them, turning their heads toward the approaching party. Miriam gasped.

"What's really odd," Ashton whispered, "is that they look so bloody familiar, but I don't know what it is they remind me of . . . or whom."

But Miriam did. It was a crude imitation, to be sure, but the skull staring at them was familiar to her. The jutting metal cheeks, the rounded depressions around the eyes, the shape of the jaw and forehead—she had worked for that skull for the past six years. It was unmistakably the face of Ernest, the Duke of Illyria.

XIII.

JACK Feste knew a lot about skin. He had studied all kinds of skin over the years: cat and dog skin, ferret skin, rat skin, snakeskin, elephant skin, horse skin, and human skin. He knew which skins were thickest and thinnest, which resisted heat or cold the best, which shed in perfect crystal shapes, and which flaked off like white powder. He knew how it flexed and clung to muscle in over a dozen species, and he knew for certain that it was quite impossible for a human being to actually jump out of his or her skin without previous scientific modification.

That didn't stop him from feeling as though he had leapt out of his skin when he saw one of the automata clamor to life, stand up, and stare directly at him. It was a monstrous thing: not really human looking, but too human to be a machine. It had long, heavy iron legs with tubes of some sort coming out the back of the thighs and back into the shins. The legs were sculpted and muscular, but the feet were heavy slabs of metal and gears. The torso was more skeletal, almost like a small tree with three branches curving out at the top. From two of the branches hung long, mechanical arms, one ending in sharp scissorlike pincers, and the other ending in what looked to be an actual hand, though it shone slightly in the light, so it could have been well-crafted copper or bronze. The head was most frightening—barren and metallic: not quite human, but unsettlingly close. It had no mouth, not even a small hole, and no eyes, just deep depressions in the skull, but Jack could still feel it staring at him, some small awareness analyzing him from those dark crevices. It seemed to pulse slightly, and let off a low hissing noise, like a snake about to strike.

Violet let out a shriek—very unmanly; Jack would have to talk to her about that later if they survived—and the automaton turned its gaze to her. Jack swallowed.

"Bloody hell," Toby whispered, then burped. Jack felt a chilly line of sweat drip down the nape of his neck. The automaton took a halting step toward them. The very sharp pincers on its right hand clanged open and then closed, its points focused on Violet. It paused and looked down at its own hand and opened and closed the pincers again, as if pleased with its killing power. Then it looked back up at them. If it had had a mouth, Jack thought, it would have been smiling sinisterly.

"Run," Miriam said, and they all took her advice, speeding back down the hall they'd come from. Jack heard the automaton take a few fast and heavy steps, following after them, then heard Toby let out a low bellow of pain. Jack looked back, but Toby was still running, and he waved Jack on. The automaton paused to look at its own feet; then it turned and stared up at them again with the same evil no-smile. He turned back around, his breath ragged, and they ran on, not following any particular path. Though the drunkenness had been scared out of him by now, Jack had no real idea where they were, and he doubted anyone else did, either.

"This way," Miriam said, dashing around a corner, lifting her skirts nearly to her knees as she ran. They followed. A few minutes later, they stopped, panting and leaning against the filthy walls. Jack listened for the sound of following metallic footsteps, but heard nothing.

"That was a very stupid idea," Jack said through heavy gasps.

"You're hurt," Miriam said to Toby, who was clutching his arm. A long bloody gash ran over his shoulder, his jacket, shirt, and skin all torn. Jack took off his jacket and shirt and tore the latter into strips, applying them carefully and silently to Toby's wound.

"Those things were less scary last time," Toby said. "I mean, last time, they didn't get up and look at us. They just sort of reached out."

"This one was new," Violet said. She was bent over and staring at the ground, trying to regain her breath. "Nothing that sophisticated was there last time."

"New?" Miriam asked. "You mean, someone only just made it?"

"Or it was behind that the door," Drew offered. He seemed to be the least out of breath, and in fact was grinning as though he was having a wonderful time. "No one could have possibly built that thing in a week, could they?"

Violet shook her head.

"Let's not come down here again," Jack offered, still patching up Toby. "Let's just leave it alone. I'm all for havin' a bit of adventure, but when killer automata start slashing my mates, it's not really 'a bit' anymore, is it?"

"Aye," Toby said, wincing.

"We could disable it," Violet offered. She stood upright now. Jack was alarmed to see that the running had apparently loosened her bindings, for her chest was swelling slightly.

"Maybe," Jack said. He patted Toby lightly on his back. "There. We should stop by the biological lab; then I can fix it up even better. But this'll hold you till we're out of here."

"Thanks," Toby said. Miriam slung Toby's good arm over her shoulder, so he could lean on her if the pain increased.

"Let's find our way out," Jack said.

"Follow me," Miriam said, and led them back to the entrance.

"How did you do that?" Toby asked when they arrived. He was grinning.

"I thought like Ariadne," she said, and kissed him on the mouth. Jack looked away, embarrassed.

"I don't know what you mean," Toby said, "but you're a wonderful woman."

"Ariadne," Miriam said. "She helped Theseus navigate the . . . It's amazing how I am surrounded by geniuses who seem to know nothing."

"I know a thing or two," Toby said, still grinning. "It is only the classics where my mind becomes fuzzy. I am too modern a man to be bogged down by the past. But I think it's time to sleep now. I'm exhausted. And we have our first of the duke's lectures tomorrow."

"Right," Violet said. "I'll try to think of a way to disable the automata tomorrow."

"Very well," Miriam said, "but you had better be sure. I do not want to go up against that, that—*mécanique du diable*—unprepared again."

Everyone nodded in agreement.

They stopped briefly at the biological lab, where Jack cleaned and numbed Toby's gash, then sewed it up. It was deep, but not very wide, and Jack didn't think it would leave much of a scar.

"No war wounds for me?" Toby asked.

"Little one," Jack said. "Just be careful, and let me know right away if the stitches open, or you start bleeding, or it turns a weird color. Don't want it to become infected. Let's head to bed now, shall we?"

"Go on ahead," Toby said to them, and clutched Miriam around the waist. Jack and Violet looked perplexed, but followed Drew into the lift and took it up to the dorms, leaving Toby and Miriam behind.

"Thomas Huxley theorizes that there's a chemical," Drew said on the ride up, "in the brain. When we get excited from stress, fear, or such, well, we also turn . . . romantic."

"Ah," Violet said. Jack looked at her. She was blushing bright red.

At the dorm hall, they parted ways with Drew. Violet fell right onto the bed as soon as they closed the door behind them. "That was frightening," she said. "It almost took my mind off how dizzy I am. Is this being drunk? I have certainly been drinking before— well not *been*, but I've drunk. Not been drunk, simply drunk things that were alcoholic—but never to such excess. I find my head is quite swimming . . . and I find I cannot keep my thoughts to myself. The drunkeness has taken my mind off how sad I was, too. Do you think I'm going to humiliate my father and drive him out of the scientific community?"

Jack looked at her. Perhaps it wasn't from blushing that she was red. "I don't think you could ever do anything that wouldn't result in your father loving you and being proud of you," he said.

Violet smiled. "You're very sweet," she said, "when you want to be."

"Your bosoms are showing," he said.

She stuck out her tongue at him, went into the water closet, and emerged a minute later in a nightgown, her face scrubbed, her hands cleaned. She stretched happily, then fell down onto her bed.

"Did you drink any water?" Jack asked her. "You should drink some water, or else you might feel worse in the morning."

"We're testing Toby's hangover cure, remember?" she mumbled, and pulled the covers up over her. Jack smiled and went into the bathroom to wash up and get himself into bed.

�֍֎◉֍֎

IN the morning, Violet did feel worse. Much, much worse. Her head banged like a poorly built engine, and her stomach spun like gears moving too fast. She lay in bed, closing her eyes at the too-bright slivers of light that came in through the curtains, and flinching at the impossibly loud grinding of the gears of Illyria.

"Come on," Jack said. "You have to wake up and change into costume before Toby shows up with his cure."

"How can there possibly be a cure for this?" Violet asked, burying her head under the pillows.

"Something I've been asking myself for quite some time. But we agreed to try it out. Go get dressed."

Violet had not yet moved, and was astounded by how rusted and sluggish her joints felt, how heavy her limbs, how weary her—

"You've been sitting there for ten minutes," Jack said. "You do realize that, right?"

Violet dragged herself out of bed and to the water closet. Binding was particularly painful and difficult, feeling the way she did, and her head throbbed under the bright electric lights. She was still dressing when there was a knock on the door and Jack opened it.

"All right?" Toby's voice came.

"Please tell me your cure works," Violet called through the door.

"Oh, you didn't drink that much," Toby called back. Violet finished her disguise and opened the door. Toby was standing in a large white nightgown, Drew behind him, sloppily dressed and apparently asleep while standing. "I don't understand you blokes who dress so quickly," Toby said. He held four vials of yellow liquid.

"Ashton is very concerned with his toilette," Jack said. "Gets up early every day to make it perfect."

"That would explain why he's always so clean-shaven," Toby said. "I'm a bit envious—when I do remember to shave, it just grows back to stubble by noon."

"Can I have your cure now?" Violet asked, extending her hand. Every part of her seemed to pulse in time, like being inside the second hand on a clock.

Toby smirked and handed out the four vials, nudging Drew awake. With trepidation they all downed the elixir and waited. Jack was the first to run to the toilet to vomit, then Violet, then Toby. Drew held out surprisingly long, possibly because he nodded off again after swallowing the brew, but a few moments later he, too, had purged himself. After the vomiting, they all felt tremendously better, though Violet wondered if that wasn't solely by comparison to how they'd felt before.

"Lucky thing the college provides maids," Jack said, smiling nervously.

"I'd better change," Violet said.

"Us, too," Toby said. "See you at the lecture in a few."

Violet and Jack closed the door and sighed. Her body really did feel a bit better.

"Drink water," Jack said. "That's what will really help."

Violet felt more herself after a few glasses of water, and after washing her mouth and face and changing into fresher clothes, she was eager to go to the lecture and hear the duke's thoughts. To understand how a person thought about the world, she reasoned, was to understand the person. And she had a desire to understand the duke. He was, after all, heir to a scientific legacy, and probably a genius in his own right, if the rabbit Shakespeare was any example.

Violet and the other students all got to the Great Hall a few minutes before the lecture was to begin. The duke was already onstage, reading over some notes. The students all took their assigned seats, and the professors sat in the back—though, Violet noticed, both Bracknell and Curio were absent. Cecily and Miriam came in last of all, Cecily dressed all in gold and red, with Shakespeare trailing behind her on a gold leash. She walked toward the front of the assembly hall, Miriam shadowing her. She paused in front of Violet's seat and smiled down at her. Jack, who was sitting next to Violet, stood, and Violet did likewise, remembering she was a gentleman.

"Ashton," Cecily said, "how very nice to see you."

"And you," Violet said. "What a lovely dress."

"Oh, thank you," Cecily said. "As you can see, Shakespeare is still running smoothly."

"I'm glad of it," Violet said.

"Ashton told me that Shakespeare is a work of mechanical genius," Jack said.

Cecily paused for a moment and looked at Jack. "Jack, was it? Are you and Ashton friends?"

"Since childhood," Jack said. "I would enjoy it if I could see Shakespeare at some time, as well."

Cecily's eyes narrowed, and she regarded him more carefully. "Of course," she said. "Perhaps if you stopped by the chemical lab at some point, I may show him to you."

"It would be an honor," Jack said, smiling.

"Well, I'd best take my seat. My cousin is glaring at me most obviously. Gentlemen."

"Till later, Cecily," Violet said.

"Miss Cecily," Jack said, and she walked to the front of the auditorium and sat in a seat up front, cradling Shakespeare in her lap. "Oh, she is the most wonderful girl," Jack whispered. "You must help her to love me."

"I'll do what I can," Violet said, trying not to roll her eyes, "but let's listen to the duke's lecture, now."

All faces turned expectantly toward the duke, who approached the podium and cleared his throat. He was dressed in a fine gray suit and wearing a green cravat, and his hair was oiled back and gleaming. He smiled at the crowd, and without realizing it, Violet smiled back.

"Travel through the æther, through space," the duke began, "is something we have long quested after." Violet shifted uncomfortably in her seat. The duke seemed to spot her, and nodded his head slightly. "The great æther of night remains unexplored, even if we have thoroughly investigated as much of our own terra firma as possible. Truly, the stars and planets beyond our own are the next realms for our scientists and explorers. But how shall we get there? It will not be as hard as you think—the principles are already established."

Violet sank lower into her chair. What the duke was saying sounded very similar to the essay she had written for her application.

"Time and funding are needed, to be sure, but if we examine some of the science of mechanical engineering, we shall find that travel to the stars is firmly in our grasp. Of course, we will also need to take from other scientific realms: Chemistry is close to, but has not yet been successful at, creating a fuel capable of sustaining . . ."

Violet could listen no longer. He was using her essay, her ideas, her theories on space travel. And passing them off as his own. How dare he! She crossed her arms and slumped lower in her seat, determined not to listen. He was prattling on about combustion, which was ridiculous, as she had said in her paper that it wasn't required for propulsion. But then, he was probably saying that, too. Violet willed herself not to listen, and found it surprisingly easy. Perhaps it was the hangover, or the hangover cure, but the grinding of the wall of gears seemed louder the more she focused on it, until it was positively overwhelming.

If she ever spoke to the duke again, she would slap him right across the face for the scoundrel he was, though she supposed that would probably get her expelled, and probably wasn't a very manly approach to the situation. She wondered how long the duke could talk. She glanced up at him. He was gesticulating wildly while describing the way one would need to determine the exact trajectory of a ship bound for the moon. He must be near the end, then; she had closed on that note in her essay, saying it was more the astronomer's job than the mechanic's. She wondered if plagarizing others was the duke's usual practice, and if that was why he had published so little. Probably even Shakespeare the rabbit was designed by someone else, perhaps his father. It was sad to see how far the apple had fallen from the tree. People were standing now, and applauding. Violet did not. Jack gave her a questioning look, but she held her tongue. They would discuss it later.

The students and professors filed out of the Great Hall and headed to the dining hall for lunch. Violet was amazed that the duke could take her paper, which was really not very long, and extend it into a two-hour lecture. He must have made her simple, precise language much more florid and grand. How ridiculous of him.

"What are you pouting about?" Jack asked, sitting down at the table next to her. She still had her arms crossed, and was not in the mood to eat.

"It was my paper, Jack! I wrote that for my entrance exam, all about space travel and what might be possible, and he copied every word I said."

"He did?" Jack asked, surprised. His eyes narrowed in disgust.

"Yes," Violet said, "and I will never respect him again."

"Whom will he never respect?" Toby asked, sitting down.

"The duke. He didn't like the lecture," Jack said. While he didn't doubt Violet, and his opinion of the duke had suddenly dropped, he didn't want himself or Violet to land in trouble for making accusations.

"He didn't?" Drew asked, also sitting down. "I thought it was bloody brilliant."

"It was," Violet said, as she rose from the table and marched out of the dining hall.

Jack looked after Violet. She was angry, and had the right to be. He would go talk to her later, when she had cooled down.

"I thought he was especially spot-on when he started talking about the need for safe combustion, and his ideas on how to create a formula for a fuel that would create it," Drew continued. "Made me want to give up the whole perfuming business and go to the moon." He smiled whimsically at them. "I won't, of course. The moon is probably terrifying. Moon people would eat me."

"Aye," Toby said. "They would."

Jack grinned at them, and started wondering how much of the lecture Violet had actually heard. He hadn't read her paper, but some of the ideas that the duke had mentioned seemed as though she could have come up with them. Other parts of the lecture, though, seemed not quite in her realm. Violet was not excellently versed in chemical combustion theory, and Jack thought she had even spoken against the need for combustion for space travel. He wasn't sure. Perhaps she was still feeling the effects of the drinking last night, or the cure this morning. Or maybe she just missed her brother.

Lunch passed quickly for the three of them, as Toby played on Drew's fear of moon people, while Jack fantasized about what he would say when he went to visit Cecily later that day. And soon enough, Jack found himself in the biology lab, staring down at Dorian, who still couldn't make much more noise than a musical gurgle. But he seemed happy, so Jack left him alone, told Valentine he needed supplies, and wandered over to the chemical lab, hands in his pockets, nervous.

Cecily was working behind one of the counters, wearing a smock over her dress and large goggles over her eyes. Her hair was tied up and back, and she was bent quite carefully over a beaker of white liquid, holding a dropper over it. Jack waved at Drew and Toby, who threw him questioning looks until he walked up to the table across from Cecily. They grinned and went back to their projects. Jack watched as Cecily worked, waiting for a time to speak.

"You need to move to the side," she said without looking up. "You're blocking my light, and I need to be sure of how many drops I put in." Jack stepped to one side silently. Cecily let three more drops fall into the beaker, then looked up and pushed her goggles to the top of her head, revealing her lovely, sparkling eyes. "Jack," she said, sounding a little surprised.

"Ah, yes. I stopped by to see Shakespeare. You invited me."

"Yes, I remember. Jack. Who is such an old friend of Ashton's. Well, I need to let this formula sit for a few minutes, anyway." She walked across the room to where Miriam was sitting and talking quietly with Professor Curio and idly stroking Shakespeare's ears.

"Miri," Cecily said, "this is Jack. He wanted to take a look at Shakespeare."

"Is that all?" Miriam asked, holding out Shakespeare. Cecily took the rabbit and gently handed him to Jack.

Jack was impressed. The way it moved, even when not active, was impressive, almost lifelike. The fur molded out of brass and gold, the beautifully rendered face; it was hard to believe it wasn't actually a rabbit.

"Extraordinary workmanship," Jack said. "I've seen many rabbits, and I don't think I would know this one wasn't real if it weren't cold to the touch."

"I love rabbits," Cecily said. "I used to hunt for them as a little girl when we went out to the country, and I once freed all the test rabbits from the biology lab. After that, Cousin Ernest made me Shakespeare. He is the king of rabbits."

"I can tell," Jack said, pleased.

"Now that I have shown you Shakespeare, will you do me a favor, Jack?"

"Anything," Jack said.

Cecily took his arm—Jack felt her touch like a chemical reaction in his blood—and guided him away from Miriam to a quiet corner. "Then tell me," she said, "about Ashton. Is there a girl whom he is courting?"

Jack grinned. "No," he said.

"And how, do you think, would be the best way for one such as myself to attract his attentions?" Jack laughed. "What is so funny?" Cecily demanded, suddenly red in the face. "Am I so below him? I have rank, too. I shall inherit Illyria if Ernest has no heirs."

"No. It's not that, dear Cecily, please do not misunderstand me. With or without your rank, any man with eyes would do all they could to win your heart. But I fear that Ashton may be . . . blind to your advances."

"I should throw myself at him, then? Like a hussy?"

"No, not that either. I think perhaps you should forget about Ashton. He will be a good friend to you, I have no doubt, but his heart belongs to . . . science."

"You are just trying to drive us apart because you think you fancy me," Cecily said, turning a lovely shade of pink. "You, just like all the others, who haven't even bothered to speak to me as though I were anything other than a simple woman made to be stared at and appreciated for her hair and eyes and nothing else. Ashton talks to me of science. When have you ever done that, or asked my opinion on some scientific theory?"

"I don't need to ask you any of that," Jack said. "I can see that you are perfect, inside and out."

Cecily said nothing in response to that, but stared at Jack wide eyed for a moment, before her eyes re-formed themselves into a glare. "Give me my rabbit," she said, grabbing Shakespeare from him. "If you were a true friend to Ashton, you wouldn't try to come between us. Good day, Mr. . . ."

"Feste."

"Mr. Feste. Good day." Cecily stomped back over to her counter and examined her beaker.

Jack sighed and left the lab, everyone now staring at him. Oh, what rotten luck for him, he thought, and kicked the wall in the hallway. To have the one he loved be in love with his best friend. Surely Cupid was laughing right now at the strange sapphic spell he had cast on Cecily. But no matter. Jack was quick to think, and he already had a plan. Jack assumed that after the woman Cecily wanted as a lover revealed her true identity, she and Cecily would still be friends. Surely if that were the case, then someone who was her friend now could later be her lover. So he would be her friend. Though, judging from the way she had just left him, that might be difficult. Jack kicked the wall again and went back to the biology lab. He sat down, chin in his hand, and looked at Dorian, who was asleep.

How best to be a friend to Cecily, and then to win her heart? Jack pondered this as he stared at Dorian, and then smiled. He was

slowly developing an idea for the Science Faire that could prove his
affections to Cecily, as well. It would take time, of course, and
plenty of experimentation, but it was manageable, if he was clever.
The love that bounded through his heart as freely as a wild winged
ferret would provide the rest.

❧❀❧

NOTHING bounded in Violet's heart. She had worked aggressively
all afternoon, pounding out her frustration on sheets of hot metal,
hammering a large piece of bronze that was to be the outer shell of
her mechanical woman. She was amazed at the duke's audacity.
When she was a woman, he wouldn't deign to speak about science
with her, and when she was a man, he stole her ideas for his own.
She should just find him now and tell him everything, how the
woman he thought unworthy of serious discussion was the one he
was now plagiarizing. She hammered even more forcefully, and
Bunburry turned and looked at her, his brow furrowed. She nodded
politely and tried to bang softer. She would save the harder banging
for the duke.

The machine was coming along nicely. Many gears and mechanisms were already in place, and the individual parts she had tested
seemed to work. Of course, she would need to make some sort of
control panel, from which they could all be operated. And then
there was the matter of finishing several pieces and putting it all
together. There was a lot of work left to do. She spent most of the
day with a hammer in her hand, focusing on little else but the way
it bent, and smoothed the metal into the curves that she demanded
of it. Metal was simple: heat it, pound it, it becomes what you want.
Violet sometimes felt it was a pity the same principles couldn't be
applied to people.

❧❀❧

VIOLET worked until supper and then ate silently with her friends,
who stared at her as if she frightened them. Toby had had plans
alone with Miriam for after that, and Violet didn't want to go out

anyway, so she went back down to the mechanical lab while Drew and Jack had gone to the biology lab and played with Dorian.

"You're in a rather foul mood," Jack said as they readied themselves for bed.

"I know," Violet said, climbing into bed and turning down the lamp so that the room was dark.

"They say that imitation is the highest form of flattery."

"Don't defend him," she said.

"Very well. I offended Cecily today."

"Oh?"

"Yes. She told me she was in love with you and I laughed at her."

Violet began to laugh, as well, which made some of the weight on her lift. "You're joking," she said. "You're just trying to make me laugh."

"Quite serious. She asked me for help in winning your heart."

"And what did you tell her?"

"That you were so devoted to science that you had little time for matters of the heart."

"Ah," Violet said, suddenly feeling sad again.

"She said I was trying to get between the two of you, because I love her."

"She is clever to notice," Violet said wryly.

"Well, she actually said that I only thought I was in love with her."

"She must be *very* clever, then."

"Don't doubt my devotion," Jack said. "I love her dearly."

"Dear boy, I wouldn't dream of doubting you," Violet said, mocking him. "After all, what truer love can exist than love at first sight? Of all the senses, sight is surely the most romantic. I have heard once or twice of love at first smell, but I don't think it worked out in the end."

"So now I must persuade her that I am her friend," Jack continued, ignoring her. "Then, at the end of the year, when you reveal your masquerade, she will realize I was the right man all along."

"I'm not sure that's a sound plan, Jack."

"It is just as sound as yours, isn't it?"

"I suppose," Violet said, then sighed. "I miss my brother."

"We shall see him tomorrow."

"I know. It just hasn't been the week I expected."

"What did you expect? Praise from all corners, appreciation of your genius, and no effort required to hide your gender?"

Violet did not answer.

"You are brilliant, Violet Adams," Jack whispered. It was the first time he had used her real name all week, "but you cannot expect everyone to know that just by looking at you, especially not when you must hide so much of yourself so as not to attract attention."

Violet sighed again. "So how are you going to befriend Cecily?" she asked.

Jack knew that entertaining his scheme was her way of thanking him. "I don't really know."

"Ask her about her work. She is a very smart scientist, but I would imagine most men who have courted her have paid little heed to anything but her face and figure."

"Actually, she said something similar when we argued."

"That is probably why she is in love with me . . . with Ashton . . . with me-as-Ashton. Because I talk to her about science. When the duke refused to discuss the scientific principles of the flowers with me, I became quite annoyed with him."

Jack laughed.

"What's so funny?"

"That all you would see in flowers are scientific principles," he said, "even when a man tried to show you their beauty."

"But that *is* their beauty," Violet said, pursing her lips. "Really, I don't know what it is with your gender, that they must divide science and beauty into separate fields. As if the stars and planets themselves are lovely, but to map the way they turn takes that away from them. In my opinion, the way a planet spins only adds to its beauty."

"Perhaps you are right," Jack said.

"Of course I'm right," Violet said.

"The duke tried to talk to you of the beauty of flowers?" Jack asked, his voice full of innuendo.

The room was silent for a moment as Violet considered what he meant. "Oh, do be quiet and let me sleep," she said, taking one of her pillows and throwing it at him, before turning over and ending the conversation. Jack chuckled in the darkness.

XIV.

ASHTON Adams, the real Ashton Adams, had had a wonderful week. He had attended four poetry readings and two séances, as well as an extraordinary art exhibit showing exclusively paintings of young men bathing. He had even met several of the models for the paintings, though he hadn't yet gone bathing with any of them. He supposed that would have to wait until summer. The house was in order: running nicely, thanks to the cook and the maid and Antony, all of them quite pretty, quite friendly, and quite discreet. He had a plate of cucumber sandwiches, cake, muffins, and bread and butter ready for Violet and Jack. He marveled at how he missed his sister, despite the short time they'd been apart, and how busy he'd kept himself.

In truth, he was also worried. Dressing Violet like a man and teaching her to walk funny had seemed amusing at the time, but a week in, he wondered if she had been, or would be, found out. And what would happen if she was. Society was not forgiving of trespasses like gender reversal. Society was only forgiving of reversals of fortune, and then only when the rich became poor, because that made excellent gossip. To have the poor become rich was rather distressing, and to have a woman become a man was perverse. Ashton himself had once been beaten just for associating with a certain sort of people, though he'd told his father and sister that the attacker had been a thief. He had always believed that the best thing you could do for your life was to live it fearlessly, and so, had done so. But how much worse would it be to see horrible things happen to his sister. He wouldn't ask her to stop, of course. He would just fret quietly from offstage and hope that she remained at her best.

She did not seem at her best when she came in, though. Ashton could see that as soon as they were through the door. Her skin was pale, her eyes red with dark circles under them. But she was smiling.

"Oh, Ashton," she said as soon as the door had closed behind her and Jack. She ran to hug her brother. "How I've missed you."

"I can see," Ashton said, the wind knocked out of him. When Violet had finished squeezing him, he also gave Jack a pat. "You don't seem to be taking very good care of her," he said.

"That's not my fault," Jack protested. "She's the one who spends all day in the lab."

"We all spend all day in the lab," Violet said. "It's required."

"Well, you didn't have to come drinking with us last night."

"You begged me to go drinking with you."

"I think begged is a little strong. We merely requested your ever-charming presence so that we might gaze at your pretty mouth and hear what clever wit next emerged from it. Like when you told us all that so much of who you were depended on where you were—if you were in a bar, you were a bar person; in the street, a street person. Or when you began to imitate how Mrs. Wilks would play the horn."

"You've gone drinking?" Ashton asked.

"She was quite the lushington the other night. But don't worry, I took her home okay."

"You took me to the basement to go hunting for vicious killer automata."

"Well, yeah, but it was at home."

"You've been getting drunk and going hunting for vicious killer automata?" Ashton asked. "That makes my first week in town seem positively dull by comparison."

"Yes," Violet said proudly. "The bizarre mechanical creatures of the basement have tried to kill me on more than one occasion."

"Me, too," Jack added.

"Why don't we sit down?" Ashton said, "There are muffins and cucumber sandwiches."

"You didn't eat them all already?" Violet asked, walking into the kitchen. She was relieved not to have to concentrate on keeping her voice low, or on how she walked. Who knew that being a gentleman would require as much effort as being a lady? She sat down and helped herself to a muffin.

"So," Ashton said, eating a cucumber sandwich, "you've been chased by murderous automata?"

"Yeah," Jack said, "during our initiation, and then again when we got knackered and decided to explore the basement to see if Volio's secret lab was behind the mysterious door."

"I'm sorry?"

"Volio," Violet continued, "is a horrid second-year student whose brother was nearly expelled for producing weapons, and who is now blackmailing Miriam because he knows that she goes out with us at night."

"Who's Miriam?"

"Cecily's governess," Jack said, and sighed, thinking of Cecily.

"He's in love with Cecily," Violet said, buttering a muffin. "Cecily is the duke's cousin and ward."

"This is very complicated," Ashton said. "Why don't you just tell me about your week, from first day to last."

"Very well," Violet said, and she did.

A few hours later, Ashton was also a bit paler with dark circles under his eyes. "This is needlessly complex," he said.

"And that's just the first week," Violet said.

"So, will you write a fake love letter from Cecily that will keep Volio appeased?" Jack asked.

"I suppose," Ashton said. "I do enjoy a good prank, but you must promise me something."

"What's that?" Jack asked.

"And Violet, too," Ashton said, his voice suddenly a shade more serious. Violet nodded. "You must promise me you will stop looking for trouble. The basement sounds dangerous. Stick to your studies. And the drunkenness."

"But if it is Volio's lab, then we'll be able to blackmail him and make him leave Miriam alone!" Violet said.

"And if your bindings come undone while you're running and he's watching, then he will blackmail you, too," Ashton said. "Not to mention the physical peril you put yourself in. Imagine how Father would feel if he returned from America to find his daughter impersonating not only a man, but a dead man. I'm sure for a moment he'd be quite impressed by your incredible impersonation skill on both fronts, but when it was revealed to him that the latter was the truth, his heart would quite shatter."

Violet looked at her feet. Jack turned slightly pink.

"And you," he said, turning to Jack. "I would hope that as my dear friend, you would perhaps be a little more careful with your life. True, you aren't hiding anything about yourself, but it would still be a great disappointment to me were you to die."

"Yes," Jack said, looking at his own feet now.

"I don't mean to be gloomy," Ashton said, "and I certainly never want to be serious—I'm not old enough to be serious just yet. I believe one must be at least sixty before one can even consider being serious. So, come, smile, and let's start on this letter of yours. That is a piece of tomfoolery I can approve of. I don't think we can have Volio change his wardrobe just yet, but I'm sure I could persuade him to always look down when Cecily enters a room, or some gesture that would cause you a little amusement. After all, when a man is truly in love, as you say this Volio chap is, then he is as easy to lead about as a bull by the nose ring."

"Actually," Jack said, "Toby, Drew, and Miriam said they'd be spending the day at White's Club on Saint James's, and that if we convinced you to assist in the letter writing and wanted company, we should send a messenger and they would join us."

"A chance to meet your new friends?" Ashton said, a wide smile on his lips. "Sounds splendid. And they sound like quite my type of rogues if they are not only members of White's, but have also somehow managed to sneak a woman in."

"I was curious about that, as well," Violet said. "Remember, though, Ashton: I'm also Ashton, and you're my cousin."

"Two cousins named Ashton? They didn't find that curious?"

"I said it was a family name. Still surprised it worked, actually. Shall we send Antony out to White's with a message?"

"Antony?" Ashton asked, looking down. "No, no. Antony is resting. I'll step out and have one of the pages run over. Besides, it's beginning to rain, and Antony looks so sad when his clothing is soaked."

Jack and Violet exchanged a glance. "Send the note however you wish, fellow," Jack said. "To Sir Toby Belch, at White's. Let them know that Mr. Adams requests their company for mischief."

Ashton nodded, and penned a quick note before running out into the rain, flagging down a young urchin, and giving him a few coins and the note. The boy went dashing off.

Jack and Violet watched this from the window. "It must be odd having a lover as a servant," Jack said.

"You mean a servant as a lover," Violet said. "What you describe is merely how most men view marriage."

Jack snorted as Ashton came back in.

"It will be quite a storm tonight," Ashton said, brushing his jacket down. "Now, let's get out some brandy and playing cards and prepare for our guests."

By the time they had set up the card table and gotten out glasses, the others had arrived. Violet greeted them at the door, and they smiled at her through the rain, Drew holding an absurdly large umbrella over them all.

"Come in," Violet said. "Ashton has agreed to help and is eager to meet you all."

"And," said Ashton, stepping up behind Violet, "I'm eager to hear how you sneaked a lady into White's."

"Ah," said Toby, taking off his jacket, "that's a clever scheme on my part. You see, you ask for a private room for a private game, but on the ground floor, in the back right corner."

"The *farceur* has me sneak in through the window," Miriam interrupted, "and duck under the table whenever one of the stewards comes in. Which is often, with the amount of hot chocolate these two *gros garçons* order."

"It's so good and creamy," Drew said, closing his eyes.

"You are already one of my new favorite lady friends," Ashton said to Miriam. "I'm afraid we don't have much in the way of hot chocolate, but we do have plenty of other refreshments. And I've set up the card table. What were you playing at the club?"

"Poker," Toby said. "Shall I deal?"

"Certainly," Ashton said, "but I need to know more about what you'd like from these false love notes to Volio, so I may write them as you play. What they should say, what you'd like him to do, and such."

"Can you arrange for him never to speak?" Violet asked. "His voice is most tedious."

"I will assist Ashton," Miriam said, then cocked her head. "Cousin Ashton, I mean. The rest of you play cards. You are all so generous in helping me. You don't need to do any more."

"Excellent," Ashton said. "Let us write, then."

Over the next hour, Miriam and Ashton worked on the missive to Volio and then joined the others in playing cards. It had begun to rain very hard outside, but there was much laughter as Ashton told them of his various adventures at the art galleries. He also praised Miriam's literary skill in writing the love letter, and soon they were all fast friends. A little before supper, the party left, Miriam clutching the note she was to deliver to Volio that night.

They hailed a cab and piled in it, heading back to Illyria.

"Your cousin's a real swell," Toby said to Violet in the cab, "but I'm not sure I liked him praising Miri so much."

Jack snickered. "I wouldn't worry about that."

Miriam nodded. "Your jealousy is attractive only if well placed, Toby," she said.

Toby furrowed his brow, confused, but decided to accept this answer.

"He's a molly, Toby," Drew said.

Toby's eyes grew wide. "Oh!" he said, and everyone burst out laughing.

⁂

AT the entrance to Illyria, Miriam peeled away from the group, Toby sneaking one kiss before heading into the college for supper. Miriam walked to the garden beside Illyria and up to the riverbank. The rain was falling even more heavily now, so she lifted the hood of her cloak and watched the storm fall into the water. She had been having trouble sleeping of late, and was haunted by the automaton in the basement with the face of the duke. Surely it had been her mind playing tricks on her. She took a deep breath, smelled the river and the wet grass and the rain, and pushed thoughts of the cellar from her mind. Let them wash off her.

As a child in Persia, Miriam had not been allowed to play in the rain. In Esfahān, the Jewish ghetto was marked by rough fences, and the streets were worn layers of dirt, which in the rain became puddles of heavy mud that splashed as the water hit them. Miriam would stare at them through the windows and long to go outside and play in them. The water from the sky looked so inviting, almost magical. To be drenched by the sky sounded delightful to her. She was only six, and was just beginning to understand that there were rules, and they were either to be obeyed or broken.

Her parents were not watching. The street outside the window was empty. Mother was sewing by the fire, and Father was going over his accounts. Business was not doing well. Recently, a group of local youths had broken into his shop and taken many of the goods. The police had done nothing, since there were no Muslim witnesses. Miriam glanced around and slowly, quietly lowered herself off the bench she had been kneeling on to look out the window. She crept to the door, reached up to the handle, and opened it. The sound of the rain intensified, droplets hitting the dirt, heavy and thick. She could barely see more than a few feet in front of her. Taking a deep breath, she ran out into the rain.

She was soaked instantly. Her dress became plastered to her body. Her long hair, which had been pinned back under a scarf, fell loose under its own weight and pressed down on her head. She laughed. The water felt cool and good, and ran down her face. She couldn't see anything besides the rain and mud. She was alone in the world, and didn't need to worry about the Muslims, or even the Jews, her family, the rules of behavior. She was free and separate. For the first time, she felt she was not like a small part of a bigger whole she'd never volunteered for, governed by its rules and standards, but like Miriam, just Miriam, completely. She laughed louder and looked up at the sky. The droplets zoomed toward her out of a silver background.

But then her father had swept her up in his arms and run back inside with her. "What were you doing?" he yelled, putting her down. Her mother had been standing just inside the door, her hands clasped anxiously, but now she went to work, stripping Miriam as her father yelled, and placing her clothes over the fire to dry. "Do you know what the Muslims would have done if they had seen you?" her father continued. "They would have killed you!" Miriam was naked now, and shivering. Her mother moved her closer to the fire. Her father sighed and lowered his voice. "To them, we are dirty. When we go out into the rain, this invisible dirt that they claim is on us washes down into the mud. They could step in it, and get their boots dirty. For that, they would kill us."

"But if they step in the mud," Miriam said, "their boots are going to be dirty even if I wasn't playing in the rain."

Her father sighed again and sat down, throwing a look at her mother. "It is different," her mother said. "It is because we are Jews."

"Then I don't want to be a Jew," Miriam said.

Her mother slapped her across the face. "Don't ever say that," her mother said, and pulled the now crying Miriam into a tender hug before dressing her. Miriam went back to kneeling at the window, and looking out at the rain. It fell heavier and heavier, but to Miriam, the thought of playing in it made her feel light.

A week later, the local boys broke into her father's shop again, and this time destroyed as much as they stole. Two weeks after that, her family left for Paris.

Miriam stared out at the sky. The rain was coming down fiercely, so that she could barely see across the river.

"When I said we'd meet in the garden, I assumed you would choose a place under the doorway, out of the rain," Volio said harshly from behind her. Miriam turned. He was not dressed for the weather, and his dark hair was plastered to his ghostly skin, giving him a slimy and cold look. His eyes reflected the shine of a nearby electric lamppost.

"I like the rain," Miriam said simply. She took the false note out of her cloak pocket and handed it to Volio, who snatched her wrist with one hand and held it, removing the note with his other hand.

He pocketed the note and grinned at her. "You have your note," she said, trying not to sound afraid. "Now let me go."

"I was thinking about it," Volio said, still holding her wrist, "about how I have devoted much of my life to scientific pursuits and thus have had little time to indulge in romantic ones. I have seen a whore now and then, but I don't like paying for something others receive for free, so I usually go to the cheaper ones, who don't know much about screwing like a lady. But you . . . you're a high-priced whore, aren't you? Fucking a baron, working as a governess. But you, I could fuck for free."

The rain had made her wrist slippery, so when Miriam pulled it back in disgust, it slipped from Volio's grasp. Volio slapped her lightly across the face. "Not the way to respect your betters," he said.

"You are not my better," Miriam said. "And the most you will get out of me are those letters. If you try to take more, I shall tell the duke of your attempts to force yourself on me, and if I lose my job, I shall not mind it."

Volio let out a single crack of laughter. "The duke?" he said. "The duke is nothing at Illyria. A figurehead. He wasn't even invited to know the school's secrets. He would be nothing against us." His words hung in the air, confident and electric, as the rain continued to fall down around them.

Miriam stared hard at Volio, trying to uncover his meaning, discern whether he was bluffing. Did he know something about the duke-automata? The rain fell hard on both of them, and a long roll of thunder vibrated the air.

"Then I'll tell Cecily you forced yourself on me. She certainly would never love you then," Miriam said.

Volio glared at her a moment, water running down his face, and then spit. "Fine," he said. "Letters only. You're a cunning bitch. I suppose most Jewesses are. I'll give you my next note for Cecily the night after tomorrow. I shall need that time to put words to the sentimentality I feel in my heart." He smiled in a way that made her shiver, and stalked off into the darkness.

Miriam let out a deep breath and turned to face the river again, letting the rain pour down on her. She had experienced things in her life that frightened her before—hate and fire and violence—but Volio seemed to be something beyond all that. He had hate, fire, and violence in him, but it was his aura of cruelty that scared her, the thought that he felt so superior to all around him that he had the right to cut them open just to enjoy the smell of their blood.

Miriam shivered again, her body becoming damp under the cloak. She was meeting Toby later at a hotel they often went to. She took another deep breath and listened to the sound of the rain a while longer before she set out for the road, thinking of Toby's warmth, of his hands gliding around her waist and down her thighs, and of the way he smiled, filled with adoration and joy as he kissed her body. She would not tell him of Volio's proposal. That would result in violence, and perhaps Toby's expulsion, and if Volio wasn't lying about his power, possibly worse. Truthfully, she didn't know who really ran Illyria. She had always thought it was the duke, but Volio had spoken with such conviction that now she wasn't sure.

She pulled her cloak tightly around her and caught a cab to the hotel. She would tell Toby that the exchange went fine, that Volio said nothing of import, and then take him in her arms and make love to him until she forgot everything but the rain.

XV.

MALCOLM Volio was about to open his presents on his eleventh birthday, when the Duke of Illyria made him his heir. It was a sticky day in August, the kind where the heat crept into the house and made it like an oven. Even with the windows open and country breezes wafting about, the air seemed heavy. Malcolm was sitting on the floor, an array of wrapped gifts around him, his father and mother on chairs behind him, his mother doing needlepoint in that fierce, artless way she always did it. Malcolm's elder brother, Ralph, was working on something in the stables, where he did most of his scientific work. He had just finished his first year at Illyria. He spent most of his time working now, sometimes with Father's help. Father would have stayed working in the stables all day, too, if Mother hadn't dragged him out.

Malcolm had just chosen which present to open first—a large box from Aunt Jenny—when a coach pulled up outside the manor.

"Who could that be?" Malcolm's mother asked, throwing her needlepoint onto the table and rising stiffly to go to the window. "Whoever it is, we will send them away. It's Malcolm's birthday."

"It's the duke," Father said, after following Mother to the window.

"Send him away, then."

"I cannot send away a duke. Besides, we have important things to discuss."

Mother sat down and began working on her needlepoint again, even faster and with more violence, the pin pushing in and out like a dagger through flesh. Malcolm decided it would be best not to open any presents just then, and instead turned toward the door and waited for the duke.

A servant came in to announce the duke, who then entered. He was not the image of ferocity Malcolm had expected, but a withered old man supported by a thick brass cane, with small spectacles perched on an angular nose.

"Volio," the duke said to Father, who rose to shake hands with the duke. "And Millie. You look well," the duke said to Mother, who looked up briefly, then went back to her needlepoint. Mother didn't like being addressed by her Christian name, not even by Father. Father was looking at the duke in awe. Malcolm wondered exactly who he was. His father hardly looked at anyone, not even Malcolm. Father paid attention to very little besides his job and Ralph. "We have things to discuss, Volio," the duke said, leaning on his cane. Father nodded, then looked at Mother, then back at the duke.

"It's our son's birthday," Father said, motioning toward Malcolm. "This is Malcolm, my second son. He turns eleven today."

"Ah," the duke said. He walked slowly up to Malcolm, looking down at him. "Good morning, Malcolm."

"Good morning, sir," Malcolm said nervously. The duke had dark brown eyes. The centers of them, which were black on other people, looked almost silvery on the duke.

"I know your brother, you know. He's a very good student at my school."

"I know, sir. I want to go to your school as well."

"I'm sure you will one day, my boy. And, as it is your birthday, I have something for you." The duke straightened up and twisted the top of his cane. It popped open with a hiss, and he reached into it. "Here you are, my boy. It's a key, if you can figure it out." He handed Malcolm what seemed to be a bent piece of brass. Malcolm took it and anxiously examined it.

"Say thank you, Malcolm," Father said.

"Let him look at it," the duke said.

Malcolm carefully examined the brass piece in his hands. It had hinges all over it, and could be bent and locked in different ways. He thought about it a moment more before bending the brass into the shape of a key. It took him less than twenty seconds.

"Very good," the duke said. "That key opens some of the doors in Illyria. Not all, mind you, but some. You have a key to Illyria now, my boy. One day, perhaps, you will have all of them, if you keep that mind of yours sharp."

"Sir, you don't need to give him—," Father began.

"Your boys are clearly very smart. I hope they make good use of their talents, instead of designing toy rabbits, like my son."

"Of course, sir. Thank you, sir. Say thank you, Malcolm."

"Thank you, sir," Malcolm said, still examining the key.

"You're welcome, boy," the duke said, and patted Malcolm on the head. "Now, Volio, we have much to talk over." Father and the duke left the room, talking quietly. Mother let out a low grumble of discontent, snipped a long piece of thread off her needlepoint, walked over to Malcolm, and took the key from him. Malcolm cried out and reached for it, but stopped when he saw what she was doing. She put the key on the thread and then tied it around Malcolm's neck.

"You'll probably end up just like them," she said, more to herself than to Malcolm, "but with any luck, I'll be dead by then." Malcolm barely heard her. He clasped the key to his chest. The rest of his presents held little interest for him anymore, but he dutifully opened them all anyway.

The duke died less than a year later, and Mother died a few years after that, but Volio still had the key, hanging around his neck by his mother's needlepoint thread. The key, it turned out, did open a few doors, and nearly all the gates, but by the time he got a chance to try it, Volio had better keys from his father and brother, ones that only the worthy received. And Volio, it turned out, was the only worthy one in all of Illyria. Not even the current duke, who Volio knew had been a disappointment to his father, had the keys Volio did. And as far as Volio was concerned, this made him the heir to Illyria. Of course, he couldn't just proclaim that, dangle some keys, and be acknowledged by all as the rightful ruler of these scholastic halls. No, he would wait. Once the Society had taken control, Volio would ask that Illyria be his. He couldn't see that anyone would object, as it would surely be his creations that took control for the Society. But there was one thing more Volio desired, the key to which he held in his hand.

———✦———

My Sweet Malcolm,

Your note to me was so unexpected. At times I have felt you loathed me, and it nearly broke my heart. For the truth is, I have noticed you as well.

I have admired your fine features and the way you use your hands to build such wondrous things. Your great machines have often driven me to ecstasies with their genius. I marvel at your passionate mind, your honest intellect, your piercing eyes.

Alas, I have seen your mind, but not your heart. Your letter has now shown me a small part of it, and I long for more. Write to me again, Malcolm.

Be warned, my cousin is jealous and possessive. He must not know of our correspondence. So, if you find yourself in my presence, it would be best to ignore me altogether, and I will do the same. Cast your eyes to the ground whenever I am near, and I shall behave as I always have, as though I didn't even know your name. But know the truth, fair Malcom: I adore you, I adore you, I adore you.

With Fondest Love,
Your Little Cecily.

———✦———

Volio was still smiling as he read the letter again. Just two hours after receiving it, it was wrinkled and stained with sweat from his palms, but he couldn't stop folding and unfolding and rereading it, though he had already memorized its contents. He had never expected Cecily to harbor secret affections for him. He had prepared himself for a lengthy courtship, almost a war. But in retrospect, it wasn't really so surprising. He was, as she said, a genius, and he did have piercing eyes, not to mention a proud masculine brow like his brother and father, a scientist's brow. It all made sense to him now. Her seeming never to know he existed was pure shyness. She could be friendly only with someone she found ridiculous, like that first-year, Adams. She dealt with those she really admired by being shy and standoffish.

Volio sighed and rolled over in bed. He folded the letter and slipped it under the mattress. He had many papers under his mattress— sketches of machines and beautiful women. The maids who changed his sheets wouldn't look closely at a new one. And his roommate, Freddy, never paid much attention to anything when he was in the room, which wasn't very often, as he spent all his time downstairs plugging Bible verses into the analytical engines.

Ah, but what did it matter? He had Cecily's letter, and soon, he would have her heart. And if all went according to plan, he would have the duke's approval by the end of the year, when he would debut his invention—his glorious invention would surely win the duke's blessing and, with it, Cecily's hand. He thought of how lovely she would be to come home to after a long day of working with his brother at the Ministry of Defense. How she would ask him about his work and massage his shoulders as they waited for the maid to bring out supper. Their children would be lovely. A son with dark eyes like his own, and hair a dark shade of gold, a fine picture of manhood; and a daughter just like her mother, sweet and feminine, a constant delight. Volio looked forward to these things. He had little doubt that they would happen.

It was Sunday night. Tomorrow would begin the second week of his second year at Illyira, and he would deliver his second letter to Cecily, through Miriam. He was surprised that Miriam had been so cooperative. He had expected something clever from her, perhaps "accidentally" dropping the note where the duke could find it, though if that happened, all he would need to do was deny the letter was his. Whom would the duke believe? The son of one of the men who helped build Illyria, or some Jewess from who-knew-where?

Despite the duke's gullibility, Volio had to be careful. Cecily was tied in blood to the duke, and wasn't something intangible like a legacy that could be taken simply by proving himself deserving. Volio would need his permission to wed Cecily. So he planned to treat the duke as he would any ass: with a carrot and a stick. Sticks he had plenty of, an army of them in progress. The carrot would lead the sticks, a shining gift to the duke.

Of course, Volio still needed to finish both parts of his plan, and he wasn't sure he had the time. Outside, the sound of a clock ringing one in the morning poured out over the clanking of the gears. So tedious, those gears, always winding, a vast metallic cacophony. The noise made his work in the lab so much more difficult. But he would endeavor, and he would succeed. With Cecily's love, nothing could stop him.

XVI.

AFTER the first week of school, time sped up considerably. Even the gears on the walls seemed to spin faster, pushing time along, propelling Illyria into the future. Jack toyed with voice boxes and tried to befriend Cecily, who glowered at him and then walked away in a huff. Violet worked on her machine and silently fumed during the duke's lectures. Cecily progressed on her clay formula and had long conversations with Violet, which she thought were signs of Ashton's love for her. Toby and Drew worked in the chemical lab and considered what strange things they would ask Cousin Ashton to write in the next letter to Volio, who worked on his own projects and treasured each false word from Cecily. Classes flowed with a more steady hand as the students got a grip on what was expected and professors began to understand their students' needs. Even Bracknell's class became tolerable as he grew bored with mocking his students and focused on the science. Days darkened, and the garden outside turned shades of bronze and gold that matched Illyria's halls.

The only one for whom time seemed to slow was Miriam. She hadn't told anyone about what she had seen in the metallic features of the automaton that night. The scheme with Volio had kept her mind off it for a while, but now that she and Volio had fallen into a disgusting system of note exchange, her anxieties turned from her position to her life, and the possible threat to it by an automaton-duke. She had tried to convince herself that she hadn't really seen the duke in the device—it had been dark, after all, and she had had a drink or two. But no matter what she tried to tell herself, a smaller voice, the voice she had learned to trust years ago, told her that she had been right. But what did it mean? Miriam found herself study-ing the duke whenever she saw him, when he called her to his study, at meals, during lectures. Was it possible that the duke him-self was an automaton of some sort? Miriam had never known the duke's father, as she had been hired just after he died, but she gath-ered he was a man completely devoted to science. Ruthlessly devoted. So was it not possible that he had produced a child with science? Certainly the current duke sometimes seemed inhuman—he needed little sleep and worked harder and faster than any man she knew. But how such a thing would work, Miriam had no idea. And she did not want to contemplate why those other machine-cousins of the duke would be made for killing. Instead, she studied the way the duke's mouth moved when he chewed, and told herself that it was impossible, that no machine could look so human.

✦

FOR his part, the duke thought things were going swimmingly. The professors all reported that the students were doing well, and that the final projects were looking particularly impressive in aim and scope this year. He was concerned that some of the students were overshooting their abilities, but there was plenty of time yet, and the Science Faire at the Crystal Palace was always a success in the end, even the time one of the machines had exploded and knocked an earl unconscious. Afterwards, the Queen told him she thought the big flash and the earl's body arcing over the crowd of people were quite a sight. She had asked if he could arrange for it again next year, but with a specific courtier.

London's autumn wasn't colorful the way it was out in the coun-tryside. The city, already grey and silver, stayed grey and silver. The sky changed from the color of blue flowers to the color of violets and steel, and in the garden outside the school, the trees shed their leaves and stood straight and tall and pale, like half-built machines. Every fall, Ernest took pots, shovels, and soil out to the garden, and carefully moved those plants that could survive into pots, kneeling in the dirt and patting the soil down around them. He had started transplanting late this year, time seeming so intent on racing for-

ward that it raced right past him. On the Sunday that he moved the
flowers, it began to snow, light, careful flakes drifting down slowly
and in small numbers, barely snow at all.

He stopped at one point, to catch his breath and look out at the
city, and saw Ashton Adams staring at him curiously through the
snow. But when Ashton saw the duke looking back, he turned and
walked off, his feet stomping heavily on the ground. The duke waved
after him.

Ernest had wanted to talk to young Mr. Adams since he had re-
lied so heavily on his work for his first lecture, but months had
passed since then and he hadn't had the nerve. How could he, the
dean of Illyria, thank a first year for his inspiration without it somehow upsetting the balance of the school? And there was something
odd about Ashton, alluring and confusing at the same time, that
kept him from broaching the subject in private. Ernest would thank
him eventually, would credit him in the paper he finally wrote.

For since writing his first lecture, the duke had grown fascinated
with space travel. Ashton Adams's essay had inspired him more
than he had been inspired in quite some time. Thanks to Ashton's
influx of energy, the duke felt newly enthused about working well
into the night, writing formulae for possible combustible fuels, tinkering with mechanical valves and a steering system through the
upper æthersphere.

He had been interested in space exploration as a child, but his
father had dismissed it. "You may be able to break through the sky,
but then what?" he said to a twelve-year-old Ernest, who held out a
model æthership for his father's inspection. "We don't know what
it's like among the stars. How thin is the æther? Will the act of flying through it cause waves through all of space that press down on
our own terra firma? No, better to stay here. Conquer this world;
then we can move on to the emptiness surrounding it."

Ernest had never seen his father's own projects until they existed
for the world to see, so showing his father his few ideas—and hearing his critique—was the only way to absorb his genius, though Ernest was never really sure how well it worked. His father always seemed
to produce, as if from nothing, some great creation or feat, some

conquering of nature, complete with a full text on how it was executed. Ernest never saw his father toiling long nights in a lab, never
saw him pound his fists on the table in frustration when some theory
didn't prove true. This is how Ernest knew, even as an adult, that he
was not like his father. His father was more conjurer than scientist.
Ernest needed a lab, he needed to keep notes, he needed to fail over
and over before he could even hope to produce something worth
showing to the world. And he never knew what to work on next.

He knew the world outside Illyria stared at him, anxiously waiting for him to fulfill the promise of his heritage, which was why
he stayed in Illyria and emerged only for the year-end faire, when the
focus was on the students' work. He never participated in scientific
conversation, always turned down invitations to parties where he
would be expected to speak about his new theories or inventions.
His life was in Illyria, and that was where he would keep it. He
waited, feeling the weight of unfulfilled promise dragging him down,
pulling him flatter and flatter, closer and closer to nothingness. He
was terrified of it, and yet longed for the day when it would obliter-
ate him. He watched his students create, while his own lab, a huge
bronze space with windows and every conceivable convenience,
stayed empty.

Until this year. Now he worked, possessed by the dreams of his
youth. He'd forgotten them, but the Adams boy had rejuvenated
him—had dared, without knowing it, to engage him. He went up to
the observatory on clear nights, walked out among the clock statues,
and stared long and hard at the promise of space.

"What are you building in there?" Ada asked on one of her Sunday
visits, as they walked past the door to his lab. Cecily trailed behind
them, pulling Shakespeare on his golden leash.

"An æthership," the duke said, smiling.

"Oh," Ada said, and she began to smile back. "Oh," and then she
laughed, until she was laughing so hard that she had to put her hand
on Ernest's shoulder to keep herself upright. "Very good," she said,
patting him on the cheek. She smiled to herself and walked ahead of
them. Cecily looked curiously at Ernest, who shrugged.

It wasn't lack of ambition that kept Ernest from working all these years, nor was it really lack of inspiration. He never sought inspiration, as he feared to do so would be an endless chase. Inspiration had to find him. His father had always been inspired. It was part of his genius. The duke hid himself, his science, because he knew he wasn't his father but didn't want the rest of the world in on the secret.

But, space travel! Impossible, his father had said. If Ernest tried to create something his father had said was impossible, there could be no comparison between them; he would just prove his father right or wrong.

Still. He wished he were truly his father's son at times, wished he could set his mind to a thing and produce it, completely, without a hint of work, without even the use of a lab. He once asked Ada how his father had done it, but she just shrugged and smiled. "He was a genius," she'd said.

A sudden chilly wind came through, and the smell of London and her rising fog swept over the duke as he knelt in the garden. He much preferred the smell of the soil that covered his hands. He wiped his hands on his trousers—old, worn ones, just for this purpose—put the last few potted plants in the wheelbarrow, and went inside.

Cecily was just inside the residence, sitting at the window, Shakespeare in her lap. "Has it stopped snowing?" she asked.

"Help me with the last of these plants," he said. She nodded and jumped up to help him, placing Shakespeare on the seat.

"I don't know why you won't just hire a gardener," she said as she lifted a pot and carried it to the small room that Ernest had turned into a conservatory.

"I prefer to do it myself," Ernest said.

"But why?" Cecily asked, selecting a shelf. The room was circular, with a glass roof. Ernest had no idea what it originally had been designed for. Cecily delicately placed her potted flower on the shelf, then twirled to face her cousin.

"I find it refreshing to work with soil and plants after a day of working with chemicals and metal. Flowers generally smell sweeter."

Cecily raised an eyebrow as though she didn't quite believe him. "We should find you a wife," Cecily said, and left the room.

Ernest stared after her, puzzled, then placed the last plant on the ground. The room was pearl colored in the fading light, and the greens of the flora seemed to glow brightly.

Ernest realized that it would be time for supper soon, and he ought to bathe. The residence was, he thought, unnecessarily spacious. Four stories, like the college, the top story set aside for his personal chambers: bedroom, water closet, dressing room, office, and laboratory. Below that were Cecily and Miriam's rooms. On the first story were additional bedrooms and smaller water closets, a library, a smoking lounge. On the ground floor was a dining room, a parlor, and the conservatory, sticking peculiarly off the side. The dining room was seldom used, so it and the parlor had become something of a classroom for Cecily, for those lessons that could not be learned by sitting in on classes in the college. So Miriam taught French, German, art, music, and various other classes that Ernest knew Cecily loathed. But, Ernest was sure, these were things a lady needed to know. His father had told him so, and Ernest had no reason to think otherwise.

The great wall of gears powered their quarters as well, forming one side of his lab, the smoking room, the parlor, and one of Cecily's rooms. He and Cecily had practically grown up with the sound of it, and he found its steady clanking hum comforting, letting him know that Illyria was functioning properly.

Ernest's water closet was tiled from floor to ceiling in sand-and-white marble, with bronze pipes running along the side, pumping water to his bath and sink. The wall facing the bath featured a small pattern of bronze circles in the tile, and within each circle, a few molded, unmoving gears, which added a touch of whimsy to the room. Ernest loved a warm bath. He loved the illicit feeling of stripping naked and stepping into a pool of steaming water. He let the soil, sweat, and grime lift from his body as he laid his head back on the stone tub. Perhaps this was what space was like, he thought— like a warm bath. If that were the case, then space was certainly worth exploring. Perhaps he would move there. He could build a small home that orbited the Earth as the moon did, a beautiful glass home with windows on all sides to look out at the stars. He could live quite happily there. Maybe with a large greenhouse to grow his flowers in, and a small lab, and rooms for Cecily, of course, and possibly a wife, a beautiful clever wife with auburn hair and clear gray eyes, much like Miss Adams. But not her, of course, he thought, shaking his head; she was confusing. No, his wife would be easy to understand, and inspiring. But certainly she could look like Violet Adams. It was just a fantasy, after all. He closed his eyes and dipped his head under the water, letting a few air bubbles escape to the surface. He loved the way the water caressed him and how he could handle his body. To live forever in the warm bath of space. How nice it would be.

After relaxing a while longer in the bath, the duke rinsed the dirty water off himself and changed for supper. The dining hall was mostly empty. On Sundays, students weren't required to be in the dormitory for meals, so many with family in London went home for supper. He and Cecily sat alone at the professors' table, joined only by Professor Curio, who seldom made conversation, and was often more distressing than pleasant when he did. Ernest didn't mind, though. He enjoyed quiet Sunday suppers.

"You know, s-s-sir," Curio said suddenly, in his quiet voice, "young Miss Cecily here has very nearly invented a q-q-quite brilliant formula."

"You're kind, Professor Curio," Cecily said, "but I do not know if it is very nearly complete."

"What formula is this?" Ernest asked.

"I've told you about it," Cecily said, looking glumly at her food. "It should harden, like a clay, but into a nearly indestructible form, like steel. So far, though, it always crumbles when a moderate amount force of is applied to it."

"Not your most r-r-recent attempt, Miss Cecily," Curio said. "It stayed quite firm until you spent several minutes p-pounding on it with a hammer."

"Yes," Cecily sighed, "but it should have held up to that."

"I'm s-sure it will soon," Curio said. "You work on it so earnestly."

"It isn't just for me," Cecily said. "I'm trying to help a friend."

"What friend?" Ernest asked, raising an eyebrow.

"Ashton. I told you. He has a genius engine planned, and I think my formula, if it works, would be a much more suitable material for it than bronze."

"I hope you're not distracting him from his work."

"I don't think I could," Cecily said. "All he does is work on it, and go see his cousin on Sundays."

"His cousin?" Ernest asked. "Not his sister?"

"I didn't even know he had a sister," Cecily said, then sighed heavily and stabbed her food, leaving the fork planted in it like a flagpole. "May I be excused?" she said. Ernest looked her up and down. She had eaten little, and was flushed, but he could tell she would put up a fight if he protested, so he nodded his assent.

He was not meant to be a father. Cecily was a little sister to him, and he knew he was indulgent with her. Miriam would have been able to coax her to eat a little more, but Miriam wasn't here. Outside the windows of the dining hall, it began to snow again, the light from the windows catching on the flakes in the darkness. The duke finished his meal in silence and bid Curio good night before heading back to his lab.

Having a giant space to call his own and to use solely for science was his favorite privilege. Ernest's lab was gigantic and just as messy or organized as he was at any given moment. Today there was a large table strewn with tools and bent metal, a board covered with sketches of his theoretical æthership, and a smaller table covered in bottles of clear liquid. He was lately more interested in shapes of potential æther vessels. Certainly, the aerodynamics differed slightly than with seafaring ships, and there was no need for sails. No, an æthership would need to be as streamlined as possible, so as to protect the riders during the initial blast of launch, not to mention any possible stellar debris. And of course, there was the aesthetic question: How could this metal sphere—or tube, more likely—be artistic? He tried to curve a sheet of metal, creating a smooth shape, something that could flow through the æther smoothly, like a fish through water. It was just a model, of course, not big enough to hold anyone, but he preferred to work with three-dimensional forms rather than sketching. He loved bolting bronze pieces together after softening them in the fire and then hammering them. It was like growing something, he felt, coaxing the shape of the invention out of the metal and heat. But tonight he didn't have the kind of bronze he wanted. He needed a thicker sheet of it to curl into a tube. He would take some from the mechanical lab. Bunburry wouldn't mind—after all, it was his school.

He could hear students coming back in through the main gate as he left the residence and headed for the mechanical lab. He liked the sound: their footfalls, their murmurings, the way genius and potential and youth radiated from them. Illyria was itself a giant machine, churning out scientists, but it wouldn't work without the students, and when they were absent, the school seemed dark and empty, switched off.

He found a thick sheet of bronze in Bunburry's lab and was lifting it when he heard footsteps at the door. He looked up and saw Ashton. "Mr. Adams," he said, feeling a little like a thief caught in the act, but also oddly happy.

"Sir," Ashton said coolly.

"I was taking some bronze up to my lab," Ernest said. They looked at each other for a moment. "I'm happy to meet you like this, though—I've been meaning to talk to you since my first lecture of the year." Ashton paused in the doorway, backlit, and walked farther into the dimly lit lab. He looked at the duke expectantly. "I wanted to say thank you. I found your paper inspiring." Ashton said nothing, but made a little huffing noise. "Yes," the duke said. "Well. I can tell you're extremely grateful for my thanks."

He picked up the bronze and headed for the door. He was suddenly very annoyed. Had a student just huffed at him? For a thank you? What incredible gall. Ernest grew angry just to think of it. Best to leave now.

"You weren't inspired," Ashton said as the duke was leaving. "You simply plagiarized my essay."

"I—what?" the duke said, turning. He leaned the bronze against the wall. This was incredible. "I did no such thing. In fact, if you have anything to be sore about, it would be that my lecture was a vast improvement on your paper. I pointed out all your mistakes in logic."

"Mistakes?" Ashton said, approaching the duke. "What mistakes?"

"Well, for starters, I said we would, in fact, need combustion to launch."

"No, we won't!" Ashton said, turning a shade redder. "Not if we launch from a high enough place. That's precisely what I said: Combustion, and the fuel you'd need to carry, weighs down the ship and severely limits the design of the ship itself." Ashton's eyes flashed. He took a deep breath and licked his lips.

"Without combustion," the duke said, stepping closer to Ashton, "we'd just end up sailing around the globe, just above it, like a hot air balloon. We can't expect to keep going in a straight line, past the horizon and into space. Gravity will hold us. We must launch right up, with as much force as possible." The duke felt sweat forming around his brow. He licked his own lips. The air seemed warmer, and the lab glowed in the light of the forge.

"How limiting." Ashton said, folding his arms, "Think of da Vinci's aircraft designs. They went directly up, using only gears and fans." The duke noticed sweat beading on Ashton's forehead as well.

"We're talking about breaking through the air and into the æther of space," the duke said. "Do you really think we can do that with fans and gears? Space travel is complex."

"I know it's complex," Ashton yelled, "I wrote the paper!"

Ashton's cheeks were a pretty shade of pink, and Ernest felt his body warm. His clothes were suddenly too tight. He breathed in the silence, frustrated beyond belief at this arrogant student, and pulled at his collar.

And then they were kissing. Ernest couldn't say how they got there. He suffered a moment without memory, where he moved from staring down at his student to pressing his lips against his, their tongues soft and salty in each other's mouths. Ernest even felt his hand clutching the small of Ashton's back, pulling him closer. His mind was blank, and it wasn't. He thought about pushing Ashton against the wall and tearing his shirt off as they kissed longer and deeper; he thought about licking Ashton's taut stomach.

Instead he pulled away. He had kissed a man. He had kissed a student. He didn't know which was more distressing. He felt shaken and surprised, as though he were suddenly falling in two directions. Ashton wouldn't meet his eyes. He took several steps back.

"I'm . . . sorry," the duke said. "That was inappropriate. I should . . ." He turned and left, forgetting the bronze he had come for.

✣⟡✣

VIOLET watched Ernest go. She wanted to say something, but couldn't. She sat down in the nearest chair and covered her mouth with her hands. She had kissed the duke! She didn't know what had come over her. But while arguing with him, she had grown hot, and started noticing the way his lips moved as he spoke, and how he licked them after he finished a statement, and then he had pulled at his collar, and suddenly she lost all sense of who she was, or what her situation was, and she threw her mouth up to his, which had apparently been waiting for it, for he had most certainly kissed her back. It was humiliating, that loss of control, and the way it expressed itself. She didn't even like the duke! It must have been Ashton's nonsense at the house today, the way he talked on and on about love as he wrote another false note to Volio. All that talk of love. And the wine, of course. It was a foolish mistake, to think for a moment that the duke was attractive, to forget how frustrating he was, how he had stolen her paper and her ideas. Although, from what he had argued with her, perhaps she was wrong about that. She tried to think back to his lecture. How much had she actually listened to?

Perhaps he had argued a different point than she. But to accuse her of being *wrong*? Ridiculous. What did he, a duke who inherited a school of science and had done little to live up to his family's genius, know about the mechanics of space travel? He was clearly passionate about it, given the way his cheeks had flushed when he spoke or the way his eyes started to glow like stoked embers, but that gave him no right to treat her like someone who didn't know science!

Violet stood. She had come down here to work, but was no longer in the mood for it. She would go to sleep. In the morning, everything would be fine again. She would forget that the whole disaster had ever occurred. She hoped the duke would have the sense and courtesy to do likewise. Though with him, who knew? She had seen him earlier today, on her way to see her brother, covered in dirt and moving the flowers from the garden into pots. Such a peculiar man.

Jack was playing with his latest ferret, Amelia, when Violet walked in. Amelia was not allowed to stay in the lab, because she would occasionally let out a horrible screech like an owl when she was sleeping, which greatly disturbed the other animals, particularly the mice. Jack was scratching her under her chin and murmuring to her as Violet closed the door behind her.

"I thought you were going to work," Jack said.

"Oh, well, yes," Violet said. "I changed my mind."

"I've been giving Amelia some syrup with her food. I think it prevents her from screeching."

"Maybe not giving her the voice box of an owl would have kept her from screeching to begin with."

"It's for science," Jack said.

"What happened to the owl?"

"It was already dead. Old age. I'm not quite so cruel about the animals as I seem, you know."

Violet walked into the WC and began to change. "Do you remember the duke's first lecture?" she called.

"About space travel? Yeah."

"What did he say, exactly?"

"You know: he argued that space travel was possible, but we'd need the right sort of craft and combustion—"

"He said combustion?"

"Yes."

Violet emerged from the WC in her nightshirt. "Oh," she said, feeling glum.

"What's the matter? I thought you said you had written it."

"I was wrong, I suppose," Violet said.

"And how do you know that now?" Jack asked.

"I got into an argument with him."

"With the duke?" Jack asked, his eyes widening.

"Yes," she said, "and then I kissed him."

"You kissed the duke?" Jack's eyes widened even further, further than Violet had ever seen them go. She could not tell if he was going to laugh or have a fit of panic.

"Yes," she said softly.

"Does he know you're a woman?"

"I . . . I don't know. We only kissed. He didn't . . . touch me."

"Is he an invert, do you suppose?"

"I don't know. But he looked rather surprised, so perhaps not. Or perhaps I am just an excellent kisser."

"Did he expel you?"

"No . . . he apologized."

"Well," Jack said, looking a little relieved, "then he probably won't expel you." He leaned back in his bed and laughed. "Of course, little Violet, her head full of science, should first fall in love when it would most ruin her."

"I'm not in love!" Violet said. "And I'm not little, either. I'm more than usually tall for my age."

"Then why did you kiss him?"

"My kissing him has nothing to do with my stature."

"I mean, if you're not in love."

"Oh . . . I suppose it was to make him shut his mouth. We were arguing, as I said, and he wasn't listening to sense; he just kept speaking nonsense, pretending it was science. So I kissed him. And then he was quiet. It was quite clever, I think."

"Certainly," Jack said dryly.

"Not everyone is a fool for a pretty face like you, Jack," Violet said, getting into bed. "Some of us value our work over petty romance."

"My love of Cecily isn't petty," Jack said, "and once she is no longer angry at me, we shall be great friends. And then, she will love me."

"She doesn't love you now," Violet said. "I mentioned you while we were talking last week, and she became nearly purple in the face."

"It will take time," Jack said sagely, "but I can wait."

"You talk of her like she's a child," Violet said. "That is no way to win a woman's affections."

"She is not a child. She is a genius."

"How do you know?"

"I asked Toby all about her work. He explained it to me, and I was quite confused, so I assume she is a genius." He rolled over in bed, away from Violet. "Ah, but those genius women, they are the most difficult of all womankind." Violet took one of her pillows and tossed it at his head, where it hit him soundly. "Oof," he said. Satisfied, Violet turned out her light and went to sleep.

XVII.

CECILY noticed that her cousin had begun to act most peculiarly. Of course, he had always been a bit strange, but in the past week, he had become even stranger. He rarely left his lab, and stopped looking in on his students' classes. At mealtime, when he was forced to be in the same room with the students, he spoke little and glanced at them nervously, as though expecting one of them to pounce. And she thought she detected a little guilt in the dark circles around his eyes, particularly when he spoke to her. She had asked him if anything was wrong, but he merely said, "Nothing . . . nothing . . . ," and walked away from her. There really wasn't much she could do besides try to be a dutiful cousin, so she brought him tea at night when he was still in the lab, and told him how classes were going for the various students, as reported by Ashton. Ernest always seemed to grow paler when she mentioned Ashton.

And Ashton, too, was acting a little odd of late. When Ernest mentioned that Ashton had a sister, she realized that she really knew very little about him. They worked together, and talked of science, but not of each other. How was she to make him love her if she didn't know him as a person, not just as a scientist? But he had become strangely reticent of late, introspective, as if something else were occupying his mind.

"Is your sister all right?" she ventured one day, taking measurements of his sketches for molds.

"What?" Ashton said.

"Your sister? My cousin mentioned you had one, and you seem distracted, so I thought maybe your sister was in some sort of trouble."

"No! No, nothing like that. No trouble. I'm not distracted. Just, working."

"You never told me you had a sister."

"Oh. Yes. Twin, actually." Ashton kept his eyes on the bronze in front of him.

"And you never told me," Cecily said, pouting a little.

"Well, I guess not," Ashton said, still not looking up.

"Ashton." Cecily looked at him, but he would not meet her gaze. "Ashton," she said again, reaching out, putting her finger under his chin, and lifting his face so he was looking at her, "are we friends?"

"Of course," Ashton said, turning red. In the corner, Miriam stood and took a step toward them.

Cecily pulled back her hand. "Then we should speak as friends do, don't you think?"

"I thought we did."

"We speak of machines, and chemicals . . . but you never told me of your sister. And you have never asked about my family."

"I didn't . . . I didn't want to be rude," Ashton said, sounding as though he was just thinking of it.

Cecily crossed her arms. "My mother's passing and my father's disappearance are tender subjects, yes, but you could ask me about my cousin."

"I don't think that would be appropriate," Ashton said, turning redder.

"You wouldn't be taking advantage," Cecily said. But Ashton seemed extremely uncomfortable at the notion, so she tried a different subject. "So, then, tell me of your sister. What is she like?"

"She's . . . very clever," Ashton said. "Not very ladylike, though. She doesn't wear pretty dresses like you do, or always behave properly. Sometimes . . . I think maybe she's a bit of a thorn in our father's side." Ashton's hands drooped and went inactive as he stared out in front of him. "Sometimes she's really very stupid, actually. She does things without thinking about them, and without knowing why. Stupid, dreadful things."

"Is she really all that bad?"

"Bad? No. She's not bad. I just wish . . . She's so smart. At science, anyway. I think . . . she doesn't realize how foolish she can be about things outside the scientific realm. She's so used to being smart that she's overconfident." Ashton looked up, seemed to realize what he was saying, picked up a nearby hammer, and began pounding on the bronze.

"Do you think we'd get along?" Cecily asked.

"Yes," Ashton said, smiling, "I think you could be great friends, if nothing came between you." He looked down again as he said this.

"What could come between us?"

"As I said, she sometimes is a very stupid girl. I don't think she always realizes how harmful her schemes can be."

"Well, I shall have to meet her sometime, and hope that she isn't in a scheming mood. Does she have a lover?"

"What?" The hammer flew out of Ashton's hand. He bent down to pick it up.

"I'm sorry. I was just wondering if she has the attentions of any particular man."

"I honestly have no idea," Ashton said. "She keeps her heart a secret from me."

"Well, perhaps she and I will become great friends, and if you're very nice to me, I'll tell you all her secrets."

"Perhaps."

"Maybe we'll visit you on Christmas. Wouldn't that be nice?"

Ashton looked up at her, surprised. "We?"

"Well, Miriam always goes away for Christmas, so my cousin would have to escort me."

"I don't think that would be appropriate," Ashton said, shaking his head.

"Don't be silly."

"And I won't even be there," Ashton said, as if suddenly realizing it.

"You won't?"

"No," he said, staring down at the metal he had been pounding, "I go to my aunt's home for Christmas. And my cousin—also Ashton—comes and stays with my family."

"An Ashton exchange?" Cecily asked, and giggled.

"Yes," Ashton said, sighing heavily.

"Well, then, there would be no point in visiting, after all."

"No," Ashton said. He turned back to his work and considered it. Cecily cocked her head at him. There was a point in going to visit, of course, but not one Ashton needed to know: meeting her future sister, who sounded quite intriguing. And Ernest needed to get outside and socialize more. A Christmas visit would be good for both of them.

"Well, I should probably go back and see how the new formula has dried. Good day, Ashton."

"Yes," Ashton said, distracted. "Good luck."

"Thank you." Cecily resisted the urge to lean forward and kiss his check. Instead she left the mechanical lab and headed upstairs, half-skipping in anticipation of her Christmas plans. Miriam shadowed her, an amused look in her eye, but said nothing. Cecily wondered what she should give Ashton for Christmas.

She rounded a corner and sighed. Jack, Ashton's friend whom she would have preferred not to think about, was coming down the hall toward her. She debated turning around to avoid him, but it was too late—he had spotted her, and was smiling. She tried to walk past him, but he sidestepped to block her path.

"Miss Cecily."

"Kindly let me pass, Mr. . . ."

"Feste."

"Mr. Feste."

"I shall, but I beg you for a moment."

"Whatever for?"

"So I might apologize."

Cecily looked up at him. He seemed sincere enough, and she thought herself a kind and forgiving person. "Very well," she said.

"You were right. I was jealous of your affections towards my friend. But as you are clearly a lady who fights for what she wants, and you want my best friend, I felt that I should be the better man and give up my own hopes of you. I was hoping, though, that as we have a friend in common, we could also be friends."

Cecily nodded. He was a good sort after all, it seemed. Perhaps a little passionate, but he came to his senses quickly, and wasn't afraid to apologize, which was a lovely quality much lacking in many of the young men she had met. "Very well," she said, extending her hand.

He shook it. "I'm very glad."

"If we're to be friends, perhaps you could help me with something."

"Anything to make up to you my past behavior."

"I thought you could advise me on a Christmas present for Ashton."

Jack raised his eyebrows, bit his lower lip, and tilted his head slightly. "Hm," he said.

"Do you have any ideas?" she asked.

"Well, normally I would suggest tools of some sort, but I assume you wish to give him something unique."

"I do," she said, nodding.

"May I think on it a bit?"

"Of course," she said, "and I shall as well."

"Thank you very much, Miss Cecily. You are as kind and forgiving as you are lovely."

Cecily raised her eyebrows at him.

"Oh, don't worry," he said, seeing her look. "I flirt with all my friends of the gentle gender. I'm quite shameless with Ashton's sister, though she is as a sister to me, as well."

"Well, mind you don't get too smart, or else Miriam will scold you," Cecily said, not quite believing him. He seemed so sincere, though. He had a boyish quality about him, as though he were honest and passionate and always looking for fun. She liked those qualities. They were so different from the usual stern, focused mentality of the other students. Perhaps, as they were now to be friends, she could find him a more appropriate match. But only if he was truly her friend. She would think on it, and see how things progressed.

Jack smiled at her again, and continued his walk down the hall. Miriam drew close to Cecily and spoke softly in her ear. "I think your cousin will find your giving a gift to a student quite inappropriate," she said.

"Oh, don't worry so much about it," Cecily said. "He would really be mad only if Ashton got me a gift, and I don't expect that from

him. Still, I would appreciate it if you didn't mention my plans to
Ernest."

Miriam raised an eyebrow, but nodded. They went into the chemical lab together.

⁘⊚⊰

ONCE out of sight, Jack leapt with happiness. All was going
smoothly. Cecily would be his, if he were patient. He chuckled to
himself as he walked back to the biological laboratory. Once there,
he went over to his workstation, which had a small floppy-eared
bunny in one cage and a pigeon in another. He put down the bottle
of ether. He wasn't all that fond of this part of his science. Cutting
the animals open always seemed to him like a particularly cruel
means to various ends that he loved. He tried to be cavalier about
it—the scientific community had long ago sanctioned, if not en-
couraged, the use of animals for scientific purposes, and he didn't
disagree with the idea in theory—but as he dosed the pigeon with
ether and carved open its chest, he shivered a little at the coldness
of it.

Art requires sacrifice, he told himself. And besides, perhaps this
bird can be taught to sing a new song, and then he will have his
pick of the birds to mate with. One never knew what could make a
better animal until one tried it. Jack found the voice box in the
pigeon and switched it out for one he had taken out of a dead
mockingbird, taking care to sew it in well so that it wouldn't choke
the pigeon. Then he closed the pigeon back up and let it rest in its
cage. Later, Jack would see if he could make it sing. He looked over
at the floppy-eared bunny, which he wouldn't operate on until he
felt quite sure of his abilities. The bunny stared back at him with
large dark eyes. He gave the bunny a pat on the head, fed it a carrot,
and the bunny anxiously took the carrot in its tiny paws and nibbled on it.

"You don't mind being part of an experiment, right, Oscar?" he
asked the bunny, who paid him no heed. "We're going to teach you
to talk, after all. What rabbit wouldn't want that?"

XVIII.

SUNDAYS had become Ashton's favorite day of the week. It wasn't that he didn't enjoy the rest of the week: supper parties at Lady MonCrieff's house, poetry readings, plays, art exhibits, drinking at taverns with various liberal-minded young men, evenings with Antony. He enjoyed it all. But Sundays were some strange new breed now. His sister and her friends were a delightful bunch of rogues. He hadn't really expected his sister to become a rogue, but it wasn't too much of a surprise. After all, she had always had the qualities of a lady adventuress—she was forthright and clever, and seldom let things get in her way. But to actually see her laughing and drinking with a group of blokes was both funny and sweet. Ashton would often find himself looking at his sister as she slapped her knee in laughter at some joke Toby had told, and his eyes would grow a little damp with pride and happiness.

He liked her friends, too. Miriam, especially. She had a dry continental wit, the morality of a Frenchwoman—which was to say, not very much at all—and she always laughed at his jokes, even when no one else did. And she had a gift with words. While the others played cards, they would go over Volio's last letter together, laughing at his poor metaphors and boorish expression of feeling, then respond in florid, girlish prose that Miriam said would be quite mortifying to Cecily if someone thought she had written it.

When the doorbell rang, a gentle snow was falling outside, and Ashton opened the door to the scoundrels with a grin. The tops of their heads were white, and Jack had an eyebrow raised, as though Ashton had been doing something scandalous instead of opening the door promptly.

"Come in out of the cold," Ashton said.

"*Merci*," Miriam said, stepping in first, and handing Ashton the latest sealed note from Volio. "I am unaccustomed to cold weather."

"You've lived here since you were sixteen," Toby said, following her in. "How can you not be used to it yet?"

"*Silence!*" Miriam said. "Cousin Ashton doesn't know my age yet."

"Not a day over seventeen, surely," Ashton said.

"Such a charmer," Miriam said, sitting by the already set up card table. The others joined her.

"There's drinks at the bar," Ashton said, popping the seal on Volio's note, "if you need further warming."

He took the note out of its envelope, read it over quickly, and felt his heart stop. He read it over again, slowly this time. But it still said the same thing. This was very bad.

"What is it, Cousin Ashton?" Miriam asked. "You look terrified. What did Volio say?"

"Oh, nothing," Ashton said, forcing a laugh. "I had merely forgotten how mortifying Volio's poetry could be."

"I wish I had forgotten as well, but it still haunts me," Miriam said. The others had poured themselves drinks, and Toby was dealing cards.

"Come play a round, Cousin Ashton," Toby said. "You can write your fake love note later. For now, let's relax a bit."

"Actually," Ashton said, narrowing his eyes at his sister, "my cousin and I have a little family business to discuss, if you don't mind. And, Miriam, as you're so sick of Volio's writing, why don't I handle this note alone?"

"Are you sure?" Miriam asked. "Of course, I would be grateful, but—"

"No bother. I'll have it done in a nick, and then we can all play cards and drink until we've forgotten not only Volio's poetry, but even his name."

"Suits me," Drew said.

Ashton nodded at Violet, who rose with a confused look but followed him to the study, the rest going back to their cards. Ashton tried not to slam the door, but as soon as it was shut, he spun on his sister. "You kissed the duke?" he hissed.

Violet turned bright red, and then very pale, and looked at the floor. "He kissed me, too," she said softly.

"Violet," Ashton said in a somewhat higher voice, "perhaps this was a bad idea. Perhaps you should just drop out of school, and no one will know a thing about this scheme."

"No," Violet said, "I can't now. I will just avoid him."

"Oh, Violet, I did hope one day you would fall in love, but your timing is . . . less than pragmatic."

"I am not in love! Why does everyone insist that a kiss must signify love?" She threw her hands up in the air, and then, seeing how ridiculous she looked, crossed her arms. "It was just an experiment."

"An experiment?"

"I had never been kissed before. I wanted to try it. Experiential learning."

Ashton smiled at this ridiculous excuse. "And what were the results of your experiment?"

"It was quite nice," Violet said softly, "but I don't need to do it again."

"Of course not," Ashton said, nodding. He plotted what he would tell their father when this scheme exploded, as it was now clear to him it would. Maybe they could just move away for a while. America, perhaps. Scandal wouldn't follow them there. He hoped.

"How did you know?" Violet asked. Ashton handed her Volio's letter.

⋙⋘

My Dearest Cecily,

    I fear I must disclose to you some disturbing news. I wish to write to you of nothing else save how beautiful you are, with your hair, yellow like the sun, and your skin, as pale as milk, but I fear I bore witness to a most scandalous encounter between two men who are close to you—one whom you call friend, and the other whom you call cousin. Yes. I saw your cousin, the duke, and

Mr. Ashton Adams in a most perverted embrace in the mechanical laboratory. I was going that way to pick up something I had
left when I heard an argument from within. I crept quietly to the
door, not wanting to involve myself in anything, and as I looked
in, I saw the duke and Mr. Adams kissing most passionately.

Such perverts should not be keeping company with a young
lady of good moral upbringing such as yourself. Of course, you
cannot avoid your cousin—perhaps you can help him to cure himself of this vice—but Adams you should remove from your life.
Such a disgusting creature does not deserve to be pulped beneath
your glorious foot.

I tell you this because I love you, and want to protect you, as I
shall when we are married. I shall spend my days and nights building for you a great castle where you and our children will be safe,
and the outside world will not intrude. But I cannot build it yet, and
so I must protect you via our letters. Until next we write, know that
I adore you, I love you, and I long to bury myself in you.

Your Devoted Malcolm.

"He really is a very terrible poet," Violet said, closing the note.

"Loath as I am to admit there is such a time, now is not when
you should be witty. You should be worried."

"It's simple," Violet said with a wave of her hand. "We tell him the
duke confessed the kiss to Cecily—said Ashton threw himself at
him." Ashton crossed his arms. "And so Cecily, being that font of
goodness that she is, is trying to cure Ashton of his perversions.
And that Ashton wants to be saved. And then whatever other nonsense you throw in there about how Cecily yearns for his arms."

"I cannot decide," Ashton said, looking unimpressed, "if you
were always so arrogant, or if it's just that in the guise of a man,
such arrogance is less appealing."

"What arrogance?" Violet asked, throwing up her arms and
speaking in her normal voice. "It will work, won't it? Hasn't this
whole scheme worked so far? Doesn't Volio believe everything you
tell him?"

"Yes, but this lie is more ridiculous. And we shouldn't need to tell it. Nor should I need to hide it from Miriam. You're very lucky she waits to read them with me. This was a risk you took, which you should not have."

"I suppose," Violet said, looking down again, which Ashton was glad to see. She was at least a little ashamed. "Had I known Volio was there, I would have postponed my experiment."

"Does the duke know you're a woman?"

"No!" Violet said. "I don't see how he could. We kissed. It was not this passionate embrace Volio speaks of. It was a kiss. I can think of no way he could suspect my gender."

"So the duke is an invert?" Ashton said, scratching his chin. This would make good gossip at certain alehouses.

"I don't know," Violet shrugged. "I've made it this far," she whispered. "Surely I can finish this without mishap."

"Let's hope," Ashton said. He rested his hand on his sister's shoulder. "Does Jack know?"

"Yes."

"Good. He'll keep a closer eye on you from now on, I hope."

"Most likely."

"No more experiments."

"Only of the usual variety," Violet said with a smile.

Ashton sighed. There was nothing to be done now. He might as well let his sister make the most of her time at Illyria. He would begin inquiries about town houses in New York, for their inevitable move there.

"May I go now?" Violet asked. "I think I can beat Toby at cards this week. I theorize he has a habit of blinking more often when he is lying—I'm not sure, but I want to test it."

"No. You will wait here with me as I pen our false missive. It is your punishment for poor judgment."

Violet pushed her lips out into a pout, waiting as Ashton wrote a note to Volio begging him not to tell anyone what he saw, explaining how the duke was an unwilling participant of the kiss, and how Ashton was seeking help in curing his perversion. Ashton felt sick after writing it, but folded it up and put it in an envelope.

"Thank you," Violet said, and kissed her brother on the cheek.

Violet was wrong about Toby blinking more when he lied during cards. Toby won half the hands, Miriam most of the others, with Jack winning once.

"I'm quite terrible at this game," Violet said, throwing the cards down.

"*Heureux au jeu, malheureux en amour*," Miriam said with a sly grin.

"What does that mean?" Jack asked.

"Unlucky in cards," Ashton said, beginning to laugh, "lucky in love." His laughter rang through the house. Jack chuckled, too, and Violet glared at them both, until everyone was laughing. The laughter couldn't dislodge the cold chills from Ashton's chest, though, as he thought of the sinister Volio, what he had seen, and what he might do.

XIX.

I N his private lab, the duke was attempting to fold softened bronze
into a shell for his space vessel, but found that his mind was not
on the work. His hands kept slipping on the edges of the metal, cutting them. Outside, the sky was turning from gray to blue, and he
could hear the river rushing faster past Illyria. He had been trying
to work for the better part of the day, skipping dinner and supper,
but had accomplished nothing. His mind kept wandering to Ashton
Adams, their kiss.

The duke had bedded many women. When Ernest was sixteen,
his father had put him in a coach and told him it was time for him
to become a man. The coach had arrived at Mrs. Williams's, a brothel
for clients of good society. Mrs. Williams herself was a woman approaching sixty, with hair dyed a bright scarlet, heavy makeup, and
a sometimes smudged fake birthmark drawn on her left cheek. She
had greeted Ernest with open arms and told him that his father had
arranged for him to have an evening of pleasure. The pleasure,
thankfully, was not provided by Mrs. Williams, but by a girl called
Ocean, with long black hair, warm tanned skin, and striking gray
blue eyes. She was about the same age as Ernest at the time, but
much more experienced than he in sexual relations. His father had
purchased several hours with the girl, so though Earnest was done
with her after a few minutes, she coaxed him into staying so that
she might give him instruction in the ways of pleasuring women.
He learned a variety of acts pleasurable to both him and Ocean,
and she was kind enough to note when they were participating in
an activity in which a proper lady would never partake. He went

back to her regularly for a whole year before she vanished, apparently purchased to be a full-time mistress to another client.

After her departure, Ernest had decided to educate himself further. Ocean had taught him the elementary lessons, but as in all the sciences, further experimentation was needed before he felt truly competent. He visited a variety of whorehouses, and a variety of whores around the city: elegant and dirty, thin and fat, young and old. He tried various combinations, once even involving another man, though he found that particular experiment to be a failure, and flagged when he attempted to pay any attention to the other man. For two years, he whored about London with a detached civility. He didn't compare whores or read guides to the best prostitutes in London as other young men did, but merely found the women on his own, sampled them as many times as he liked, and moved on.

Then, after he turned twenty, his mother began to throw elaborate parties and invite the families of various eligible young women to them. She held thirteen of these parties, one a month, until she was found expired in the kitchen, a bottle of her favorite whiskey still in her hand, her body slumped, as though she'd just fallen asleep drinking again.

The parties were uncomfortable for Ernest. The young women he knew he was supposed to mingle with were for the most part insipid, with overly large teeth and a tendency to giggle whenever he talked about science.

"Oh, you do go on, don't you?" said Miss Murchison-Pinch, at the third party. "Wouldn't you rather tell me how pretty my eyes are?" She batted her eyelashes. Her eyes were a dull brown color, lacking in both luster and intelligence. Ernest sighed and walked away.

After the first party, Ernest's father had insisted on being able to invite his own friends, so he had something to do at the parties besides talk to the equally stupid parents of the stupid girls the parties were for. He stood with a group of his scientist friends in a corner, and Ernest joined them after leaving Miss Murchinson-Pinch, who stood in the middle of the family parlor, looking confused.

". . . but that is not the point, is it?" said one of the men, a Dr. Rastail, as Ernest approached. "The point is that if we, as a people, think bad decisions are being made on our behalf, we have the right—no, the responsibility—to speak up, to demand that the right decisions be made. And if we are not heard, we must make ourselves heard. And we being brilliant men of science"—and here the men all chuckled knowingly—"we have the means to make ourselves heard, not to mention the intellect to make the right decisions." Ernest sidled behind his father, unnoticed, listening to the men's argument.

"I think you're being idealistic, Rastail," said the cranelike Dr. Knox in his low voice. "Why bother talking with the Queen at all? Or with anyone else? If you have the power to take more power— just take it. We may be a . . . group of highly intelligent men, but we don't agree on everything. So we waste time fighting each other. If Algernon here would just help Alfie instead of fighting him, all our plans could progress, and we could succeed in—"

"And we'll all be destroyed in the process," interrupted Ernest's father with some cold anger. "The idea is madness, Knox, and—"

"Look who's joined us!" interrupted the massive Dr. Pluris, his voice booming from behind Ernest.

"Ah, young Illyria," said Dr. Rastail, looking at Ernest. "What do you think? Should we not make ourselves heard, if poor decisions are being made in our name?" Ernest felt his face go warm at being addressed by one of his father's peers. He looked to his father, who stared at him, waiting.

"I think that when decisions are made for us, we must talk with the ones making them, discover why such decisions have been made, and then we can come to an understanding, the best decision for everyone."

"For everyone?" Dr. Rastail repeated, as though the words were new to him. He paused, and then started to laugh. "Right so. Every-one. Everyone who is our equal!" All the men began to laugh around him, and his father stepped forward, pulling Ernest by the arm out of the crowd.

"Why don't you go entertain the womenfolk, Ernest?" his father said coolly. "They're here for you, after all." And then he turned back to his peers. Ernest had turned from them, his face warmer than before, and looked to the women all hovering at the other side

of the room. They looked over at him anxiously. Ernest turned from
them, as well, and left the room for the garden, hoping to take some
fresh air.

Outside, it was dark and cool and smelled of flowers and dirt.

"Oh, bloody 'ell." A voice came from behind the willow tree. Ernest walked toward the voice, curious. A girl around his age sat on a
low stone wall, trying to roll a cigarette. She was in a maid's uniform,
but her long orange curls fell loose over her shoulders.

"Need some help?" Ernest asked. The girl looked up at him with
a grin, but seeing his face, her eyes widened in panic. She stood
quickly and looked at the ground. "Sorry, sir . . . Your Grace . . .
young Illyria. I was just trying to roll a cigarette—I only snuck off
for a few minutes—the kitchen gets so hot, you see, and—"

Her stammering made Ernest smile. "I can roll your cigarette, if
you'd like," he said.

She looked up at him curiously. "That would be wonderful," she
said with a sigh of relief. Ernest sat down on the low wall, took the
tobacco and paper in his hand, and rolled it quickly and simply.

"Cor, you're good at that."

"My godmother taught me."

She took the cigarette, stuck it in her mouth, produced a match
from her pocket, and lit it. She inhaled deeply, and blew the smoke
out her nose. "Ah . . . thank you, Your Grace. I've been needing a
smoke since I got here."

"You're new?"

"Arrived day before last. Kitchen maid. Adelaide Moth." She
looked at him, an honest, friendly expression on her face, and brought
the cigarette back to her lips.

"I'm Ernest," he said, taking out a cigarette case from his pocket,
producing a cigarette, and lighting it.

She laughed. "As if I'd call you that," she said. "You can call me
Del, though. I mean, if you want to. Miss Moth, too. But if you want
to call me Del, you're welcome to. Cor, that's a nice cigarette. You
roll that one, too?"

"I did. Good tobacco, too. Want to try one?"

"One of your cigarettes? I'd die, I would."

"I hope you won't," he said, took out another cigarette, and gave it to her. She took it, and he lit it for her. She inhaled deeply and closed her eyes. "I wish I were a duke," she said.

He laughed. "Now you have to call me Ernest," he said. She nodded. He liked her smile, her freckles, the leanness of her body. They finished their cigarettes in silence, and she stood up.

"I have to go back to the kitchen," she said, leaning down and kissing him on the cheek. "Thanks for the cigarette, Ernest." She grinned, and he leaned up and kissed her on the mouth. She kissed him back and left. Ernest had another cigarette before going back to the party.

Del came to his room that night, and many nights after that for the next year and a half. She was a wonderful lover with a quick mind. She listened to Ernest talk about his inventions, asking questions when she didn't understand him, the long fan of her orange curls on the pillow, her arm around his chest. She was the one he cried in front of, when, eleven months later, his mother died, and the one whose arms he slept in after the funeral. He never thought he loved her, and she told him quite clearly that she wasn't fool enough to let herself fall for a duke, but they were friends, and they laughed together, smoked, and made love. Then she left the house, married a butcher, and moved to the country.

She couldn't meet his eye when she told him she was getting married, but he could tell she was happy, which made him smile as he lifted her chin to look at her. "Course, I'll be sad to leave you behind," she said, pinching his cheek. "You're a good fella, Ernest. A nice bloke. You're almost like a big brother, I think. Except for when we're naked. I think I do love you a little. But don't think I'm going to call off this wedding."

"I wouldn't ask you to," Ernest said honestly. "I just want you to be happy."

"I am," Del said, glowing.

"I'll miss you, too."

After she left, Ernest quit smoking and went back to paid sex, sometimes indulging in another maid, or a young widow, but he rarely made any sort of connection as he had with Del.

And then, one day, he decided it had all been enough for him, and he turned all his energies to science and the school. He had been chaste for nearly two years now. He dragged himself to his quarters and prepared for bed. He wondered if he had ever experienced passion. He had read a poem or two in his time, and the way they described love seemed quite absurd to him—the longing of hearts and bodies, the need involved. Ernest had never felt need like that, never felt a desire he could not quell with reason. Why, then, when his lips reached for Ashton's, did it feel as strong as magnetic force, completely unavoidable? Is that what the poets meant? How horrible, to have every love affair be so overwhelming and out of one's control.

Kissing Ashton did not make sense in the list of his experiments, either. Even now, lying in bed in his pajamas, he was aroused by thoughts of Ashton in ways he could not explain. He had never felt this way toward other women, and he had *certainly* never felt this way about any man. He reimagined the argument, and then the kiss, and touched his own lips as he did so. But as he thought more and more about it, Ashton blurred, his hair growing longer, his body curvier, the passion in his eyes unchanged—and taking on a guise strikingly similar to Ashton's sister, Violet. He was no invert, Ernest told himself, tossing in bed; it was just the confusing nature of twins. The thought was quite a relief. True, he had behaved badly with a student, but he hoped that awkwardness would pass with time. He would just have to avoid Ashton for a while.

He was suddenly aware of how hungry he was. Cecily had brought him a dinner plate, but he had left it in the lab. He glanced at the clock. It was nearly ten. Supper would be cold, but edible. He walked downstairs to his lab and turned on the lights. Miriam stood alone in the room, looking surprised and guilty for a moment before her face returned to its usual passive gaze.

"What are you doing here, Mrs. Isaacs?" he asked, heading for his dinner plate.

"Miss Cecily asked that I retrieve certain materials from your lab for her experiments, sir," Mrs. Isaacs said, bowing her head slightly. The duke wondered when she changed out of her black high-collared dresses, or if she ever let her hair out of its tight bun.

"Well, take what you need from the cabinets. But not from the tables, please. I'm working with what is on the tables."

"I already searched, sir; you don't have what she needs. I will need to go to the chemical lab."

"Very well. Good night, Mrs. Isaacs."

"Good night, sir."

Mrs. Isaacs bowed and swept out of the room like a shadow while the duke took a bite of his chicken.

❧✦❧

OUT in the hall, Miriam headed for the basement. She had lied to the duke, but she had her reasons. She had been searching his lab not for materials, but for evidence, an explanation for what she had seen in the basement.

Miriam had tried to repress her curiosity. She had tried to distract herself by making Cecily's German lessons harder for both of them, by studying Cecily's complex chemical formulae, or in long weekends in bed with Toby and his achingly skillful hands, but the truth was, Miriam wasn't very good at being restrained. She could cover things up, but actually restraining of any part of her for very long wasn't in her grasp. She couldn't restrain her desires, she couldn't restrain her confidence, and she couldn't restrain her curiosity.

And unfortunately, she thought, wandering the basement halls alone, she couldn't restrain her stupidity. Ashton had gladly made her a mechanical torch, but hadn't explained that to keep the light constant would require constant squeezing of the trigger. Miriam nervously squeezed it every other second or so, more often than she needed to, so that the light stayed steady, though her finger was tight and cramped. She spent some time trying to find the mark she had left previously, an uneven line through the dust on the walls. Already it had begun to fill in with more dust, but it was still visible with the light shining on it. She ran her finger through it again as she stalked through the halls, making it deeper, easier to see. The friction of the rough stone and dust made her fingertip raw. She had come alone because she needed to see the automata again, needed to verify that it was the duke's features she had seen, but she couldn't tell anyone that. It implied a secret too dark for her to share with anyone, even Toby. And she liked the duke. He was a good man to work for, and if her fears were proved true—if he wasn't entirely human—then she would weigh that information against what she knew of him as . . . if not a man, as a being. And a good one, overall. She didn't need to reveal his nature to anyone else. She just needed to know for herself.

Miriam wasn't a scientist. She didn't know how one could make a mechanical man as lifelike as the duke, or if it was even possible, but she had seen many things she thought previously impossible since coming to work at Illyria, and one more didn't seem out of the question. There was one time last year when she had walked in on him in his lab with what seemed to be a metal thigh on his own leg. He had seemed flustered, and told her that he was merely making a part for Bunburry, in case he had another accident, which at the time seemed reasonable, but Miriam wondered if maybe she had been seeing something else—the duke making a new part for himself, or perhaps his actual skin, under his clothes.

Miriam stopped walking as something brushed against her dress. She pointed the torch at her feet, but saw nothing. The beam of light seemed very small compared to the vastness of the basement. It seemed to get darker every time she was down here. Distantly, she heard a door swing shut, and something that sounded like giggling. She could hear the sound of the wall of gears, too, pulsing dimly in the darkness, like soft footsteps.

What else was happening in the basement? She had asked a few of the other servants about it, but they just shrugged or walked away. The only one who had spoken to her, the girl who made her bed, told her that she didn't think anyone went very far into the basement. Anything that was stored down there was a few yards from the stairs. The other servants weren't fond of Miriam. They didn't like that a Jew with dark skin seemed to have more rank than they did, that they had to change her sheets and serve her meals. She wished now that she could have made the servants like her more. Perhaps one of them had made a map of the basement, or at least knew something about it, but all of them claimed it was unused.

But it wasn't. There were closing doors and laughter with no sources and warm, unseen things that brushed against her dress and a cluster of skeletal automata. Except—Miriam saw as she came to the point where the line in the wall ended—those seemed to be gone, too. It was definitely the right place, a turn in the hall with a small alcove sticking out of it and a strange handleless door. But the automata were gone.

Quietly, Miriam crept forward, pointing the torch at the floor. It was clean all around the door and alcove. Everywhere else, inches of dust lay undisturbed. Someone had swept. And taken the automata away.

She approached the door. It was more like a doorway, sealed over with metal. There was no handle, no gap, just a great archway with smooth bronze behind it. If it was a door, the door behind which the automata were taken, she could see no way to open it. She swept her palm over the front of the door, searching for some sort of keyhole. In the center, she found a slight circular depression, about the size of her thumb. The back of the depression seemed to have some sort of engraving in it, and when Miriam shone her light directly at it, she could see a small pattern of gears. The pattern seemed familiar, though, so Miriam leaned in closer. Then she heard footsteps behind her. She froze, and her torch flickered out. She held her breath, waited for another noise.

More footsteps, from somewhere down the hall. Miriam backed into a corner, pressed herself flat against the wall. It was almost completely dark, but she could see a shadow—the shadow of a tall man, she thought—at the end of the hall. He walked slowly, but because he was only a shadow, Miriam did not recognize him. She swallowed, wondering if it was the duke, come down here to check on his brothers. But the shadow passed by, leaving her alone in the darkness. She put her hand on her chest, feeling her heartbeat pound quickly. It was time to leave.

After waiting for what seemed a long enough time—maybe five minutes, maybe an hour—Miriam walked slowly back to the entrance. She turned her torch on only when she absolutely needed to, and listened carefully for footsteps. When she finally emerged from the basement, she was coated in dust, grime, and sweat. Her hair, normally bound back tightly, had fallen loose and was wet. Her hands shook and her back ached. She walked back to her room and drew a bath for herself.

Christmas break would be upon Illyria soon. Toby was going to take her to the south of France, where they could pretend to be a married couple, and no one would really care anyway. She was looking forward to leaving behind eerie basements and blackmailing students and the constant grinding of gears. Illyria was beautiful and wondrous when she first arrived. Now she saw beyond the brightly lit bronze-and-gold halls filled with genius, and into the shadows produced by the tooth of each turning gear, the shadows themselves turning, sliding over the walls and gears, like a net wavering in the breeze.

XX.

LONDON in winter wasn't white like the country in winter. It was gray and silver, the color of iron and stone. Outside was steadily falling snow, heavy fog, specks of white on a pewter background, and through all that, a depth of monochrome, smoke and shadows of buildings, all shimmering, all unreal. This was lost on Gareth Bracknell, who did not care much about the beauty of the physical world. Even though he had been studying the stars since he was a child, he saw them only as points of light, like marks on a map. In fact, he hated snow. Hated the way it covered the dome of the astronomy tower and didn't slide off, creating strange gray shadows in the classroom. Hated the way it blotted out the sky at night, creating confusion over whether things were a falling star or snowflake. And he hated the cold. He had on several thick sweaters, a scarf, and mittens, and it was still cold in the astronomy tower. He tucked his hands under his arms and felt his teeth chatter. The students looked at him from their desks, waiting for him to start, apparently unaffected by the cold. They had on little jackets and shirts, and the fat one wore a ridiculous-looking sweater, but none of their teeth chattered, none of them shivered. Bracknell hated them for their warmth.

"Fuck all," Bracknell said. Violet had stopped trying to pay attention in Bracknell's classes since discovering that he was going to be nasty either way. When she tried to please him by studying hard and getting every answer right, he called her a sissy, and when she didn't pay attention or got an answer wrong, he called her stupid. Not paying attention was easier.

"I don't see the sodding point in trying to have an astronomy class in the snow," he said, "but your headmaster, the bloody Duke of Idiocy, said that I have to do something. He paused, looked out the window. A smile crept onto his lips. Violet didn't like it.

"I know," he continued. "How's about a little test? A test-y. Oh yes. It won't be your final exam, of course—those aren't until the third trimester—but a test. You have to work. I don't. Sounds perfect. Everyone take out a piece of paper."

With audible groans, the students all took out paper and readied their pens.

"Good," Bracknell said. "Draw me a map of the stars as they will look on Christmas from the observatory this year. Use your books if you need to, but if you do, do realize that you have shit for brains and haven't learned a thing." With that, Bracknell sat down at his desk and pulled out a book—some serialized adventure novel for boys—and began reading. The class, feeling a little thrown off, waited a few moments before starting their work.

A map of the stars on Christmas. Violet thought it over and began to draw. Christmas was only a week away. This was their last class before they went home for Christmas holiday. It would be sad this year without her father there. Mrs. Wilks would be there, and Ashton, of course, and probably Jack, but they had no extended family who visited, and no neighbors who would visit for more than a few minutes. Violet drew star after star, dot after dot of ink, and labeled each constellation. Looking around the room, she was happy to see that no one had opened their books. She saw Bracknell looking up and noticing the same thing, but with disappointment. Their eyes met and he glared at her before going back to his book. Violet wondered how such a man had become a scientist—or a professor.

When the class was over, Bracknell stood, grabbed each piece of paper from the students, even if they were still writing, and left. Violet felt she had drawn the stars correctly and easily, and hoped her success would irritate Bracknell over the holiday.

"Happy Christmas, Professor!" Merriman called after Bracknell as he vanished down the stairs. Bracknell's grumbles echoed slightly before the door slammed shut.

"Well," Jack said, "time to go home, then."

Fairfax stood and left the room in silence.

"Happy Christmas, Roger!" Merriman called after him. Fairfax did not reply. "I love Christmas," Merriman said to no one in particular.

Violet smiled. "Have a very Happy Christmas, Humphrey," she said to Merriman, who beamed. "You, too, James."

"Thank you," Lane said, standing. "To all of you as well." He gathered his books and left.

"I want to go out on the tower once before we leave," Violet said to Jack.

"It's slippery," Jack said. "That's a bad idea."

"I'll go," Merriman said.

"Good," Violet said. She walked over to the glass door and opened it, letting in a whistling rush of cold wind that scattered loose papers.

"Bracknell's not going to like it," Merriman said.

"Bugger Bracknell," Violet said, stepping out onto the snow-covered rooftop. Jack and Merriman followed. Jack was right: It was slippery, and the wind was strong, but it smelled fresh and felt cold and wet on Violet's skin. She walked slowly over to the statue of Leonardo da Vinci atop a lion and rested her hand on it for support as she looked out over the city. Behind her, she heard Merriman try to follow and slip and fall with a thud. Jack helped him back up. The wind pressed into Violet, and she wished that she still had her long hair or her skirts so that they could be blown around. She wished her breasts weren't bound, so that her whole body could be as loose as the wind. She took a deep breath and turned back.

Merriman beamed at her. "It's cold out here," he said, "but it feels great."

"It does," Violet said. "It feels free up here. And we're surrounded by geniuses," she said, patting the lion on the head. Merriman laughed, and Violet and Jack each supported him on one side as they went back in.

"I really had a good first trimester," Merriman said in the lift down. "I never thought I'd get in here, and then I thought for sure I'd flunk out, but . . ."

"It's been good for me, too," Violet said.

"That is because you're both brilliant," Jack said, slapping them both hard on the back, "but I could give a ferret's arsehole about that. I want to get home for presents," he said, and darted out of the lift when it stopped at the dorms.

"Happy Christmas, Jack!" Merriman called after him as he ran down the hall. "Happy Christmas, Ashton." Violet walked after Jack. "Happy Christmas, Ashton," Merriman repeated.

"Happy Christmas, Humphrey." Violet smiled then hurried to her room. She had forgotten for a moment that she was Ashton. She clearly needed a vacation from this ruse. In the room, Jack was throwing clothes haphazardly into a case. Of course, going home and pretending to be the perfect lady for Mrs. Wilks was just another ruse, but for some reason, she found herself looking forward to it. Which ruse, she wondered, was more true to her own character? Woman or scientist? And why did she have to choose?

With a sigh, she sat on her bed.

"Why so glum?" Jack asked, throwing something else in his case. "We're going home."

"I'm just not sure what to pack," Violet said. True, though not the real answer.

"You barely have to pack a thing," Jack said. "Leave all your clothes, bring whatever books and tools you'd like."

"Right," Violet said, taking out and opening her own case. She threw in all her books and her tool case and organized them. It took her a few minutes. Jack was still packing. "There," she said.

"Great," Jack said. "Want to do me a favor, then? Antony is supposed to meet us downstairs in about twenty minutes. Could you take Amelia down to the biology lab? Valentine said he pays a man to feed all the animals in the lab over the break and clean their cages. It's sad to think she'll be locked up all that time, but mum would kill me if I brought her home. She hates ferrets. Says they're like tall rats."

"You don't say," Violet said, picking up Amelia's cage. Amelia bounced around for a moment and then screeched. "Can't imagine why your mum wouldn't especially love this one, though." Jack stuck his tongue out at her, and Amelia screeched again.

Caged ferret in hand, Violet headed down to the biology lab. Illyria was almost empty already. Her footsteps echoed through the halls. Even the electric lights had been dimmed slightly, giving the already bronze and stone walls a golden tint. All the lights were shut in the laboratories she passed, except for the biology lab, which was dark, save for an eerie glow. Violet palmed blindly at the walls in the dark, looking for the light switch. The lights in the biology lab revealed Volio, working by a dim gas lamp over an apparently empty table covered with nothing but a bloody sheet. When the light went on, he looked up. Seeing Violet, he growled with annoyance and went back to his work. Violet felt her body go rigid and as cold as a steel rod. Volio had seen her kiss the duke. She had tried to tell her brother it was nothing, an easy problem, but she remembered the hate in his eyes as he blackmailed Miriam, and shuddered to think of it directed at her. There was nothing Volio wanted from her, though. She was safe from his machinations for now.

Volio seemed to be grasping at the air in front of him. Despite her fear, Violet peered forward, curious. "What are you doing?" Violet asked without meaning to. She took a breath and walked into the lab as though she wasn't afraid of Volio, as though she didn't know what he knew. She placed Amelia on a table that already held a few animals sleeping in cages.

"Research," Volio said, not looking up. "Go away."

Despite the part of her screaming not to, Violet crept closer and peered over Volio's shoulder. The white sheet was covered in a spray of blood as though something had been killed on it, and he was moving the empty air in front of him back and forth.

"You've killed one of the invisible cats!" Violet exclaimed.

"Your voice sometimes becomes disturbingly shrill," Volio said. "I suppose it's a side effect of the imbalances within you that make you want to be a woman."

"I didn't think they were real," Violet said nervously, ignoring Volio's taunt.

"You were down in the basement, weren't you? What, did you think the scratching noises and pressure against your leg was the wind? Reading too many romances, are you, Ashton? Perhaps some gothic book about a young pervert corrupting a nobleman?"

"When were you ever in the basement?" Violet asked, ignoring his questions. If this was the worst he was going to do with his information, she could handle it.

"Every class goes down in the basement for initiation," Volio said, clearly disappointed that Violet was unaffected by his accusations. "Did you think you were special? They've been doing it for ages."

"And you killed one of the invisible cats," Violet said, making her disgust obvious.

"We kill animals all the time for research," Volio said.

"But not intentionally. We try to keep them alive when we can. We don't murder a thing just to study why it's invisible."

"I know why it's invisible. I want to study its joints. The inside of the cats, it turns out, is not invisible." He smiled and lifted a hand up over the corpse. It dripped with sticky red blood. He waggled his fingers.

Violet clenched her jaw. "And I suppose the cats up here weren't good enough for you?" Violet asked, crossing her arms.

"It's easier to study the joints when the cat is dead, and Valentine gets upset if we a kill a thing without trying to give it feathers first."

"Why are you studying the joints?" Violet wondered if she could figure out what exactly he was up to.

"Go away," Volio said. He didn't sound like he would be any more forthcoming. Violet was shocked he had said as much as he had. Perhaps he wanted someone to brag to.

"Happy Christmas," Violet said as she left. She was still frightened of what Volio might do, or what he might say, but it was Christmas. There was nothing he would do until the new year, and he didn't seem keen on doing much besides mocking her.

"Shut the light," Volio said. Violet left it on and headed back to her room, where Jack was ready to leave.

"Home!" he said, lifting his bags in the air. A clanking sound came from one of them. Violet took her case and headed downstairs.

The last few students were straggling out into waiting coaches. The duke and Cecily stood at the door, waving good-bye to everyone. A light snow tumbled around them.

"Happy Christmas, Ashton," Cecily said as Violet and Jack came out. "Happy Christmas, Jack." She smiled warmly at both of them. Violet had to bite back a laugh as Jack grinned like an idiot.

"Happy Christmas, Cecily," Violet said. The duke stood by silently in a top hat, watching them. He offered no words. Neither did Violet.

"Have a lovely Christmas, Cecily. And you, too, sir," Jack said.

"I plan to. Thank you, Jack," Cecily said. The duke nodded slightly. Cecily waved a mittened hand at them as they spotted Antony and headed for him and their coach.

Antony smiled as they approached. "Eager to change out of those things?" he asked.

"I'd stick my tongue out at you," Violet said, "but people might see. And besides, I think you get quite enough tongue from our family."

Antony turned bright red and looked away, taking their bags and strapping them to the coach. Violet and Jack got in, and soon they were off across London. In the snow, the city seemed pale and serene. The Thames was a cool blue and black and rolled merrily along next to them, froth crowning its small waves.

"She wished me a Happy Christmas," Jack said, sighing as he settled back into his seat.

"Yes," Violet said, amused.

"You're jealous because the duke said nothing to you."

"I couldn't care less what he said or didn't say," Violet said, turning to look at the river again.

"Oh, don't pout," Jack said. "It's Christmas."

"I'm not pouting," Violet said, and crossed her arms. Jack laughed.

The coach pulled up in front of the town house, and Antony opened the door to let them both out. He was still blushing.

"Don't be so bashful, Antony," Violet said. "I was only teasing."

Antony said nothing, just went about refastening their baggage to the coach. Violet and Jack went into the house.

"Oh good, you're here," Ashton said as Violet and Jack came in.

"Go upstairs and change," Ashton said to Violet. "One of Mrs. Cap-shaw's dresses is waiting for you in your closet, and I already packed the rest of them. Quickly, please."

"Why the hurry?" Violet asked. She had been hoping for a cup of tea to aid her transition back to womanhood.

"Your maid will be here soon. Do you want her to see you dressed as a man?"

Violet sighed and hurried up the stairs. As promised, in her closet was a very fashionable dress of blue and gold, which she changed into as best she could alone. Her men's clothes she left lying on the floor.

"Ashton!" she called, leaving her room and heading back down-stairs. "I need your help fastening the dress in the back!"

At the bottom of the stairs, Jack, Ashton, and a strange woman looked up at her.

"I see what ye meant," the woman said in a heavy Scottish accent.

"Violet, this is Fiona Gowan. She's an actress, and has agreed to play the part of your maid."

"I've played maids before," Fiona said, walking up the stairs and standing behind Violet. "And queens, too," she said, fastening the dress. "But the theaters usually close down for Christmas, and I have no family, so when your brother offered me this . . . peculiar job, I figured why the 'ell not? Seems a lark, eh?" She finished fastening Violet's dress, and Violet turned around to face her.

"Nice to meet you," Violet said, extending a hand.

"And you," Fiona said, shaking it. Fiona was older, perhaps in the midst of her thirties, with a pointed face, jutting cheekbones, and large heavy-lidded eyes of a startling ice blue. Her hair was brown and pulled back in a tight bun, and she wore a black maid's outfit, though it was perhaps a little too tight, so her excellent figure could be too-plainly seen. A black ribbon adorned with sparkling jewels was tied tight around her neck. "We're going to have to do some-thing about your hair. But don't worry, I know some stage tricks for that. I used to have to do me own makeup. Aye, this'll be easy."

"Thank you," Violet said.

"Your brother says you're just not the sort to have a lady's maid, but that your keeper back home wouldn't approve of that. So I'll act like your maid and help you with your dressing, but I won't really *be* your maid, so don't treat me like one. I'm an actress. You're going to have to pick up your own clothes and the like."

"Of course."

"Frankly, your brother didn't mention you looked like something out of the wilds of Africa, but I imagine it shouldn't be too hard to fix you up. You have a pretty face, under all that wild hair and messy dressing. Come on, let's get you up to your room and make you up proper. You won't convince anyone you're a lady looking like that." Fiona turned and walked up the stairs. Violet bit her tongue and followed, turning back once to glare at Ashton and Jack, who were snickering.

In her room, Fiona glanced at the men's clothes on the floor, but said nothing. She ordered Violet to undress, tightened her corset, and sat her down in front of the vanity. She ran her hands through Violet's hair.

"So, how should we do your hair, then? There's not much of it . . . but that can be fixed with some false hair, which I just happen ta have. So how do you want it done? Jug-loops? A Molly's Flip? The Bearer Updo? A Downy Dahlia?" She leaned her head down so it was next to Violet's and smiled toothily at her in the mirror. "Maybe Miss Laycock's Crown?" She wiggled her eyebrows.

Violet creased her forehead in confusion. "Are those all real hairstyles?" she asked.

Fiona stood up straight again, and began to play with Violet's hair. "Oh, aye," she said with a wave of her hand. "I mean, I made up the names, is all. And some of the stylin'. Except for the jug-loops. But you don't want those. I'll give ye the Judy's Jolly—that'll look just fine with your pretty face."

"Just something simple," Violet said nervously. Fiona took out a bunch of pins and a lock of false hair, all of which she stuck in her mouth as she started do Violet's hair. Her fingers moved nimbly, taking the pins—and false hair—from her mouth when she needed them. Soon, Violet's hair was done up in thankfully simple style. When she was finished, she brushed Violet's face with powder, which made her sneeze. She was having trouble breathing and walking, her skin felt odd, and her head was on fire—except for the distressingly moist parts of the false hair that had been in Fiona's mouth—but when she looked in the mirror, she could see it was worth it. She looked like a gentlewoman in a play or painting. Her skin was perfect, and her eyes were bright. Even her hair seemed full of color, and matched the dress perfectly.

"Your coat is downstairs, miss," Fiona said with a wry smile.

"Thank you so much," Violet said. "You're amazing."

"It's not hard. I'll show ye how to do it yourself so I don't have to every day."

"That would be wonderful, thank you."

"We'd best be off, though. Your brother was looking impatient."

"Yes," Violet said, following Fiona out the door. She admired the way Fiona's body moved, like flowing liquid. Violet's body felt like rusty gears. Fiona stopped at the top of the stairs, took a small flask out of her bodice, and drank from it.

"I'm not fond of carriages," she said to Violet, "so I like to prepare a little."

She walked down the stairs and Violet followed, clinging to the banister for support.

"Wow," Jack said as she came into view. "You're gorgeous."

Ashton ran up the stairs to take Violet's other arm and lead her down.

"Don't let Cecily catch you saying such things to other women," Violet said.

"You're a miracle worker, Fiona," Jack said.

"Aye, you should see me onstage. If I can do all that to her, imagine what I can do to myself." She grinned wickedly at Jack, who laughed.

Violet eyed Fiona, who also laughed and took her flask out again for another drink. Ashton gave Violet her coat and hat, then walked her out to the coach and helped her into it. Antony tipped his hat. "You look lovely, miss," he said.

"Are you teasing me, too? Am I normally so ugly?"

"No, miss," Antony said, turning pale.

"Ignore her, Antony," Ashton said. "She's just annoyed she has to wear a corset."

In the coach, Violet crossed her arms. "Am I ugly?" she asked her brother.

"Not at all," Ashton said. "You come from the same stock as I do, after all. You're just usually . . . untidy."

Violet didn't know how to respond to that. She tried to settle into her seat, but her back was held tight by the corset, so she was forced to sit stiffly. Jack and Fiona got into the coach next, snickering. Ashton tapped the window, Antony whipped the horses, and they headed home.

Violet stared outside at the softly falling snow, turned gray by the smoke of the city. A horseless carriage passed by, its engine clanging and hissing and clearly in need of some repair. Violet imagined the duke seeing her like this. It would be interesting, but the last time he'd thought she was a woman, he treated her like a child, and when he thought she was a man, he . . . well, he kissed her back. If she had to choose between being treated like an idiot and being kissed, she would choose being kissed.

When they arrived home, Mrs. Wilks was waiting outside for them in the snow, which had turned orange in the dusk. The house glowed merrily behind her.

"Welcome back," Mrs. Wilks said, smiling slightly. "You look very lovely, Violet."

"Thank you, Mrs. Wilks."

"And how do I look, Mrs. Wilks?" Ashton asked.

"Your usual self," Mrs. Wilks said, bringing a hand to her mouth and faking a yawn.

"Which is to say, far too pretty for her liking," Jack said. "She much prefers her men brutish."

"As you may recall, Jack," Mrs. Wilks said, "Mr. Wilks was a very refined man. Your father is waiting for you at your home. Once Antony has unloaded Ashton and Violet's luggage, he can drive you over."

"No need, Mrs. Wilks," Jack said, sweeping his suitcase off the coach. "I can take myself."

"The snow is three feet deep," she said.

"I shall simply keep an image of you in my heart, Mrs. Wilks, and then I shall float above it all." Mrs. Wilks rolled her eyes, and Jack gave both Ashton and Violet a great hug before heading home.

"And this is Laetitia," Violet said, nodding at Fiona, "my lady's maid. She's been indispensable."

"Yes. I'm Mrs. Wilks, Laetitia." Mrs. Wilks said, stepping forward and looking Fiona up and down with an audible sniff, "I run the household. I like to think that my relationship with the children is close enough that they have grown fond of me, in a motherly sort of way—though, of course, I could never replace their real mother. You will stay in the room next to Violet's, so that you might tend to her needs. It isn't a very big room, and you'll have to share the bath with our cook, but I don't think she bathes very often, so that shouldn't trouble you much. There are a number of rules, but I assume you're familiar with them, having been in good houses before?"

"Aye . . . but good Scottish houses."

"Oh," Mrs. Wilks said, looking confused. "Then we'd best go over the rules."

Ashton grinned at Violet, took her arm, and led her inside as Mrs. Wilks listed the multitude of house rules. Inside, a fire was going and the house smelled of roasted pheasant and potatoes. Servants took their coats and showed them into the dining room for supper.

"It's good to be home," Violet said. "And even though I have to wear this damned corset, it's good to be a woman again, as well."

"Is it?"

"Certainly. Though I'm sure it's much more convenient to be a man, I find that after living as one for a while, I actually become rather attached to my femininity, or at least to the honesty of being myself."

"And this," Ashton asked, gesturing at her outfit, "is your honest self?"

Violet looked down at her skirts and rustled them slightly with her hand. "Perhaps a little fancier than usual, but when I look in the mirror, I feel quite at ease."

"Really? I would have imagined you wouldn't recognize yourself with all that powder on you."

"I can see myself clearly through it. The powder merely . . . highlights my features."

Ashton chuckled as Mrs. Wilks and Fiona entered.

"You will dine with the other servants, of course," Mrs. Wilks said. "I have the honor of dining with the family, if only to ensure proper table manners. I will show you to the servants' table. Children, you may begin without me."

Violet and Ashton nodded as Mrs. Wilks escorted Fiona out of the room.

"Did you tell Fiona what she was in for?" Violet whispered as their supper was served.

"I may have taken poetic liberties," Ashton said.

"Let's eat," Violet said. "I want to change into my night dress."

"I bought you a new night dress," Ashton said, grinning wickedly.

"Oh no. Is it horrid?"

"I suppose that depends on how you feel about lavender bows."

Violet cocked her head. "I don't feel any way at all about them. As long as it's comfortable."

"Oh," Ashton said. "Well, yes, of course it is."

"Will the bows make me look ridiculous?"

"Perhaps a little."

Violet shrugged. "A small price to pay."

"You are changing, sister, into someone quite different."

"Perhaps being a man has taught me a little about being a woman."

"No," Ashton said. "No, I don't think that's it at all."

XXI.

WHEN Ashton awoke and went downstairs, he was happy to find the tree up and decorated with gifts underneath it, but also sad, because his father wasn't sitting there, examining all the presents and trying to figure out what his children had gotten him. There were gifts under the tree from him—sent from America, Ashton assumed—as well as a long letter, but toys and words were no replacement for their father.

Ashton made a mental note to thank Mrs. Wilks for laying it all out. He was shirking his responsibilities as man of the house, and he knew it. It was difficult to think of himself as an adult. True, he lived alone in town, but he spent his days writing poems and his nights playing on the town. He had even coaxed Antony into coming with him to some art shows, theater, and poetry readings, after which they would go to Ashton's bedroom, where Ashton would write poetry about the lines of Antony's thighs.

Ashton sat on the floor in front of the tree and stared at the presents. They couldn't open them until Christmas Day, or Mrs. Wilks would be quite upset, but he could inspect them, and guess what they were. The tree shone with glass and copper ornaments, several made by Violet. When wound, they performed little clockwork routines, such as a man twirling his cane, or Father Christmas digging into his bag of toys. On top of the tree was a shining angel, ash branches in her hair and violets in her hand.

Christmas was in a few days, which meant the next few days would be filled with baking, decorating, and caroling. Ashton and Violet would have to string the house with ivy and hang cookies and berries on the tree. They would go caroling tomorrow, and to the masquerade pageant at the church that evening. He wondered if Violet could stand to do all that in a corset.

Ashton loved his sister dearly, and understood her passion and her unwillingness to be forced into the role society had carved for her: woman, keeper of the home, wife and mother. Ashton wasn't all that fond of the role society had set for him, either. But he had seen more of the world than Violet had—his gender had afforded him that much—while she had worked away in the basement, with no company but himself and Jack. Now she was out in the world, and he enjoyed watching the effect it had on her. She had always been fearless, but before, it had seemed that she was fearless because she didn't know better. Now she was fearless because she chose to be. She was growing, like a flower moved from a greenhouse to the outdoors.

And it seemed distinctly possible that she was falling in love. He doubted she knew it. She hadn't read much about love, he thought, aside from the poems he'd read aloud to her, and she probably hadn't really paid attention to those. She was probably as willing to listen to his advice on matters of the heart as he was eager to hear her recite the proper way to fix a horseless carriage. She'd have to learn in her own way.

"Oh! For a moment, I thought you were your father," Mrs. Wilks said, appearing in the doorway.

Ashton turned and stood. "Sorry, no," Ashton said.

"Well, of course you're not. I laid out all the presents he sent us, though. The presents you sent up a few days ago are here, too."

"My presents are here, too!" Violet called from upstairs. She bounded down the stairs in her nightgown and a housecoat, a bushel of poorly wrapped packages overflowing her arms. "Sorry!" she said, coming to the foot of the stairs. "I meant to put them down here last night when no one was looking, but I forgot."

"That's all right, dear," Mrs. Wilks said, taking the packages one by one from Violet and placing them under the tree.

"I hope everyone likes them," Violet said.

"I'm sure you picked out lovely presents," Mrs. Wilks said.

"Oh no, I made them."

"You made them? Where?"

"Violet set up a little lab in one of the empty rooms in the town house," Ashton said, standing. He shot a look at Violet, who had the decency to look momentarily ashamed.

"Still tinkering with your mechanics?" Mrs. Wilks asked.

"Well, yes," Violet said. "I don't see what's wrong with it. Everyone should have a hobby. And I think you'll agree that the perambulator I made for your cousin is far more useful than a needlepoint doily."

Mrs. Wilks raised an eyebrow and smiled a little. "It is at that. Just mind you don't get grease stains on your nice new clothes."

"Of course not," Violet said, looking a little surprised. Ashton was surprised, too. He had expected a nervous lecture from Mrs. Wilks on how ladies who invented didn't find husbands.

"As long as you behave like a proper lady, I'm sure I don't mind what your hobbies are," Mrs. Wilks said, seeing the surprise on their faces. "You're a very clever girl, Violet. I just want you to pay as much attention to being a girl as you do to being clever."

"Your present I worked especially hard on, Mrs. Wilks," Violet said, kissing Mrs. Wilks on the cheek.

"I'll be glad to see it, then. Now, we'd best have breakfast so you can go and change. I imagine there'll be visitors from the neighborhood today, and with your father gone, you two will have to host them."

"When is the church masquerade pageant?" Violet asked.

"Tomorrow night, dear," Mrs. Wilks said, patting them both on the back to herd them in the direction of the dining room. "Tomorrow you can go caroling, if you'd like."

"Sissy Travers already sent me a note telling me as much," Ashton said. "She's gotten quite the group together. You will come this year, won't you, Violet?"

"I can't sing a note," Violet said.

"Neither can Sissy, and if she doesn't mind her own lack of musicality, she certainly won't mind yours."

They were in the dining room now, but did not sit. Mrs. Wilks sighed and pulled out a chair for Violet. "It amazes me how you can both still get so caught up in your own banter that you forget where you are and what you're doing. Or do I need to ask you to sit down?"

Mrs. Wilks said. "The cook will bring out the buffet in a moment. And Violet, you must go caroling. It will make the neighbors positively glow in astonishment to see you dressed up and so pretty. I'm not sure they know what you look like without grease on your face."

Violet stuck her tongue out at Mrs. Wilks, who sighed again.

"I suppose I can't expect you to become a complete lady so quickly," Mrs. Wilks said, and walked to the kitchen to check on the cook. Ashton chuckled.

"Why is Christmas so busy?" Violet asked. "Was it always so busy?"

"We have to receive visitors, maybe go visiting ourselves, go to church, go caroling, give to charity, and finish decorating the tree and house. It has always been this way."

"Has it?"

"In the past, you just shut yourself up in the lab for long bouts."

"I miss Father," she said.

"Me, too."

"I think Mrs. Wilks does, as well."

Violet paused. "The duke's cousin, Cecily, seems to be in love with me," she said. "She wanted to visit over Christmas."

Ashton burst out laughing. "The one that Jack is in love with, whom you have me write those fake love letters from?"

"Yes."

"I must visit Illyria. It sounds more like a farce than a college."

"I don't know what to say to her. I like her, and wish we could be friends, but—"

"But you are not the man she loves."

"Yes."

"I think you should do what you can to be her friend. Then, maybe, after she learns the truth and her heart is broken, she can look back and realize you were good to her, despite the lies."

"I suppose. She asked me about my sister. It was very awkward. And she is the duke's ward. I told her I don't think its appropriate for us to be so close, but really I'm afraid it will draw the duke's attention." Violet looked down at her lap. Ashton smirked, but there was a flutter of worry in his stomach. He said nothing, though. They both worried when they thought about Violet's kiss with the duke.

"The cook will be out in a moment," Mrs. Wilks said, emerging from the kitchen. "She hasn't had to cook a proper meal in a while, so she's moving a mite slower than usual. Violet, does Laetitia normally have breakfast?"

"Oh," Violet said. "I don't think so, no." Mrs. Wilks looked at her quizzically. "She's very Scottish."

"Well, I'll ring her bell anyway," Mrs. Wilks said, and went back into the kitchen.

"It's Christmas," Ashton said. "Let's try to be merry, and forget all about Illyria, at least for a little while."

Violet took her brother's hand, and squeezed it.

⋇✺◈✺⋇

THE next few days passed in a blur of holly and snow. Violet felt as though she were experiencing Christmas for the first time. In the past, she had opened presents and caught snowflakes on her tongue, but spent most of the day making ornaments for the tree or, one year, a pair of huge feathered wings which opened at the push of a button for the angel to wear in the Christmas masquerade pageant. But this year, she sang carols and visited the neighbors, bringing them cookies she and Ashton had baked. They all cooed over her and told her how pretty she looked and what a fine young woman she had grown into, and those neighbors with eligible sons told her they would make sure their sons paid particular attention to visit her and her brother over the holiday. Violet found it all breathy and strange, wonderful and uncomfortable. Never had she been the center of such attention. She sometimes wanted to shout at them "I am a genius!" when they told her she was pretty, as though their noticing only her beauty made her dumb in their eyes, which was what she most feared.

"I suppose it is nice of them to pay me compliments, though," she said to Ashton as they rode home in the coach.

"Let them tell you you are pretty at first, then talk to them about machines you've invented and let them see your cleverness. No matter how coated in oil you are, or if you're holding a wrench aloft, no one sees genius. They see pretty or ugly. Be thankful that you are pretty." Violet bit her lower lip and furrowed her brow. She couldn't see a flaw in Ashton's logic, but she didn't like it, either. "I bought a present for Antony," Ashton said gently. "You must tell me if you think he will like it."

"Are you still at that?"

"He is a kind and gentle boy," Ashton said.

"But won't taking up with a coachman bring scandal on the family?" Violet refrained from also asking if Antony felt quite as invested as Ashton seemed to.

"Taking up with a man of any profession, stable boy or barrister, would bring scandal on the family. Which is why I am very discreet."

"You aren't in the least bit discreet."

"I am discreet when I need to be. Everyone may know of my proclivities, but I do not advertise them. I do not hold hands with Antony in public, or propose marriage to him. That is the way it is with men like me, and the way it will always be."

"That seems unfair."

"Most things in life are unfair, sister. Now, you must come with me to my room and tell me if you think he'll like the present."

The present was an exquisite silk scarf, a pair of leather gloves, and a duster, all of the highest quality. Violet fingered the scarf and told Ashton she knew Antony would love them, but the idea of him giving this beautiful present to the coachman saddened her in some small way. Ashton had no way of fighting for his equality as she did. If he were to perform some grand gesture, as she was currently undertaking, it would still never give him the public acceptance he deserved. It would only result in his being ostracized, and most likely imprisoned.

She didn't sleep well that Christmas Eve, but fretted on her pillow, uneasy without knowing why.

✦⚜✦

FIONA knew why *she* was uneasy. Mrs. Wilks was in every shadow, behind every corner, apparently watching her. "Is that how a lady's maid behaves?" she asked when Fiona slept in one day, or when she helped herself to a drink of brandy at supper.

Fiona had thought this was going to be an easy bit of work. Play lady's maid for a few weeks to some rebellious young rich girl. Good money, room and board in the winter, and maybe even a gift. Sure, the girl's hair had been strange, but easy to cover, and she seemed like a nice enough young lady, as rich girls went: she didn't judge Fiona for being an actress and was perfectly polite, if a little odd. Rich people were usually odd, though, so that wasn't unexpected.

But the house, that was unexpected. Servants, who were supposed to be her chums, eyed Fiona fearfully and scurried away from Violet as if she were a ghost. The only one who seemed to have any authority was Mrs. Wilks, a jumpy storm of a woman who felt no one could do anything properly, so she did it all herself, with a cloud of discontented sighs and visible disapproval.

This is not how good houses were run. At least, not in the plays that Fiona performed in. When she played a maid in those, she usually wore a much more comfortable outfit and talked about her mistress with the other servants. Sometimes she said something funny under her breath, always getting laughs from the audience. More often than not, she and a cook's boy or stable boy ended up rolling about together onstage, which was great fun if the men playing those parts were good-looking and not mollies. Sometimes she rolled around with them offstage.

But that was not the case here. Here, when she tried going down to the kitchen late at night to pour herself a drink, Mrs. Wilks was already there, asking her what it was she thought she was doing. When Fiona told her she was just looking for a drink, Mrs. Wilks looked scandalized and told her to go to bed. Told her to go to bed! Fiona hadn't been told to go to bed by anyone since she was six. But Fiona trudged back up the stairs, because what else could she do? She worked for that horse-faced idiot. At least for now.

This was not at all what she expected. So, on her third night, Christmas Eve, when she really couldn't go any longer without a drink, she crept slowly down the stairs to the kitchen again. She wasn't an expert at sneaking—usually it was her job, and her gift, to draw attention to herself—but she found it wasn't so hard to do. The manor did take on an eerie air at night, but she had walked the streets of London alone after dark. If she could survive the drunks and murderers there, she could certainly survive anything this place could put her through.

The kitchen was blissfully empty. She poked around quietly, looking for a bottle of spirits: ideally scotch, but anything would do. And then she heard a noise. Crouching against a shadowed cupboard, she tracked the room with her eyes. There was no movement in the kitchen. Then the sound came again: a loud clanging from the wine cellar, then a woman's voice, muffled but clearly angry.

Fiona walked over to the cellar door and pressed her ear against it as the sounds continued. Well, there was no liquor up here, so it was probably down below, where good families kept it. Which meant she'd have to go down there anyway if she wanted a drink. May as well investigate the commotion, too. She pushed the door open slowly. It creaked softly, but was drowned out by the steady, frustrated clanging. She crept down the stairs the way she'd been taught to onstage; arms up in the air, legs bent into nearly right angles and lifted carefully before being placed down again, but found that it made quite a bit more noise than she expected.

There were two doors at the bottom of the stairs. Light shone out from under the one that the noise was coming from. The other, Fiona reasoned, must be the wine cellar. She opened that door first. It was a grand affair as she had expected, but filled with rather more wine and rather less scotch than she was hoping for, but she found a small bottle of something that smelled like scotch. After a few swigs, it tasted like scotch, too, so that was good enough.

After finishing half the bottle and taking another for later, she wandered back out of the cellar. There was still light and noise and swearing coming from behind the other door. With her ear pressed to it, she recognized Mrs. Wilks's voice. Sensing that she was about to discover something that would allow her to drink as much as she liked, Fiona pushed the door open.

Mrs. Wilks stood in the middle of a great stone room, a fire roaring behind her and a table in front of her laid out with gears and metal parts. She was in a simple housedress, the sleeves rolled up, and her hands stained with grease and oil. Her hair was pushed back into a tight knot, and she wore large round glasses too big for her face.

"—and fuck it all!" she was saying as she threw a piece of metal on the table. It made a clanging noise. Fiona smiled and leaned against the doorframe, the bottle of liquor swinging in her hand. Mrs. Wilks looked up. "Shit," she said.

"An' good evenin' to you, Mrs. Wilks," Fiona said. Her Scottish accent grew stronger when she drank.

"I—," Mrs. Wilks began to say. Then shut her mouth. Fiona looked at what she held in her hand—a long column of smooth bronze with a rounded tip on one end, and what seemed to be a series of interlocking gears on the other. She looked back up at Mrs. Wilks, who sighed. "When Violet went off for the season, I thought I would come down here and clean up," she said, "but as I was cleaning up, I found that . . . I enjoyed putting things together. I liked the way the gears all fit into one another to make things work. And, since Violet was gone, I . . . thought it wouldn't harm anyone if I studied what it was she spent all day on."

Fiona didn't quite know what Mrs. Wilks was talking about, but she kept her eyes slightly squinted and focused on her. The drink had begun to have a strong effect on her, and there wasn't much she could think of saying at the moment.

"So," Mrs. Wilks continued, "I started to work a little. More of a game. And clean up, of course. But then, one night, I was sitting here, and some of the pieces I was tinkering with fell into my lap and . . . I had an idea. So, I've been working on this," she said, nodding at the odd device in her hand. "You won't tell anyone, will you?"

"What is it?" Fiona asked.

"It's . . . an oscillation therapy device," Mrs. Wilks said, turning bright red. Then, half ashamed, half proud, she brought the device up, turned a key on the end with gears, and released it. It was handheld, and pulsed slightly. Mrs. Wilks demonstrated by placing it on her shoulder, where it massaged her skin. "It relieves stress," she said, and then slowly broke into a wry smile.

Fiona grinned. "You're a right genius, Mrs. Wilks," she said. Mrs. Wilks blushed and looked at the floor. "And if you're willing to make more, I know plenty of ladies who would pay good money for that sort o' thing." Fiona stepped into the room, her feet slightly unsteady.

Mrs. Wilks looked up at Fiona, her eyes curious. "Do you?" she asked. Fiona nodded. This little job was going to be much more profitable than she had expected.

XXII.

JACK loved Christmas. He loved making garlands from berries and stringing them around the tree. He loved caroling with his mother and dressing the field mice he caught in little red or green coats and hats. He even loved going to church for the pageant and for Christmas morning services. But most of all, he loved the presents. This year he had gotten his father a fine wooden pipe with an ivory handle, and for his mother he had found a silk wrap. From them he had received a leather-bound copy of Mrs. Shelley's *Frankenstein* and a collection of bird whistles. They had all hugged one another and eaten Christmas breakfast; then Jack had put on his warm jacket and mittens and taken a bunch of wrapped boxes from his mother to deliver to the Adamses.

Jack knew the lands of Messaline well, probably better than Violet and Ashton did, as his father had supervised them and taken Jack out on his runs since he was little. The estate was lovely, particularly in the snow. At the top of a hill marking the end of the apple orchard and the beginning of the last long field before the manor itself, Jack paused and leaned against one of the trees. Below him rolled sheets of diamond-like frost, which stopped at the gardens surrounding the house proper. The sky glowed a soft white, like the color of a damp pearl, and snow seemed to fall from it without needing any science at all. Science seemed far away from here; Illyria, too. Thoughts of killer automata and blackmail and disguises had all been swept under the snow. There was no need to worry about any of that here. It was Christmas, after all. The skies were becoming darker as the clouds overhead thickened. Jack breathed in deeply and caught a snowflake with his tongue before finishing his walk.

"Jack, my fellow!" Ashton called when Jack came into the sitting room. Their tree was up, decorated and sparkling, and it looked as though they had only arrived back from church a few minutes ago, probably from a much later church service. "We were about to open presents, so your timing is perfect."

"Everything about me is perfect," Jack said, laying his presents under the tree. "I bring gifts from my parents."

"And we have gifts for you to take to your parents, as well," Violet said, grinning archly. "But first you must stay awhile. After we open gifts, we will eat and drink eggnog."

"Well, I would never say no to eggnog," Jack said.

"I'd imagine not," Ashton said, clapping him on the back. "Mrs. Wilks!" he called. She appeared in a doorway, where she had probably been waiting. "Let the servants know that we will be opening gifts and that they all have a gift under the tree as well."

"Of course," Mrs. Wilks said, and vanished again into the shadows. The servants all filed in silently and stood around the edge of the room. Mrs. Wilks went to the tree and handed out their gifts to each of them. Violet poured eggnog into glasses and handed them to Jack and Ashton.

"How has your Christmas been so far, Jack?" Violet asked.

"Quite lovely," Jack said. "Da' and I built a snowman yesterday. It was fun."

"I don't think I've ever built a snowman," Violet said. "At least, not since I was very little."

"That's because you'd probably use clockwork parts made of ice to bring the thing to life," Ashton said. "So we tried to keep you away from snowman building."

The servants opened their presents quietly save for small gasps of delight. Ashton had done the shopping this year, and he had excellent taste. With murmured thanks, the servants, except for Mrs. Wilks and Fiona, retired to the kitchen to admire each other's gifts and drink their own eggnog.

"Mrs. Wilks, have I ever built a snowman?" Violet asked.

"I'm sure you did once, yes, when you were five or so."

"I wish to do it again."

"Well, there's plenty of snow. But why don't you open your gifts first?"

Violet grinned and walked to the tree and sat beneath it, picking out her presents. Mrs. Wilks poured glasses of eggnog for herself and Fiona before they joined the children and opened their own gifts.

From America, Mr. Adams had sent a turkey feather hat for Mrs. Wilks and a book of American poems and a jacket for Ashton. For Violet, there was a set of American tools, supposedly used by the great American train engineer Matthias Forney, along with the full schematics of the airship he had taken to America. There was also a large set of arrowheads for the twins to share. Violet pored over the schematics as though her father were there looking at them with her, and rubbed the arrowheads in her fist. For a crushing moment, she felt a sense of loss at not having him there, but then she read his letter and felt better. It was a short letter, lacking in poetry and detail, but it described his travels in America, and his meetings with various astronomers.

"I wish he would describe America," Violet said. "I think it must be very lovely."

"Certainly not lovelier than England," Mrs. Wilks said, adjusting her hat.

"No," Violet said, "but I have never left England. A description of exotic places would be nice to hear."

"Well, when he returns, you can question him in as much detail as you like."

They opened the rest of the presents next. Jack had gotten everyone lovely articles of clothing: scarves and gloves of fine quality, soft to the touch, as well as a leather-bound journal for Ashton and a lady's pocket watch for Violet. Everyone agreed, though, that Violet's handmade gifts were the best of the lot. For Jack—and, truthfully, for herself as well—she had created a cage with an enclosed bottom level that had been carefully soundproofed. For Ashton, she'd made a lock that even her automatic skeleton key could not open, and a music box with an image of their mother and father inside, dancing. And for Mrs. Wilks, she created an umbrella that opened with the press of a button, and spun itself dry and closed with the press of another.

"What a marvelous mechanism," Mrs. Wilks said as the umbrella spun around again.

After opening presents and drinking their fill of eggnog, all of them went out into the snow, which was falling quite heavily now, and built a snowman. And though she thought hard about it, Violet could not see any way to properly mold ice into gears to make the snowman live.

⚜

CECILY and Ernest were also building a snowman, in the barren garden next to Illyria. Ada, who stayed with them for Christmas— she had two living children of her own, but Anne was always in Arabia with her horses, and Ralph's wife, Mary, talked of nothing but conservative politics since her father's death—did not feel like joining in the building, so she sat on a bench nearby, sipping warm eggnog.

Cecily giggled as she packed the head on top of the creation. "What shall we use as eyes?" she asked.

"Coal is traditional," Ada said, and held out two lumps of coal.

Cecily kissed her for her foresight. "Thank you, Auntie Ada," Cecily said, smiling at the snowman as she gave him eyes.

"I'm cold," Ada said. "Let's go back inside and play with our presents again."

Inside, in the sitting room, their unwrapped gifts lay amidst a pile of wrapping paper under the tree. Their tree was very traditional, with a Nuremberg angel sparkling on top, and strings of berries, paper chains, and garlands wrapped around it. Here and there, a few German glass ornaments shone.

From her cousin, Cecily had recieved an automaton dog that would chase after a magnetized ball, and, from Ada, a book on early chemical development. Ernest had recieved a book on plant life as well as a small glass terrarium filled with exotic plants from Cecily.

Ada had given him a new suit. And Ada now had an automatic card shuffler and a new deck of cards from Ernest, and a locket from Cecily with both of their pictures in it.

Supper would be served soon. Ada lit a cigar, sat down in one of the chairs in the sitting room, and pressed the button on her machine, causing the cards to shuffle themselves. She laughed, delighted. "Anyone want to play cards? If you think I'm cheating, blame Ernest."

"I'll play cards," Cecily said, "though we don't have enough players for bridge."

"Let's play cards after supper," Ernest said. Ada snorted and inhaled deeply on her cigar. Cecily picked up the silver ball and threw it. The dog chased after it until it was close enough to grab it in its jaws, then sat down.

"Sorry I couldn't think of a way to make it return the ball," Ernest said.

"It's quite delightful the way it is," Cecily said. "And besides, running after it is good exercise." Ada laughed. "Ernest," Cecily said, taking the ball from the dog's mouth, "tomorrow, we should go for a ride in the country. Through the snow. I think it would be lovely." The automaton dog's head followed the ball—almost hungrily, Cecily thought.

"I don't know," Ernest said. "I should prepare for the next trimester."

"You'll have days to prepare," Cecily said. "And we haven't been out in ages."

"We were just out."

"Out of the city." Cecily pouted, then dropped the ball at her feet. The automaton dog picked it up and held it out for her.

"Oh, go for a ride, Ernest," Ada said, blowing smoke out over the room. "You're in here too much, and Cecily wants to go."

"Will you come with us?" Ernest asked.

"No. Riding isn't fun when you're as old and your bottom gets to be as thin as I am and mine is." She puffed on the cigar. "Besides, there's a poker game I'm already committed to."

"Please, Ernest?" Cecily said, "I know exactly where we could go, as well."

"You do?" Ernest asked.

"Yes," Cecily said innocently. "It's a lovely landscape, and I'm sure the trees will look quite pretty covered in snow."

"Very well," Ernest said. "But I'm bringing my books with me, in case we stop and I have time to work on them."

"Don't be such a bore, Ernest," Cecily said, smiling. A servant rang a bell to let them know that supper was ready. They ate roast goose and cranberries and a dozen other Christmas delights before they all went off to bed, Cecily dreaming of her trip to Ashton's home tomorrow.

⁕⧁⁕

BY morning, the snow had stopped falling and frozen, so all of London looked like a great ice sculpture, or a city of glass. Cecily dressed alone, as Miriam was still gone, and she didn't think she needed a maid to help her. If she could have it her way, she would wear her nightshirt all day, but she knew she was pretty enough to be noticed no matter how she dressed, and she preferred to be thought well of at first glance, and not as disheveled or insane. She tied her corset a bit looser than was fashionable so that she could breathe easily, but otherwise she looked quite presentable. She pinned her hair up in a bun, chose a blue hat to match her dress, and went downstairs for breakfast. Ernest was already there, and Ada, too, eating and reading their newspapers. Cecily sometimes wondered if normal families talked over breakfast, or if they all just read the newspaper in silence as hers did. Cecily helped herself to eggs and toast and took out her diary to reread at the table. Often, when bored, she found the sensationalism of her diary to be a great diversion.

After breakfast, Ada left them to return to her own home in town, and Cecily, barely able to contain her excitement, got into the coach with Ernest and whispered their destination in the driver's ear.

The drive was quite soothing, Ernest had to admit. He had nearly told Ada about his kiss, asked her what it was that she felt was so striking about Ashton. But that, he decided, would have been awkward, and most definitely won Ada their bet. So he had remained quiet. In fact, he was quite determined to avoid thinking of young Adams ever again, if he could. The rolling, snow-covered countryside helped him to feel good about this decision.

The manor whose driveway they pulled up into did not. "Cecily, where are we?" he asked.

Cecily was glowing. "This is the Adams estate," Cecily said, smiling. "I thought we could call on them."

Ernest felt his breath wheeze out of him. "Call on a student? That would be most undignified!" he said. The world seemed to be spinning around him. "Quite inappropriate."

"Don't worry, Cousin," Cecily said as the coachman opened the door. "Ashton won't even be here. He is with his aunt and uncle for the holiday. We are calling on his sister, Violet."

"His sister?" Ernest asked. Cecily noticed the corners of Ernest's mouth briefly perk up at this before his brow settled into a scowl. She felt quite sure, all at once, that Ernest was in love with Violet, and it delighted her.

"Do you know her?" Cecily asked coyly. She was now standing outside the carriage, though Ernest was still sitting inside.

"She delivered her brother's application."

"Well, then you must come with me, if you know her already," she said, and started for the house, leaving Ernest to hop out of the coach and chase after her.

✥⊚✥

INSIDE, Violet, Ashton, and Jack were playing darts in the lounge. Mrs. Wilks was the one who came in to announce the unexpected arrivals. "There is a Duke of Illyria and Miss Cecily Worthing here to pay a visit," she said, apparently just as surprised as they were that the word duke had just come out of her mouth. Violet, Ashton, and Jack stared at her, stricken. Jack began to chuckle. "How do you know a duke?" Mrs. Wilks whispered. "Did you meet him through your father's friends?" Her eyes were larger than Violet had ever seen them.

"Well, send them in, then, Mrs. Wilks," Jack said. Mrs. Wilks waited a moment longer for an explanation, but when it was clear none was forthcoming, she nodded and left the room.

"I suppose we're lucky you're not the sort of girl who faints," Jack said to Violet.

"I told her I—I mean, Ashton—wouldn't be here. I said that he would be away and our cousin Ashton would be here instead."

"I'm the cousin again, am I?" Ashton said.

"This is . . . ," Violet began.

"Quite amusing," Jack said.

"No!" Violet nearly screamed. Ashton and Jack stared at her, now much more nervous. "We will be polite. But not too polite, so that they leave quickly," Violet said, her hands out, palms down and bouncing, as if motioning them to sit down, "and so that we give nothing away." She thought for a moment. "In fact, I may have to be rude."

Ashton raised his eyebrows, but he poured himself a glass of brandy and said nothing.

Mrs. Wilks came in to announce the guests once more. Cecily and the duke entered and looked around. Everyone stared at one another in silence.

"Perhaps you'd leave us alone with our guests, Mrs. Wilks?" Ashton said. Mrs. Wilks narrowed her eyes. She clearly wanted to stay. But Ashton knew she was far too intimidated by the presence of a duke to argue her case, so she curtseyed slightly and vanished into the kitchen.

"Pray let me introduce myself to you," Cecily said, approaching Violet. "I am Cecily Worthing." Violet shook hands with Cecily. "Perhaps your brother has mentioned me?"

"No," Violet said, sitting again, "he has not."

"Ah," Cecily said, "well, let me introduce the Duke of Illyria, my cousin and guardian."

"We have already met," Violet said, her voice cool. Ashton and Jack stared at Violet. She had taken on a demeanor they had never seen before. Her back was arched, her chin high, her face pale. "You surprise me, sir," Violet said to the duke, "by your visit here. While I did say our gardens were lovely, I am afraid that in winter they look just like everyone else's."

"Ah, yes," Ernest said, clasping his hands behind his back. He didn't miss the coldness of her tone. No one in the room did.

"But we do have—that is, there is an astronomy tower," Ashton said, stepping forward. "I'm Ashton, Violet's cousin. I've heard of you, of course, sir. Perhaps you'd like to see the tower?"

"Yes," Cecily said. "You ought to take dear Cousin Ernest to see the tower. You as well, Jack. Violet and I will talk as ladies do." Jack snickered at this, but Violet shot him a look that quickly made him stop.

"Yes," Jack said, "let's all go see the astronomy tower. Of course, it cannot be compared to the one at Illyria, sir." The three men left the room, and Cecily sat in the chair next to Violet.

"Something tells me we're going to be great friends," Cecily said. "I already like you more than I can say, and my first impressions of people are never wrong." Violet found she could not stop staring at Cecily, at her audacity. She had to force the panic from her throat as she nodded. "And I hope you will call me sister," Cecily said. "You see, I love your brother, and I am going to be his." She sighed and leaned back into her chair.

"May I offer you some tea, Miss Worthing?" Violet asked, standing. She felt extremely uncomfortable, and suspected that Cecily could see it in her body. "Perhaps some cake, or bread and butter?"

"No thank you, Miss Adams," Cecily said. "But I fear what I have said has caused you discomfort. I suppose I was too brusque in my manner. I should say that your brother has not yet proposed. But I do hope he will. I have come here with the express purpose of becoming your friend, so that when your brother and I become engaged, you and I will already be thick as thieves."

"Ah," Violet said, sitting down. She hoped Mrs. Wilks was not listening. She was unsure of what to do—she could probably break Cecily's heart with the right lie, but she did want to be her friend. "Well, I hope we shall be great friends, too," she said carefully, "but let us not talk of my brother."

"Are you arguing?"

"Yes," Violet said, thinking fast. "We had quite a row when he got back. He wanted to take the letter our father sent us from

America with him to read on his trip, but I had been saving it for him, so we could read it together." Violet was ashamed of how well she could lie, but relieved.

"That does seem rather selfish," Cecily said, her brow creasing with confusion. Violet suddenly realized how she could break Cecily's heart and still be her friend.

"He is quite selfish," Violet said. "I should tell you, Miss Worthing, for I like you as well, that my brother can sometimes be quite a brute."

"No!" Cecily said.

"He has a great many lady admirers," Violet continued. "I suspect I may already have an illegitimate nephew." Cecily gasped. "My poor, wounded, Cecily," Violet said, and laid a hand on her knee.

Cecily clasped it in her own. "But he seems so sensitive."

"He is," Violet said. "But men are many things, aren't they?"

"Yes," Cecily said, looking up at Violet, her eyes wet, "and thank you for telling me. I now know what I must do."

"Yes?" Violet said, clasping Cecily's hand.

"I must change him," Cecily said with complete resolve. Violet held back a sigh. "Like a poor, diseased plant, I will take the good parts of Ashton, the parts I have seen, and help them to grow, while cutting off the disease. Yes. I understand now that love is a difficult thing, but I am prepared for the battle ahead. And I hope you will aid me in it, my sweet, wronged Violet," she continued, clasping Violet's hand to her chest, "for he has hurt you, too. But with you as his sister and me as his friend, we will change his deceitful ways, will we not?"

"Yes," Violet said weakly. Her plan had failed her.

"And now," Cecily said, dropping Violet's hand and standing, "if you don't mind, I *will* have some bread and butter."

"Of course," Violet said, defeated, and rang the bell.

When Mrs. Wilks came in, Violet asked for some bread and butter for both of them. Upon her return, Mrs. Wilks stared at Cecily for a long while before setting down the bread.

"How do you know Violet, if I may be so bold?" Mrs. Wilks asked, forcing her mouth into a clownish grin.

"Oh," Cecily said, "we've only just met. I know her brother, Ashton."

"Oh," Mrs. Wilks said, and nodded, as though this somehow made more sense to her.

"Perhaps you could leave us to talk, Mrs. Wilks?" Violet asked sweetly. Mrs. Wilks nodded again, and left.

As they were eating, Cecily started to tell Violet about her scientific projects, which Violet knew about already, but managed to seem interested in nonetheless. A few moments later, the men came back in and Violet felt herself stiffen.

"It's a lovely astronomy tower," the duke said, "and your cousin knows all the details of the construction."

"As do I," Violet said.

"I'm sure," the duke said, coloring slightly.

"We were just having some bread and butter and tea. Would you gentlemen like anything?"

"I will have some," Jack said, sitting down next to Cecily. "Do you have any muffins?"

"We do," Ashton said. "I'll get them myself."

"I thought perhaps you would honor me with a tour of the grounds," the duke said to Violet. "I saw what looked to be a lovely cluster of ash trees by a pond."

"Yes," Violet said. "It was my mother's favorite spot."

"And Ashton said that violets grow there in spring—is that what inspired your name?" the duke asked, smiling.

"Yes. I'm afraid the violets are not in bloom, however," Violet said.

"I'm well aware, Miss Adams."

"And yet you bring them up anyway. Tell me, Miss Worthing, does your cousin talk of nothing but flowers to you as well? When I met him, it seemed he was quite incapable of discussing anything else."

"Well, Ernest does like his flowers . . . ," Cecily began nervously.

"I believe you overestimate my interest in botany, Miss Adams," the duke said with an arched eyebrow.

"I believe you overestimate mine, sir," Violet responded, her eyebrow equally arched. Her heart was beating quite rapidly, and she felt her face flush.

"Oh, just show him the trees, Violet," Ashton said, coming back in with a plate of muffins. Mrs. Wilks followed with a tea tray and several more cups. They placed their respective platters down on the table.

"We've never had such grand company here before," Mrs. Wilks said. "Ashton, how is it you know—?"

"Very well," Violet said, standing, "I'll take you outside, if Miss Worthing doesn't mind being left alone in the company of two such rogues."

"Jack is perfectly harmless," Cecily said, "and I'm sure your cousin is quite charming."

"Cousin?" Mrs. Wilks asked, looking at Ashton.

"I am," Ashton said, with a wink. "I'm very little besides, in fact."

"And I am harmless, as she says," Jack said with large eyes.

Violet rolled her eyes.

"Who is your cousin, Violet?" Mrs. Wilks asked again.

"Why don't you put on the kettle for more tea, Mrs. Wilks," Ashton said, grasping Mrs. Wilks's shoulders and directing them toward the door. Mrs. Wilks walked out, shaking her head.

"She sometimes becomes confused around the holidays," Ashton said. "But she's been working for us for so long, she's like part of the family."

Cecily nodded sympathetically.

"Will you show me the grounds, then, Miss Adams—even if they are covered in snow?"

"I suppose," Violet said.

The duke offered his arm to her, and she took it lightly, nearly pulling away as their bodies touched and a strange sensation crept from her arm to her spine and made her shiver. She kept her face stern, however, and tried to look bored. Nonetheless, the cold wind that blew over them as they stepped outside was a relief to her, as it cooled her face, which had grown quite warm. Violet felt confused. She was angry with the duke. Seeing him again while in a woman's guise, she remembered the last time they had so met, and how he had talked of nothing but flowers, as though she were a silly-minded girl. But she also remembered the experimental kiss, and though she could see no logical reason to continue that experiment, the results of it lingered in her mind and body.

"These, then, are the trees," Violet said when they had reached the cluster of ash. She pulled back her arm to gesture at them.

"They look quite lovely," the duke said. "I should like to come see them in the spring, perhaps."

"You should feel welcome to, sir. You needn't even bother stopping in. Just drive your coach up, look at the trees awhile, and leave again."

"I sense, Miss Adams, that you do not like me."

"I do not like that you seem to only be capable of broaching subjects floral or arboreal when you speak to me."

"I apologize," the duke said sincerely. "What would you prefer to talk of?"

Violet looked at him for a moment, evaluating the situation. "My brother," she said, "wrote a most clever essay on space travel. He tells me you disagree with his points. Why?"

"Ah," the duke said, looking a bit hurt by the bluntness of her statement. "It is not that I disagree with his points. I feel only that his scope is limited. While a spaceship powered by a mechanical spring and electricity is possible, a better craft could be made by using all the sciences harmoniously. And I do feel quite strongly that a chemical reaction of some sort would be required for launching such a vessel."

"You don't agree that a large enough spring could propel such a craft out into the æther?"

"I think it could work, but the energy required to turn such a spring is tremendous. Why not just use a chemical reaction?"

"It could damage the ship, and carrying fuel will weigh it down more."

"You and your brother seem to feel that a chemical reaction necessitates some sort of damage to the ship. But we could easily account for such a thing, and for the weight. The chemical sciences make such a thing fairly easy to predict and prepare for. Besides, then the ship would be able to take off again from the planet's surface, something you haven't taken into account at all."

Violet smiled. He was finally treating her with respect, but she was too cold to enjoy it fully. "Let's continue this inside, by the fire, shall we?"

"Of course," the duke said, offering his arm. Violet took it in hers and laid her other hand on his elbow. "You really don't like flowers, do you?" he asked as they walked toward the manor.

"I like flowers just fine. I dislike being thought the sort of lady who thinks of nothing but flowers."

"Ah," the duke said, looking contemplative. "I apologize for ever having given that impression."

"Argue with me some more," Violet said as they reached the door. "Convince me that my brother's theories are wrong."

They debated for about an hour longer, while Cecily, Jack, and Ashton played cards. When the sun turned a deep orange, the duke and Cecily bade everyone a friendly farewell. Violet admitted that the duke's reasoning on space travel was well thought out, but would not concede that it was better than her brother's theories.

"May I write you, and try to convince you in my letters?" the duke asked.

"You can try," Violet said.

The duke grinned and stepped into his coach, and he and Cecily rode off into the snow.

"WHO were those people?" Mrs. Wilks asked after they left. "And why did they think you were cousins?"

"I'm the cousin," Jack said quickly. "I confess, I masquerade as their cousin in town when we go out. Much more regal sounding than son of their estate manager. You won't tell, will you, Mrs. Wilks?" Jack got down on one knee and looked pleadingly at Mrs. Wilks.

"But she said 'Jack and your cousin,'" Mrs. Wilks said, looking confused. "Which would mean Jack and your cousin were different persons. I'm almost sure."

"No," Ashton said, "she said I was charming, and that Jack was harmless."

"Yes . . . ," Mrs. Wilks said.

"Dear Mrs. Wilks," Jack said, taking her hand, "I would be ever so grateful if you didn't mention this to anyone." He looked up at her imploringly.

She blushed slightly and nodded. "Of course not," she said. "Goodness, if I met a duke, I'd be so flustered, I might say I was the Queen." Mrs. Wilks shook her head and went back into the kitchen for more tea. Violet, Jack, and Ashton breathed in deeply and let their shoulders slump in relief. Mrs. Wilks came out and refilled their cups. "What a Christmas. My sister will never believe me when I say there was a duke here."

Ashton chuckled. "Have some tea, Mrs. Wilks," he said. She nodded, sat down, and began to sip the cup of tea she had just poured for Jack. Everyone laughed, drank, and enjoyed the heat from the fire. In the sparks from the logs, Violet thought she saw the arc of a launching æthership, leaping away from earth.

XXIII.

THE New Year came and went quickly, and then it was time to drive back to London. Fiona left them there, with her payment, a promise to play the part again come Easter, and a kiss on the cheek for Violet. She had, in the end, enjoyed her Christmas, and Violet had never once asked her to pick up her clothes, or treated her like a maid in any way.

The next day, Violet trimmed her hair, bound her breasts, and dressed in men's clothing once more. She had forgotten how uncomfortable it was, and gasped as she pulled the cloth tighter and tighter around her bosom. Then, with an odd feeling in her stomach, a mix of excitement and dread, she and Jack walked back into Illyria and returned to their room.

Little had changed. The gears still cranked on in their spots, and the bronze halls were still filled with the sound of them. Violet was surprised by how easily she slipped back into her routine of lying. She made up elaborate stories about her trip to her aunt's for Cecily, who now often worked statements about following one's "natural goodness" into conversation. She went out drinking with Toby, Drew, and Miriam, and they all talked of their various holidays. Classes proceeded as they usually did, though now the work was harder and faster, and sometimes even Violet had to work on Bunburry's assignments during her independent time.

About three weeks into the new trimester, Cecily came rushing into the mechanical lab, so excited that Miriam had to run to keep up with her. Panting, Cecily placed a shining white gear in front of Violet. "It works," Cecily said. Violet stared at the gear a second or two before it sank in, then she picked it up. It was smooth, light,

and felt like glass. She slammed the gear down on the table. It didn't
break. It didn't dent. It was completely undamaged.

"Brilliant!" she said, forgetting to lower her pitch for a moment,
which probably made Ashton seem manic with excitement. "Can
you make the rest of the pieces?"

"I have already begun creating the molds for them."

"This is quite amazing, Cecily. You should go show your cousin.
I'm sure he'll be very proud."

Violet had received one letter from the duke, sent to the house in
London, then sent back to Illyria by Ashton. It was an oddly dry letter,
filled with scientific argument, almost cold. Violet had responded in
kind.

"I will show him, but I wanted you to see it first. Now you can
create your engine."

Violet was so excited she nearly jumped. "Thank you so much,
Cecily! Together, we will outshine everyone at the faire."

"You will outshine them, Ashton. And then, when the world
sees how brilliant you are, you can truly become the man you were
meant to be: one of noble mind and noble spirit."

"Perhaps," Violet said, "but I must do my part, now that you have
done yours." Violet turned to the metal on the table before her as
she said this. She was barely halfway finished with creating the actual machine.

"I trust you shall, Ashton," Cecily said, laying her hand on Violet's briefly. "Now I am going to tell my cousin of my achievement."

"Thank you again, Cecily," Violet said as she walked away.

Cecily looked back over her shoulder coyly. "No need to thank
me, Ashton. It is indeed a pleasure to work with you."

And then she left. Violet picked up the gear again and dropped
it on the floor. It clanged, but didn't break. Violet was impressed.
And now she was all the more aware that she had to work harder.

❊❖❊

THAT evening, she was going over plans in her room, figuring out
how best to proceed with her work, when Jack came in, holding
a larger-than-average cage. In it was a nervous-looking mottled

gray-and-white bunny with floppy ears and a twitching nose. Violet dropped to her knees to look more closely at the rabbit, which was adorable, with large black eyes and soft fur.

It looked back at her and twitched its nose curiously. "Fuck off," said the rabbit in a squawking voice.

"This is Oscar," Jack said as Violet backed away, frowning. "Valentine said I couldn't keep him in the lab because his language is undignified."

"Oh, bugger," said Oscar.

"I transplanted the voice box of a parrot into him. But the parrot was brought to England by sailors, and apparently picked up a few things."

"Oh, bugger," repeated Oscar. The voice was definitely parrot-like.

"The parrot, meanwhile, can no longer talk, but seems to sniff a lot, and has shown a sudden fondness for carrots."

"So the foul-mouthed rabbit stays with us?" Violet asked.

"I hope it won't offend your delicate sensibilities too much," Jack said.

"Shite," said Oscar, wiggling his nose. Jack set the cage down and opened it. Oscar nervously stepped out, sniffing the room, then bounded under Violet's bed.

"Fuck off," came the muffled voice from underneath.

"Well," Violet said, looking at her bed, "that's going to make sleeping a little more difficult."

"I find it soothing," Jack said.

Violet shook her head in exasperation and turned back to her plans. They were for the engine itself. Cecily had finished the pieces, and it was now up to Violet to assemble them.

❦

WHICH she did, a few days later. Violet and Cecily stood over the finished engine and stared down at it, breathless with anticipation. The final product was not very impressive to look at: just a bronze orb, about the size of a head. Out of one end came a stem-winding key, and out of the other, a rod with a gear on it. Cecily had a pocket watch out and was looking at it. With a nod, Violet turned the key three times and then stood back. The engine started to tick and rattle slightly, but did not roll off its stand.

Cecily laid her hand on it for a moment. "It produces vibrations," she said dreamily.

"Of course it does," Violet said. "It works like clockwork: all the pieces turning together, while a pendulum swings back and forth and back and forth."

They stared at it awhile longer. After twenty minutes, it showed no signs of slowing down, and Violet took out more gears to assemble for the rest of the machine. Cecily continued to time the engine. When the period was over, Violet took it to bed with her. It was still going in the morning, so the next night, Cecily took it. It ran for nearly three days.

"One turn will keep it running for a day," Cecily said, amazed.

"It can keep any machine going, as well," Violet said. "Imagine the possibilities of it."

"You have to keep it a secret until the faire," Cecily whispered. "Otherwise people will tamper with it and steal it. Reveal it at the faire in front of everyone, so no one can doubt it is your invention."

"I plan to," Violet said.

"Where will you hide it until then?" Cecily asked. "Would you like me to keep it?"

"I can store it in my room," Violet said. "Jack is trustworthy."

"Perhaps you could keep it in one of the storerooms in the basement," Cecily said.

"Oh no," Violet said. "I have been in the basement, and it is entirely too mysterious to keep anything safe. I'll put it in my room."

"What do you mean, 'mysterious'?"

Violet smiled and took out more pieces of her machine. As she assembled them, she told Cecily the story of their initiation the first night. Having once encountered Cecily while a woman, Violet now found it harder to remember that she was supposed to be a man when interacting with her, and sometimes found her voice slipping, or her mannerisms getting sloppy. But she also found herself thinking more and more of Cecily as a close friend. It was only after Cecily was gone that she would remember that she was not a close friend of hers, but a close friend and admirer of Ashton's. And then there was the matter of Violet's growing admiration for the duke, admiration she hoped was reciprocal, although she couldn't be sure. After all, it was Ashton who had kissed the duke, and now the duke avoided him. But the duke didn't avoid Violet. He wrote her letters, and instead of fluff about flowers, these letters were now filled with real scientific argument: it was a correspondence between two great minds. The duke wrote Violet that he was building a prototype of an æthership, and asked for her opinions on how things should work. She sent him sketches of parts, and he sent her back his corrections to them, some of which she accepted. But he made no romantic overtures in his letters. Violet wondered if perhaps he was an invert like the real Ashton, and was writing Violet only in the hopes of winning the fake Ashton's favor. She told herself that such things didn't matter in an intellectual relationship, but sometimes, during his lectures, Violet found herself staring at the duke's lips and remembering the softness of them, and imagining his hands around her waist.

Violet kept the engine in her room, and Oscar grew particularly fond of it, often rubbing up against it and murmuring affectionate obscenities. Jack didn't seem to mind, but Jack had grown oddly distant. Not unfriendly, just very involved in his work, staying in the lab until late to perform odd experiments on his menagerie.

Which is why, about five weeks into the new trimester, when Toby suggested they all go out to a show, Violet agreed, and demanded that Jack go as well. Violet didn't ask what sort of show it was, just piled into the coach with Toby, Drew, Miriam, and Jack, and let Toby tell the driver where to go. She sat across from Miriam, who had seemed a little nervous lately. Violet knew that she and Toby had spent the break together in France, and wondered if perhaps Miriam was pregnant and hadn't yet told Toby, which would account for her anxiousness. But that anxiousness, Violet saw, dwindled the farther and farther they drove from Illyria, so Violet supposed it was probably only Miriam's fear of being caught. She patted Miriam on the back and said, "Don't worry, no one will recognize us where we're going."

Miriam gave her an odd look, but smiled. "I'm sure," she said.

The theater, if it could be called that, was a ramshackle old building with one poster outside advertising Mr. Pip's Prancing Ponies. It showed a circus ringmaster with a whip circled by beautiful young women clad in very little besides saddles, but with the heads of horses. Violet paused, unsure of what she had gotten herself into.

"Oh, come now," Toby said. "Or are your sensibilities more sensitive than Miriam's?"

Drew, Jack, and Miriam snickered at this, so Violet followed them in, her chin held high and her swagger as masculine as she could make it.

The inside of the theater was as broken down as the outside, with an unsteady-looking balcony and a small stage with a tattered purple curtain. It was lit with old gas lamps that smelled of kerosene and smoke. The seats were just chairs set up around small tables. The whole place smelled of ale, and the wood floors were stained and sticky. As they sat down, a barmaid collected their tickets and gave them each a mug of ale.

"Free drink with your seat," Toby said, raising his glass in a toast. He drank deeply from it. "More drinks cost extra."

Their seat was close to the stage, which Violet was happy about, because it meant that when the balcony fell—which could clearly happen at any moment—it would not fall on them.

After a few minutes of drinking, one of the barmaids went around dimming the houselights by hand, and the stage lights came up. A man in a top hat came out from behind the curtain, and the audience applauded. It was a large audience, and a rowdy one. The man onstage, who Violet supposed might once have looked like the man on the poster outside, about twenty years and sixty pounds ago, introduced himself as Mr. Pip, and said that he was pleased to present to the audience his precious prancing ponies. And with that, the curtain was pulled back, and the ponies were revealed.

They were not ponies, of course, but girls. They were dressed most scandalously, in very short skirts that showed their knees and thighs, brown leather corsets, and each with a unique array of tassels, bells, and feathers. Mr. Pip cracked his whip and they pranced in a circle around him in a convincingly horselike manner, their feet making the sound of hoofbeats. Violet watched, her stomach churning with disgust, though Drew, Toby, and Jack seemed to be enjoying it, as they were cheering. Miriam looked more amused than anything else. Violet thought the whole thing perverse. An obscene show, clearly, and one in which women were made into animals. She felt herself flushing, and she was about to walk out when she made eye contact with one of the ponies onstage, and all the color drained from her face.

It was Fiona. She was dressed in costume, of course—her hair pulled back into a tail, feathers tied into it with a chain of bells, tassels around her neck and ankles, a saddle on her back, and a bit in her mouth—but it was definitely Fiona. And just as Violet saw Fiona through her costume, she could tell that, even galloping onstage, Fiona had seen Violet, and recognized her through hers.

Violet swallowed, realized her throat had gone dry, and quickly downed her ale. A barmaid came by and gave her another. For the next hour or so, Violet watched as the "ponies" jumped through hoops, stood on one leg, and even let various men from the audience ride them. Fiona, it turned out, was a very talented pony, and she let Mr. Pip brush her hair and slap her bottom in front of everyone as she nibbled happily and with great enthusiasm on a carrot. Drew particularly liked this part.

When the curtain closed and the lights were turned back up, Violet didn't know what to do. She leaned in toward Jack and hissed in his ear. "It was Fiona!"

"I know," Jack said happily. "We know a real talented actress."

"She recognized me," Violet said.

"Oh, don't be silly. She might 'av recognized me. But that's 'cause I'm a lot handsomer than you." His breath had the distinct odor of alcohol.

Onstage, a piano was rolled out, and an old man to play it. Men and women of questionable repute began to dance together. Toby and Miriam joined them.

"Well, well, well," said a Scottish accent from behind Violet. Violet felt a hand rest on the back of her chair and willed herself not to turn around. "Did you lads enjoy the show?" Fiona asked, sitting in Miriam's empty chair. She had changed out of her costume, but was still revealing more skin than Violet had ever seen on another woman before the pony show.

"Oh yes," Drew said. "I love horses."

Fiona laughed. "How about you?" she said, looking right at Violet, who stared at the table.

"It was somewhat . . . that is . . . not quite to my tastes," Violet stammered.

"No?" Fiona asked. "Well, that's a pity. Come and dance with me, tell me what ye didn' like about it, and maybe I can get Mr. Pip to make some changes. I have a bit of pull with the old man. Got a hold on his reins, you might say." Violet swallowed.

Fiona stood and held her hand out to her. "Aw," said Fiona when Violet wouldn't rise. "Come on now and dance with me, else I might become a wee bit upset, and who knows what I might say then?"

Violet finished the rest of her ale in one gulp and stood unsteadily. Fiona took her hand and led her to where the couples were dancing. "Now, put your arm here," Fiona said, placing Violet's hand on her waist, "and do try to lead a little." The dancing was awkward. Violet knew little of dancing and less of dancing as a man, and so Fiona was often adjusting her hands or moving her feet quickly out of the way to keep Violet from stepping on them.

"What do you want?" Violet asked after a moment.

"Oh, don't mind him," Fiona said to a couple they bumped into. "He's just had a mite too much to drink." She turned back to Violet. "So this is why your hair was so short."

"Yes," Violet said, "I'm masquerading as a man. But it's not what you think."

"I dunna think it's anything just yet, except the sort of thing ye'd like to keep secret from your mates." Fiona nodded at Drew and Toby, who were seated again. "And from dear Mrs. Wilks. Did you know she asked me to write her? I dinnae think I'd have much to say, but now—"

"It's for the good of women everywhere," Violet said desperately. "Really. See, I've enrolled myself in Illyria—it's an all-male college of science—and I'm going to reveal myself at the end of the year, and then they'll be forced to let women in. And that's good for you, see?"

Fiona raised her eyebrows. "Well, that certainly isn't what I thought was going on. And I'm not unsympathetic to your situation. But . . ." She let her sentence trail off as they danced a bit more.

"What do you want? Money?" Violet asked.

Fiona tilted her head, considering, then focused on the table Drew, Toby, Jack, and Miriam were at. "Tell me, which of those men is richest?"

"Richest?" Violet asked, looking back at the table. Toby waved at them.

"Well, Toby is a baron, but I think Drew's family probably has more money. His family is the Pale family. Of Pale Perfumes."

"You dinnae say!" Fiona exclaimed. "I use their soap. With the lavender in it. I love the smell of lavender, don't you? So feminine."

"I suppose," Violet said.

"Well, as I am a woman, and you seem to feel you are doing a great deed for all womankind, I won't ask you for money to keep your little secret. I'll ask you for information."

"Information?"

"On how to win the affections of Mr. Pale, over there. He's handsome, and apparently rich. If you answer all my questions about him, I won't ask you for any money, and you can keep your scheme going until the very end, when you win a victory for rich girls who finished school and want to go on to college, and through them, all womankind."

Violet paused. She didn't quite understand. "So you want me to tell you what Drew likes?" she asked.

Fiona nodded. "I think he's attractive," Fiona said, "and it would be nice if he could fund a show for me in which I didn't play a horse."

Violet nodded slowly, then said, "He falls asleep unless he's constantly excited. He likes bright shiny objects and strange smells. He's a chemist, and is trying to work on a perfume that will increase the intensity of its scent as the wearer sweats. He may be looking for test subjects." Violet stared at Fiona to see if any of this was odd to her, but Fiona just smiled a little, apparently unfazed.

"Good start," Fiona said. "I can work with that. And where do you and your mates usually go drinking?"

"The Well-Seasoned Pig," Violet said with a sigh. "Usually about nine o'clock, but it varies which nights we're there."

"Oh, I'm sure I'll find you if I stop by every day for a week. And if I don't, well, I suppose I should write dear Mrs. Wilks back. It's rude not to keep up one's correspondences, isn't it?"

"Yes," Violet said through locked teeth.

Fiona stepped away and bowed. Then she and Violet headed back to the table. Fiona rested her hand on Drew's shoulder and asked him if he'd like to dance. Drew nodded happily and they headed for the dance floor. Violet wondered if she had just betrayed her friend, giving a woman of questionable morality the tools to seduce him. But he seemed quite happy on the dance floor.

Jack patted Violet on the back. "There's too much blackmail going on around here," Violet whispered to him. He gave her a sad look, one filled with his sorrow at not being able to help, and also with the several mugs of ale he'd drunk. Leaning back in her chair, Violet sighed and looked out at Fiona and Drew, who were still dancing.

XXIV.

I T was difficult for Volio to work on his projects in the mechanical lab. He had to make sure that none of the pieces revealed the more violent aspects of his work, and of course, he couldn't assemble anything in the lab itself, not in front of Bunburry and the other students. But he was required to be there, and not being there would be suspicious, so he worked on the more innocent pieces. Thankfully, Bunburry ignored him most of the time, probably intimidated by his genius, but he'd often noticed Adams glancing over at him in a nosy and infuriating manner lately.

Volio knew he had Adams under his thumb, but wondered if maybe that was the sort of thing Adams enjoyed. He'd heard that sodomites were often mincing and effeminate and enjoyed being dominated by their masculine counterparts. Perhaps his power and genius had worked as a siren song on Adams, and he was now fostering a little infatuation. Disgusting.

Today, Volio was working on one of the arms, human looking but not violent looking in any way, testing its range of movement. Each piece had a trigger, which he would test later, in private, but for now, he wanted to make sure that the arm could move in all the ways he envisioned: each finger moving separately, and the arm bending in many different ways. The trick was making sure each gear wasn't too tight or too loose, or else the arm wouldn't move, or would fall apart trying to.

He hooked the arm into the wall of gears and tested each movement until it seemed to be working properly, and noted the exact tension on each joint, so he could replicate it later. All the while, Adams kept looking over at him.

"Do you want something?" Volio finally asked, unable to take Adams's eyes on him any longer. Adams looked up, surprised. He wasn't looking at his body, Volio realized; he was looking at his machine. Probably trying to steal his ideas.

"No," Adams said, and turned away.

"Then stop glancing over here."

"Sorry," Adams said back angrily. "It's just that your invention has an audible flaw, and the sound of it is giving me a headache."

"A flaw?" Volio asked, incredulous.

"Yes, you see, the gear on the . . . elbow, I suppose . . . it's supposed to be an arm, isn't it? Well, if that were the elbow, the gear is far too tight. You can hear it in the way there's a slight high-pitched squeal when it straightens from a bent position. If any pressure were applied to force it back farther, the entire forearm would break off like a twig." Adams crossed his arms and looked proudly at Volio.

Volio glared back. "Your jealousy is unbecoming," Volio said. "I would think the duke might find it . . . unattractive."

Adams blushed bright red at this, opened his mouth as if to say something, and turned back to his own work, finally ignoring Volio. Volio looked down at his mechanical arm again and bent every joint. He heard no squeak, and was quite sure each gear was perfectly tightened. Not surprisingly, Adams was an idiot. Perhaps that was why Cecily assisted him so much of the time. She felt sorry for the poor, stupid boy and helped him improve his inventions so he wouldn't be an embarrassment to the duke and Illyria at the faire.

Volio knew she felt sorry for Adams's inability to resist his perversions. She had told Volio so in her last letter. In fact, her cousin had told her of them, after being accosted with the unwanted kiss Volio had witnessed. Volio suspected that the duke had led his cousin to believe the kiss was less mutual than it clearly had been, so as to keep his own reputation clean. Now, Cecily spent her time trying to cure Adams of his illness. Volio didn't know why the duke didn't just expel Adams, but there would probably have to be an explanation for such an expulsion, and accusing someone of being a sodomite had a nasty, unnecessary storm of scandal around it.

There wasn't much else to do with the information, except mock

Adams. He couldn't blackmail the duke as long as the duke claimed the kiss was forced upon him, and besides, Volio couldn't refute such a claim. He had no proof. Still, if the duke refused him Cecily's hand, even after the gift Volio was planning, then perhaps a mention of it might convince the duke of Volio's dedication to Cecily. But better to try to win him over first, before resorting to unreliable blackmail.

Volio watched as Adams tried to attach what seemed to be a wheel to a large grooved hoop. He put the hoop on the ground, balanced on the wheel, and gave it a slight push. The wheel went flying off. Volio snickered as Adams kicked the floor. He wondered how Adams had gotten into Illyria in the first place.

When independent time was over, Volio left to eat supper quickly and alone, then retired to his room, waiting for night to fall. He had another letter ready for Cecily, which he read over once more before sealing it in the envelope. Volio was smart enough to know he wasn't a poet, but he felt he managed to express some small part of his romantic feeling in words that, if not beautiful and florid, were beautiful in their directness.

He sealed the envelope with golden wax and his family's signet ring, and left his room to meet Miriam in the gardens and give her the note. Cecily, he knew, often worked alone or read or spent time with her cousin after supper, and so it was easy for Miriam to get away then. She was waiting, as she always did, along the edge of the river, a long dark cloak sweeping around her as she looked at the rushing water. Volio walked up to her quietly, resisting the sudden urge to push her, and watch her drown.

"Mrs. Isaacs," he said. She turned, and he thrust the letter toward her. She took it from him, her face expressionless, and it vanished into the pockets of her cloak. She turned back to the river. Volio hated the way she ignored him, the way she seemed to retain the power during their meetings, though it was clearly all his. He stepped next to her and looked at the river. "Do you think if you look at it hard enough, it will wash away your sins?" Volio asked.

"I have no sins I wish washed away," Miriam said without looking up. "I have your letter. You may leave now, Mr. Volio."

"When Cecily and I are married, I think I shall forbid her from seeing you ever again. You are uppity for a servant, and the fact that you are also a Jew and a woman makes it worse. You should be more docile, not less."

"The Jews would agree with you," Miriam said, with a low, murmuring sound, maybe a laugh.

"Just remember, a word from me, and you'd be finished," Volio said, then turned around and left Miriam standing alone in the dark.

Miriam wished it were raining, that the water could run down her face and neck and ease this clutch of muscle in her chest. She wished she were back in France. Every day there had been spent lying blissfully alongside Toby by the beach or going bathing in the hot springs, and every night they had made love in their private villa with the windows open so they could hear the crash of the ocean on the shore. It had been cold some nights, but neither of them had cared. Toby just brought more blankets to the bed, and Miriam wrapped him around her for warmth.

Here all she could hear was the constant sound of the gears of Illyria, turning and grinding away. She got away from it as often as she could. When Toby was in bed or working late in the chemical lab, she often stole out into the evening and lingered in the fog-heavy garden, watching the river. It felt good to be out of Illyria, even if she was still standing beside it. Illyria had become too fraught with darkness: blackmail and a possibly mechanical master who spent his nights lurking in a labyrinthine basement were more than Miriam could handle at once. She considered herself strong. She had endured a lot, after all: her move to Paris, then London, the death of her parents and her husband, being spit on in the streets. But the mysteries of Illyria were exhausting. A fire she could put out, a dead husband she couldn't bring back; these were simple difficulties. What lay beyond that door with no handle was something else entirely.

She had begun having nightmares since they came back from France. In them, she was chased by clawed automata with the duke's face until she was pressed against the door with no handle and couldn't open it, their claws closing in on her. She would wake up from them, startled and sweating. Every night she walked through the basement to leave the building, and every night, the hallway to the rest of the basement seemed to call out to her. Curiosity warred with fear. She did not want to go the rest of the year like this. And so, that night after receiving Volio's love note, she returned to the basement and walked into the dark hall, determined to confront her fears and solve the mystery.

Her torch flickered in the hall as she aimed it ahead. It was just as she remembered, filthy and full of shadows, with soft shuffling noises and dimly lit lamps placed seemingly at random. But almost immediately after turning the corner, she heard footsteps in addition to her own. She couldn't decide whether to run away or just shut her torch and press against the wall.

A moment later, before she could decide, Professor Curio came around the corner, holding a gas lantern. He looked at her, clearly surprised. "Mrs. Isaacs," he said.

"Professor Curio."

Miriam was never entirely comfortable being alone with a professor. She wasn't a student, nor was she a professor. She ate with the professors often enough to know them, but did not socialize with them. She was not their equal, but she was not clearly below them, either.

"What are you d-d-doing down here, at this hour?" he asked. His eye twitched in the dim light of his lantern.

"I remembered just before retiring for the evening," Miriam said, a lie forming in her mind, "that Cecily asked me to pick up some more tree sap for her project tomorrow. There was none in the duke's lab, nor yours, so I thought I would come down here and claim it from storage."

"Ah," Curio said. Miriam could not tell if he believed her. The hand that was not holding the lantern suddenly spasmed violently, and Miriam took a step back. Curio had never seemed dangerous, just twitchy, but in the basement at night, his small, uncontrolled movements took on a sinister aspect. "Sorry," he said as she jumped back, "c-can't help it. Well, the tree sap will b-be just in this room, here," he said, opening a door. He stepped into the room, and Miriam leaned over to watch him. The room was just for storage, lined with crates and barrels. He took a large bottle out of a crate on the floor and handed it to her. "I'll try to keep a better stock of it in my lab from now on," he said. "You s-s-shouldn't have to come down here alone. It could be q-quite d-dangerous."

"Oh?" Miriam said, trying to appear fearless. "Well, thank you for the sap."

"Of course," Curio said, bowing slightly. "What Cecily has d-d-done with it is most impressive, isn't it?"

"Yes," Miriam said. "She's quite a brilliant girl."

"Indeed," Curio said, suddenly looking distracted. "Well, g-good night."

"Good night," Miriam said as Curio locked the door again. She headed back to the entrance to the basement, her heart pounding furiously. Her hands shook, so that the bottle of sap nearly slipped from them and she had to react quickly to catch it. As she rose in the lift, she realized that while Curio had asked her why she was in the basement, he never revealed his own reasons for being there. Could he have some relation to the handleless door, or the automaton that so resembled the duke? Miriam tried to think back on what she knew of him, but it wasn't much. He had been here longer than she, and spoke little. She didn't even know his first name. From what Toby said, he was mostly a quiet man, and a good instructor, though he would sometimes have fits of rage and violence. And of course, there was his twitching.

It was worth mentioning to Toby. She hadn't told him anything, not about her going back to the basement, or about the duke's odd resemblance to the automaton. Nor would she—he would be distraught to hear of her going there alone—she would simply tell the same lie she had told Curio about the tree sap. She didn't want to make an accusation against the duke and be wrong.

The clock was tolling when she reached the ground floor, and she paused, watching a shadow walk slowly up the stairs ahead of her. She didn't know who it was, but decided it was best not to be found out of bed after dark anymore. The shadow shrank away, and the clock stopped tolling, so the only sound now was the clanking gears and the soft buzz of the few electric lights that were still on. Gathering her cloak tightly around her, Miriam headed to her room and soon fell into a fitful sleep.

꘠꙰꘠

THE next day was filled with the usual business. Cecily had lessons in French and German, and the duke had asked that she be taught "Domestic Skills," so Miriam devoted an hour to needlepoint and crochet, which neither she nor Cecily enjoyed very much. Then, after lunch, Cecily was free to pursue learning on her own, usually by working in the lab, but sometimes by convincing one of the professors to tutor her, and sometimes just by reading. She chose to work in the lab this afternoon. Though she had finished creating the gears for Ashton, Cecily was still exploring the properties of her new formula, seeing if it was still as strong when molded into very thin sheets, among other things. Miriam sat beside her at her table in Curio's lab, occasionally eyeing Curio to see if he was in any way suspicious, and sometimes, when no one else was looking, smiling at Toby, who worked beside Drew at his own table. She had not brought a novel today, as she sometimes did, but she did have her lesson book, so she went over what she would be teaching Cecily for the rest of the week. The gears moved particularly quickly that day. Before long, supper was over and night had fallen again, and Miriam stole out of Illyria to the gardens, where Toby, Drew, Ashton, and Jack were waiting for her.

The bar was curiously quiet that night. The serving girl leaned against the bar reading a penny dreadful, occasionally glancing up to see if anyone needed her, and usually finding that they didn't. Miriam leaned back in her chair and into Toby's arm. She reached out and squeezed his thigh. Ashton was looking around nervously, while Drew and Jack were discussing the pony show from the weekend. It was as good a time as any.

"I saw Curio in the basement," she said. At the word basement, everyone looked at her. "I was down there to get some supplies for Cecily and he came around a corner, from deeper in."

"You think he has something to do with the automaton?" Ashton asked, his voice oddly high.

"I don't know," Miriam said. "I don't really know Curio. But I think we should go back. Explore some more."

"Mmm," said Toby. "Curio's an all right fellow. He has his fits, sure, but he's not a bad man. And those automata had something right sinister about them. I don't think they're connected. He was probably just in the basement for supplies, same as you."

"Nonetheless," Miriam said, "I'd like to go look again. I want to know what's going on down there."

"I don't," Ashton said, then took a long drink. "I promised my sister I wouldn't go back down there. I told her all about it, and she said it was dangerous and made me promise."

Sometimes Miriam felt that there was something not entirely honest about Ashton. It wasn't that she thought he was lying, but that the truth had somehow gotten cluttered in his mouth and needed to be reassembled on the table like a puzzle. She liked him, sometimes felt an odd kinship with him without knowing why, and she trusted him, but the details never seemed entirely correct. She believed only two things: that he was a genius, and that he was a good man. She wasn't sure about the rest, but then, it didn't matter much to her. There was nothing sinister about Ashton's secrets, whatever they were. They would unravel of their own accord, in time. But the secrets of the basement needed further prodding.

"Aw," said Drew, "c'mon now, mate, y'ain't gonna let your sister boss you about, are ya? Doing that will give ye a woman's character. Be a brick, eh? I'm curious to go down there again." Drew took a large swig of his drink. Ashton watched him with half-open eyes, which seemed a little sad to Miriam.

Jack looked carefully at Ashton, as if deciding whether to side with him, or convince him to change his mind. "There's no reason your sister would ever know," he ventured.

"I don't like breaking my promise to h-er," Ashton said.

"Tell her you were drunk and I forced you. Blame me. Let her slap me around a little. I don't mind."

Ashton sighed, finished his ale, and then nodded slowly. Toby clapped his hands. "Adventure!" Toby declared. "It is the one call we men, and Miriam here, cannot ignore. And since we're not anywhere near the jungles of Africa, then to the basement of Illyria shall we go. I plan to prove Professor Curio innocent of all wrongdoing and behavior that would suggest him to be in any way eerier than he actually is."

" 'Ere, 'ere!" Drew said.

"I think we should bring paper this time," Miriam said, "and ink. So we can make a real map of the place."

"We'd need light for that," Jack said.

"We have the torches Ashton made," Miriam replied.

"And something hard to write on," Ashton said, looking thoughtful. "Can it wait until tomorrow? I have an idea."

"I suppose it is a bit late," Miriam said, disappointed.

"Don't worry, love," Toby said, putting an arm around her. "We'll catch all the bogeys in the basement."

Miriam nodded. It was something, anyway.

⁂

THE next day passed in a flurry. Miriam taught Cecily her lessons and helped her work in the chemical lab. Outside, the fog was extremely heavy, and a pale yellow color, like preserved human skin. Looking out the window on the second floor, Miriam couldn't see more than three feet. All of Illyria felt disconnected from the world.

That night, they all met in the basement. Ashton had brought with him a new invention: a brass tray of sorts that he hung around his neck with a leather cord, so it lay flat in front of him. It had a handle on the side, like an organ grinder, which, when wound, caused the top of the box to light up. Ashton had placed a piece of parchment over this light, so the parchment glowed, and he could sketch a map of the basement in charcoal. Everyone agreed it was quite brilliant and stood about at the edge of the basement hall, discussing it for a few moments.

But Miriam did not want to delay much longer. She turned toward the darkness and headed into it, and the others followed. Miriam wanted them all to see the door and the missing automaton, but as they headed forward, she found she had no idea where it was. Her lines in the dust of the walls were gone, as if someone had swept them clean, but not the floors. Ashton carefully mapped each hall, noted each door. They found halls that curved oddly and seemed to slant downward slightly, as though they were going lower, but they found neither the door nor the train that they had found previously. At one point, they came upon the wall of gears, which apparently extended deep into the basement. Water dripped down on them, and they were rusty and covered in moss, but they still ground, slowly, almost silently. It was a vast wall, Miriam thought, longer than Illyria itself. It seemed to stretch on forever.

"What would they need these here for?" Jack asked.

"I—I think I remember," Ashton said, marking something on the map, then looking up at the gears again. "It was in one of my books on Illyria. They originally built the waterwheel, then extended the gears down here to power some machines that helped build the building itself, from the ground up. It was a brilliant idea. Some engineer friend of the duke's came up with it. . . . I don't remember his name."

"Hm," Toby said, gazing at the wall. He reached out and touched one of the gears, then drew his fingers back and looked at them, rubbing them together. "Well, it's barely working now. And it's slimy to the touch." He wiped his hand on his trousers.

"I bet the algae is something special, though," Drew said, then reached out and tore some of the green stuff off a gear. The gear vibrated at the movement and, for a moment, turned much faster, speeding up the gears around it and sending a small shock wave and the sound of clanking metal down the wall. Everyone stared silently at the point where the wall faded into darkness, as if waiting for something to come out of it, alerted by the shaking gears. But nothing did.

"We should go," Toby said. "It's late." Miriam sighed. "We can continue this later," he said, taking her hand. She flinched, trying not to think of where that hand had just been, but nodded.

"Let's try to space it out a bit," Ashton said. "We don't want to go every night. Let's head to the pub again tomorrow. We can decide our next route by looking at the map. I want to find the train again, and mark it down."

"Good idea," Jack said. "Best to go in with a plan, right?"

Everyone agreed, and Ashton wound up his light-box again, examining the map and pointing the way out.

XXV.

FIONA Gowan had a knack for selling things. She understood the ideas of exchange rates and relative value. She knew how to make a person want something, and how much they would pay for it. But being born the only child to a tanner in Inverness, all she had to sell was herself. Not in the sense of prostitution—though she did dabble in that from time to time, if a gentleman seemed wealthy and enjoyable, or to get a better part in a play—but in the sense that she could show people what they wanted to see. As an actress, some might have called her a ham, but she knew what the audience wanted from her, and she delivered, perfectly.

But she was getting to an age, the kind never spoken aloud, where parts were fewer. She needed a steadier income. An audience of one with full and generous pockets. Becoming a mistress seemed the best option; even better would be mistress to a man who invested in theater, and cast her as all the leads. But she'd settle for anything that got her a clean room for a while.

Violet was a great source of information in preparing for her new role. Despite the extortion, Fiona rather liked Violet. She had a wild impetuousness that Fiona had only played onstage a few times, but which she secretly hoped she also possessed. Pleading sick from Thursday's pony show, Fiona returned to the small boarding room she shared with two other girls, and fished out her small satchel of glass and paste jewelry. She had bought some new pieces with her share of the profits from peddling Mrs. Wilks's Oscillation Therapy Devices—an easy sell—and she put them all on to prepare for the night, and for her great audition.

That new role was to be the lover of Drew Pale, heir to Pale Perfumes. He was an ideal audience for many reasons. He was rich; she found him genuinely attractive, and he her; and he wasn't so complex that she would need to be constantly tweaking her performance. He was excited, or he was asleep, Violet said. If he was asleep, then she was not keeping him entertained; therefore, she needed only to keep him awake. From what she understood, Drew was kept awake by sparkling lights, noises, and smells. Like a baby. Fiona smiled at that idea.

Thursday, at nine o'clock, Fiona walked into the Well-Seasoned Pig dressed for her new part. Glass jewels sparkled down the front of her chest and over her very low neckline. Her fingers and earlobes glittered. She had her hair up in an ornate style she called the Fancy Pork Belly, of the kind usually seen only on Wagnerian sopranos. Her dress was a shining purple, and tight down to her feet, and she was wearing a combination of three different perfumes, which caused her to sneeze occasionally because they didn't mix particularly well. She paused for a moment in the doorway of the pub, because as an actress, she knew that the audience would need a few moments to take in her entrance. Then, spotting Violet, Drew, and the rest of them, she glided purposefully toward their table.

"Well, 'ello," she said, smiling her broadest smile and posing with one hand on her waist and the other bent up as though she were holding a serving tray. She had calculated that this position showed off her jewels to their best possible effect without taking her clothes off. Everyone looked up at her. Violet's eyes widened slightly, and the rest of them looked confused. But it was Drew on whom she was focused, and it was Drew who stared at her as if transfixed, his eyes flashing from her face to her ears to her wrists to her bosom and then starting over again. "'Ello, Drew," she said, leaning toward him so that her necklace fell away from her chest and hung in the open air, swaying back and forth, "care ta buy me a drink?"

"Oh, yes," Drew said, looking confused at having been addressed. He stood and offered her his chair, then went and got another of his own and sat down next to her. She laid her braceleted hand on his knee. He stared at it. The others watched this interaction with expressions between fascination and shock, not speaking.

"I'm Fiona," she said to them. "We met the other night. I was in the pony show."

"Of course," said the dark-looking woman Fiona had not been introduced to. "I'm Miriam. This is Toby. We weren't introduced, because you were dancing most of the time."

"Oh, aye," Fiona said, "I do fancy a bit of dancing." Fiona sneezed, then shook her head and stared at the table. There was a piece of paper laid out on it, and everyone had been careful not to put their drinks too close to it. It had lines running all around. As she looked closer, she thought maybe it was a map, but not of London, or any part of it she knew. "What are ye workin' on?" she asked.

"Just a project," Violet said in her ridiculous man voice, rolling up the map.

"Ah," Fiona said. She ran her fingers up and down Drew's leg, and felt it shudder slightly under her nails.

"You smell most extraordinary," Drew said to her.

"Aye," Fiona responded, "I like ta . . . experiment with scents." She smiled at him, then sneezed.

"It's wonderful," he said.

"You'll have ta excuse me," she said, sniffling. "I seem to 'ave a bit of a cold."

"Oh," he said, taking a handkerchief out of his pocket, "please."

"Thankee," she said as she took the handkerchief and dabbed at her nose. The handkerchief smelled heavily of sweat, but she tried not to react.

She started to hand it back to him, but he shook his head. "Keep it," he said, closing his hand around hers, which held the used and sweaty handkerchief. She felt it squish in her hand.

"You're too kind," she said, batting her eyelashes.

"Perhaps . . . since you already experiment with perfume . . . you'd be willing to let me test some of my own perfumes on you. I'm a scientist, but I'm also of the Pale family."

"Pale Perfumes?" Fiona asked with perfect shock on her face—she'd played perfect shock on at least seventeen different occasions and felt sure she was good at it. "Why, I love your products! When I can afford them."

"You do?" Drew asked, excited. "Well, if you let me test my perfumes on you, I'll name the one you like best after you, and you will have it for life."

"That would be so very kind of you," Fiona said, squeezing Drew's thigh.

He squealed slightly, and sighed with contentment. "No," he said, "it would be an honor."

Miriam cleared her throat loudly. Fiona looked up, saw everyone at the table looking at them, and realized she had begun to lean in, almost predatorially, toward Drew. She drew back and smiled. "So tell me," she said to the group. "Was that a map I saw? What is it ye all are planning?"

"We're mapping the basement of Illyria," Drew said, eager to please her. Fiona noticed the others glaring at him, as if he had disclosed a secret.

"The basement?" Fiona asked.

"Yes," Violet said with a sigh.

"That sounds messy," Fiona said.

"It is," Jack said. He was grinning, as if terribly amused by something.

"Well, don't mind me," Fiona said. "Just keep on mapping away. I'll just drink a little and be on my way."

"Oh, you musn't go so soon," Drew said.

"I have a show tomorrow," Fiona said with an excellently formed look of regret. "Otherwise, I'd stay with you all night."

"Where are you staying?" Drew asked, and then, in a slightly quieter voice, "I can deliver your perfumes myself, and put them on you, if you'd like. Some oils need to be smelled just as they touch the skin."

Fiona rasied an eyebrow. He was more debonair than she thought. She gave him the address of her boarding house, finished her drink, and kissed him lightly but lingeringly on the cheek while stroking his thigh. Then she left, looking back once from the doorway. Drew was staring at her, while the others pored over their map. She winked at Drew and left.

She hadn't stayed more than half an hour, but had done a very effective job, she thought. He'd be thinking about her for quite a while, and with any luck, would keep his promise to deliver her oils and soaps. Which was a start. Not quite a private set of apartments and unlimited income, but free soap was better than no soap. She'd need to know a bit more about him, though. So once she was home, she wrote a letter to Violet at her address in town, requesting additional information on Drew's appetites, particularly those in the bedroom, and sent it off. She'd be prepared for him by the weekend. Having taken off her fake jewels and tight bodice, she changed into her old ragged nightshirt and lay down on the straw mattress the boarding house provided. She put her hands under her head and gazed up at the ceiling. Drew was a very nice boy. And he had very nice thighs. Fiona knew her acting came from her ability to forget herself in a role. Was she forgetting herself so quickly, smiling at the thought of settling down and taking care of the boy with the nice thighs and pretty, nervous lips? She didn't know. But it was a role she could play. Fiona breathed in deeply and shut her ice blue eyes to the night, hoping that this show would be her last.

XXVI.

THEY kept mapping the basement for the next few nights. The map was developing nicely, though they still had yet to rediscover the train or the mysterious automata and the door they guarded. Miriam had been leading the group on this endeavor, and Violet had been impressed. She had been encouraging and energetic, the romantic figure of the lady privateer that one usually found only in books, hair windswept, skirts worn and rippling with movement. And they had mapped a lot. It seemed the basement did have a few levels, though there were no stairs, only sloping halls, so it was hard to tell if they were one level below the ground or two, unless they were looking at the map. Every night, Violet came back to the room and, after bathing, translated her rough charcoal map into a more elegant one of ink and parchment, which she kept rolled up in the closet, so Oscar wouldn't eat it.

Something had been bothering Violet. Since seeing the rusted gears in the basement and remembering their purpose, it had been like a feather tickling the ear of her memory. She lay in bed, flipping through her books on Illyria, trying to find the section on the basement. Finally, in the third book she tried, she found it, several pages into the description of the college's creation: ". . . construction of the basement was overseen by the engineer Adam Volio, an old school chum of the duke's . . ." She leapt up off the bed.

"Fuck!" Oscar, alarmed by the sudden movement, hopped off Jack's bed and under it.

"What?" Jack, who had been feeding him carrots, asked, looking up at her. She thrust the book in his face and pointed at the line. He read it. "Well, now we know how the little bugger got into the school," he said, "though I don't see how it helps us."

"Bugger-balls?" said Oscar cautiously, sticking his head out from under the bed.

"Yes," Jack said, holding out a carrot. "C'mere." He wiggled the carrot, and Oscar leapt back onto the bed, took it from his hand, and began nibbling it.

"It helps," Violet said, "because it means Volio must know the basement—he probably has a map or something. I'd say the automata were his, but they could be his brother's. Certainly it explains how his brother hid everything when he was a student here. I'll bet Volio is hiding things down there, too. The automata are his . . . security or somesuch."

"That seems like a leap to me," Jack said, petting Oscar. "I mean, yeah, it would make sense that Volio is the son or grandson of this Volio"—he pointed at the book—"but we can't prove that. And do you really think there could be a place in Illyria so secret that even the duke didn't know about it? I mean, his da' oversaw the construction of the college, too. I don't think there's much he doesn't know."

"Then maybe he does know. Maybe he's sanctioning it for some reason."

"Don't trust your lover?"

Violet felt herself blush crimson. "He's not my lover!"

"I've seen you reread his letters at least seven times now," Jack said.

"I was studying them," Violet said quickly, "so as to argue my points better when answering his questions."

"Shite," said Oscar.

"I agree with Oscar," Jack said, "I don't see why you need to deny it. Love, my dear Violet, is a beautiful thing."

"Shite," repeated Oscar.

"Hush," Jack said, stroking Oscar's ears. "Well, whether you love him or you don't," he said, "do you really think him capable of assisting Volio? Anyone can see Volio is a blight on Illyria."

"Maybe he's being blackmailed," Violet said. "It seems to be a much more common occurrence than I had once thought."

Jack shrugged. "It doesn't explain Curio, and what he's doing down there," he said.

"Oh, bugger," said Oscar.

"I suppose not," Violet said, sitting back down on her bed. Oscar, done with his carrot, hopped off Jack's bed and onto Violet's and nestled against her, burrowing his head into her waist. She reached down and petted his soft, floppy ears.

"But it's something," Jack said, trying to be encouraging.

"We'll see what the others make of it tomorrow."

Jack nodded. "So, you think Fiona will nab Drew?"

"Probably. I got a letter from her today. She sent it to the house in town, but Ashton sent it along. She wants to know about his . . . bedroom proclivities."

Jack laughed and clapped his hands. "She'd be a cad if she were a bloke."

"How am I supposed to ask Drew about that?"

"I'll do it," Jack said. "Hell, he's already said a few things, and I can guess the rest."

"He has?"

"Sure. You're just not listening proper. It's the way we menfolk talk. When he says he likes a girl with shape to her, it means he likes a large bosom. Which, luckily, Fiona has in spades."

"Ah," Violet said. She felt herself blushing slightly, so she looked down at Oscar, who had fallen asleep. "Well, you write it down, then. I certainly don't want to hear about it."

"You're a funny one," Jack said. "You can swear like a man now, and swagger like one, but when it comes to talking about fucking, you clam up and turn red."

"I'm a virgin, Jack. The rest of you are not. It's a different matter for men."

Jack considered this, then nodded. "I suppose that's true. I guess you're so good at the rest of it, that I'm starting to forget you're just a proper lady underneath it all." Violet glared at him. "What? You don't think you are? Wasn't that you in the lovely gowns caroling with us at Christmas?"

"That was different. I wasn't always so proper," Violet said.

"Mm," Jack said, sounding as if he didn't quite believe her, pulling the blankets up over himself to go to sleep. Violet rolled her eyes, took the books off her bed, and lay down as well.

"Bugger," Oscar said, waking up, and hopped off the bed. Violet turned out the light and lay down in bed. Jack was already snoring softly.

She fell asleep and dreamt of caroling with the duke and a troupe of musical automata in a snow-filled basement, Ernest smiling at her over the music.

⚜

AT breakfast the next morning, she told Drew and Toby about the Volio link. Toby nodded slowly, eating his toast. "Helps explain why he's such a prick."

"Doesn't it also mean that he's responsible for the automata in the basement—that they're his brother's leftovers from when he marched an army of them out of here?" Violet shuddered to think of the mechanical demons again, and the cold, violent intellect behind them.

"I dunno, Ash," Toby said. "I mean, it could be that, sure, but this is Illyria. Could be from anything, really. But I do like the idea that Volio is behind it. Then we can get him in trouble. Although," he continued, rubbing his shoulder where his wound had healed, "I don't like the idea of his being in control of a bunch of the aforementioned killer automata. What do you think, Drew?"

"Hm?" Drew said. He had not been asleep, but staring dreamily into space.

"He's thinking about that Fiona again," Toby said. "Never thought I'd see the day Drew fell for a lady twice his age, but I can say quite certainly that older women are often a good bit of fun. Less squealing, more experience." He laughed loudly and elbowed Drew, who looked at him, confused.

Violet looked at Drew, a bit baffled by the effect Fiona had had on him. She had been out drinking with them two nights now, she and Drew talking quietly together while the rest of them had planned further expeditions into the basement. Violet didn't feel quite so guilty for feeding Fiona information anymore—Drew seemed happy, after all. Perhaps it would be best if everyone's friends told potential mates the best way to please them.

Breakfast ended, and they went off to reckoning, where Professor Prism flipped the many lenses on his glasses back and forth several times while watching the students feed information into the great analytical engines. Violet found the whole class dull. Create a sheet of metal representing the information and the question and give it to a machine to decipher without doing any actual problem solving yourself. It was like looking into a crystal ball, but with none of the mystique and a lot more heat. It made sense to her that Roger Fairfax was so enthusiastic about it, and always finished early, though he never helped his classmates once he finished. After all, it was a lazy sort of science, and Fairfax was a spoiled and lazy man. The creation of the engines, improving on them, and teaching them new ways to solve new, more complex problems—all the realm of Lady Byron— were things that sounded exciting to Violet, but these subjects would not be approached until her second year. If she had a second year.

Prism looked at the answer Violet's machine had given her—an estimate of the number of Catholics that would be living in London in three years' time—and nodded before clicking another lens of his glasses down. Violet sighed and went to help Jack, who was actually quite dreadful at using the analytical engines. With Violet's help, he managed to finish by lunch.

Lunch was mostly spent mulling over their plans to further inspect the basement that evening. Drew would not be going with them—he and Fiona were going to "test perfumes" at a hotel. Without Miriam, their plans were only halfhearted, and conversation soon turned to teasing Drew about what sort of perfumes he planned to test, and where on Fiona's body. Violet spent much of the time blushing, laughing occasionally, then blushing some more.

In the mechanical lab, Violet's creation had become so large that it now sat in the corner covered with a cloth while she worked on additional pieces. It was all coming together smoothly, and she noted with pleasure that Volio would sometimes look up at her creation in the corner and glare at the sheet nervously before going back to his own work, which he always kept out of sight.

Cecily visited and bent over all of Violet's pieces, inspecting them, while Miriam stood in the corner. "It's really looking wonderful, Ashton," Cecily said when she was finished.

"Thank you," Violet said. "Though I still have loads of work to do. You're really driving me to work harder since you built the engine."

"You built the engine."

"You made the material. We should test this part, though," Violet said. The part in question was a door mechanism that would cover the driver, shielding her from harm. The doors had been constructed and mounted on a platform, but they needed to close tightly and lock with the press of a button. "Go around and stand on the other side of the doors," Violet said, "and I'll stand here and activate them. Tell me if they don't look right."

"Okay," Cecily said, and stood in front of the doors, inspecting them. Violet went through them, then turned to face them as well. Cecily waved, though they were only a few feet apart. Violet grinned, then hit the button.

A loud, horrible shrieking noise arose from the doors as they tried to close. One of them seemed to twist from the inside, and began to fall forward, off its rails, onto Cecily. Cecily screamed, and Violet tried to run around the doors to get to her in time, but when she got there, Cecily was already safely out of the way, with Miriam's arm around her waist. The crushed door fell to the ground with a clang. In the back of the lab, Violet saw Volio leering at her failure and snickering. She resisted the urge to spit at him.

"Sorry," Violet said, "I'm so sorry. That should have worked."

"It's all right," Cecily said. "Worse has happened. And Miriam saved me. Thank you, Miriam."

"*Mon plaisir*," Miriam said, brushing dust off her dress. "But next time, stand a little farther back, please?"

Violet let her shoulders shrug, and felt tears pricking at her eyes. She was not used to failure. "I'm really sorry, Cec," she said again.

"It's not your fault, Ashton," Cecily said, laying a hand on Violet's arm. "There was an error. It happens. I should have stood farther back, like Miriam said. No need to be so upset."

"It's just been hard, what with being up so late," Violet said, and yawned. "But I'm going to finish it in time. I know I will."

"Why have you been up so late?" Cecily asked.

"We're mapping the basement," Violet said, not really thinking. Miriam coughed loudly and shot Violet a look. Violet realized what she had just said.

"After hours?" Cecily asked.

"You won't tell, will you?" Violet asked, looking up.

"Of course not," Cecily said. "How could you think I would? We're friends. And I keep my friend's confidences. Have you found anything interesting down there?"

"No," Violet said with a sigh, "nothing yet. The wall of gears, is all. It's a huge basement. Nearly bigger than Illyria proper, I'd wager."

"I remember you said your initiation was frightening." Cecily said, "I can understand the need to map the cellar, though. If my cousin knew, he might actually be pleased." Violet looked at her anxiously. "But I won't tell him, don't worry." Cecily smiled and batted her eyes brightly. "Anyway, I'd best be off. You have lots of work to do, and I think the wrench I made from the formula should be ready by now. I hope it works."

"I'm sure it will," Violet said, turning back to her work. She was so very tired.

"Good-bye," Cecily said.

"Bye, Cecily," Violet said, and nodded at Miriam, too, whose lips were pressed tightly together in a look of mild annoyance.

⚜

"YOU shouldn't have told her about the map," Miriam said to Violet that night in the basement.

"I know," Violet said. "I'm very sorry. I just wasn't thinking."

"Well, I think she's in love with you enough that she won't mention it to anyone. But she does like to talk." Violet and Miriam were leading, Miriam with torch in hand, Violet with her light-box around her neck, while Toby and Jack walked a bit behind, still making jokes about perfume testing. They were exploring what Miriam had said was the western part of the basement.

"I'm really very sorry, Miriam," Violet repeated.

"You were tired and distracted," Miriam said. "I know a bit about that."

Miriam stopped as they came to an intersection and shone her torch down each passage. Violet saw something reflect down one of them. "There," she said, pointing. Miriam headed toward the reflection.

As they stepped into the room, the air around them changed, their footsteps echoing differently. Miriam's torch traced the object. It was the train. They were in the station as before, but the lights that were on earlier in the year had died out, leaving the station dark. There was a faint sound of rushing water from the tunnel beyond the train, but the train blocked the way, fitting the entrance to the tunnel like a key in a lock.

"The train," Violet said, making a note on her map.

"I didn't imagine it was this big," Miriam said, shining the torch around. The station was huge. Violet had forgotten how huge. Their steps echoed in the emptiness of it, and the air was chilly and smelled of water.

"Think you can make it work?" Jack asked.

"Do you think I should?" Violet said. No one answered her, but they all silently headed for the train. It was beautifully designed, like a smooth cylinder of copper, with benches along either side, lined in moldy red velvet. There were windows and chairs facing out both ends.

"Monorail," Violet said, looking around. They had all piled inside it now. An open arch was the only exit onto the platform, and it didn't have a door attached. In front of the back chairs were a series of levers and switches. Violet handed the light-box to Jack and sat down at one of them. Miriam shone her torch on the console while Violet examined it. Like the train, the design was smooth and beautiful. The switches looked as though they were incapable of rusting. But Violet couldn't figure out what the power source was. There was no engine she could see, no place to feed coal, no key to turn. She tried one of the switches and the lights in the train went on, flickering a little. The train was now lit from the inside.

"That's something," Toby said.

"Electric," Violet said, impressed. The train was old. Electricity was just being experimented with when it was made. An electric motor seemed highly unlikely, but the lights suggested that it was possible. Violet stood and examined the floor for a hatch or panel, hoping to find an electric motor underneath, but there was nothing but wires and tubes. She went outside the train, looking for an external power source. The others followed her in silence. She could not find anything to make the train go.

"Ashton, it's really late," Jack said. "You've been at this for two hours." Violet looked up at him, confused. Had it really been that long?

"We should go," Miriam said, nodding. "We'll take tomorrow off. You need your sleep, Ashton. I'm sure you'll be able to figure this out when you're rested."

"Yes," Violet said. Her eyes did feel tired. "Of course."

She turned the lights in the train off, and they left the station, Jack leading the way, Violet half-asleep. Their footsteps echoed in the train station.

They had walked about ten minutes, and were probably only another ten minutes from the lift back to the college, when Jack stopped dead in his tracks and hissed, "Listen."

The rest of them stopped, Violet swaying with exhaustion on her feet. A faint stomping noise could be heard, growing louder and louder.

"The automata?" Miriam whispered. Toby nodded. The echoing of the halls made it hard to tell where the sound was coming from, so they froze in the middle of the passage, moving their torches back and forth, looking for the source of the noise.

"There!" Jack shouted, catching sight of metal reflecting off his torch. The first of a line of at least six automata marched down the hall toward them with frightening purpose and speed.

"Run!" cried Toby, and darted down the hall away from the marching metal soldiers. The others followed, but Violet was dizzy, her energy spent on exploring the train, and she lagged behind. The others were ahead of her, and she was frightened. Her heart was pounding, but not fast enough to lift the great weight of her feet, and the automata were gaining on her, their talons out in front of them and gleaming.

And then she tripped. She felt her foot catch on a loose stone in the floor, and she fell forward and to the side, crashing into the wall of the hallway and rolling down it, so she lay against the edge of it. She was stretched out and vulnerable, and the first of the monsters was upon her. She would be gutted like a fish. A taloned hand would reach down and tear her open from her gut to her chin, slice through bone and all the major organs, and the automaton wouldn't even need to stop moving. It would be bloody, painful, and over in moments. She took a deep breath and flinched as the line approached her.

But nothing happened. Violet squinted as the line marched by her in perfect unison, apparently taking no notice of her. She counted the pairs of gleaming metal feet—a dozen. All of them marched by her and continued down the hall.

"Ashton?" came a voice. She pushed herself up and looked for its source. Jack and the others poked their heads from around a corner a few yards down the hall. The creatures had passed them by, too.

"I'm okay," she said. They ran to her, helping her up. "Just bruised, I promise," she said. "They didn't hurt me. I don't know if they even saw me."

Jack propped Violet's arm around his neck and his arm around her waist so she could lean on him and walk.

"They were marching," Miriam said. "Military formation."

"But they ignored us," Toby said.

"Practice," Miriam said. "Drills. My husband used to march like that. Ignore everything, march forward, prepare for war." Her words hung in the air, silent except for their ragged breathing.

"They've never acted quite like that before," Jack said.

"A malfunction?" Toby asked hopefully. "I mean, they're not invading Illyria or anything."

They looked around at each other and silently walked to the lift. It was empty. The automata were nowhere to be seen.

"Not a malfunction, maybe," Violet said, leaning on Jack. "Maybe just patrolling the area. Could be that's what they were designed for originally—keeping the basement safe."

"Then wouldn't they have attacked us?" Miriam asked.

"It's not how they behaved before," Toby said. "And I don't like it."

"Should we tell someone?" Jack asked.

"What, that we've been sneaking into the basement and we found some marching mechanical creatures?" Toby said. "People would just laugh—say that's part of Illyria, and what were we doing down there, anyway?"

"I need to go to sleep," Violet said. She could feel herself falling asleep on Jack's shoulder. "My brother says we all think better after we've slept," she said, and closed her eyes.

"Brother?" Miriam asked.

"He means his cousin, I'm sure," Jack said. "He's like a brother." Violet wanted to open her eyes, but she couldn't. There was silence.

"Sleep, then," Toby said. "We'll come back to work on the train later, maybe. And if we see the automata again . . . we'll figure it out then. Maybe it was just a fluke."

"J'espère ainsi." Miriam said, and helped the mostly sleeping Violet onto the lift. "But in any case, let's wait awhile before coming back—at least until Ashton is recovered enough." Jack and Toby nodded, and they all went to their respective rooms. Violet fell asleep almost immediately, but the rest of them stayed awake awhile longer, staring into the individual darknesses of their bedrooms.

XXVII.

BUNBURRY was quite pleased with the way the first-year students had been progressing thus far. They were all quite clever, but more importantly, they worked well together. Well, with the exception of Fairfax. But Bunburry chose to ignore him, much as he often seemed to ignore Bunburry. Ashton, who was clearly the mechanical specialist of the group, assisted his classmates, but he didn't just do the work for them. Rather, he helped them to figure out how to do it themselves. Mostly, anyway—he sometimes indulged Jack, but Bunburry tried to put a stop to that. Ashton would probably make a good professor one day, but was also probably too brilliant to be satisfied with such work.

Yes, the year was progressing nicely. His shopgirl had let him take her to supper twice in the past month. Her name was Jess, and she was Irish. She had an extraordinary accent, and probably an extraordinary mind . . . though he wasn't entirely sure, since when she got very excited, he sometimes found it difficult to understand her. But she smiled at him often, and didn't seem to mind that he had to bend at his waist for her to kiss him on the cheek.

Today, though, he was a bit worried. He was really pushing his expectations for the first-years. They were to construct serving automata. It was a general assignment, meant to test their creativity and ingenuity: What sort of serving would each automaton perform, and how? But it meant large scale, which meant large pieces of metal which occasionally flew about the room.

Bunburry tried to observe from a safe corner, but it was difficult. After twenty minutes, he didn't feel as though he would be worthy of being called professor if he did not go out among the students and look at their work. They were all doing surprisingly well. Ashton had a barrel-shaped clockwork-powered table with an arm that poured drinks and handed them out. "I would have made it steam-powered," he said, "but that would heat up the drinks." Bunburry nodded, impressed.

Jack Feste had made a set of arms meant to tighten a woman's corset. "What's this on the front?" Bunburry asked.

"A place for a camera, to take photos," Jack replied with a smile.

But before Bunburry could respond with a disappointed sigh, the accident occurred. It was, unsurprisingly, Merriman's fault. He was trying to make a steam-powered cart that would water a row of flowers, consisting of a simple waist-high bronze box to hold water with a hose out the top. But as he was attaching the first side of the device, a sharp-edged sheet of bronze, to the steam-powered gears on the bottom, he lost control of the creation, and the brake came lose, sending the sharp, metal L-shape flying at Bunburry's bottom, edge first. Bunburry jumped, but not quickly enough, and suddenly felt an odd breeze on his behind.

"Oh my," Bunburry said. It had happened in less than two seconds.

"Professor!" screamed Ashton in a high voice. Ashton always did have such a high voice when he was excited, Bunburry thought, turning around. And there, on the floor behind him, like a chop of meat, was his left buttock. And part of his pants.

"Oh my," Bunburry said again.

"Someone get the duke!" Ashton screamed.

Bunburry didn't mind losing his left buttock. Of all the things to lose in that general area, the left buttock was really his least favorite. He even preferred the right buttock, because it had a lovely star-shaped birthmark of which he was quite fond. But his pants had been cut up, too, and that was probably inappropriate; and besides, he seemed to be losing blood, and he felt quite light-headed. Wait—was it the right buttock with the star birthmark? Or the left? He looked at the flesh on the ground. It was blank, aside from a few hairs. Bunburry smiled and passed out, his head falling with a clang next to his ass.

✦❖✦

BUNBURRY opened his eyes to a white room and the face of the duke staring down at him.

"Oh, thank goodness," said the duke. "I was afraid you might not wake up this time."

"I didn't lose anything particularly vital," Bunburry said weakly, "though I suppose it was a comfort to have it. A comfort I took for granted."

"You also lost quite a lot of blood. Young Mr. Adams was nearly in hysterics, trying to bandage you with the cloth that had been covering his machine."

Bunburry blinked, looking surprised and grateful. "That was very kind of him."

"The doctors say that you'll have to remain lying on your side for a while, and they want to keep you in hospital. I've brought in a few of my own doctors, of course, to make sure you heal perfectly."

"You're too kind, sir," Bunburry said with a cough.

"Not at all," the duke said. "You're part of Illyria. I'll take over your classes for the rest of the trimester, if you tell me where your lesson plans are."

"Same as where they are every year: far left-hand drawer of my desk." Bunburry stared at the wall. He was lying on his side, and had begun to feel a thick and unpleasant pain behind him.

"Good," the duke said.

"And, if I were to draw up some plans," Bunburry said, "for a— well, a replacement for what I am now lacking—would you be able to construct it?"

"Of course."

"Thank you."

"The doctors aren't sure when you'll be ready to teach again," the duke said slowly. "Certainly by next year, but . . ."

"You shouldn't have to teach my classes for the rest of the year. I will not be offended if you bring in a substitute."

"Anyone you recommend?" the duke asked.

"Not particularly. You have excellent knowledge of such things, sir."

"Well, I will consult with the doctors and hope for the best, but I shall arrange for a substitute as soon as possible and teach your classes in the meantime."

"You're too generous," Bunburry said. He wanted the duke to go. He wanted to take some morphine and go to sleep.

"Is there anyone you'd like us to tell about your accident?" the duke asked.

Bunburry thought for a moment, then coughed. "There is the shopgirl, sir . . . ," he began, smiling.

The duke left the hospital feeling a bit annoyed. Of course it wasn't Bunburry's fault, but the man always did seem to get himself hurt, and then Ernest had to teach, or find someone else to teach. It was an annual tradition, a yearly bother. But Bunburry *was* part of Illyria—Ernest had meant that, and he had affection for the broken man. A shopgirl, though. That was a surprise. Ernest grinned to himself and buttoned his collar against the cold February mist. He walked a block before seeing a cab, which he waved down.

He stopped off briefly at the department store where Bunburry's shopgirl worked. She was a sweet, pretty little thing, with fair skin and round eyes that grew wet when he told her of Bunburry's accident, but which did not spill over into tears. She thanked him for the news, and he gave her a little money for a cab to go see Bunburry when she was done at work.

When he was finally back at Illyria, supper had already begun. He took off his coat and went into the dining hall, which was murmuring, but quieter than usual. All eyes turned to him as he walked in.

"Professor Bunburry," he announced, "has had an accident. But he is in good condition, and the doctors feel he will make a full recovery. However, it will take time. I will find a suitable substitute for him, and until then, teach his classes myself. If you'd like to visit the professor, you may do so during lunch, but please do not visit him after dark, as he needs his rest. I'm sure he'd be very thankful for all your well-wishes, and even more thankful if you continued to work your hardest in your scientific pursuits." The duke nodded and headed toward his table, where the teachers were eating quietly.

A servant brought out a meal for Ernest, but he was not terribly hungry. He found himself feeling dumb, as he often did after making impromptu speeches. He was never sure what to say. He wasn't a leader. He didn't know enough. All these thoughts trickled into him to replace the worry he had been feeling for Bunburry, as though somehow, if only he had been more prepared, he would have been able to prevent Bunburry's accident this year. But he didn't know enough. He was not his father. His father would have been able to stop it.

Cecily seemed unable to stop talking that evening. Ernest recognized this as her way of dealing with the accident—how she tried to put everyone at ease with pleasant conversation. He admired her for it, and was thankful, for he was not in the mood to talk.

"I confess," she was saying to Professor Curio, "I am now quite curious about the basement beneath Illyria. I have lived my whole life here and have never seen it."

"Not m-much to see," Curio said, and grunted. "Dust, doors, d-d-darkness."

"But I have heard that more lurks down there as well," Cecily said. "Ashton was telling me about his initiation at the beginning of the year, how they all went down to the basement, and it was quite frightening."

"I'm sure he was exaggerating," Miriam said, "to impress you."

"Though that is a lovely thought," Cecily said, "I doubt it. Ashton is not prone to exaggeration. He said that while they were down there, he and the other students discovered a virtual labyrinth of rooms, and that they felt things brush up against them which were not there, and that they found what looked like a pile of lifeless but still twitching and vicious-looking automata, and even a large train."

"What?" said the duke, who hadn't really been paying attention.

"I said that there were things brushing against them, and—"

"Those would be the invisible c-c-cats," Curio said. "My p-predecessor's mistake, using his invisibility tonic on a p-pregnant cat."

"Not that," the duke said. "About the train."

"Oh," Cecily said. "Ashton said they found a large train."

"And where did it go?" the duke asked.

"Oh, they didn't ride it. Just saw it. It was impressive, though, I think. It sounded impressive. I would so like to see it. Perhaps we should organize our own hunting party?"

"No," the duke said. "That place is dangerous. Filled with forgotten experiments. The dark side of science dwells down there. Let's hope it stays there."

"But—," Cecily protested.

"No," the duke said. "That is my final word." Cecily crossed her arms and fell back into her chair glumly.

"My d-dear," Curio said, one eye enlarging slightly, "your cousin is q-q-quite right. It is v-very d-d-dangerous down there, and not a-at a-a-all well lit. P-perhaps, sometime in the future, we c-can attempt to c-c-clean it up and then take you d-down there. But right n-now, it is no p-place for a young l-l-lady to be."

"Yes," the duke said. "One day, when it is cleaned up."

"But when shall that be?" Cecily asked.

"I shall hire some men to take care of it this summer. Is that soon enough?"

"I suppose," Cecily said, the corners of her mouth turning up a little.

The duke was happy to have pleased Cecily, but inwardly, his mind was churning. He had heard rumors about the train under Illyria, read the ridiculous books by men who had never set foot in the college, but he had assumed they were all lies. After all, if there had been a train under the school, his father would have told him, wouldn't he? When his father died, Ernest had searched all over the residence for his notebooks, any unfinished theories or inventions or notes, but had found nothing. The duke's only possessions, it seemed, were his clothes and the books in his library. Ernest had been unsatisfied, angry. His father had seen death coming—he was old and bedridden—and still he told Ernest nothing, only to run Illyria well, and to keep its gears well oiled and moving.

He didn't think to mention that there was also a train in the basement.

Ernest scowled and dropped his fork. His food remained uneaten in front of him.

"I find I am not hungry," he said, rising. The professors and Cecily all looked up at him, then went back to their conversations. The duke walked back through the dining hall and across the bridge in the Great Hall to his residence.

In his study, he opened drawers and cabinets, searching for the original blueprints of the college. He tore the room apart, opening every book and looking behind each shelf, but he couldn't find them. He thought his father had shown them to him once, but it was so long ago, Ernest wasn't sure if the memory was real. He sat down among the dust and strewn books and papers, and then sneezed.

"Ernest?" Cecily said, suddenly in the doorway.

"Yes?"

"What happened?" she asked, surveying the mess.

"I was looking for something," he said.

"Oh. Did you find it?"

"No."

"That's a pity. And you made such a mess."

"Yes, I suppose I did."

"And you're quite dusty. You should really go take a bath and then go to bed."

"Thank you, Cecily, you're quite right. That's exactly what I'll do."

"Good."

"Except . . . ," Ernest said, suddenly thinking. The students stumbled on the train accidentally. Surely he could find it if he was looking for it.

"Except?"

"I promised I'd visit Bunburry in the hospital."

"Oh, well, you ought to do that, then. But at least wash your face before you go. It's positively gray."

"I will. Thank you, Cecily. Good night."

"Good night, Cousin. I'll be reading. Do send Bunburry my warmest wishes."

"Of course," Ernest said. Cecily left for her own quarters. Ernest leapt up and went to his chambers to wash his face and change.

Bunburry was a convenient excuse, so that Cecily wouldn't catch him doing the very thing he had forbidden her to do. He would explore the basement tonight, find the train, and take it to its mystery destination, if he could. Another of his father's secrets would be uncovered, he was sure.

⁎❦⁎

THE basement *was* in need of repair, Ernest thought after a few minutes of walking through it. Lights were burnt out, and walls were cracked and filthy. He stretched his gas lantern out in front of him, but it barely dented the darkness. He was going far deeper than he had ever gone on a monster-hunting expedition. After walking for two hours, it seemed he was back where he started, only tired and filthy. He was going to have to keep coming back until he found the train, and keep searching his father's things for a map.

Ernest spit the grime out of his mouth and headed back up to his rooms. This was not a mystery to be solved in one night. It would take time, and he had to use his time wisely now. He would have to balance searching for the train with his own work, which now included teaching Bunburry's classes until he found a replacement. He washed quickly and went to bed. At least he wouldn't have the first-years for a week. He had avoided Ashton since the kiss, and was not looking forward to seeing him in class.

⁎❦⁎

THE next few days went smoothly. He taught or worked for the first half of the day, and worked in his own lab after lunch, leaving the mechanical students alone, Prism looking in on them occasionally to make sure they weren't dead. After supper, he would tell Cecily he was going to see Bunburry and then head down to the basement, where he found nothing. Cecily never questioned him, only praised him for his kindness, which made him feel a bit guilty—perhaps he *should* go to see Bunburry now and again. Bunburry's lesson plans were complex and thorough, written as if he knew they would be passed on to someone else at some point. And when Ernest finally had to instruct the first-years, Ashton was polite and clever, did his work and helped the others. Really, Ernest had hardly any reason to talk to him at all, though he always left straightaway, so as not to end up alone in the room with Ashton again.

Up in his lab, Ernest had a pile of letters from Ashton's sister. And though he carefully avoided Ashton, he found he could not indulge enough in Violet. Her mind was as spectacular as her eyes. While he knew that what they were writing to each other wasn't love poetry, it often felt to him as though it was better. Words on a page, no matter how much sentiment they contained, were still words. But her arguments, and suggestions for his æthership, showed much more than sentiment. They showed her inner workings. He found her a woman of brilliant intellect and integrity, of humor and creativity. But he still did not know what she felt for him. For the letters were not, after all, romantic, and while he knew her mind, he did not know her heart. For fear of rejection, and for fear of what her brother would say, Ernest could not bring himself to ask her if she felt for him what he had begun to feel for her. So instead he worked on what was no longer just his æthership, but *their* æthership, and as he molded the metal around the frame of it, he pictured his hands caressing her, and her flashing eyes.

Weeks passed, and still the duke could not find the train. There were whispers in the dark, sounds like footsteps that went silent as he got closer—Curio? The invisible cats Curio said were roaming the cellar? He didn't care. He only wanted to find the train. He had narrowed down a list of possible replacements for Bunburry and was nearly finished with the model æthership, but the basement was unsolvable, an impossible maze keeping him from his father's secrets and intruding on all his thoughts. He would have to find a replacement for Bunburry by Easter holiday, and he wanted to find the train before then as well. He would find the thing, and ride it wherever it took him. Illyria was his, after all, not his father's. He needed to see what secrets were buried under it.

XXVIII.

ERASMUS Valentine had a fondness for women of a certain age, and that age was at least sixty. He loved their soft, stretched flesh, hanging off their arms like wings, and the look of surprise in their eyes when he made love to them. He loved their stiff gray hairs, which stuck straight out from their scalp and were often dyed a strange false shade of lavender or orange, and he loved their long beaklike noses. If he was particularly lucky, their cries of passion would even sound like squawks.

He was often successful in his amorous quests. Though sometimes surprised, or confused, Valentine had loved many, many women of London, none younger than fifty-seven—and that one looked quite ancient for her age. But one bird had escaped his net, and it was the bird he wanted to catch more than any other: Ada Byron, the Countess of Lovelace herself. She was a different sort of bird. Ada had been famous for being wild and brilliant in her youth, and age hadn't tempered her with caution—as it often did—but with confidence. She still smoked cigars, gambled, and wrote tracts on the future of analytical engines with just as much fervor as—if not more than—she had when she was in her twenties. When her husband died thirty years ago in an accident involving the steam presses he made to shape wooden ceilings into cathedral-like patterns, she hadn't sought a new husband. Not out of grief, but because she didn't see the need for one. She was independent. She laughed at bawdy jokes, and drank with the men after supper. And she had rejected all of Valentine's advances. But she was coming to Illyria today, and Valentine was determined to persevere.

Ada always came early for Easter and stayed at Illyria for the few weeks before the holiday began, usually giving a lecture in the duke's place. Valentine was waiting when her coach pulled up, and was there to help her out of it.

"Lady Byron," he said, "such an honor to have you with us, as always."

"Erasmus, shouldn't you be teaching a young person something about how to make an elephant into a bird, or how to apply rouge?" She pursed her lips, and, taking his hand, stepped down out of the carriage. "Although, on second thought, you shouldn't be teaching the latter. Wouldn't want all our students looking like circus clowns." Valentine smiled at her. Her remarks stung, but she was often this way with him. He assumed it was how she expressed affection.

The duke and Cecily came out of the college, and Cecily ran up to hug Ada.

"Good day, dear," Ada said, stroking Cecily's hair. Valentine bit his lower lip. No chance of escorting her anywhere now.

"Good day, Godmother," the duke said, kissing Ada on the cheek. "So glad you've come to stay with us."

"Ernest, dear, always. How is Professor Bunburry doing? I heard his accident this year was really a kick in the trousers."

The duke held back a grin and extended his arm to escort Ada inside, leaving Valentine alone with Cecily. "Shall I escort you inside, Miss Cecily?" Valentine asked.

She raised her eyebrows at him. "Why would I need an escort?" she said, and followed her cousin and godmother, leaving Valentine to trail behind her.

※◎※

CECILY was very happy that Auntie Ada had come to stay. Ernest had been distant lately, or busy teaching, or off visiting Bunburry, and Miriam had become distracted and tired. Auntie Ada was sure to bring some energy back to Illyria, and Cecily had certain questions about love, questions she could not ask Ernest or Miriam, on the nature of the heart and how one knew one was in love. For though she had loved Ashton, and felt quite sure she still did—it would be unladylike to waver in her affections, after all—she also now had a certain affection for his friend Jack, who paid her more attention than Ashton did. Just last week, Jack had come to visit her while she worked in the chemical lab, something Ashton had never done.

Jack had apparently lost a ferret while performing surgery on it. He spoke haltingly, explaining that he was hoping to make the ferret speak, but when he had begun the surgery, he discovered a cancerous growth inside her, so he'd stopped and put her to sleep. She only would have had a week of pain and suffering before her, but he still felt quite terrible about it. Cecily saw the red lines circling his eyes and knew his sorrow was genuine. They hadn't said much after that, but Cecily was touched by Jack's delicate soul. Usually, he just seemed like a playful boy, without a care in the world, but she knew now that that was just the outer layer. And she was touched that he had come to her, had known instinctively that she was someone who had comfort to give, had seen that she was generous and understanding.

Ashton had never made her feel that way. It was Ashton she was in love with, though. Jack was just a friend. Still, she was beginning to wish that Ashton would reveal a little more of himself, as Jack had done. She would just have to work harder. Most men were not as open as Jack.

Inside the Great Hall, a few students were milling about expectantly, but most were already at lunch. Cecily followed Ernest and Ada to their table, Valentine trailing behind them, fussing with his hair. They were served as soon as they sat down, the servants anxious to please the countess.

"So, Godmother, what will you be speaking on this year?" Ernest asked as lunch was served.

"Don't bother Aunt Ada with work rightaways like that!" Cecily said. "Ask her how her trip was. How was your trip, Aunt Ada? Was the coach very comfortable?"

"It was fine, Cecily dear," Ada said with a wry smile. "Thank you for asking."

"And now," Cecily continued, with a look at Ernest, "what do you hope to do while here? I hope you and I can talk. I have some things I wish to speak to you about. And I must show you my most recent chemical achievement."

"It really is quite extraordinary," Ernest said.

"Miss Cecily promised to make me a birdcage with it," Valentine said, eager to participate in the conversation.

"I look forward to seeing it," Ada said, nodding at Cecily. "And I hope to give a lecture to the students on passion in the sciences, and overcoming obstacles."

"That sounds oddly rousing for you," Ernest said.

"I have spent too much time in the gambling houses lately, so I didn't decide on it until day before last," Ada said. "But I assure you, it will have scientific merit and shan't lead your dear students astray, Ernest."

"Of course not," Ernest said. "I would never expect anything like that."

"Perhaps the countess would care to play cards with some of the professors after supper tonight?" Valentine said from down the table.

"If I recall correctly, Professor Valentine, none of the professors here are very good card players. Consequently, they're good for taking money from, but not much else."

"Perhaps you would find it more interesting if we wagered with more than money?" Valentine asked. The duke cleared his throat.

"I will be here awhile," Ada said. "I'm sure I shall play cards at some point. But tonight I will be spending with my dear Cecily," Ada said, patting Cecily's hand, "and making sure she is up to date on her studies."

"Of course I am," Cecily said in protest. Ada smiled at her to make it clear she was teasing. Cecily crossed her arms. "I am a young woman now. I am not to be teased."

"Of course not," Ada said, patting Cecily's hand. Cecily knew Ada was still teasing her, but didn't care. She was happy to have her there.

Unfortunately, Cecily couldn't get Ada alone for several hours, as Ernest insisted on touring her through the school she'd seen so many times before. Valentine continued to suggest a card game, and said he would gladly gamble away articles of his clothing instead of currency, which Cecily didn't understand at all. Ada spent a long while checking the analytical engines and going over some improvement plans that Professor Prism showed her. Cecily didn't mind waiting for this, as she got to watch Ada correct Prism's work, make suggestions, point out things that wouldn't work, and see Prism defer to her in all regards. It was reassuring to see the power Ada wielded simply by being the best in her field.

Finally, after supper, Ada and Cecily retired to the sitting room of the residence, while Ernest went to visit Professor Bunburry, and Miriam vanished for the evening, as she often did. Ada had the servants light a fire in the fireplace, poured herself a glass of brandy, and sat down in the large divan by the fire. Cecily sat in an over-stuffed armchair next to her, the one that was so large that her feet didn't touch the floor unless she leaned forward slightly.

"Now," Ada said, lying back with a sigh, "what did you want to talk to me about?"

Despite having waited for many hours, Cecily found it difficult to form her question. "Have you ever been in love?" she finally asked. She knew, of course, that Ada had been married, but she also knew that Ada didn't bear much fondness for her late husband.

Ada grinned slightly, took a sip of her brandy, and lit her cigar. "You don't mind, do you?" Ada asked, holding up the cigar. Cecily shook her head. She was quite used to Ada's cigars and, in fact, rather liked them by now. After a moment, Ada said, "Yes, I've been in love."

"How do you know when you're in love?"

Ada took another sip of brandy to cover her amused expression. "Well, I suppose it varies with each person. Do you think you're in love?"

"I'm quite sure I'm in love. Or I was. Now I'm less sure."

"Anyone I know?"

"Ashton Adams. He is a first-year student."

Ada went pale, then red, then tried to hide a smile behind a cloud of smoke from her cigar. "I don't think Ashton is the man for you, dear."

"But I adore him!" Cecily said, feeling a bit annoyed at Ada's condescending tone. "He's gentle and sweet and talks to me like I'm an equal and not like I'm just a pretty girl for him to admire."

"I'm sure he does all that," Ada said. "But if you once thought you loved him, and now you're not sure, I think you should realize that that means something. . . ." She waved her cigar, making lazy smoke circles in the air. "Think of it as a hypothesis, where, after testing the hypothesis, you find it didn't hold up the way you originally thought."

"But Ashton has never been anything but what I thought he was. His sister told me that he's had some bad times, but—"

"You met his sister?" Ada asked.

"Yes. I wanted to meet her, so I convinced Ernest to go with me to their manor over Christmas, remember?"

"I thought you were just going for a drive."

"To their manor. But Ashton was away."

"And Ernest, he met the sister as well?"

"Yes. I think he was quite taken with her. They have been writing to each other."

"Oh," Ada said, taking a long drink of her brandy. "Well, that's very nice."

"I think I'm in love with Ashton. No, I know I'm in love with him. But I don't think he's very much in love with me."

"Perhaps you're in love with him only because he's the first boy in this school who hasn't fallen in love with you on sight."

"Oh, don't be silly, Auntie," Cecily said with a wave. "There have been plenty of men here who haven't given me a second glance."

"Inverts, probably."

"Oh, I don't think Ashton is an invert, if that's what you mean," Cecily said. "I just wish I knew how to capture his heart as he has captured mine."

Ada sighed and sat up straighter. "I have often wished," she began, as though making a speech, "that love had simple formulaic qualities, like science. A man and a woman of like mind and similar attractiveness could combine, and a chemical reaction would take place: love. But there are no formulae, no guarantees, no science involved." Ada stopped and poured herself another glass of brandy. She seemed both happy and sad, as though the two emotions were playing tug-o'-war within her.

Cecily found it somewhat worrying, and not at all helpful. "So, I will never know if Ashton loves me?" she asked cautiously.

"Forget Ashton," Ada said. "That's the best advice I can give you. As for love . . . Well, you'll know when you're in love. But love comes and goes. You asked me if I've ever been in love, and I said yes. Many times, in fact. Most times, though, it faded. As you grow older, it becomes harder to fall in love, but it fades more slowly, too. Forget Ashton. Fall in love with someone else."

"Oh," Cecily said, feeling suddenly a bit sad, and perhaps a bit angry. "Who else?"

"I wish I could tell you," Ada said. "There are plenty of handsome young men in this school who would treat you well. I'm sure, if you think about it, several of them already do."

"Well, yes," Cecily said, thinking of Jack, "but I don't love them."

"You'd be surprised," Ada said. "But enough talk of love. Show me the wrench you made with that astonishing formula of yours."

After Cecily had shown Ada her accomplishments and gone to bed, Ada stayed awake, drinking and smoking and worrying by the fire. The situation at Illyria had become more complex than she anticipated. Ada was usually fairly good at seeing all the possible results of a scenario—it came from working with the analytical engines. But she had not foreseen Cecily's infatuation. Of course, she should have: they were kindred spirits, Cecily and Violet, girls of the same age. It was only natural that Cecily would identify that and—seeing Violet as a man, and being only sixteen—mistake it for love. If Cecily was correct in her assessment of Ernest's feelings for Violet, that was . . . less unexpected. She had secretly been hoping for it, though she hadn't really expected it to happen until after Violet's secret was revealed. But Cecily was an unaccounted for variable, and the equation could come out very differently now. If Ernest and Violet did fall in love in the end, and Ernest could see the brilliance in Violet's deception, then what would happen to dear Cecily? Ada did not want to see her family torn apart by the confusion of love.

But she had nearly finished the bottle of brandy. She pushed herself up from the divan, a little dizzy, crept out of the residence, and down to the reckoning laboratory. The great analytical engines rose around her, tall as houses. She found them soothing, and caressed the metal of their sides. Though drunk, Ada was still the First Reckoner, and it didn't take her long to create a series of plates, all with possible factors, and run them through the machines. The machines couldn't really help, of course—she had told Cecily the truth about that. But she found the sound of their internal calculations soothing, as though they told her that in the end, there was a great calculation, that the world was a functioning machine, and she was just a cog in it who couldn't see the whole thing.

Each equation gave her a different answer, always in numerical form, which she would have to translate back into words. The engine spit out the answers to her three equations: Two. Five. Twenty-nine.

Sighing, Ada crumpled the thin papers the numbers were printed on and threw them into the fire.

XXIX.

VIOLET and her friends sat around a table at the Well-Seasoned Pig, drinking cheerfully. Violet settled back into her chair, feeling relaxed for the first time in a while. She was surrounded by friends, something she had never expected when she came up with her plan. But here she was, with Jack, Toby, Drew, Miriam, and even Fiona. She felt somehow warmer than she had before, and not from the fire or alcohol.

The past few weeks had not been so warm, as Violet had been too busy working. She was closer to completing her project than she expected to be at this point. She didn't know why she spent all her time in the lab, working so furiously, so that her back ached and her eyes strained; why she spent her nights exploring the basement, or trying to figure out why the train wouldn't run. She had lost some of the joy she had felt upon first coming to Illyria. The only time she felt truly at ease—even more so than she was here, with her friends—was when writing letters to the duke. It seemed that in that context she could be free, and truly herself, and have her ideas respected even though she was a woman. She would think over his ideas throughout the day while working, or now while drinking at the pub. And thoughts of his ideas often led to thoughts of him, of his eyes and lips, and made her feel like melted copper, bubbling liquid. She thought of him kissing her neck, and it made her sigh.

Fiona leaned over and whispered in her ear. "I know that look. If you need a particular device to help relieve certain urges, I can sell one to you."

"What?" Violet asked, confused.

"Nothing," Fiona said, shaking her head. Violet shrugged. She'd enjoyed having Fiona around lately. Socializing with another person who knew the truth was somehow a relief to her. Some nights, she thought of just telling Drew, Toby, and Miriam. She didn't think they'd care a bit, but every time the urge came on, she bit her tongue. She just couldn't be sure. Still, it would be nice. She hoped that when she finally revealed the truth, they would still be her friends. On nights like this, she didn't want anything to change. She finished her ale and ordered another, and Jack clapped her on the back and smiled.

⁂

ADA finished her brandy at about the same time, and set the empty glass down on the card table in the professors' lounge. Valentine refilled it for her. He had taken off his jacket and put it in the center of the table as part of his bet. Ada could tell he was hoping she might do likewise, but no amount of liquor was going to inspire that sort of behavior from her. Especially not in front of present company, which included Professor Prism, Ernest, and Cecily, who had insisted she be allowed to stay up to learn how to play poker, but was now curled up in an armchair, half-asleep.

Prism played with his glasses, and a blue lens fell over his left eye as he examined his cards. "You're bluffing," he told Valentine.

"What? Do your glasses let you see through the cards?" Valentine asked.

Prism scowled and laid his hand down. "Call," he said.

Valentine was indeed bluffing, but it was Ada who won the hand. Ada always won the hand. She slipped Valentine's jacket on over her gown. It fit surprisingly well, but then, Valentine did have a womanish figure. Valentine grinned and pushed some of his hair out of his face. Ada resisted the urge to roll her eyes. Instead she took the cards and put them in the reshuffling machine.

"Ada," Ernest said, leaning back in his chair and taking a sip of wine, "do you happen to know where my father might have put the blueprints to the cellar?"

Ada dealt as she answered. "I didn't think the cellar needed blueprints," she said.

"Oh, it's a maze down there," Prism said, looking at his cards. "I once needed some supplies and went down there to search. I was lost for what seemed like hours. It was a wonder I made it out at all."

Cecily stirred in her chair and made a slight snoring noise. Ada and the gentlemen looked over at her and exchanged glances, all resisting the urge to snicker.

"Cecily," Ada called softly. "Cecily?" she said, louder this time.

Cecily sat up in the chair. "An ace, a king, a queen, a jack, and a ten, all of the same suit," Cecily said.

Ada stifled a chuckle. "Perhaps you ought to retire, dear," Ada said. Cecily looked around and blinked, then slowly got to her feet and headed for the door.

"What I really need," Ernest continued, looking at his cards and frowning, "is a map of the cellar. Because of problems such as the one Prism just mentioned. I've been through all of Father's things, but I cannot find any such map. I don't know how I'm expected to keep things running smoothly when I don't even know where to find supplies."

Ada noticed Cecily stop in the doorway, then turn back slowly, thinking. "Cecily?" Ada asked. The gentlemen turned to look at Cecily, who was standing nervously in the doorway.

"A map of the cellar?" Cecily said carefully.

"Yes," said Ernest, looking surprised. "You haven't found one, have you?"

"Well," Cecily said, stepping back into the room, "no." She looked at her feet.

"So, then why—?" Ernest began.

"You must promise no one will be punished," Cecily said.

"Punished?" Ernest asked. "Did a student steal something from the residence?"

"Oh no!" Cecily said, stepping forward, "nothing like that. It's just . . . I was sworn to secrecy. So if I am to trust you, you must promise no one will get into trouble."

"I promise, then," Ernest said.

"Ashton and Jack," Cecily said, "and some other students. They've been exploring the basement. And mapping it. Ashton has a map. It's not finished, though."

"They've been mapping it?" Ernest asked, unbelieving. "When?"

"After hours," Cecily said softly.

Prism chuckled. "Very enterprising of them, really."

"No one will be in trouble, right?" Cecily asked.

"No," Ernest said, "no one will be in trouble. Thank you, Cecily. And good night."

"Good night," Cecily said, and kissed Ernest on the cheek before exiting the room.

"There's the answer to your problem, then," Valentine said. "A map, all prepared. Ideal situation, really. If it hadn't turned out this way, I would have suggested sending the students down there to map it anyway. Let *them* crawl through the dust."

"Ah, yes. Heaven forbid your jacket get any dust on it," Prism said. "Although, if I had as much hair as you, I think I'd be more concerned about the cobwebs."

Valentine shuddered.

"Gentlemen," Ada said, "dealer takes two."

The men turned their attention back to the game. Ernest smiled to himself. A map, already drawn! Of course, it was only really useful if they had marked the train on it. And if they had, they'd better have refrained from riding it. Those secrets, Ernest knew, were for him alone. Of course, now he'd have to talk to Ashton in private, which he'd been avoiding. It would be worth the awkwardness, though. Things were coming together quite well.

Ernest won the game, and Ada won the next two. Valentine had lost his tie and shirt by then, which everyone knew was completely inappropriate, but they'd all had quite a bit to drink, and social niceties seemed a long way off. Ernest stumbled to bed after Ada had retired and Prism and Valentine had gone home. He fell asleep as soon as his head hit the pillow.

❦

ADA'S lecture the next morning was as she said it would be: inspiring. She didn't focus on any one topic, really, talking instead of her love of science. "Invention is Humanity's Greatness," she told the students, her own translation of the school's motto, "and so is love. For invention is a sort of love. A love of the way things come together, of our ability to form wondrous new things. Two liquids that form a solid. Two pieces of metal that can move things ten times heavier than one piece could move alone. Don't forget the love that goes into your work. Science without love is just pieces of metal, never bringing anything good to humanity. But invention with love is the best of us—our joy and our greatness—and we should not be afraid of greatness," she finished. Though old, her voice had none of the tremble usually associated with the elderly. It was firm, and brought her conclusion down as solidly as a stone wall. Everyone applauded, and Ada looked pleased, bowing deeply while supporting herself on her cane.

By then, it was time for lunch, and everyone was hungry and filled with energy, so they tore through their meals before heading off to work on their individual projects.

Ada and Ernest sat alone in the dining hall with full bellies. "It really was a grand speech," Ernest said.

"You've said that three times already," Ada said. "But as I told you before, it was easy. No real content. Just some inspiration. Inspiration is easy enough, and important, though sometimes people forget it."

"I've been very inspired lately," Ernest said.

"Oh?" Ada said. "On your æthership?"

"Yes," Ernest said. "I've been corresponding with another scientist, and I've found her insight to be . . . stimulating."

"Her?" Ada asked.

"Ah. Yes. Ashton Adams's sister, in fact. A lovely young woman. Violet."

"And is she as brilliant as her brother?"

"More so, I'd guess. Though I haven't seen much of Ashton's work. She's very brilliant."

"Pity she can't be a student here," Ada said.

"Yes," Ernest said, nodding. "Though, truthfully, she would be too much of a distraction. She's quite lovely of person, as well as of mind." He looked off at the wall, his thoughts somewhere else. Ada raised an eyebrow. "She doesn't seem to care much for flowers, though," he said, furrowing his brow. "What do I give a woman who doesn't like flowers?"

"Give?" Ada asked.

"I . . . I looked at her brother's file. They're twins. Their birthday is the day before Easter. I thought I could send her a present, as a thanks for all the inspiration she's given me."

"That would be very generous of you," Ada said carefully.

"But not flowers."

"I'm sure you'll think of something," Ada said, standing. "I'm off to the reckoning lab," she said. "Prism asked me to look over a new design of his."

"Shall I escort you?" Ernest asked.

"Don't be silly," Ada said. "Besides, you'd best start work on that present if you want to finish it in time."

"You think I should make her something?"

"Nothing captures a woman's heart more than something well crafted."

"Heart?" Ernest said. Ada chuckled and began walking across the dining hall, not looking back. Servants were cleaning up, walking to and fro, taking plates away, and mopping parts of the floor. Ernest ran to catch up with her. "We'll walk together," he said. "I need to go to the mechanical lab to speak to Mr. Adams about a map." Ada took his arm.

✵◎✵

VIOLET was hard at work in the lab, feeling relaxed and happy. She had received another letter from the duke that morning, in which he had called her brilliant. She had carried that word around with her all day, glowing with it. So when she looked up and saw the duke staring at her, she instantly blushed and looked away to hide her smile.

"Ashton," the duke said, "may I have a word with you in the hall?" Ashton, she thought. Of course. He's here to speak with Ashton. She nodded and went out into the hall. She saw Volio sneer at her as she left.

"Yes, sir?" she said when they stood outside the door. He took her arm and pulled her toward a darker part of the hall.

"Ashton. I . . . Well, first I should apologize for that incident that happened . . . it was a while ago, and it was quite inappropriate of me. And frankly, I had been thinking about someone else."

"Oh," Violet said. Her stomach felt suddenly heavy.

"I hope you'll forgive me."

"Nothing to forgive, sir," Violet said, keeping her eyes on the ground.

"And there's one other thing. I hope you won't hold this against Cecily, but she told me about your evening forays into the cellar." At this, Violet looked up, suddenly very worried. "Don't worry," the duke said, laying a hand on her shoulder, "you're not going to be punished. The truth is, I have no map of the basement. So I was hoping I could borrow yours and copy it for myself."

"Oh," Violet said. "Of course, sir. I'm sorry for breaking the rules, sir."

"Ah, you're lucky," the duke said. "For in this case, your breaking the rules works in my favor, and so I am inclined to say boys will be boys. If you give me the map."

"Of course, sir. Now?"

"Yes, if you can."

"It's in my room, sir."

"Well, then let's head there, shall we?"

Violet was very aware of the duke's nearness as they rode the lift together and walked down the hall to her room. She opened the door to it and looked around. She never left any clues to her identity out, but the place was still a bit messy.

"It's not quite clean," Violet said apologetically, opening the door all the way for the duke. She took a deep breath. Being alone in her bedroom with the duke made her skin feel warm and her scalp damp. She smiled at the duke. After all, she wasn't a woman alone with a man. She was a student alone with his headmaster.

"Don't worry about it," the duke said, coming in. "If I didn't have servants cleaning everything, my place would be much worse, I assure you." He grinned and closed the door behind him. Oscar, seeing someone new, bounced out from under the bed and began sniffing the duke's shoes.

"He's a cute one," the duke said, reaching down to pet Oscar.

"Fuck off!" Oscar said. The duke quickly retracted his hand.

"One of Jack's experiments . . . ," Violet said, then opened her closet and reached up for the map. The duke came up behind her and saw what she was reaching for, then leaned over her and took it, their bodies nearly touching.

"Ah," he said, "so this is it?" He unrolled the map. Violet nodded and closed the door behind her. The room was small and dimly lit, and suddenly very warm. "Amazing detail," he said, examining it. "Is this a train?"

Violet nodded. "It doesn't work, though," she said.

"You tried it?"

"Yes," Violet said. "I tried fixing it, too. But I haven't gotten it to work."

"You'd ride a train when you didn't know where it would take you?"

"It's a train," she said with a shrug, as if that explained it.

In truth, Violet had worked on the train only a handful of times since they first spotted it. They had ventured into the basement more cautiously after that, fearing the marching machines, but hadn't encountered them since. Toby had suggested that it was a fluke—that the automata rose up once a year to make their rounds, and that they'd just been unlucky enough to see it. Violet wasn't sure, but she wanted to work on the train, so she decided to accept it.

"Well, you have to be careful," the duke said. "I can't take responsibility for what happens down there, and I'm sure your father would be very upset if he returned from America to find you injured." Violet nodded.

The duke turned to go, but then stopped and turned back. "Mr. Adams . . . I should tell you. That is. I've been corresponding with your sister."

"She told me, sir."

"And I confess I have grown very fond of her . . . of the way her mind works."

"I'm sure she'll be pleased to hear that, sir."

"When the school year is over, I was hoping to see more of her, if you catch my meaning."

"Meaning?"

"I'd like to court your sister."

"Oh."

"But as you're my student, I wouldn't want to make anything awkward for you, so if you object—"

"No, not at all, sir."

"Of course, you wouldn't get any preferential treatment from me, either."

"No, sir." Violet was blushing violently and looking down. Her heart was pounding twice as loud as the gears. She could power that train with her heart.

"Well, good," the duke said. "And thank you for the map. I shall copy it and return the original to you after Easter, if you don't mind."

"No, sir. You should be careful, though, if you plan to go down there. There are many creatures, and some seem quite violent."

"All the more reason for students not to wander," the duke said, pursing his lips. "But I'm sure I can handle it. Escaped experiments, old devices that cling to their mechanical lives—I've seen them all."

"Of course, sir."

"Thank you, then," the duke said, and exited.

Violet leaned on the wall and pressed her hands to her face, feeling the warmth. Then, realizing she had not done so in a while, she breathed in deeply.

"Bend over so I can bugger your arse," Oscar said.

XXX.

CALVIN Curio had never sought fame. His parents gone by age three, he was raised partly in a city orphanage and partly on the streets by children just a few years older than he. When a well-to-do scientist found him loafing about one afternoon and offered to pay him to fetch some things from market, Curio agreed, if only because he had never really had money of his own before. The older boys often did, and bought things with it, like penny dreadfuls and marbles. He had one marble then, a blue one with a stripe around it like Saturn's ring. So he had run the errand for the scientist and helped him carry his purchases back inside.

The inside of the scientist's apartment seemed elegant and rich to Curio at the time, though he now knew it had been shabby at best. But the basement, where the scientist kept his lab, was a place of wonder. Glass beakers were on every surface, and there was a fire with a heavy copper pot over it, boiling with something that smelled like mold and dust. Some of the glass beakers and tubes were filled with liquids of a hundred colors: blue like his marble, red like blood, green like the trees outside the city. The lab felt as though it were constantly shifting, as though, if he looked away, the beakers or their contents would dance about, only to hold still again when he turned back. Potions bubbled and smoked, hoses filled with liquid and poured it out again. Curio stood staring at it all, openmouthed.

"Do you like it, boy?" the scientist had asked. Curio nodded. The scientist introduced himself as Dr. Henry Voukil and told Curio he would gladly apprentice him if he was willing. Curio, fascinated by the lab, was willing, and for the next several years served as errand boy, apprentice, and test subject for Dr. Voukil. At first, it seemed fun. Voukil taught him to read, and the odd-smelling elixirs the doctor gave him to drink did little besides make him tingle or vomit, which was amusing. Then, as Dr. Voukil realized just how obedient Curio was, and that no one would know what he was doing, he became more daring in his experiments. Curio lost all his hair, fell asleep for a week, cried blood, and could suddenly do complex calculations in his head. He was dizzy and confused most of the time. Dr. Voukil began to teach him the properties of various elements, tell him what he was trying to achieve, mix the ingredients together, and then give the concoction to Curio to drink, which Curio did willingly. After all, he was an apprentice.

When Curio was sixteen, after testing a potion made to enhance strength, nothing seemed to happen for an hour or so. Then Curio started have a throbbing pain in his head and blacked out. When he woke up, it was on the floor of the lab, which had been destroyed: shattered glass everywhere, colored liquids mingling into odd patterns on the floor, and, among them, Dr. Voukil's blood. He was quite dead, nearly pulverized like one of his roots in a mortar and pestle. Terrified and unsure of what had happened, Curio sneaked out at night and tossed the body in the river. The next day, he cleaned up the lab, telling everyone that the doctor had gone to a scientific conference in France.

He ran the lab as Voukil had done, experimenting and reading the library of books he'd never been able to read before because he had been so busy drinking potions. And from the books he learned science. It was slow going, especially when, after a frustrating day of trying to understand a formula, Curio woke up at the docks one morning, his hands covered in blood. He knew then that the dark suspicion he harbored—that he was responsible for Dr. Voukil's death—was true. He began working late into the night, consulting the books and using what he remembered of the doctor's teachings to try to find a cure for his murderous blackouts. After three months, he found that it crept into his personality, that he could be calm one moment and filled with rage the next.

354   Lev AC Rosen

But he was also gaining a reputation as a scientist. He found cures to other diseases, if not his own; perfected a tonic for sore throats; and created formulae that could repair broken glass.

So when the Duke of Illyria came to him to offer him a job, he confessed his dark secret and begged the duke to help him. The duke died before he could cure him, but he also set up a chamber for Curio in the basement, the walls all lined in velvet pillows, the floor a giant mattress, with a solid steel door that would lock itself shut and keep itself shut until the sun rose. In this way, Curio saved himself from causing more harm.

He tried to remove himself from people as best he could. No one knew his secret, not even the current duke—though he did know of Curio's chamber, so he might have had an inkling. Curio had come to enjoy his evening solitude. He took books down to the chamber with him, even if he sometimes found them torn to shreds in the morning. It was quiet down there, except for the soft winding of the gears.

But recently, it had become much more crowded in the basement. Last year, he found footprints that weren't his in the dust, and heard odd clanging noises from time to time. He had ignored them, but this year, there were people going to and fro all over the cellar. He had to peer around corners before turning to make sure he wouldn't be caught. He stopped quietly at any sound, wondering if it was someone else, and who. He dodged beams of light that seemed to shine out suddenly from the darkness. It had become stressful to maintain his secret.

As it was definitely students wandering about after hours—he could tell from their muffled giggles and the smell of cheap ale— he decided to wait one night, and to scold them. The basement was not a place for students to play. Instead of dodging their lanterns, he would follow them. After all, he was the professor, and they the students. They were violating rules by being down here, and if they asked what he was doing, he was not obliged to answer.

Since the door would lock behind him if he entered his chamber, he instead waited in the hall beside it, staring up at its handle. It was a good door, built to look like the others, with a wooden front. The special lock was well hidden.

The students came early this evening, just after supper. Curio stood in the hallway, listening for the sounds of their feet, then ran toward their light. "Ah ha!" he bellowed in triumph.

"Professor!" said the duke, surprised by Curio's sudden appearance.

"S-sir!" said Curio, equally surprised by the duke. "I'm s-sorry, s-sir, I thought you w-w-w-were a s-student. I was going to ca-catch them, sir, and send them t-t-to you for d-discipline."

"Ah," the duke said, looking a little nervous. "Well, that won't be necessary, will it? They've all gone home already, Curio. Easter break begins tomorrow."

"Oh," Curio said. He had forgotten. All his nights were the same. He had no break from Illyria.

"Curio, let me introduce Mr. Matthias Forney," the duke said, stepping aside slightly. The man standing behind him in the shadows stepped forward into the dim light. He was a large man, smoking a large cigar and wearing a top hat and long black duster, which made him seem even bigger. A gold watch chain hung between his black vest and his trousers. Matthias had a thick black mustache, hardly any lips to speak of at all, and a rectangular face with bright gold eyes. He looked, to Curio, like a great black train, steaming and ready to run him over. "Mr. Forney will be teaching Mechanics until Professor Bunburry returns. Mr. Forney, this is Professor Curio, who teaches Chemical Sciences."

"Good to meet you," said Forney in a voice like coal. He had a peculiar American accent, flat and heavy. He extended his hand and shook Curio's heavily.

"I was just . . . showing Matthias around," the duke said.

"It's a m-m-m-marvelous building," Curio said, nodding. The three of them stood a moment in silence, save for the gears turning and Forney sucking on his cigar. "Well, since you're not s-s-students in need of frightening," Curio said, "I'd b-best b-be off."

"Have a happy Easter, Calvin," the duke said. Forney tipped his hat in Curio's direction, and the pair of them set off.

"Happy E-easter," Curio called after them. He lingered in the shadows, still confused, then headed back to his chamber. Easter already. Time was moving quickly.

XXXI.

A NTONY lay in bed with Ashton, stroking his hair. Ashton was still sleeping, so Antony was soft as he kissed the nape of Ashton's neck, then down his spine and around to his navel. By then, Ashton was more awake. He pulled Antony's mouth up to his and kissed him long and hard, their bodies pressing together. Which is when Violet burst into the room.

"Oh!" Violet said, turning bright red. "Sorry!" She closed the door and they heard her steps running down the hall. Ashton laughed.

"Happy birthday," Antony said.

"Thank you," Ashton said, kissing Antony once more before rolling out of bed. He pulled on his dressing gown and winked at Antony before leaving the room.

Having their birthdays just before Easter had made the holiday more festive for the entire Adams family. They still went to the long, somber church service, but paid little attention to it. Instead, they painted eggs and ate cake and German candy bunnies.

Mrs. Wilks had decorated before they came home. White lilies were in every vase on every surface, so that the entire house smelled of their chocolate perfume and seemed to be blooming with light. Mrs. Wilks had accented this with sprigs of violet flowers and ash tree leaves. All the linen was white, and all the wood was polished till it shone in the bright morning light. Violet went to the dining room and started eating breakfast. She looked up when Ashton came in and blushed again. "Sorry," she said.

"Not to worry," he said, looking over the buffet. He chose a few muffins and some eggs.

Lev AC Rosen

"Happy birthday!" Violet said after he sat down.

"And happy birthday to you," he said.

"Thus far, I suspect yours has been happier," she said with a smirk.

"Well, it certainly had potential," Ashton responded.

"I wonder where Mrs. Wilks is hiding our presents from Father," Violet said, ignoring her brother's last remark. "He must have sent us some, yes?"

"Of course."

"So where could they be?"

"Her room, maybe. The kitchen?"

"Fiona already checked the kitchen."

"You asked Fiona to check the kitchen?"

"Yes."

"I'm still surprised she came at all, considering your new arrangement with her."

"She's really a very lovely person," Violet said.

"Who just happens to be blackmailing you."

"She's making Drew very happy. And she said she would come because she had made a promise. That's noble, isn't it?"

"We're still paying her."

"True, but I think Drew has begun paying for most things for her, so she doesn't need the money. I like having her here. She may be a bit . . . cunning, but she could do far worse with the information she has."

"Who could do worse?" Mrs. Wilks asked, suddenly sweeping into the room, a bouquet of lilies in her arms.

"Uh, it was a character," Violet said after a pause.

"In a play we saw," Ashton finished. "She was a redeemed villainess."

"Sounds lovely," Mrs. Wilks said. "And happy birthday to you both. I know Jack will be here later, and I've invited a few of your father's friends, who will want to wish you good tidings on your eighteenth birthday. And of course, there will be a cake. Some packages have already come for you in the post, but I thought you should wait until you're dressed."

"Why?" Violet asked. "What if one of the presents is a new dress?"

"Then you should wear it tomorrow. Wearing new clothes for the first time on Easter is good luck," Mrs. Wilks said.

Ashton couldn't say exactly what had changed about Mrs. Wilks, but she seemed more at ease. Her hips swayed slightly when she walked, and she had exchanged her aura of anxiety for one of grace.

"Now, finish your breakfast and get changed," Mrs. Wilks said. "People will probably begin to arrive around noon, and it is already nearly eleven. I shouldn't have let you sleep so late, but it is your birthday . . ."

Ashton and Violet both changed quickly and met in the hall. Ashton was surprised to see that Violet was wearing a dress of light blue and purple, which their father had gotten her before he left and she had made fun of behind his back. She had also clearly done her own hair and powder. It was charming, perhaps a little romantic, with her hair pinned out of her face and falling down her neck in curls, and her skin pale and fine, her natural color coming through at her cheeks, as though she had just come in from the cold.

She smiled at him as he studied her. "What is it?" she asked.

"You look very lovely," he said.

"I have found," she said, taking his arm, "that all this isn't very troublesome at all. It's almost a pleasure how easy it is to put on a little powder and do my hair. Even the corset is simple, if I don't tie it too tight. It's all rather a relief, actually, compared to what I have to do to disguise myself at Illyria. And looking like this . . . seems to make everyone else rather happy. Even Fiona smiled when she saw me, and I was waking her. I find I like it when people are made happier by my presence."

"I assure you, your toilette has nothing to do with that," Ashton said. "That's just a family talent." He took a walking stick from the stand and picked up the bouquet of lilies that Mrs. Wilks had left on the entry table, and they walked out the door.

Since their mother had died giving birth to them, their birthday had a bittersweet air about it. Growing up, they had dealt with this by trying to fit the sorrow into one moment, and spending the rest of the day as happy as possible. That moment was when they walked out of the house and past the bench where their mother used to sit. The violets were blooming and lent the air a heady scent, and the ash tree was green, waving in the chilled spring air. They paused there a moment, arm in arm, and looked out over their estate, each wrapped in their own thoughts. They continued around to the back of the manor, walking another ten minutes or so before they came to the family graveyard. Ashton didn't know what it looked like the rest of the year, but he was sure Mrs. Wilks arranged for the gardeners to make it look pristine on their birthday. It had a low stone wall around it, and a wrought iron fence. Inside, it was all elaborate tombstones and bright green grass. A few vases with fresh flowers were placed at the corners. They walked to their mother's grave, and Ashton laid the flowers down on it. They stood silently for a few moments, the wind running through the grass and trees the only sound, like rushing water.

"We're here, Mother," Violet said. "We just wanted to talk with you. And say we miss you. I miss you very much this year, I think. I have been . . . Well, from where you are, you can see what I've been up to. I hope you're proud of me, and not ashamed. I wish you had been around more. I wish you could tell me how to behave, especially with . . . if the duke plans on courting me, as he said he would—I don't really know how to behave. I think I might be in love with him, but if I embarrass myself, or him, when he comes round . . . I don't want to ruin anything. But I'm trapped now. I have a plan, and if I don't fulfill it, I'd have to spend the rest of my life lying to him, and I don't want that. I wish I knew how to make sure he will want me after I show him the truth. I wish I knew how to act around him. And I think you could have taught me that."

Ashton was staring gape-jawed at Violet when she looked up at him, blinking wetness from her eyes. "Don't you have something to say?" she asked him.

"I have a great many things to say to you," he said, "but, as for Mother . . ." He turned to the headstone. "I hope you would be proud of me, too," he said. "I had a poem published. Not in a major journal or anything, but people read it, and liked it, I think. I hope you can read it from wherever you are. I miss you deeply, Mother. We both do."

They stood a few moments more, sniffling and regaining their composure. There was a light breeze that wavered through their hair and over their faces, comforting them. Then they turned around, looking back at the house.

"The duke plans to court you?" Ashton exclaimed.

"You had a poem published?" Violet countered.

"Well," Ashton said, smiling, "yes, I did."

"That's fantastic, Ashton!" she said, and threw her arms around him in a loving embrace.

"Thank you. Now, tell me about the duke." He took her arm and they began walking back to the house.

"He asked my permission," Violet said. "Really your permission, I suppose."

"And you gave it on my behalf?" Ashton asked. "How very kind of you."

"I felt sure you'd approve."

"Did you?"

"Well, I approve, and the thought of someone needing your permission for something to do with me is absurd."

"Of course."

"But," she said with a sigh, "it might all be for naught. Once I reveal myself at the faire, he probably won't want to have anything to do with me any longer."

"You said he kissed you when he thought you were me."

"Yes, but he said he was thinking about someone else at the time. I think it was me. I mean, me as Violet. I hope it was."

"I suspect that your revelation may bring him more relief than anxiety, but it is a difficult spot."

"Which position do you think is more difficult? An awkward courtship, or being rejected?"

"Dear sister," Ashton said, "your courtship was bound to be awkward, even if you hadn't met your beau when he thought you were a man. If he doesn't reject you after the faire, I suspect your courtship will go very smoothly, as you discuss mechanics, science, and such. The way you talk about it, it may as well be love poetry."

"Oi!" came a call from the distance. They were nearly back at their mother's bench, and Jack was coming toward them, holding two large boxes.

Ashton and Violet waved. "Don't tell Jack," Violet said softly. "I'm not sure how he'll react. And besides, I don't want him thinking he and the duke are now friends, and winking at him, or such."

Ashton snickered. "Of course."

Jack reached them and held out the two boxes. Each had a ribbon wrapped around them and a bow on top, one in green and the other in purple.

"Happy birthday!" Jack said. The box with the green ribbon suddenly shifted, as though something inside it was trying to escape. Ashton sighed.

"Let's get inside before Ashton's present suffocates," Violet said, heading toward the house. Inside, Mrs. Wilks had hung looped paper ribbons and set up a large cake on one side of the dining room table. The other side had a mountain of presents on it. A few guests who had arrived early were milling about in the drawing room, staring through the open doors at the cake.

"I'll put these with the rest," Jack said, and headed for the presents.

"Shouldn't Ashton open his now?" Violet called.

"Nah, don't worry. It's got air holes," Jack called back. Ashton sighed again.

"I hope he didn't give you Oscar," Violet said.

"Who's Oscar?" Ashton asked.

Mrs. Wilks appeared before them and took their coats and hats.

"People are waiting in the sitting room," she said. "I know they're your father's friends, and it might be a bit awkward since he isn't here, but try to be sociable." She looked at them both proudly, then headed back to the kitchen to oversee the serving of drinks. Violet and Ashton looked at each other, then headed for the sitting room.

Ashton was surprised by how well Violet handled herself. He had expected her to become shy and talk little, but she managed to keep the conversation going nearly as well as he did. She was complimented on how fine she looked, and she told them it was all her brother's influence. Their father's friends were kind, and usually of the befuddled scientific type, whom Violet could engage in intellectual conversation while Ashton charmed their friendly and overly protective wives. Jack joined Violet in entertaining the scientists, so that when Fiona poked her head in, she saw a swath of gray-bearded men laughing at something Violet had said, and a group of tittering ladies fanning themselves around Ashton. She grinned and went back into the kitchen to have a drink with Mrs. Wilks.

Mrs. Wilks was very happy these days. She was no longer picking up after the children, and her invention had eased her anxieties, both physical and, with Laetitia's help, financial. Mrs. Wilks had no intention of retiring, and her pay was probably more than fair, but now she had a little extra that she could use to buy herself things, such as pearl earrings. She felt lovelier than she had in years. And as she relaxed, so did her mannerisms, so she and Laetitia got on quite well.

In short, the birthday celebration was perfection for everyone. Cake was eaten, wishes made, and presents opened. Jack had not given Ashton Oscar, but rather a small bluejay that had been trained to rest quite passively on the shoulder or wrist, and whose feathers had been replaced so that the bird was not just blue, but also purple and green—a beautiful creature. Finally the guests returned to their homes, remarking to one another what fine young adults the Adams children had grown into.

Jack lounged in one of the sitting room armchairs with his legs over one of the arms and a lit cigar in his hand. He, of course, had not gone home. Violet lay on a divan, staring at the unexpectedly tasteful bracelet that Fiona had given her. She had been surprised by the gift when she saw it, and looked up questioningly at Fiona, but Fiona had only winked, and gone back into the kitchen. Ashton was feeding his new bird. Mrs. Wilks swept into the room with a tea tray, removed the cigar from Jack's hand and stubbed it out in a nearby ashtray in one movement, and left.

"Hey!" Jack called, a little late. Mrs. Wilks swept in again, this time with a few more presents that Ashton and Violet had not seen yet.

"You shouldn't smoke in front of ladies," Mrs. Wilks said to Jack, then turned to Violet and Ashton. "These gifts are from your father, and these are from me. I thought you'd want to wait until the others were gone."

"Thank you, Mrs. Wilks," Violet said, "and I don't mind Jack's smoking."

"I do," Mrs. Wilks said, pouring tea for all of them. Fiona came into the room and stood quietly. Mrs. Wilks handed her the teacups to pass out, and then they both sat. "So, open them!" Mrs. Wilks said.

Ashton leaned forward and took the two boxes marked for him. In the first, from Mrs. Wilks, was a silk smoking jacket. "It's lovely," Ashton said. "Thank you." He leaned forward and kissed her on the cheek. The gift from his father was an assortment of pipes and tobacco, with a card explaining the make of each pipe and the origin of each tobacco.

"When I saw your father's gift," Mrs. Wilks said, "I decided to give you something complementary."

"Thank you. It's splendid."

Violet reached forward and opened her own presents. From her father was a large mechanical globe, around which were glass rings with the constellations marked on them in jewels. When a button was pushed, the globe and stars rotated, and a light came from within the globe that shone out on the constellations, making them glow. Violet loved it instantly. From Mrs. Wilks was a beautifully crafted dress of copper and purple. Violet held it up and stood, pressing it against her body.

"Check the sides, at your waist," Mrs. Wilks said. Violet did so. There were pockets, surprisingly deep ones, which led to a series of well-concealed padded pouches. "I had it especially made for you," Mrs. Wilks explained. "You can keep all your tools and gadgets in the pouches. But don't go getting grease stains on it!"

Violet was astounded. It was clever and beautiful. Why hadn't she thought of this? She hugged Mrs. Wilks tightly.

"There was one more present," Fiona said, sipping her tea.

"There was?" Mrs. Wilks asked.

"Oh, aye," Fiona said, "it arrived late, by personal messenger. For Violet. Shall I go an' get it, then?"

"Well, of course," Mrs. Wilks said. Fiona grinned, got up, and left the room. "Could it be from one of your new friends in town, Violet?" Mrs. Wilks looked intrigued. Violet shrugged. Fiona came back in holding an elegant package. It was well wrapped and had a seal pressed into its side. Violet recognized the seal instantly: it was from the Duke of Illyria.

"Oh," she said, and took the box from Fiona. "It's from the duke."

"The duke who visited over Christmas?" Mrs. Wilks asked. "I thought it was the girl you were friends with, Violet."

"I . . ." Violet didn't have a good explanation, so she just opened the present. Inside was a cluster of bronze pieces and a note. She dumped the pieces out onto the floor with a clatter and knelt beside them.

"Not very well packaged for a duke if it broke on the way," Fiona said.

Violet read the note to herself.

≈

Miss Adams,

I hope you do not think me too bold for sending you a present on your birthday. Knowing, as I do, the workings of your mind, I thought perhaps the best present for you would be one that you found stimulating and intriguing, as I find you. I will tell you no more than that. When you have put the pieces together, the rest of your gift will be clear.

—Ernest, Duke of Illyria.

≈

"It's a puzzle!" Violet exclaimed, her heart beating quickly. "A mechanical puzzle."

"Oh," Mrs. Wilks said, sounding a little confused.

"I have to figure out how it goes together. I don't know what it is, or what it will do or look like—I have to intuit all the pieces and the way they fit." She started picking up the pieces and examining their mechanisms. "And I suspect that as I assemble it, I shall have to alter the pieces. Attach a few, pull a switch, and the pieces will re-form so I can add on more. It's brilliant. Incredibly brilliant."

"Sounds more like a test than a gift," Fiona said.

"Oh no," Violet said. "It's perfect." And it was. Violet's mind was already assembling the pieces before her, trying combinations, examining what could happen when two were joined. She smiled broadly to think of the duke creating the present, bent over his table, working out the best disguise for each piece, imagining her all the while. She suddenly felt as if she could not breathe: her heart seemed to become full and light, and her eyes became watery. Then she picked up a piece and began trying to fit it to another.

"No you don't," Mrs. Wilks said. "We have to eat supper. You can start on this after that. Why don't you take everything up to your room for now?" Violet stared at the piece in her hand for a moment longer, then put it down in the box it had come in. She gathered the rest of the pieces and the note and put them in as well. Then, with Fiona's help, she brought all her presents up to her room and went back down for supper. Down the hall, Ashton delivered his own gifts and found a bouquet of red roses on the bed. He put one in his buttonhole. He would thank Antony after supper.

Violet did her best to pay attention to the conversation during supper, but everyone could tell her mind was on the puzzle. Ashton chuckled to himself. This duke really knew Violet. He would make a good match for her.

After supper, Violet went straight upstairs to work on the duke's puzzle. It was intoxicating, like being a young inventor again, attempting to figure out how things worked, or how a certain effect could be accomplished. And, like a young inventor, she fell asleep at her desk, the pieces scattered around her elbows.

The next day, Violet wore the dress Mrs. Wilks had given her, with a purple hat with a flower in it, to Easter Mass. Ashton wanted to wear his smoking jacket, but one look from Mrs. Wilks told him that it would probably be better to wear his morning suit. The service, as always, was long and tedious. Afterwards, they walked back to the manor surrounded by a group of their neighbors, all in their pale Easter finery.

Violet had long ago created a machine that would dye eggs quickly and easily while still allowing them to be creative. Cranberries, beets, spinach, and lemon peels were ground and mixed with water and vinegar to dye the egg, which a small mechanical hand would grip and dip into each color at the press of a button. Fiona found the contraption delightful, and played with it for the entire afternoon, while Violet worked on the duke's puzzle. They were together at the table in the sitting room, the windows open to let in the breeze. Ashton had gone off for a walk with Antony, and Mrs. Wilks seemed content to lie back on the divan, sipping tea while Fiona and Violet tinkered around her.

By supper time, Fiona had dyed two dozen eggs, and Violet had assembled what seemed to be the base of the contraption. It was a beautiful base, the pieces of bronze weaving together as they reached upward. After dinner, Violet continued working, even when Jack appeared and asked her if she wanted to go out fishing with him and Ashton. Mrs. Wilks tried to tempt her away with a sugar candy bunny, but Violet just took it and munched on it as she worked. Her heart and soul had plunged into the puzzle. It was more than delightful; it was an actual pleasure every moment she worked on it, and she longed to know what it was the duke had sent her. Eventually she was persuaded to go to bed, but when she woke the next morning, she went straight to work.

She finished it on the third day. It was a large bronze flower with an unopened bud and a key to wind the mechanism. After the key was turned, the flower bloomed and a soft melody played. The flower twirled, and suddenly, seemingly from nowhere, a small envelope emerged from the petals and fell to the ground.

"It's beautiful," Mrs. Wilks said, clasping her hands together. "A beautiful piece of art." Violet nodded, and opened the envelope. Inside was another note.

Violet,

I do not mean to tease you with more flowers. I only wanted to show you the beauty of them, and thought that you would see it most clearly if you built one for yourself. You'll find that the con-

struct is true-to-life, the petals all perfectly placed so that it is a large replica of your namesake. I wished to show you that violets are beautiful, though not as beautiful as Violet. I hope you do not hate me for this.

Ernest.

Mrs. Wilks saw that Violet's cheeks were flushed after she read the letter.

"Is anything the matter, dear?" Mrs. Wilks asked.

"No," Violet said, smiling. "Everything is lovely."

XXXII.

MATTHIAS Forney could have been back home in Pennsylvania. He could have been celebrating Easter with all his friends and relatives, and with Annie, whom he'd loved since they were children. Being with Annie was like riding atop one of his trains full speed, hair whipping around him as though he were flying. But then, being with Annie also meant remembering that she was married to his cousin Phil, and that was like being shoved off the top of a train going at full speed, which he had suffered too many times already. It was why he built trains to begin with, to get away from them faster and faster, though he always came back as fast as he could, because being away from her too long was even worse. It was like not having a train at all.

He was running now. Had run all the way to London, a place no train could take him. And he was spending his Easter underground, trying to repair an old train that hadn't run in years, with an unknown destination. Ernest had crawled under the train and walked down the tracks while Forney worked, but came back an hour later, saying they went on too long to walk them.

Forney had already figured out that the train was powered by a combination of electricity and Brunel's previously unsuccessful "atmospheric railway"—all air pressure and vacuums. That was the easy bit, just turn on some lights, explore the tracks a bit. And he had figured out the brakes. But he couldn't figure out how to make the damn thing start. The vacuum and electricity went on and the train shifted a little, but it was locked. The brakes were off, so there must be some secondary brake system, but damned if he could figure it out. He missed steam engines. Those were simple.

So, he went under the train. He didn't want to be there, but there didn't seem to be any other options.

"Anything down there?" asked the duke. He had told Matthias to call him Ernest, but he was a duke, and Matthias wasn't used to people with titles, so he just called him duke.

"I'm still lookin'," Matthias called back. The vacuum within the tracks sucked and the brakes were off, but the train didn't go. Why would that be? There was a large winding key sticking out of the bottom of the train. A spring-engine train? Then why the atmospheric railway and electricity? "There's a winding key down here. Like it's spring run," he called.

The duke poked his head down to see, then frowned and got down under the train next to Matthias. "Why would this be here?" the duke asked.

Matthias wanted a cigar. "I wouldn't know."

"Shall we turn it?"

"You ain't afraid of getting run over?"

"It would be a rather large design flaw if turning what seems to be a vital part of the train resulted in the turner being run over."

"Depends on what kind of man built the train to begin with."

"My father built it."

"Ah. Oh. Sorry, Your Duke . . . sir."

"No need to apologize. Just help me turn."

Together, the two men shoved the key in one direction. Above them, the train made a clicking sound and seemed to shift in its tracks. For a moment, Matthias was sure it was going to roll down the tracks, taking them with it and grinding them to dust underneath, and he would never get to tell Annie he loved her. But then the train stopped.

"Well," the duke said. Matthias scrambled out from under the train, felt in his pocket for a cigar, found one, and anxiously lit it. The duke came out after him and wiped his hands on his trousers. They were in work clothes, but the duke was still dressed finely enough that Matthias thought it was a shame to dirty himself up. "What do you think that did?" the duke asked. Matthias shrugged and inhaled deeply on his cigar. The duke stepped onto the train, and Matthias watched as it lit up and made a slight buzzing noise as the duke turned it on. Then came the great creak of the brake being released and tracks humming with compressed air, which sent a huge gust of wind and dust around the station, blowing out Matthias's cigar. The train, however, did not move.

"Matthias!" the duke called from in the train. Matthias went in. "What do you suppose this is?" The duke was pointing at a small circular depression in the control panel, which Matthias hadn't seen before. He bent in and looked at it closely. Inside the depression seemed to be a few gears, but he couldn't understand what they were doing there.

"I don't know," Matthias said. "Looks like you need another piece to fit in it."

"Like a key?" the duke asked. Matthias thought for a few seconds, wishing his cigar were still lit, and nodded. "A key," the duke repeated. "Of course a key."

"The switch on the bottom must have opened up the panel," Matthias said, then walked to the control panel on the other end. "Yep, there's one here, too, now. And I'm pretty certain they weren't there before."

"A switch hidden on the bottom to hide keyholes?" the duke asked.

"If you knew you weren't going to be using the train awhile, and you didn't want nobody else using it . . ."

"Yes, I see. Well, I think we're done, then. I just have to find this key."

"Probably won't look much like a key," Matthias said.

"Indeed. Let's go upstairs and bathe and change, shall we? I'm curious to see if Cecily's chickens have laid colored eggs yet this year."

"Sure," Matthias said, nodding and bringing his cigar to his lips, forgetting that it was unlit. Chickens that laid colored eggs for Easter—he had come to a very strange place.

⁂

CECILY's chickens had not laid colored eggs. At least, the shells were not colored. But when she accidentally broke one, she discov-

ered that the yolk had turned a stunning indigo. In each subse-
quently broken egg was a yolk in a new vibrant color: lavender,
bright pink—there was even one that sparkled like gold. While the
results were interesting, Cecily couldn't think of anyone who would
want to eat such things, so she considered the experiment a failure
and went about coloring the eggs the old-fashioned way. Aunt Ada
and Miriam assisted, though Cecily thought her eggs were by far
the most artistic.

When Ernest and the new mechanical professor, Professor Forney, appeared for lunch, they were both most impressed with Cecily's eggs. "Did a chicken lay them?" Professor Forney asked.

"Yes," Cecily said with a sigh. "But the shells of the eggs didn't
turn colors. Only the yolks did."

"Ah," Forney said, "a disappointment—but I wouldn't give up.
That's impressive enough, I'd say."

"Thank you, Professor. You're kind to say so. But a failure is still
a failure. I shall try again next year."

Forney was impressed with this little girl and the stern set of her
jaw when she talked about her experiments, but he didn't understand the golden rabbit that followed her about, and found it a little
eerie.

"Should we have supper?" Ada asked. Forney saw with some jealousy that she was smoking a cigar. He felt around in his pockets for
another of his, but he had none left. Besides, it was rude to smoke at
meals.

The food they served was delicious, rich, and perhaps a little
heavy, in Forney's opinion. But the company was enjoyable. They
all discussed the various states of the sciences with such intelligence, even the little girl and her Turkish-looking governess.

"Now, Matthias," the duke said when dinner was finished, but
before dessert was served, "as for your teaching: Professor Bunburry,
whom you'll be replacing for the rest of the year, left a very detailed
plan for what he intended to do in the rest of his classes. Of course,
you needn't follow it, but it should give you a good idea as to where
all the students stand. In each class, you'll find one student particularly gifted in regards to the mechanical arts. Of the third-years, it

is Mr. Cheek; in the second year, it is Mr. Volio; and of the first-years, it is Mr. Adams."

"Ashton is wonderful," Cecily said.

"Yes," the duke continued. "I'm sure Mr. Adams will be happy to assist you if you need help deciphering Bunburry's notes, or locating anything. Mr. Cheek will also be quite helpful."

"I wouldn't count on much friendliness from Volio, though," Miriam said. The duke raised an eyebrow at her. "Not that it's my place to comment on any of the students."

"Regardless," the duke said, "Mrs. Isaacs is correct. Mr. Volio is more . . . withdrawn than the others. I would ask someone else in his class for assistance if you need it. Probably . . . ah . . . That year is a bit . . . Ask Mr. Comte, if you need to. He's relatively harmless, and not overly distracted."

"Distracted?" Forney asked.

The duke nodded, then licked his lips. "You'll find," he said, "that many of our students, due to their extreme genius, also have certain . . . eccentricities. Mr. Volio's antisocial behavior, for example. Or that Mr. Adams's gestures can be a bit womanish, or that Mr. McCrief will speak of nothing but the intelligence of cats, if given the opportunity."

"Don't mention cats," Forney said, a little nervous. "Got it."

"You'll be able to outmaneuver the students soon enough," the duke said, "I'm quite sure. And if you have any difficulties with any of them, just let me know, and I shall either recommend the best solution, or give the student a sound thrashing."

"A verbal thrashing," Cecily said.

"And he's not very good at those," Ada said. "Better to thrash the upstart yourself."

"Is that allowed?" Forney asked.

"No," the duke said. "We do not issue corporal punishment."

"I've never taught before," Forney said, "except for other mechanics."

"You'll do fine," Ada said. "Just think of the students as other mechanics. Small ones."

"Ashton isn't small," Cecily said with a sigh.

"He's the smallest out of all of them," Miriam said, sounding confused.

"But his heart is large," Cecily said.

"Ah," Miriam said.

After dinner, Forney was shocked when they all proceeded into the drawing room, even the little girl, and had brandy and cigars, except for Cecily, who instead ate a candy rabbit, and Miriam, who rolled herself a small cigarette that smelled like roses.

While the others talked among themselves, Ernest leaned back in his armchair, feeling satisfied. He hoped Violet was enjoying her puzzle. He had worked hard on it, coming up with it in a dream one night, and then laboring all the next day to complete it. He had been quite delighted with it. He thought it was his second best creation, aside from Shakespeare. He hadn't received a letter from Violet, but he felt mostly certain she would love it. And though the note he inserted in it was perhaps a bit forward . . . he had made his intentions known. That was what he was most nervous about. Would she turn him away? He had soothed his nerves by working on the train with Forney or working on the æthership, which was proceeding quite brilliantly, thanks in large part to Violet. He had never felt like a genius except when arguing with her. She made him one, just through writing to him. He couldn't imagine what he had done without her.

But the train was becoming easier to understand, and the æthership was nearly finished, and he was relaxing in a chair quite contentedly, so he was anxious for a letter. Just a note from Violet—a simple thank-you would be enough. He tried to turn his mind to other things, like the strange key he would need to run the train. It had to be somewhere in Illyria. But he'd been over his father's things a hundred times, and nothing looked like a key. He would have to go over them again. If it didn't look like a key, what *would* it look like?

That night, the duke slept well, but awoke early and suddenly, knowing he had seen the key in his dream. But just as the image started to make sense, all details of it faded away.

XXXIII.

FIONA lit a cigarette and smoked it lying in bed, staring at the ceiling. She didn't usually smoke, especially now, as Drew would smell it on her, but she always kept a few cigarettes in her purse and some matches in her corset. They made her feel better when she was lonely, which was more often than she'd care to admit. Not as much lately, though. But tonight she was startled by how much she missed the feel of Drew's hair. Though he seldom spent the night at the small apartment he had bought for her, he often fell asleep in her arms after making love to her, knowing she would wake him after an hour so he could get back to the college. As he slept, she would reach out, take the soft curls of his hair, and wrap them gently around her fingers. It hadn't seemed like much at the time, but alone in her bed at the Adams estate, she found herself missing the feel of it, and his soft breathing on her shoulder.

The first man who had paid her for sex was a scientist. He had been a gentle lover, like Drew. He was older than she—she was only fifteen—but kind, and not bad looking. His name was Henry, and he smelled of chemicals and glass. He had taken his time with her, finding out which sensations caused her pleasure or laughter, trying to create the formula that would put her most at ease. The night had had its good moments, for what it was. He paid her and kissed her on the forehead, told her she was beautiful and that he would be back. She never saw him again.

The memory of him lingered when she made love to Drew, but with Drew, she always enjoyed herself. She liked his sweet round eyes and the feel of his hair. He had been sad when she said she was going away on family business for Easter, but she did what she could to cheer him up. At the time, she'd been focused on him. But now she realized she was a little sad about it, too. She liked the way she cradled his head in her lap as he slept or stared up at her. She liked how she could enchant him with the simplest of little games. Again, she thought of how he was sweet and child-like, somehow innocent and debauched all at once.

Fiona took a long drag on her cigarette, letting the smoke hang over her. She had never thought of herself as the motherly type. A long time ago, she had had a baby, but it died. She hadn't really prepared for it, and the father claimed it couldn't be his, so she feared it as it grew inside her, afraid that it would squeeze life out of her. But when he was born, fragile and hairless, with her same clear blue eyes and pointed nose, she had softened, tickled his belly and smiled as his eyes bulged in delight. So she slept with the baby every night, cradling him in her arms, until the fourth day, when she woke and found his dead body nestling into her still-breathing one. She had wanted to stop breathing with him then, but couldn't, because of the ragged gasps her body took as she cried. The other girls she lived with gathered around her, massaged her shoulders, and took him from her arms. A priest came by, told Fiona it was all in God's plan, and then took her son and buried him; Fiona still didn't know where. And then, Fiona had gotten on with life. There was nothing else to do, after all. But she still dreamt of holding him sometimes, and would wake up, her arms cradling the air.

A soft rap on her bedroom door woke Fiona from her thoughts. She found she'd been twisting her own hair around her finger, in lieu of Drew's. She looked at the door. The soft rap repeated itself. "Aye?" she called out softly.

"Fiona, it's Violet. May I come in?"

"Aye," Fiona said, sitting upright, stubbing out her cigarette on the bedframe. She was wearing only her nightshirt, but the room was dark. Violet softly opened the door and came in. She was in her nightshirt as well.

"May I turn on a light?" she asked Fiona.

"Aye," Fiona said again. "What's this about?"

Violet turned up a wall sconce so the room was cast in soft light. "I need your help."

"Oh?"

"I know you have no reason to help me, but I hope you still will."

"Course I will, if I can," Fiona said. "You've been very friendly to me."

"Because you blackmailed me," Violet said with a raised eyebrow.

"I prefer ta think of it as an exchange of ideas. A meeting of minds. And that maybe ye'd have helped me even if I hadn't known your secret."

"Are you going to hurt Drew at all?"

"No," Fiona said, a little offended.

"Then, yes, I would have helped you. If I'd known how happy it would make Drew."

"Well, good. So how can I help you?"

"I . . ." Violet kneeled on the floor next to Fiona's bed, as if she couldn't bear to stand and puzzle through her request at the same time. "Well, I need to know how to change quickly from my costume to a dress."

"That? Oh, that's easy. Ye dinnae need my help with that. You can already change yourself right quick; just practice till it's quicker. I mean, I could maybe alter some of your clothes so that they come off faster—like theater clothes."

"That would be wonderful," Violet said, then paused and looked at the ground.

"Was there something else?"

"Yes. I want . . . That is . . . there is a man. And he intends to court me. And I think I would like that very much. But I don't know how to . . . how to behave. I don't know anything about making love."

"You want me to teach you about sex?" Fiona asked.

"No!" Violet said, her blush apparent even in the dim light. "I want you to show me how to attract a man's attentions. How to keep him . . . how to make him fall in love with me."

"Well, if he wants to court ye, I think you've already gotten that bit right."

"But we've only spoken—that is, we've spoken when he knew who I was only twice. And I'm afraid I've been quite rude to him both times. It's in our letters that I can be kind to him, but that is because the letters are filled with science. I don't know how to behave in person. And I'm afraid that after a few days of talking to me as I am, he will realize his mistake and flee."

Fiona snickered and Violet glared at her.

"It's easy for you," Violet said, "you know how to be a woman. How to walk in a dress."

"Ye just walk," Fiona said, "and try to forget that the dress is there. Men are always tryin' to forget that your dress is there. But of course I'll help ye. It's going ta take a bit o' practice, though. Lessons. We'll do them in your room, as there's more space there. But, Violet, I dinnae think you really need it. Sure, knowing the best way ta show off your wrist, or ta wave your fan about is useful at times, especially onstage, but you won't be onstage. You'll be with a fella who it seems already cares for you."

"I just want to be able to be a fine lady for him," Violet said.

"We'll start tomorrow after breakfast, aye?"

Violet stood and sighed. "Thank you, Fiona,"

"It'll be fun for me," Fiona said. Violet shut the light and crept quietly out of the room again. Fiona smiled in the dark. It was easy to forget that Violet was just a young girl, what with her being so full of passion and fearlessness. But she had just turned eighteen, and had never had any women around her, save for the flighty Mrs. Wilks. No wonder she thought she needed lessons on being a lady.

❧◉❧

THE next morning, the first thing Fiona instructed Violet to do was to write back to the duke. In plays, ladies were always revealing their hearts in letters. Also, they were often carrying fans, which they could use to coyly hide their faces or gossip behind, so she and Violet went and picked out a few fans and practiced opening and closing them with a flourish. She showed Violet what to do with her hands while walking with a man: loose, but down, with the wrist slightly extended, and always pointing out something interesting.

For days they went over how to walk; enunciation—though Violet didn't feel Fiona was quite on the mark in this regard; flirting; dancing; how to accept compliments and make interest known; what not to say; what not to do.

By the end of the four days, Violet felt dizzy. "Are you certain," she asked Fiona one night as they lounged with Ashton in the sitting room, "that this is the way to behave when being courted?"

"I cannae be certain about anything, really," Fiona said. "This is just acting. Genteel manners, so you don't trip over yourself when dancing or wearing a dress. How to wear your hair. I like the Downy Dahlia best on you, though the Queen's Best Castle was fine, too—"

"Everything she's taught you has been quite correct in the world of plays and books," Ashton interrupted. He had been finding much amusement in occasionally watching Violet's Lady Lessons, as he called them.

"But, how do I behave like a real lady? The kind he'll love?"

Fiona laughed. "He already loves ye," she said, "so be yourself. These are just the, shall we say, tools of womanhood. I've only been showing you the proper ones, mind you."

"And we thank you for that," Ashton said. "Imagine what terrors Violet would wreak upon the men of the world if she had access to the improper tools. But, Violet, you do seem more like a lady now: the way you walk, how to be subtle in conversation. These are life skills Fiona has taught you."

"Just don't tell him he's a brute and ye think he's ugly, and ye should be fine," Fiona said with a wave of her hand.

Violet arched an eyebrow. "What about the part where I tell him I've been disguised as a man the whole time?"

"Ah, well," Fiona said. "I've never played that part. My Bristol Cities are too big." She cupped one of them, emphasizing her point. Ashton laughed.

"I feel confused," Violet said, crossing her arms, "and I don't often feel confused." She wanted the duke to feel for her as she felt for him—she didn't want to be the greasy girl in the nightshirts any longer. She wanted to be something else.

Her brother smiled sympathetically at her. "I think you'll be fine, sister."

"Being in love can make anyone feel unsure of themselves," Fiona said, grinning. "It's even happened ta me, once or twice."

Violet sighed and went to bed, leaving Ashton and Fiona, Ashton smoking his pipe and Fiona drinking brandy.

"Think she'll be all right?" Fiona asked. "I mean, when she tells the duke her secret an' all?"

"Oh, yes," Ashton said. "No matter what you've taught her, Violet is incapable of being anything other than herself. She's just unsure of herself because she's been playing a man all year. But once she tells the world who she is at the faire, and everyone sees that she's a genius, and a woman, and a thousand other things. I feel quite sure she'll regain all her old confidence, and plow ahead with anything— even romance—entirely as herself. You've showed her a few tricks, and she'll use them as she would a wrench, but in the end nothing will stop Violet from being Violet."

"An' the duke will love her for that?"

Ashton shrugged and puffed on his pipe. "Some people fall in love with lies, some with the truth. When you love a lie, you will always end up disappointed. When you love the truth, you will most likely be happy. I hope, that as the duke is a man of science, he is also a man who loves the truth."

"Aye," Fiona said. She had realized as she instructed Violet that somehow, unexpectedly, she had begun to love Drew. The part she played with him was who she was, and who she enjoyed being. She had played so many different parts that somewhere along the line she'd forgotten which was her. But not anymore. Ridiculous, brilliant Drew had helped her remember all the pleasures of not playing a part, and she loved him for it. She gazed over at Ashton, who was puffing contendedly on his pipe, and then she looked up at Violet's room, hoping that the girl might one day experience some happiness like her own.

XXXIV.

GARETH Bracknell had not had a nice Easter. It was the same as his past seven Easters, wherein he and his wife went out to see his mother in the country. His mother, who had been both fathered by a barrister and widowed by one, had never really felt that stargazing, as she called it, was real work, or a profession worthy of any member of her family, so she spent most of the time criticizing him, or talking about the remarkable deeds of his brother, the diplomat to Switzerland. Or, for some reason, asking after Valentine, whom she had apparently met once or twice at charity functions and thought of very highly. Valentine was a scientist; Bracknell just looked at stars.

And his wife, who was quiet as a mouse at home—just a slip of a thing in a white dress who always had a headache—would join in with his mother, picking apart the little pieces of him that his mother had dislodged, like a rat feeding on carrion after the lion had had its fill. The Mass had been dull, and the vicar had come back to the house and been dull there, too, except when he had fallen asleep and drooled a little. A dreadful Easter all around.

And so, coming back to London, Bracknell was in a dreadful mood. Looking about at the cheerful, relaxed expressions of his students, all of whom had clearly had wonderful Easter holidays, filled him again with a sense of rage about how unfair the world was and how, in all the vastness of the universe, of which he was keenly aware, he was the thing that was always pissed upon.

It seemed only right for him to piss back on the students a bit.

"All right, you little buggers," he said when they were all sitting down, "let's see if your brains haven't run out your ears during that little holiday. Adams—what is the gravitational pull of Saturn?" He liked picking on Ashton in particular, since Ashton's father had once made a joke at Bracknell's expense at an astronomy gathering.

"Pardon me, sir, but I don't believe we've covered that."

"'Pardon me, sir, but I don't believe we've covered that,'" Bracknell repeated in a high squeaky voice. "I don't give a fuck. Check your book, and we'll all wait for you to find the answer."

Merriman's hand shot up, squirming in the air with the answer. Bracknell ignored it.

"I think Mr. Merriman has the answer, Professor Bracknell," came a voice from the door to the roof. Bracknell looked over, ready to spit venom, but swallowed when he saw it was the duke.

"Oh! Sir," Bracknell said uneasily. "I didn't see you there."

"I often go out on the roof to think, once spring has turned the air fresh enough for it."

"How . . . pleasant for you, sir," Bracknell said. "Very poetic."

"I suppose," the duke said with a furrowed brow. "Well, don't mind me. But, as I said, I think Mr. Merriman has the answer."

"Yes," Bracknell said. "Mr. Merriman?"

The duke left as Merriman recited the answer in an excited rush. He certainly wouldn't be asking Bracknell to substitute if Professor Cardew left again, not after that performance. But the duke had suspected this sort of unprofessional behavior from Bracknell for ages; this had merely been confirmation. Ernest had hoped to interrupt the class and find it going well, but he wasn't surprised by Bracknell's brutish teaching style. However, he had not lied when he said he had gone out on the roof to enjoy the air. In spring, he found that the smell of the water and flowers from the garden below often drifted up and overwhelmed the usual stink of the city. The flowers weren't quite strong enough yet, probably because many of them were still in pots in his residence. He would fix that today. It was a nice day for gardening, and he enjoyed gardening in a good mood. And his most recent letter from Violet had put him in a very good mood.

But how to respond? With the faire coming up, he had little time for courtship in person. Could one declare one's romantic intentions through a letter? Certainly it was the sort of thing that happened in books. But it seemed to Ernest that it wasn't quite right to say "I love you, and shall do whatever it takes to win your hand" in a letter. He wanted to say it to her face, and see her gray eyes gleam. He knew they would gleam, but he still wasn't sure what she would say. The last letter had said that she adored the gift, that it was the best present she had ever received, and that she was flattered by how well he knew her, but she hadn't said that she adored *him*, only the gift. But perhaps she was being coy. Women were often coy, weren't they? He didn't care. He would pursue her anyway. He knew that there was a spark between them, and if she rejected him now, it was only because he'd done something wrong. He had never felt so content as when he thought about Violet.

In his apartments, he changed into work clothes, filled his wheelbarrow with potted plants, and took them out to the garden. The April air was damp and fresh, and the soil came up easily as he dug places for each plant and fit them into their holes. It was when he was replanting the dahlia bulbs that the idea came to him: He would court her at the faire. He would send her an invitation, and put her down as the co-inventor of his own exhibit, the æthership. "A Model of a Craft Built for Traveling the Stars, presented by the Duke of Illyria and Miss Violet Adams." That would surely win her heart. He felt light and airy to think of it. Next year, their exhibition at the faire could simply read "Presented by the Duke and Duchess of Illyria."

He packed the soil tightly around the dahlia and looked up to survey his work. The garden was full again. He went back to the residence and found a watering can, which he filled and brought back to the garden. It was a nice enough day that some of the students were going out for lunch, trying to hold on to the last bit of their holiday. Ashton was one of them, and he smiled at Ernest. Ernest smiled back.

"What are you doing, sir?" Ashton asked.

"I just transferred some plants back to the garden," Ernest said. "Now I'm going to water them."

"Only some plants come back after the winter," said Merriman, who was standing with them. Ernest nodded, and curbed his desire to pat Merriman on the head.

"May I help?" Ashton asked.

Ernest stared for a moment in surprise. "Why, certainly," he said, and handed Ashton the watering can. "Come do. I'll show you." He led Ashton to the garden and instructed him in pouring water—not too much—on each of the plants.

Violet listened carefully and did her best. She had asked if she could help without thinking, just trying to be close to him for a bit longer. He grinned at her as she poured the water, and she tried not to blush.

"There, that's enough—more is too much; you'll drown the plant."

"Sorry, sir."

"No need to apologize." He would enjoy having Ashton as a brother-in-law, now that the awkwardness of the kiss had been explained away. Mostly explained away. The duke was still very aware of Ashton's smooth skin, but he felt almost positive that this awareness was because Ashton's smooth skin reminded him of Violet's.

"Sir, if I may ask, why do you maintain the garden yourself? You have servants who I'm sure would do it for you."

"That's true," Ernest said, "but I think it's important to work in the earth, to understand the plants and ground personally, not just scientifically. When I create something, I try to work with nature, not against it. Why, in a few letters between your sister and me, we quite argued over the shell of the craft I'm building—we're building, really. You see, I wanted to follow an organic pattern of metal sheeting, somewhat like a pineapple—it would make the structure sturdier, I think. The way the shell of a pineapple grows, or how petals bloom in a flower: their overlap is nature's genius, a brilliant mathematical design. Much more resilient than the simple sheets of metal your sister argued for."

"Simple?" Violet asked, slightly offended.

"I didn't mean your sister was simple. Anything but; she's incredibly brilliant. But on this point I disagreed; the layering of the metal may make the device a little heavier, but it will also keep it stronger."

"I see," Violet said, pleased with his answer. "You study nature to improve your science."

"Well," Ernest said, "yes. That, and I like it. Nothing smells sweeter than a flower you've grown yourself."

Violet considered that. "Like building something yourself," she said.

"Yes, like that. But when you grow a flower, you don't work alone, you work with nature. It is less controlled. And because of that, I enjoy it. I think I've kept you from lunch, Mr. Adams."

"Oh, don't worry, sir."

"Nonsense. Everyone should eat. Come inside, I'll have the chef prepare something simple for both of us."

The dining hall was nearly empty when they entered it, as lunch was almost over. Only Cecily and Miriam remained.

Cecily grinned as Ernest led Ashton to the professor's table. "Are you hiring Ashton, Ernest?" she asked.

"He helped me in the garden and skipped lunch for it," Ernest said. "I thought he should eat."

"I think Ashton would make a fine professor," Cecily said. "You should have had him replace Professor Bunburry, instead of that mysterious Professor Forney. He smokes in class, did you know?"

"He does?" Ernest asked.

"He does," Cecily said. "At least, that's what the students were saying at lunch."

"Well, we all have our quirks," Ernest said. A servant approached them and, after a murmured conversation with the duke, ran back to the kitchen.

"How was your Easter, Ashton?" Cecily asked.

"Very good," Violet said. "And yours?"

"Well, Ernest was working for most of it, but Miriam and Aunt Ada kept me company."

"Do you celebrate Easter, Mrs. Isaacs?" Violet asked.

"Oh no," Miriam said, "but I like painting the eggs."

The servant brought out some sandwiches for the duke and Violet, and they ate them happily. Violet was quite content to be eating, drinking, and socializing with the duke, Cecily, and Miriam. She felt pleasantly at ease, as though they all knew she was Violet, and not Ashton. She could see Cecily as a sister, Miriam as a friend, and Ernest . . . the word husband was a heavy one to her, weighed down with implications of ownership and captivity, but if anyone could wear it and have it mean something else—have it mean partner, equal—then it was Ernest. Violet wanted to grasp his hand and declare the truth, and not just the truth of her gender, but of her adoration of him. Instead, she bit down on her sandwich.

·⚜·

AFTERWARDS, Ernest walked Ashton down to the mechanics lab to explain his tardiness to Forney, who was indeed smoking as he supervised the students working independently.

"Eh? No problem, then," Forney said. He was poring over engine plans.

"You're Matthias Forney?" Ashton asked. "The American train designer?" Ernest smiled, proud that his student knew international scientific figures.

"Yep, that's me. And you're Ashton Adams, right?" Ashton nodded. "Good to meet you. If you want me to look over whatever it is that you're building, I'd be happy to, but if you want me to mind my own business, I'm good at that, too."

Ashton grinned. "If you'd like to look over my plans, it would be an honor, sir."

"Sure," Forney said, taking his cigar out of his mouth.

"But the duke has to leave first," Ashton said with a sly look. Ernest widened his eyes and looked at Ashton. "I would prefer that you didn't see it until it's finished, sir," Ashton explained.

Ernest shrugged. "Very well. See you at dinner, Matthias. Mr. Adams."

Ernest left, shaking his head. Other students would have jumped at the chance to have Ernest critique their work early. Ashton was confident, like his sister, whom he owed a letter. He would write it tonight, but now he had to work on the craft, and then he had to search for that damned key. The key didn't worry his thoughts much anymore, though. He felt as though he knew where and what it was, and that if he just relaxed, it would pop into his mind like an old memory. So he worked on the æthership, thinking as he did so of what he would write to Violet that evening, and what she would say when she saw her name on the exhibit at the faire.

XXXV.

VIOLET liked Forney. By May, they had grown quite friendly, and Violet had even accepted a cigar from him on more than one occasion during her independent working time. His view on mechanics was different from Bunburry's: more forceful, more about pulling as much energy as possible out of every gear, every piece of coal. He enjoyed embellishments on the outside of a device, and clever functions, but the core was how good an engine a machine had. Which is why he was so enamored with Violet's engine, with its extreme functionality.

Cecily, though, did not seem to take to Forney, and started to avoid the mechanical lab, claiming the cigar smoke made her dizzy. The one time she came down to find Violet smoking, she grew quite upset, until Violet put the cigar out. Afterwards, Forney had come up to her and patted her firmly on the back. "Women, eh?" he said. "Can't handle a little smoke, shouldn't be living in London. But I guess we love 'em for being so sweet and dainty." Then he got a far-away look in his eye for a moment. "Well, better get back to work," he said, and clapped Violet on the back again.

Violet didn't think she was ever going to be sweet and dainty, but then, Ada Byron smoked cigars, and her many affairs were well known in the scientific community. It wasn't a cigar that was going to make the duke reject Violet. It wasn't even how well she behaved like a lady. It was how well she behaved like a man and, more important, that she had claimed to *be* a man while doing so.

It was at night that the lie really began to wear on Violet. Lying in bed, not really dressed as a man anymore, but not really a woman, either, she felt unfixed, and guilty. She wanted to tell everyone the truth. She started having trouble sleeping, tossing back and forth in time to the gears.

The duke's letters became kinder and more loving. He soon invited her to the faire at the Crystal Palace in less than two months, to see the model of the æthership that she had helped him create. Violet wrote back that she would be there. It wasn't a lie, of course, but it was one more untruth she felt uneasy about. The duke had begun to pour out his heart to her, slowly, subtly, but she still hadn't told him the one great secret that could drive them apart.

It was a Sunday when she and the duke next spoke in person. She had spent most of the day with Ashton and Jack, writing the false letter from Cecily for Miriam to give to Volio. They lunched together, but Violet had wanted to go back to Illyria to work, so she and Jack left a little early. When they got to the campus, Violet saw the duke standing in the garden, looking out at the river. Jack looked at her warily, then at the duke, and then headed inside without saying anything.

Violet walked to the garden and stood beside the duke. "I love the river," he said. "I know it's polluted, and if I were really up near it, it would smell quite bad, but I like the idea of it. Of ever-moving water. It strikes me as peaceful, even just the sound of it."

"I find the sound of the gears in Illyria soothing," Violet said.

"Do you?" The duke chuckled. "I'm sure your sister would, too. But you should take some time to consider the water, too. Brilliant in its own way. Forever moving, and very deep. Underneath it, I'm sure you wouldn't hear anything."

"Does that appeal to you, sir?" Violet asked.

"Well, yes, though not as morbidly as I said it, I suppose. I don't mean the idea of death. I just find the idea of a life without expectations refreshing. Under the water, it would just be me. Not my father's voice telling me to do better, or the scientific community saying I'm not good enough." The duke sighed. "But this is more than you asked."

"You wouldn't want to hear my sister's voice as well?" Violet asked awkwardly.

"Oh, no. Her voice is perfect," the duke said, placing a hand on

Violet's shoulder. She shivered. "No, her voice I wouldn't want to escape. It is encouraging, honest, argumentative, brilliant."

"I think," Violet said, looking down, "I think she feels similarly about you, sir. From what she's said."

"Thank you for that," the duke said, and patted her on the back before heading into Illyria. She watched him walk back inside, glowing a pale orange in the fading light.

✻⦿✻

VOLIO did not see the fading light, though he probably wouldn't have cared for it if he had. He had been working all evening in his own lab, and it was now past midnight, and he wanted to go to bed. But he had lost something, and it was important that he find it. The basement was as dark and clanging as it always was, and its sounds were giving him a headache. He held a gas lamp out in front of him, walking slowly down the halls, trying to be quiet, because a sound might cause what he sought to run away from him.

He groaned slightly, and rolled his neck, hearing it crack. He was tired. He'd been working all night, and he was in a foul mood. His eyes were dry from staring. He stopped walking to rub them.

Which is when the duke came around the corner at a very brisk walk. He saw Volio and stopped short. Volio lifted his lamp to see the duke better. His face was red, his eyes large and surprised. He wore a bronze jacket, and his hair was wet. "Sir?" Volio said.

"Volio?" the duke yelled. "What are you doing down here? Students are forbidden in the basement; you know that! And so late."

Volio clenched his jaw. He was in a foul mood, and being scolded by this pretender to his throne was not helping. "I was just looking for something, sir."

"In the basement?" The duke looked at him as if he were stupid.

Volio glared. "Yes, in the basement. Did you think I was confused about where I was?" Volio said with more venom than he intended.

The duke had been tapping his foot, as if irritated, but now he stopped. "Get out of here, Volio, before I expel you for violating the rules," the duke snarled. He sounded angrier than Volio had ever heard him, which only made Volio madder.

"Expel me?" Volio said, and then uttered a harsh laugh. "You? Expel me?" The idea was outrageous, offensive to all Volio's senses, and yet funny, too. As if the duke really had that power. As if his blood, weak and watered down, really gave him the rights to this school, which was so obviously Volio's. He had the key, after all. He was the better scientist. He was part of The Society. The duke was nothing. Volio laughed again, and then spit at the duke's feet.

In one fluid movement, the duke's hand flew out and grabbed Volio by the neck, pinning him to the wall. "You've always been an arrogant prat, Volio. Perhaps you feel more entitled because of your father's friendship with my father, or because your brother got away with breaking the rules. But, rest assured, you will not. I will expel you, regardless of your relations, and I will take a very great pleasure in doing it. Now, leave the basement."

Volio felt his face turning red from anger and lack of air. "Or what? Or you'll kiss me?" Volio asked in as nasty a voice as he could muster. The duke's hand went slack, and Volio felt his body relax.

"What?" the duke asked.

"I saw you and Adams fighting. I saw you kiss, too. Is that the sort of thing you really want people to know about? The headmaster who snogs his male students. Wouldn't go over very well, would it?"

The duke let his arm drop, color draining from his face, and Volio folded his arms in victory. The duke stared long and hard at him. "Leave now," the duke said in a low, cold voice, "and I will do everything in my power to forget this entire night ever happened." He stared at Volio in a way that made him feel as though he were shrinking.

"Fine," Volio said, turning from the duke's eyes. He stomped toward the lift, angry at the duke for thinking himself above him. He hated that no one knew—no one was allowed to know—how superior Volio was to all of them. He didn't like waiting on his father and brother, on the society of slow-moving old men. He wanted to take Illyria now, and to take Cecily, too.

That thought made him angry at himself. If he had made an enemy of the duke tonight—and he had, unless the duke really could forget everything—then Cecily's hand would be impossible.

Perhaps he could bargain for it. When he ruled Illyria, he could let the duke keep his title, and his apartments, in exchange for Cecily. A marital truce, like royal families did to end wars. Certainly the duke wouldn't be having heirs of his own, not if he was off buggering boys like Adams.

What was the duke even doing down in the basement? Volio felt a growl rising in his throat as he rode the lift up to the dormitories. It was unexpected. The duke had no right to be poking about where he didn't belong, either.

He opened the door to his room and closed it with a slam. Freddy snorted in his sleep and mumbled the beginnings of the Hail Mary. Volio rolled his eyes and sat down in his bed, pulling off his shoes. He would have to continue his search tomorrow. Hopefully, his lost object wouldn't cause trouble. It had the capacity for great violence, but only if activated the right way, and no one knew how to do that but Volio.

He lay his head down on his pillow, closed his eyes, and tried to fall asleep, and stop the grinding of his teeth.

❧❀❧

THE duke ground his own teeth in frustration, but remained awake, working his way through the dark basement halls to the train. The encounter with Volio was unfortunate, and the duke felt guilty for letting his temper get the better of him. But he had been in such a rush that Volio's appearance was an overly aggravating delay. And Volio, of course, had been an ass. But now that he had sent Volio to bed and shrugged off the blackmail—after all, who was going to believe a bitter student over a duke?—he gained control of his emotions and headed to the underground station, fondling the ring on his finger.

After his conversation in the garden with Ashton, the duke had retired to his water closet. He often did this after long conversations with Ashton, for they felt like long conversations with Violet, and long conversations with Violet made him feel in need of the relief only a warm soak could provide.

It was in the bathroom that the key to the key's location had finally come to him. He lay in the tub and stared at the tiled wall, and noticed the fanciful adornment of gears that had been there for as long as he had occupied his father's chambers. While he had always found the small circles with the gears inside them charming in a way that did not suit his father, that night they caught his attention in a new light, for he suddenly realized that they were the right diameter to fit into the small circles in the train. Naked and wet, suds rolling down his back, he knelt in the bath and tried to pry one of the circles out of the wall, but his hands were slippery and the tiles would not budge.

However, the gears in the circles would turn. He stopped trying to pry them out and looked at the pattern more carefully. It was a grid of circles, three rows of three, and each circle depicted a few gears, already interlocked. All but the center circle rotated, so he could turn the gears to face any way he liked. After a moment he noticed that if he imagined the outside gears as butting up against one another and not in separate circles, they could be made to fit together, and in doing so, they would also fit with the gears in the immobile center circle. He carefully turned each bronze disk so that the gears faced one another in a continuous system.

As soon as he moved the last gear into place, the center circle popped out slightly with a small ping. Ernest carefully removed it from the wall with a satisfied grin. It was a ring. A bronze ring with a large circle on its front, containing a number of small gears, like those in a pocket watch. Also like a pocket watch, there was a small knob on the side. Ernest twisted it a few times, and the gears spun slowly for moment, with a small buzzing sound.

Ernest finally understood. He hopped out of the tub, dried himself off, threw on some clothes, then headed to the cellar. He knew the way to the train well enough by now that he didn't need a lantern to find his way there, but he brought one anyway and, after his brush with Volio, finally arrived at the train. He smiled as he stood on the station's platform. Here, finally, was the door to his father's secrets, and now he had the key.

Inside the train, he pushed all the switches and buttons. The tracks hummed, the train lit up, and the brake released, but still the train wouldn't go. So Ernest took the ring from his pocket, wound the knob, and fit it into the small depression in the control panel before it could stop winding. A small click came from somewhere below him—a secondary brake?—and the train pushed forward on the tracks, into the darkness.

The train ride took longer than he had expected. It was dark outside the train, and he couldn't see much, but it smelled like stone and wet earth. At least twice, he was sure that the tracks went over an underground river, and once, he thought that he had somehow gone *through* a river. Sometimes the train would squeal and totter, and Ernest would have to grab a wall for balance. Sometimes he thought he heard animals outside screeching. Where was he? Where was he going? He stared out the windows, but could see nothing but the darkness into which he was plummeting.

✳✿❀✿✳

THAT night, like so many, Violet couldn't sleep. All she could think about was her constant lie to the duke, and how much more wonderful life would be without it. She wanted to tell him the truth now. When she did finally manage to drift off, she had two dreams: In one, she told the duke, and he thought her clever for it and told her he loved her. In the other, she told him and he stood there openmouthed before telling her he could never love a girl so twisted and arrogant as she.

She got out of bed slowly and softly and crept from the room. She sometimes found the cranking of the gears to be a comfort, so she went to the students' lounge to hear them better, but tonight, after an hour of listening, she did not feel soothed. She stood, spine rigid, headed to the lift, and took it down to the ground floor, and walked to the Great Hall. It was nearly empty and dark, lit only by a few golden lamps, but the sounds of the gears was strongest here.

Still in her nightshirt, she approached the central gear in the darkness. "Invention is the greatness of man" or, as Ada had said it, "humanity's greatness." In either case, she was surely a great inventress. She had invented an entire persona, a series of lies, and now all she wanted was to shrug them from her body and have the duke embrace her. She couldn't keep up the façade much longer. She knew the end was in sight, less than two months off, but she still felt as though time could not move fast enough.

A sound came from the darkness, and the duke stepped slowly out of the shadows. "Sir!" she said in her man's voice. "Sorry, sir. I couldn't sleep, and I thought a walk would help me." The duke said nothing, just stared up at the central gear. In the dim light, his skin seemed bronze. Violet looked down at herself. She wondered if it was light enough for the duke to see her, between disguises now: not quite a man, not quite a woman, her breasts unbound but her hair short, wearing just a white cotton nightshirt hanging to her knees.

And then, suddenly, it was like one of her dreams: She got down on her knees before the duke and confessed. "I need to tell you something, sir," she said, the words pouring out of her unbidden but with great relief. "I am Violet Adams. That is, you have known me as both Ashton and Violet, but I am just one person. One woman. Violet. My brother was the man you met over Christmas, who said he was my cousin—also named Ashton. It was a stupid lie. That one, I mean, not the one where I disguised myself as my brother and came here as your student. That was necessary. You wouldn't let women into Illyria, but I am worthy of being here. You know I am worthy of it, from my letters as Violet, and from my work as Ashton. And I just wanted to prove to you I was worthy . . .

"But then you started writing me letters, and talking to me about flowers, and I didn't just want to be worthy of Illyria anymore. I wanted to be worthy of you. I . . . I love you, Ernest. And I hope, despite my gross deception, that you still love me as well. For I know you love me. You haven't said so in your letters, but you asked me, when I was Ashton, if you could court me as Violet. And I said yes, because I love you."

The duke said nothing. Violet felt tears begin to spill from her eyes, and she clasped her hands together. "Say something . . . ," she begged softly. "Anything."

The clock in the hall began to chime three in the morning, and the sound of it echoed through the hall, louder than the gears. The duke looked away, and then suddenly ran from the room. Violet reached an arm out after him. "Ernest!" she sobbed. But he was gone. She cried awhile longer in the dark room, and must have fallen asleep for a while, because when she next had a thought in her mind, she was lying on the floor, her face sticky with salt. She pulled herself up and crawled back to her bed, not wanting anything but to close her eyes and make the evening end.

XXXVI.

I T wasn't until morning that Violet really realized what she had done. She woke up suddenly and gasped.

"What is it?" Jack asked. He was already awake, wearing a towel around his waist.

"I told him," Violet said, not quite believing it. "Maybe it was a dream."

"What?" Jack asked.

"Bugger," said Oscar.

"Last night . . . I went walking, and I found the duke, and I told him the truth, about me being Violet and Ashton."

"You what?" Jack screamed.

"Bugger!" Oscar screamed.

"At least, I think I did," Violet said. Her memory was hazy. All she could remember was the unfeeling face of the duke, bronze in the light, and the chiming of the clock.

"You better remember," Jack said. "This could affect me, too, Vi. I could be in trouble."

"I know. I'm sorry," Violet said. Jack and Oscar stared at her. "I did. I think I did. I need to leave!" Violet sprang up and opened all the drawers on her armoire, then took her bags from her closet and began shoving everything from the drawers into them.

Jack and Oscar continued to stare at her. "Bend over so I can bugger your arse," Oscar suggested.

"No," Jack said to Oscar, "not what I would recommend." He walked over, knelt beside Violet, and laid his hand on her shoulder. "I wouldn't recommend running, either," he said.

"I'm not running. I'm leaving before I'm kicked out. It lessens the scandal. And this way, I won't have to see him again. I don't think—" She stopped packing. "—I don't think I could stand that."

Jack saw her eyes shimmering. "Maybe he won't expel you," Jack said. "Maybe your plan worked, just a little earlier than expected."

"He didn't say a word. He just ran off," Violet said, now leaning into Jack's arms. "As though he couldn't bear to be around me. Oh, I've ruined it all," she said, and started weeping.

Jack had never seen her cry before, so he wasn't sure how to comfort her, but he wrapped his arms around her, let her cry into him, and stroked her back. "He's had a whole night to think it over. And to expel you. But he didn't. Go to class. Act like nothing happened. Let fate come to you. Perhaps it won't be as bad as you think."

"I'm sorry," she said, her tears dying down. "I know this could get you in trouble, too."

"Well . . . I'll just claim extreme stupidity. If they didn't find you out, I don't know why I would've, just because we share a bedroom. What man pays attention to the person in the bed next to him, anyway?"

"Don't let Cecily hear you say that."

"Is this really the time to be mocking me about my undying-but-considerably-more-constrained-than-yours love for Cecily?"

"I don't love Cecily."

"For Ernest, then. I assume that's why you told him."

"Yes," Violet said, looking down.

"Well, hopefully you just dreamed the whole thing. If so, you most definitely should not tell him in real life. Go dress. We'll get breakfast."

The duke was not in the dining hall at breakfast, and no one stared at Violet any more than usual, or ran up to her and shouted, You're a bloody bird, ain't cha? She still found herself walking through the dining hall hunched over, as if expecting a blow.

Jack elbowed her as they sat down. "Maybe it *was* just a dream," he whispered.

She knew, of course, that it hadn't been a dream. It was easy to think of it as one, it had all been so unreal—the chiming of the clock, the shadows, the hard angles of his face as he turned from her. But there were also concrete things, like the dust from the floor she had found in her hair when bathing. It had not been a dream. She had confessed her secret to the duke, and he was surely not at breakfast because he had called the police to arrest her for fraud. Or maybe he was locked in his bedroom feeling hurt and betrayed, and he would come down later and quietly banish her from Illyria, and from seeing him again.

Violet didn't know which she could stand the thought of less. She worried not just for herself and her family—the shame she'd bring on her father and his reputation, the collapse of her scheme, and the end of her goals—but for the pain she might have caused the duke. Even if he stripped her of her right to be a student, she hoped he could still love her. To lose both would be terrible. She wondered if he was sitting alone in his lab staring at her letters, before throwing them into the fire and watching them burn.

When they got to the astronomy tower, Bracknell was tapping his foot nervously and looking out at the duke, who was standing on the roof, still as a statue among the various figures. The morning light turned him a bright gold.

"He's been out there all morning," Bracknell said anxiously. "I think he's testing me." He turned to look at the students, who were all sitting at their desks. "All right. Well, let's give him a real good show, then. Kind, gentle teacher; studious, intelligent students. We'll both be lying through our teeth, but if I can do it, so can you."

The duke didn't move for most of the first part of class, but Violet kept looking at him anyway. His back was to them, and he was looking out over London. At ten o'clock, the clocks all through Illyria began to chime, and the great clock of statues that the duke stood among started to move. The duke moved with them. First he just stood on the platform, but then his head moved down, staring at his feet. And then, as suddenly as he had last night, he turned and ran for the edge of the roof overlooking the river.

Violet was out the door to the roof in a second, but she wasn't fast enough. "Ernest!" she shouted after him. He turned at the last minute and looked her silently in the eye, his expression cold and empty, and then he fell.

The other students had by now come out onto the roof, screaming and unbelieving, running to the edge to see where the duke had fallen. "Christ!" Lane said.

Violet was the first to reach the edge of the roof. She looked over it just in time to see Ernest plunge into the river and not come up again. She felt dizzy, but Jack was beside her, leading her away from the edge.

"Bloody hell," Bracknell said.

"Why would he do that?" Merriman asked. Violet knew the answer, but she couldn't say it aloud. Instead, she just leaned against Jack and said nothing. But in her mind, she was saying the answer over and over: He did it because of me. He jumped because of me. He killed himself because of me.

XXXVII.

WORD spread quickly around Illyria that the duke had thrown himself into the Thames and not come back out again. Classes stopped immediately. Servants began cutting black armbands for themselves and the students. All of Illyria was in mourning.

Cecily broke down crying in Miriam's arms when she heard, and Miriam had Professor Curio send for Ada immediately. After crying awhile, Cecily finally gave in and fainted, which meant Miriam and Curio could move her to a divan in her residence. When she came to, she was groggy and confused about where she was, but she heard Miriam and Ada speaking.

"It can't be true, can it?" Ada was saying. "You didn't see it with your own eyes, did you?"

"No, ma'am," Miriam said, "but several students did, and so did Professor Bracknell."

"Bracknell!" Ada said with disdain. "That man can barely pick out the stars. I'm sure if Ernest did throw himself off Illyria, then it was only because he couldn't stand another moment breathing the same air as that loathsome brute."

"I don't know why he did it, ma'am," Miriam said softly.

"I know, Miriam. I'm sorry. I'm just . . ."

Cecily opened her eyes and saw Ada wringing her hands in front of her. "Cecily!" Ada said, hugging her, and pressing her face close to the young lady's. Ada's cheeks were wet—she had been crying, too.

"Where's Shakespeare?" Cecily asked. She very much wanted to hold the rabbit, knowing that Ernest had made it. Miriam quickly left the room, came back a moment later with Shakespeare in her arms, and handed him to Cecily. Cecily cradled Shakespeare, pushing her face into his cool fur and listening to the ticking gears that served as his heartbeat.

"I suppose," Ada said, resting her arm around Cecily's shoulder and sitting beside her, "that I should make some sort of funeral arrangement. I'll make sure it's a good service. And I'll make sure that when they find his—" She started to cry. "—when they find his body, that it is treated with respect." Cecily burst into tears again, which caused Ada to cry harder. Even the stoic Miriam had tears running down her face.

The rest of the day passed in a haze for Cecily. She didn't seem to eat, or do much of anything besides lie on the divan and stare vacantly into space. Once, she thought she heard Miriam turning someone away at the door. She asked if it was Ashton, come to comfort her, but Miriam only shook her head.

In fact, it had been Jack, who had spent much of the day convincing the grief-stricken Violet it was not her fault that the duke killed himself, that there were clearly things they did not know or understand about him. When Violet fell asleep, Jack had instantly gone to check on Cecily. Miriam met him at the upper door to the residence, on the bridge over the Great Hall.

"Please, Miriam, we're friends. Just let me talk to her."

Miriam shook her head sadly. "I'm sorry, Jack. Ada is here, and I need to keep my job if I'm going to be able to be a comfort. Ada told me no visitors, so no visitors. As soon as Cecily is up to seeing people, I will let you know, I promise."

Jack kicked the edge of the bridge. The sound echoed through the empty hall. He put his hands in his pockets. "All right," he said, "I understand."

"*Je suis desolée*," Miriam said, looking down.

Supper was served to a noisy dining hall. Everyone wanted to know why the duke had done such a thing. Some thought he might have discovered a dark secret about his father, some thought he was merely insane, but most felt he had thrown himself off the roof because he felt he could never live up to the family name. The professors ate silently, except for Valentine, who sobbed dramatically over his plate. No one knew what to say.

❧❀❧

LATER that night, it began to rain dark heavy drops. They bat-
tered the windows and ceiling, and the sound of them, hammering,
almost blocked out the sound of the gears. Cecily was asleep, but
Miriam found herself restless. The duke's suicide was another mystery she couldn't solve, and this one so much more awful than the
others. Why had he done it? How could he do this to Cecily?

Miriam donned her cloak and looked into Cecily's room to make
sure she was still sleeping. She loved the girl. It was a silly thing to
admit to herself, but it was true. She was like a little sister. The closest thing to family she had, besides Toby.

Miriam used the secret passage to get out into the garden, the
cloak of her hood up, the rain falling in heavy curtains around
her. She walked up to the river, where she normally stood, and stared
into the water. It was a tomb now, and yet it looked so alive, the
rain rippling it in a furious dance. Interlocking, ever-widening
circles overlapped in strange hypnotic patterns like a language she
didn't know.

The rain made thick sounds when it hit her cloak, like the beating of a far-off drum. For a while it was her alone with the river and
the sound of drums. She felt sad, after all that had happened, but
happy, too. The rain always made her happy; it washed everything
else away. It made her feel apart from the world. Alone.

Then she felt Toby's arms encircle her from behind. She didn't
mind that, though. Of all the people in the world to be alone with,
Toby would be her first choice. She sighed and leaned back into him.

"I thought you'd be out here," he said. She didn't reply, but leaned
back into the weight of him. "What are you thinking about?"

"The rain," she said. He knew what she meant.

"Ah," Toby said, "the rain." They stood in silence for a while before he spoke again. "Days like these, it makes you realize you need
a roof to protect you from the rain. Maybe I could buy one for you.
And a house to go with it."

"I rather like standing in the rain," Miriam said. "And I don't mind
getting a bit wet."

"Please, Miri, why won't you let me buy you a flat, near mine?" He stepped around to face her. "You wouldn't have to work at all. I'd take care of everything for you."

Miriam turned around, smiling, and put her hand on his cheek. "Do you love me?" she asked.

"Wildly."

"Why?"

"You're unlike any other woman I've met," he said. She raised an eyebrow, but kept her hand on his cheek. "Other birds, they're either stuck-up women of high society—some are smart, sure, but not smart enough to be really different from the dumb ones. And the lower class girls are often uneducated, and just want my money. But you . . . you're separate, different from any of them."

"And if I began taking your money, and living off you, would I still be different?"

"It wouldn't matter," he said.

"It would matter to me."

"Miri, you can't be Cecily's governess for the rest of your life. Especially now. Is it . . . do you want to get married? Because you know I—"

"No," Miriam said, staring past Toby at London. "I've been married." They stood in silence after she'd said it. They rarely talked about her husband, her life before Illyria. "I'll stay on as long as Cecily needs me, but I should leave next year, I think. She'll be inheriting Illyria. She doesn't need a governess. I have plenty of money saved up. I should have enough to rent my own apartment for a year or so, until I find new work."

"But—" Toby began to say.

Miriam put her finger over his lips. "Can't we just love each other, and be independent, too? Isn't that enough?"

"As long as you love me," Toby said, "it will always be enough."

Miriam reached up and kissed him softly on the lips, and let her breath pass into him. The rain soaked them through as they held each other. For that moment, they were both under her hood, and all she could hear was the beating of rain and her heart.

CECILY finally felt up to eating again at dinner the next day, so Ada and Miriam led her to the dining hall. Classes had started back up again, on Ada's orders, but everyone was somber. Cecily was colorless with sorrow and dressed entirely in black. When she entered the dining hall at midday, it instantly fell silent, something she was keenly aware of as she walked to her table. Before sitting, she turned to the students, who stared up at her expectantly.

"My cousin"—her voice was weak, but it still echoed through the dining hall—"would not have wanted us to be so dreary. He would have wanted us to continue learning. To finish the school year, to do our best. His memory will live on in all your works this year, so don't disappoint him by saying your sorrow stifled your intellect. Work harder in his honor. We shall all recover."

Then Cecily turned and sat down at the head of the table. Ada reached out and patted her hand gently. "That was a fine thing you did," Ada said. "Ernest would be very proud."

The servants brought out turkey and salad, and Cecily ate, though she did not feel hungry. She did not even eat much of the strawberry shortcake they made for dessert, knowing it was her favorite. She felt oddly uncomfortable in the head chair. It was for a bottom larger than hers, and longer legs. She looked out at the students. Jack was patting Ashton on the back, as Ashton, who looked as bad as Cecily felt, cried silently over his plate. Such a sensitive soul, Cecily thought; such a good young man. Her heart leapt weakly in her chest, like a crippled deer. Even romance was dulled by Ernest's absence. She stared vacantly out over the students as they ate. The soft sounds of clinking glasses and silver seemed hollow, louder than usual. She let the noise of them enter her mind, and tried not to think.

When dinner was nearly over and the students had begun to stand to leave the room, the doors burst open with a resounding and enthusiastic slam, and in walked Ernest, Duke of Illyria. Cecily stood with a gasp. The hall once again fell silent. Cecily felt quite sure that she was hallucinating. Perhaps a side effect of one of the chemicals in the lab, or perhaps she had merely fainted with sorrow and was now dreaming up what she longed for the most.

"Ernest?" she said, and reached out a hand.

"Cecily?" Ernest asked with a smile on his face. He was covered in grime, and his face was dirty, but glowing with happiness. "I trust this garb of woe does not betoken some terrible calamity?" Ernest asked.

"You're alive," Cecily said, and then turned to Ada. She was staring at Ernest as well, equally shocked. So was Miriam, whom Cecily had never seen shocked in her life. Everyone was seeing him.

"Of course I'm alive," Ernest said.

"Oh, Ernest!" Cecily exclaimed, and ran forward and held him hard and fast in front of the entire school.

"Ernest!" Ada followed suit, rushing up and throwing her arms around Ernest's waist.

"While I am delighted by such an enthusiastic reunion," Ernest said, "I see little cause for it. I've been gone only two days. I apologize for not telling anyone I was going, but it was quite unexpected and—"

"You were dead!" Ada exclaimed. "The students, and Professor Bracknell, saw you leap off the roof and into the Thames. And you did not resurface."

"Dead?" Ernest asked, and began to laugh. "What nonsense. Why would I leap off the roof and into the Thames?"

"We didn't know," Ada said. "We had no idea."

"When was this supposed leap of death?"

"Day before last," Cecily said, "in the morning."

"Well, I don't know what they all saw," Ernest said, "but here I am, as alive as you."

"Oh, Ernest," Cecily said, burying her head in his chest. She was crying again now, with relief and joy. She looked up, and her eyes searched for Ashton's, so that Ashton could share in her happiness. But when she found Ashton's eyes, they were locked firmly on Ernest, wet with joy, and no matter how long Cecily looked, they would not budge. Instead, to her surprise, she found Jack staring back at her, smiling broadly, and his green eyes sparkling to see her once again filled with delight.

XXXVIII.

T HE night before last, Ernest had stepped cautiously out of his
father's train. The ride had been long—he had forgotten to put
his watch back on after the bath, so wasn't sure how long—and he
might have fallen asleep once or twice, he wasn't sure. He was eager
to explore, but his brain told him to be wary—he did not know
where he was, or who for certain had built the train to begin with.

The room was dark, but from the feeling of the air and the echo
of his footsteps, he could tell it was large. The light from the train,
and from his lantern, barely made a dent in the darkness. He
walked forward slowly, lantern in front, and soon came to a set of
elegant but dirty stairs that seemed to be made of marble, with
graceful curved banisters. He laid his hand on one of them, intend-
ing to start climbing, but the moment he touched the banister, the
room sprang to life with an audible electrical snap. Lights came on
from wall sconces and a chandelier that hung from the ceiling. The
platform was large, and many boxes were piled up on one side of it,
as if they had recently been delivered. Up the stairs was a landing
lined in marble columns that went from floor to ceiling, giving it
the appearance of a cage. From somewhere beyond that, the sound
of an out-of-tune violin scratched softly in the air. After a moment,
an out-of-tune piano joined it. Ernest felt a bead of sweat run down
his neck, and heard his heart beating faster. Where had he come to?

Nervous, Ernest clenched and unclenched his hand, then climbed
the stairs. The tune the violin and piano played was one he recognized, an old tune from his father's childhood that he would often
hum while walking about Illyria. At the top of the stairs, beyond
the landing and marble columns, was his father's lab. Ernest knew

it instantly. It was giant, a tower that plunged upward with a huge circular staircase in the center and windows all along the sides, many of them stained glass. Scientific accoutrements—beakers, bottles, gears, electrical engines, bones—were scattered around the open floors of all the stories but the ground story, which was covered in dust. A large banner hung from one wall bearing a version of the Illyrian seal—a shield against a red background with a gear inside it. Normally, the gear bore the symbol of one of the five sciences Illyria taught and it was worn on the jackets of graduates to show mastery in their scientific form. But this version of the seal showed a globe, seeming to suggest mastery of the earth itself. And the motto, written on the image of the gear, had been changed to *ARTIFICES DOMINATORES HOMINI SUNT*—"Inventors Are the Greatest of Men." No . . . not quite greatest. More like rulers. Ernest clenched his jaw and frowned. This banner felt like a mockery of everything he loved about Illyria.

Under this banner was a stand, and on that, an open book. Ernest approached the book, blew the film of dust off it, and read the top page—a list of signatures:

Algernon Illyria	Pierre Frett	Gremio Walle
John Snow	Jan Weever	Tarquin Whittaker
Alfred Kingsberry	Adam Volio	Beau Dogberry
Henry Voukil	Orlando Canterville	Uriel Barbicane
Marcus Pluris	Marcellus Knox	Walford Cowper-Cowper
Arnost Bonne	Randall Grey	Kingston Pontefract
Langston Verges	Franz Umney	Howard March
Abelard Alroy	Quimby Rastail	Daniel Ghatan

Ernest recognized some of the names: his father's, a few of the professors who had taught at Illyria years before. Many of the names he knew belonged to men who were dead now. After the top page was a manifest of sorts, saying that the group had been formed to rule the world, to impose their superior intellect on humanity for its own good. In many places, various hands had gone back, crossed things out, and written more in between the lines. The manifesto had clearly been changed over the years. After that, there were monthly meeting minutes, each in a different hand. There were notes on the progress of various members' experiments, notes on arguments among members of the group, notes on ways to overthrow the Queen, and the best way to conquer Ireland. The minutes were all dated, but ended a year or so before his father's death. It seemed that by that point, the group had fallen into disarray. Members stopped coming to meetings, some were kicked out, and several had mysteriously vanished, probably the victims of other members' machinations. Then, the book went blank.

Done with the book, Ernest climbed the central spiraling staircase. Each level was open to the floors below it and hugged the walls, more like a very wide balcony than like an actual floor. One floor was a library, and another was a place for storing supplies like bottles of chemicals and eyes floating in jars—human eyes. On another floor was a huge slab with arm restraints and various wires hooked up to it, and a single human bone lying still on the surface. Another floor was covered in gears and metal parts and had a huge forge. And another floor had a small analytical engine, and another, half taken apart, or only half put together. On the very top floor were the violin and piano, both being played by mechanical hands, and both sadly out of tune. Ernest looked out one of the windows of the top floor. It had a crack in it, and a strong draft came through, blowing his hair back. He was in a tower in the middle of the countryside, but where, or which countryside, he could not tell. It was all green, with nothing but woods and plains in every direction. He could see no sign of other people, except for a wandering cow, which he supposed might have escaped from a nearby farm.

He spent a day thoroughly exploring the tower. His father had left notebooks everywhere—piles and piles of them, all meticulous, far more detailed than Ernest's own notes. Ernest read them all in a huge dusty armchair on the top floor, and when he finished, he knew something new: His father was not the genius Ernest had thought. He had been a genius, certainly, but what Ernest had thought had set him apart—his ability to pull his inventions seemingly from the air already perfected, as though he had just thought of the idea and then calculated how it would best work—did not exist. His father had worked at least as long and hard as Ernest did before he even announced an invention. Keeping his workings secret had been intentional, to enhance the appearance of his genius, as well as his mystique.

Ernest found philosophical notes written in the margins of the notebooks, as though, when his mind couldn't stand scientific computations any longer, he would step back to muse on science in a more general sense. "Always keep your working secret," his father had written. "No one wants to see science made. It makes people think they can do it themselves, that it is just a matter of hard work and trying over and over until they get it right. It is not. Some men are born with the genius for science. Some are not. Therefore, a society in which those born with that genius rule over those born without it, or at least those born with some genius rule over those without any, would be for the betterment of mankind." Ernest did not agree with his father on any of these points, but he felt satisfied to be delving into his psyche.

In other notebooks, he found more scribblings, such as "The stupid should be sent to Australia and kept in cages" and "Ideally, the Queen would cede power to us willingly, but if taking it is what we must do, it shouldn't be difficult. And once we have control of England, the continent shan't be far off."

In the final notebook, the one dated a few months before his father's death, Ernest found a note in the margin about him. "Ernest—should I let him into the Society? There is so much infighting. They would eat him. Better to let him live happily, making his little toy rabbits. He does not have the spine for real science." Ernest bit his lower lip when he read it and, for a moment, swelled with rage, but then it subsided. He knew what the Society was now, knew his father's dark secrets, his philosophy and goal of world domination, and Ernest knew that even had his father offered this legacy to him proudly, he would have wanted no part of it.

Most satisfying, though, were the places in his father's notes where Ernest could see his father struggling to understand something Ernest grasped easily. Of course, in many instances, it was due to the progression of the sciences since his father had written the notes, but there were many principles that Ernest knew innately which his father seemingly had to discover. Ernest wouldn't venture to say he was smarter than his father, but knowing his father was only human made Ernest gasp deeply, as though suddenly rising off the ground. He started to laugh, loudly and for a long while, drowning out the playing of the disharmonic instruments.

His father had also left many experiments unfinished, such as a new analytical engine that did not just predict numerical equations, but also retained information from previous equations, and built on them, interacting with the user to figure out a problem. He had attempted many experiments on human resurrection, which Ernest found distasteful and only glanced at; and many chemical experiments attempting to find a cure for, as well as a replication of, what he called "Curio's Condition."

After finishing his inspection of the lab and reading many of the notebooks, Ernest returned to the banner and the list of names. This had to be the "Society" to which many of his father's notes referred. The Society was long gone now, and held no more threat to England, or anywhere else, than a bunch of disgruntled old men, working away in their labs and mumbling about how they had almost ruled the world.

It took him another day to look at everything, but when he was done, Ernest felt completely changed, as though he had somehow dissolved a layer of himself in acid and emerged fresh and stronger, uninhibited by whatever had been clinging to him. He began thinking of new things he could do with Illyria, things he wouldn't have tried before, because his father would have disapproved. His father was dead now, and Illyria belonged to Ernest. Changes could and should be made.

As he rode the train back and walked through the college, he was lost in his plans, unaware of the dreary silence of the place until he walked into the dining hall, and saw everyone staring at him, and then felt Cecily squeezing him with joy. He felt happiest at that moment, and wished only that Violet could be there as well, to make it perfect. And somehow, he thought, he felt she *was* there. He would write to her immediately, to tell her of his plans for Illyria. There were so many changes to be made, and he knew she would bring out the best ideas in him, if she didn't come up with them herself.

XXXIX.

THE one person who was not pleased by the duke's resurrection was Malcolm Volio, because it confirmed what he had feared: that his automaton, his final project for the faire, had fallen into the Thames. When he heard Ernest had jumped, he should have been joyful, because it meant that Cecily was free to give herself to him—for though she was quite willing to marry him, she was a dutiful girl, and would never do anything to displease her cousin and guardian. But he refrained from rejoicing, suspecting the drowned man was not actually the duke.

A few nights ago, Volio had taken his automaton out for a test run through the basement, but when the clock started chiming, his machine ran off suddenly, and Volio had been unable to find it, though he had searched until dawn. And the next morning, it had thrown itself off the roof. Volio couldn't figure out how his creation had gotten to the roof, but it was well designed enough to be capable of anything. Including, it seemed, suicide. He had worked so hard on it, crafted it perfectly in the image of the duke, dressed it in the finest clothes, even given it glass eyes. He was sure it would have won the duke's approval, and with that, Cecily's hand in marriage. It was his last honorable attempt at winning approval to marry Cecily, which would have been so much faster than waiting until the Society had taken over.

But instead the worst-case scenario had come to pass. As the rest of the students crowded around the duke to win his approval by telling him how sad they were at his apparent death, Volio stalked out of the dining hall and down to the cellar, making sure no one was watching him. Losing his project was a setback, but not a major one. He had more automata, just as carefully built as the one modeled on the duke, but without all the superficial detail. They would still be impressed with his accomplishments at the faire; he was sure of that.

He crept through the cellar without a light, knowing the way by heart, and came to the door—if it could be called that. Really, it was a sheet of metal with a small depression in the center. Volio turned the knob on the ring on his finger, thrust it violently into the depression and then pulled it out again after he felt it tremble under his hand. The door slid open into the wall, and Volio stepped through quickly, so that it didn't close on him when it slammed back into place a moment later.

The room, his brother had explained to him when he had given him the ring, was once a holding area used by the late duke, who kept various supplies here before shipping them off to his private lab via the train that was down the hall. Volio's brother had tried to operate the train once, but couldn't decipher it, and didn't really need to. The former holding bay was huge, and still had many supplies in it when Volio's brother first invaded it. It hadn't taken much work to turn it into a huge and well-equipped lab.

Volio had been worried that the current duke would discover him, but his brother had assured him that only members of the Society even knew about the room, much less how to open it, and the duke had never been initiated into the group. But then, neither had Malcolm. His brother had been, and his father was a founding member, but Malcolm wasn't good enough yet—he had to prove himself, they told him, prove that he had the scientific abilities to create something worthy of their Society, and the passion to use it for the good of mankind.

Volio agreed with their philosophies, of course: The intelligent should rule the stupid, the strong should rule the weak; it would make things run more smoothly. But Volio also felt that any supposed geniuses who didn't agree with this philosophy—like, he suspected, most of his fellow students—were not bright enough to be good rulers. They would have to be ruled, along with those of simply common intelligence.

Volio surveyed his automata. There were nearly eighty of them now, all laid out on their own slabs. These did not look like the duke, more like metal skeletons, but they had also been perfected, and wouldn't run off as his duke-automaton had done. What was brilliant about them was their ability to take orders, like soldiers. Normally, an automaton had just one function, or had to be manually reset if it were to be switched between two functions. Even his brother's army of automata had been capable of little besides rushing forward and shooting. But Volio's could take orders at the ring of a bell. The sound of each bell produced vibrations, and those vibrations resonated within his automaton, which activated a gear, and so on. Ring this bell and they walked forward; ring that one, they turned left; ring another, they began to run; ring yet another and their clawed hands reached out and began slashing. Perfect soldiers. Unfortunately, with the duke-automaton, which he had given more commands and functions, trying to make it look human, Volio had been having trouble making sure that the vibrations produced by the bells were not produced by anything else, like a grandfather clock. That was what had cost him his gift to the duke: It was confused by those ringing clocks, those clicking gears, the two grand clocks atop the astronomy tower—so many sounds that the automaton had taken on a life of its own and apparently leapt to its death.

Volio's lab was the one place in all of Illyria where you couldn't hear the gears, and Volio loved it. The constant clatter of them sometimes made him feel insane, but until his testing of the duke-automaton, he hadn't thought they would affect his science. As a controlling device, Volio had been using a xylophone, which hung by a strap around his neck and which he played carefully, as each note gave a new order. He needed to adjust his automata, make them hear notes that nothing else produced, possibly ones too high for the human ear. It would have to be a small xylophone indeed, it seemed. But making musical instruments was easy. It was the adjustment of all the automata that would take time. He couldn't wait to see all their faces at the faire when an army of automata, gleaming and skeletal, marched into the Crystal Palace, ready to obey his every command.

For the rest of the day, while the other students rejoiced at the duke's return, and cake was served, Volio worked on his army, pausing only occasionally to reread his latest letter from Cecily. He was sorry to have caused her sadness with the false death of her cousin. She was a gentle girl, and he appreciated that. He wanted to explain and apologize in a letter, but he did not know how to phrase it. So he focused instead on his bronze soldiers, for matters of metal were easier for him to navigate than matters of the heart.

It was three weeks later when he saw his chance to apologize. He had not written to her, unsure of what to say. He was returning home on a Sunday from lunch with his father and brother, who had ignored him. They had spoken only of their weapons research for the Queen, and how she did not appreciate it, and how they should just turn the weapons on the Queen. Then they both laughed the low chuckle that they shared, making their twin mustaches bob. Malcolm had inherited his mother's appearance: frail, with pale skin and dark hair. His father and brother were of heartier stock, balding, but with fine thick reddish hair where they weren't. They often pushed him out of the way, and when he tried to speak of problems with the automata, they would say, "You'll figure it out, old boy; now let's talk of the more important work, shall we?"

He descended from the coach that had brought him back to Illyria, and had intended to go right inside to the comfort of his laboratory, but he spotted Cecily in the garden alone. As no one else was around, he thought it would be a good chance to speak with her. She was in a beautiful white dress, holding a matching white lace umbrella over her to shade her from the late afternoon sun. It was early June by now and the weather had turned warm, but the breeze off the Thames was a comfort. She stared out at the river, idly stroking Shakespeare, who sat in her lap.

"Cecily," Volio said, sitting down next to her.

Cecily frowned. She didn't think it was proper for him to be addressing her by her Christian name. "Yes, Mr. Volio?" she said.

"You must call me Malcolm," Volio said. She did not reply, or even look at him. Maybe she knew what he was about to say already, he thought, or was just upset that he hadn't written to her lately. "I wanted to say I'm sorry."

"For what?"

"Well, I haven't written you in three weeks, but besides that—"

"Written to me?" Cecily said, turning to look at him, confused. "When have you ever written to me?"

"Cecily," Volio said, putting up a hand to interrupt her, "there is no one around. We may speak freely."

"Sir," Cecily said, standing, "I do not suppose it would be proper for us to be free with each other." Volio stared up at her, his hands shaking. "And you have certainly never written to me."

"But—," Volio said, reaching into his jacket pocket to take out her most recent letter. A strange sinking feeling had welled up in him, and his lips felt dry. He held the letter out to her.

She took it and read through it briefly, and then began to laugh. "Mr. Volio," she said, still giggling as she handed the letter back to him, "I believe someone has played a trick on you. This is not my hand." When he wouldn't reach out for the letter, she shrugged and dropped it at his feet before walking back into Illyria.

Volio sat for a moment longer in the garden, hunched over, heart-broken, and completely still. Then he reached down and snatched up the letter, crumbling it in his hand. Something inside him trembled. He felt as though his eyes were made of glass, and they had broken, exploded into a thousand tiny shards, and underneath were new eyes, real, fleshy ones that saw so much more. He felt the wind blow around him, and felt in it the potential for hurricane and light-ning. He heard the river wash by, and heard in it a swelling tsunami that would flood all of London. He saw in his own hands the throb of his blood, rushing inside him like a war chariot. He had the power to make these floods and storms, and he knew now that there was no reason not to. Cecily's love for him had been the one good thing in this world. Without it, he felt the ground quake and the globe shatter. Without Cecily's love, Volio felt no need to hold back the madness inside him, no need to spare the fools of the world for whom he had suffered all his life. In the garden, the only movement was Volio's lips parting to let out a breath, and the breeze that blew his dark hair from his face.

Of course it was a trick! He was a fool not to have seen that. His brain hummed like electrical wiring. Love was a blinding disease from which he was now recovered. It was a trick perpetrated by that bitch Miriam and her idiot men.

The only solution was to end her life entirely.

And then he could simply take Cecily.

It might not have been Cecily writing those letters, but it could have been. He could be sweet, and kind, and loving, and she would see that if she had the chance, but that chance would not come unless it was thrust upon her. Yes. It would be easy. He would kill Miriam and make Cecily love him. And if she wouldn't, then he could kill her, too. Until then, he would play their game, write their notes, and dream of Miriam's blood running over cold bronze.

Volio slowly shredded the letter into small strips and then walked to the river and opened his hand over it. The strips flew out over the water, some into it, most into the wind. He would have his revenge, and he would have what he desired. He just needed to take it.

XL.

THERE were few things Lothario Prism loved more than the Crystal Palace. His wife, of course, and his children, and his newborn granddaughter, whom he felt guilty for loving more than his own children; but the Crystal Palace was a close second below them. He loved how it shone, and how he could appreciate it as well as anyone else, despite his vision difficulties. For the glass of the Crystal Palace was not colored; it was all light and air. Lines, forming the outline of the great structure, a series of arches forming a pyramid with a great arched roof at the top, and flags flying high. It was huge, long as a train, and tall enough that inside, trees grew and fountains splashed. The balconies indoors were draped with velvet curtains, so it was at once a garden of delights and an Oriental opium lounge. It was indoors and outdoors, light and water, air and iron, all wound together, like something from a fairy tale. Even though he knew how it was built, and how it held together, it seemed a miracle.

He stood before it in the evening light and looked up at its beautiful, complex interlocking glass pieces. He flipped down the red lens over his right eye, and two clear lenses, so he could get a better look at the flags.

Without his colored lenses, he often could not tell the difference between red and green, blue and yellow. His eyes had always been weak. He needed lenses now to see things far away, and close up, and he often found that, in his work of punching very small holes in the sheets of metal for the analytical engines, the magnifying lenses were very useful as well. He knew the contraption on his face looked odd, but he didn't mind it, and when he held his baby granddaughter in his arms, she often reached up and flicked the lenses down, one at a time, giggling as she did so. For that alone, and for the ability to see her smile, the lenses were worth it.

Prism had a few laborers with him, who were growing impatient as he stared at the palace—he could feel them tapping their feet and sighing behind him, so he waved them forward. He was in charge of directing the setup of the exhibition area for the faire, a task for which he always volunteered.

"Lottie!" he heard as they were approaching the great arch that led into the palace. He turned. His wife was scurrying forward, walking as quickly as she could at her age. He marveled at her plump, wiggling figure and her large eyes, still so beautiful. They were gray, she promised him when they had first met, the same gray as he saw them. "Lottie," she said again, and waved a handkerchief. He waved back, and she came up to him.

"Hullo, darling," he said, grasping her hand tightly.

"Sorry I'm late," she said. "I know how you like it when I come to watch you set up, but Jess is quite sad and needed some cheering up. Some good friend of hers is in hospital." Jess was her sister's daughter, a nice girl who worked at the toy department of Whiteleys Department Store and often brought them little toys for their granddaughter.

"Why, that's dreadful. Did you comfort her?"

"As well as I could."

Prism looked around. No one was very close or paying attention, so he gave her a quick kiss on the lips. She giggled. "Lothario!" she said, mock-shocked, as she waved her handkerchief.

"Come, darling," he said. "Let's go see if the laborers have set anything up correctly this year."

The Crystal Palace shone over them as they entered it, holding hands and smiling.

⟞⟜◉⟝⟞

THE Crystal Palace also shone in Violet's dreams. Since the return of the duke, Violet had had nothing but sweet dreams. Dreams in which her scheme—revealing herself at the Crystal Palace, at the faire—went off perfectly; in which she emerged from her machine beautiful, with her hair and toilette done perfectly, her dress a long soft purple; the duke staring at her after her demonstration, crying out to her, "My own Violet!" and she ran to him and they embraced, because at that moment, he knew all that had happened and why she had done it, and not only understood, but thought her brilliant for it. After that, the dream often skipped ahead to their wedding night, the light bronze and his fingers running along her stomach while she pressed her palm into his bare chest and the gears of Illyria whirled around them, humming a soft melody.

She had not felt guilty since the duke returned. He seemed to know nothing of her ruse, leading her to believe she had confessed to the same phantom that threw itself off the astronomy tower. She also now knew that her secret needed to be kept until the right time, and that time was not three in the morning in the Great Hall. She didn't know what or who it was that had gone off the roof, but she knew that it was a sign of some sort, that if she told the duke too soon, she would not accomplish her primary goal, which was to prove she deserved to be in Illyria. It had to be at the faire. Sooner than that could be disastrous.

His return had filled her with joy. She had nearly cried when he walked into the dining hall, feeling her heart leap up from its own ashes, from gray dust to red muscle, throbbing harder than it ever had before. She had longed to run up to him and to embrace him, to lay her hand on his cheek, to bury her face in his chest, but she was so shocked, so speechless, that she could not move, and when she could, she had regained herself well enough to know that any such demonstration would be a mistake. Still, she kept the memory of his return with her, and at night, she went to sleep thinking of how one day she might be allowed to run to him whenever she wanted.

Everyone was looking forward to the faire. Jack, all his various experiments complete, had written a working theory on transplanting organs between species, and how he hoped to one day be able to use a chimpanzee to save a human life, though he couldn't test this, as there were no humans volunteering for chimpanzee parts—and besides, chimpanzees were very expensive. He had created as examples a ferret and a bird, both alive and well, but using each other's lungs and heart. He also wanted to present Oscar as part of his final project, but Violet told him that the Queen might not appreciate Oscar's brand of speech, and Valentine positively forbade it.

Toby had indeed perfected a hangover cure, a strange bright blue concoction that smelled like the ocean and tasted like honey. They went out several nights in a row, getting as drunk as possible, and the next morning, all with pounding headaches, they would drink the stuff at breakfast, clinking their test tubes together before downing the brew. Each time they tried it, they were all feeling much better within three minutes, and often very hungry as well.

Drew's perfume, though still occasionally too heady when activated, was also a success, and he was working now on finding the ideal scent with which to demonstrate it at the faire. Fiona had graciously agreed to be his model, and was saving up a bottle of her sweat in preparation.

Further explorations of the cellar were few, as everyone had been so busy finishing their projects, and shortly after the duke's resurrection, he had begun locking a large gate in the hall leading to the cellar to which only professors had the key. By that point, Miriam had puzzled out that the duke was most likely quite human, and someone had been creating automaton duplicates of him, one of which had pitched itself off the roof. She was more than content when they all went out to the pub where they could drink and laugh.

Miriam knew her time at Illyria was nearly through. Cecily didn't need her any longer, and she had grown tired of the place. It held mysteries which it seemed could never be solved, and while Miriam loved a good mystery, she knew the only truly good mystery was one with a solution. She thought perhaps she would become a schoolteacher, or maybe even a professor of French at one of the women's colleges.

Thoughts of darkness had slipped away from all inhabitants of Illyria since the duke's return, because after such a happy miracle, it seemed nothing could go wrong. Illyria and her occupants were beacons of merriment, and nothing could put them out.

Even Volio had become merry, in his own way. Not happy, but satisfied and resolved. The old gates that were used again to lock the basement made his nights quieter. He still had access via the key he had received from the late duke. Every night, he had his creations stand up from their slabs and march in perfect lines around the room as he played notes no one could hear. Often, after he had them all lie back down, he cackled with glee.

And late one night, a few days before they were to move their projects to the Crystal Palace, Violet finished her own creation, which she had lovingly taken to calling "Pallas." The other students had left the lab, as it was late, and she stood alone with Professor Forney, looking up at her work.

"That's impressive, Mr. Adams. Very impressive," Forney said, and clapped Violet on the back. Violet, even at her most modest, agreed. Pallas stood twice as tall as a tall man, and was a beautifully crafted woman of bronze. She wore a corset with silver lace patterns over it, and the hem of her dress fell low to the ground, hiding the series of wheels underneath. Her face was immaculate, looking heavenward, and coils of golden hair fell around her face from the loose bun they had been pinned into. Her hands were out of proportion—incredibly large, and with visible joints, but as she was already made of metal, this bit of inhumanness lent her a powerful air. On her chest was a brooch—really a glass window from which the pilot could see out. At the press of a button, Pallas's corset would open and reveal a large operating chamber with steps descending from it, which Violet climbed, ready to demonstrate her device for Professor Forney. She sat in the pilot's seat and pulled a lever, closing the corset over her and pulling back the steps. Then Pallas came to life. Violet could make her move and spin, and lift the tables and chairs in the room. At Forney's insistence, she even lifted him, while he smoked his cigar and looked about the room from on high, satisfied. It was everything Violet had hoped it would be—and it had enough room inside it for her to change clothes quickly.

The duke had also completed his display for the faire. He felt quite positive that his and Violet's æthership could easily reach the moon, and hoped that the Queen would agree. He had never before had a display of his own at the faire. He was nervous and excited, and he often felt like jumping up and down like a child. Cecily, who had never presented before either, felt similarly, though she felt like spinning, and when she didn't indulge in that feeling, she felt as though the world were spinning around her. Her experiments were going well, and while Ashton had become distant, caught up in his work, Jack had become even more welcoming, and she found herself visiting the biological laboratory at least once a week, as she once had the mechanical. It wasn't that she loved Jack, she thought—for her heart had settled on Ashton, and was steadfast—but that Jack was more talkative, and very funny. He showed her his ferrets and she showed him her chemical formula. She'd made several tools from it, including an entire pocket watch, which Ada—who had decided to stay on after the duke's reappearance—thought was very handsome, all white and gleaming.

One night, after Cecily had gone to sleep, Ernest told Ada what he had found in his father's laboratory tower. Ada, who was smoking, with a glass of whiskey in her hand, leaned back into her armchair. They were in the parlor of the residence, and though it was warm, Ada had had the servants start a fire because she liked the crackling sound of it. She sighed and looked at Ernest with a sad smile. "Your father," she said, "was a good man. The best of men. And also the worst. His intelligence made him smarter than everyone around him, and he knew it, and often grew frustrated by having to explain himself over and over. So yes, I could see him involved in some . . . cult bent on world domination. He would occasionally say things to me when we were alone—odd cryptic things about the future. Thank goodness he died before he had a chance to act on those desires. He could barely run Illyria—I hate to think what he would do with the world."

"He could barely run Illyria?"

"Oh my, no. He was not an organized man, your father. Kept it hidden, of course; wanted everyone to think he was smart and sharp as a blade. That's why Illyria accepts so few students. There's certainly room for more, but more than fifteen students was too confusing for him. Science, he could manage. Bureaucracy was beyond him. You've done a much better job with Illyria."

"I want to do more," Ernest said, leaning forward, his eyes shining. "When I found everything in my father's lab—the worn-out flag, the notes—I realized that he was just as human as I am. His shadow shrank, and thankfully, it shrank so that I was no longer in it. Illyria is mine, isn't it? To do as I please?"

"It is," Ada, with a wry expression.

"Then yes, I think we should begin admitting more students. And you were right when you said we don't admit students without social graces—we should. I'll teach them manners if I must, but there is surely untapped brilliance out in the wilds. And I'd like to reorganize the way classes are handled, maybe even have more classes, and certainly more guest lecturers."

"Those all sound like wonderful ideas."

"I have more, too. Those are just the beginning. Perhaps I could let in women, at some point. Did you know there's a girl from one of the Spanish colonies who has been applying to Illyria every year for the past five? And she's quite brilliant, too. Her stellar cartography theories and skills are finer than mine . . . than anyone's, I think. And every year I write her back, telling her I'd love to accept her, but Illyria doesn't accept women. Illyria has a reputation, but it could be so much more."

"It could."

"I have your support?"

"Fully."

"And . . . do you have any suggestions yourself?"

Ada pursed her lips and smiled. "I do," she said, "but there will plenty of time for that later. For now, worry about the faire. You'll have all summer to re-create Illyria." Ernest nodded and sat back in his own chair. "And after you're done with that," she said, "you can go to the moon."

XLI.

VIOLET was stunned by the Crystal Palace. She had seen it in pictures, of course, but to have it looming over her, like a sky of diamond, and to be in it as it was filled with people, fountains, trees, flowers, exhibits, and a faint, indescribable perfume like rose-water, incense, and ice. And to have her invention here among it all! It was enough to make the mechanics of her body stop, and to pause the machinery of her soul.

The Palace was crowded, and the booths were set up and ready. Each booth had not just the invention or demonstration, but also papers explaining the science behind the invention. Violet had a carefully executed, oversized drawing of the engine within her machine, and a large sign directing them to Cecily's booth across the hall to find out about the materials. Each booth shined in its own particular way.

Merriman had cages set up, each with plants growing inside to demonstrate his theories on using the celestial realm as additional farmland, and the possibility of growing plants on other planets. He had even worked up a model of a small farm on the moon. Lane had a series of vials of what looked like water, and many large graphs explaining the effectiveness of his anti-anxiety elixir. Jack's booth chattered and chirped as the bird and ferret examined each other from their white cages. Toby's booth had not just vials of his tonic, the chemicals he had used to create it, and explanations of the science behind it, but many barrels of ale and some glasses as well, so that those interested could test his potion. At Drew's booth, Fiona stood as the centerpiece, done up in a long black evening gown, each arm extended, one slick with her own sweat, one kept dry. She

would pose with her head slightly back and to the side, as if smelling her arms, and she had managed to take all her hair and put it up
in a column of curls, her few stray grays rising like stripes from her
temples. Drew would dab a bit of his perfume on each of her arms,
and the onlookers would then smell each arm to see the difference
in the scents' intensities. For effect, Fiona tossed her head back and
moaned slightly when they did so.

This was as far as Violet could see, and she had not yet had time to
wander, for since setting up, she had not had a lull in onlookers. Most
seemed to be men of science, who asked her questions about the engine. A few asked her why she had chosen to make her device in the
form a woman, to which she replied, "Women can do more than
dance, gentlemen," which produced a few chuckles. She was pleased—
people seemed to be impressed with her engine, and Professor Forney,
just before he left to go back to America, had slapped her on the back
and told her that if she ever came across the pond he would hire her in
a heartbeat. It was late morning when a familiar voice from the crowd
asked, "Are there any other brilliant members of your family?"

Violet raised an eyebrow. "Just my father," she said to the scowling
Ashton as he stepped out of the crowd. The other scientists looked
at them and wandered off, sensing a personal moment, which as
scientists they knew was bound to be messy.

Ashton gave his sister a hug and then stepped back to admire
Pallas.

"My," he said softly, "that's quite splendid. But don't you worry
that when you step out of her in a dress, that standing next to her,
woman next to woman, and ready for comparison, that you'll end
up being the ugly one?"

"A risk I'm quite willing to take. She may be more lovely, but I
am less likely to crush a man. Slightly less likely."

Ashton laughed and stared at Pallas awhile longer. "Listen," he
said after a moment. "I've something to tell you."

"Yes?"

"Father will be here."

"What?" Violet asked. She felt her back tense, and a light ringing
began in her ears.

"He apparently missed us terribly, and has seen quite enough of America, so instead of seeing the southern territories, he's come home to spend the summer with us. He says he'll go back to the conference in September. And, because he misses us, he thought he could take us to the Illyria Science Faire. A note came by messenger this morning."

"What time will he be here?" Violet asked. Her pulse was rising and she could feel sweat trickling from her brow.

"Just before teatime, I believe."

"Oh, that's all right, then," Violet said. Ashton looked at her curiously. "The Queen will be surveying the faire just after dinner, or so we were told. The duke will personally be escorting her to each booth, and we are to save our best presentation for that time. Father will arrive after that, so by then all the drama will be over with."

"You're really going to reveal yourself in front of the Queen?"

"Can you think of a more understanding person to present myself to?"

Ashton cocked his head and then nodded his assent. "Fair enough. Just after dinner?"

"That's when it begins."

"I'll be back for it, then. I should go check on Antony, though. I left him by Toby's table, and I'm not sure what that could result in. I'm not a scientist." Violet grinned. "Oh," Ashton said as he walked away, "one more thing—did you see the duke's exhibit? At the other end of the hall?" Violet shook her head. "You should make it a point to see it before you go," Ashton said with a grin, and then walked off into the ever-thickening crowd.

By midmorning there were plenty of non-scientists exploring the faire, a great many of them governesses or mothers with children. Several little girls came up to Violet's booth and stared wonderingly up at Pallas, which made Violet grin, but when she knelt down to ask them if they wanted to see it work, they scurried back to their caretakers.

"Does it dance?" asked a man staring up at Pallas. "It's awful big to go about dancin'."

"No," Violet said, "she doesn't dance. She works. She can move in all directions and her hands can lift up to the weight of a horse, each."

"So she doesn't dance?" the man asked. Violet shook her head. The man shrugged and walked off. Violet frowned after him.

"Can I see it work?" came a small voice from below her. Violet looked down to see one of the little girls who had fled earlier. A woman in a severe navy dress stood a few feet away, looking on warily.

"Of course," Violet said, and gave a demonstration of Pallas lifting one of the chairs. The little girl clapped as Violet stepped out of Pallas again.

"How did you build it?" the little girl asked.

"It took a lot of hard work," Violet said. "I had to figure out which parts go where and how to make them. I bet when you're older, though, you can make something even better."

The little girl put her thumb in her mouth and shook her head, looking down, then giggled.

"Sara," the little girl called to the woman in blue, "this lady says when I grow up, I can be an inventor like her!"

"That's a young man, Carlotta," Sara said in an even American accent. Carlotta turned back to Violet, a confused look on her face. Violet knelt down so only Carlotta could see her, put a finger over her own lips, and winked. Carlotta giggled again and ran back to Sara, who took her hand and led her to the next booth.

Violet was so busy demonstrating Pallas's abilities and answering questions that she didn't have a spare moment to see the duke's booth. The Crystal Palace was quite full until lunch, when the crowd began to taper off. When she could see through the crowd again, she cast glances at her friends' booths: Toby seemed to be out of ale, and quite upset about it; and Fiona's hair had begun to topple, probably due to her constant sneezing; but otherwise, everyone looked happy, proud, and tired. Violet waved at Jack, who shot her a grin. Which is when she saw the large crowd at the other end of the hall. It was flanked by guards and people in particularly fine dress, and moved deliberately, stopping at each booth; this was surely the Queen and her entourage.

Violet swallowed. Her palms were sweating—would they be too slippery to operate the controls, or put on the dress she had hidden inside Pallas? And what about her hair? Fiona had shown her how to quickly put her hair up with a false bun, and she had practiced until she could do it in under half a minute, but she hadn't practiced with sweaty palms. Could the duke love her with short hair? She glanced over at Toby's table. He was definitely out of ale. Everyone was staring at the Queen's entourage now, as it came down the Great Hall of the palace. All the commoners had been cleared out, and the nobility and scientists flocked around the Queen, wanting to catch a glimpse of her, or see the demonstrations in her honor.

Time passed slowly. She looked at each booth after the entourage had passed. Each time, the student looked as though he had been stampeded by the nobility, not merely interrogated. When Toby's turn was over, he was red faced and nervous looking, and when they were done with Drew's exhibit, Fiona was fanning Drew, who had apparently fainted into her arms. Remarkably, Merriman seemed unscathed and happy when they were done with him, but Violet had little time to examine him, for they were upon her next.

The Queen was not a tall woman, nor were her looks terribly imposing. She more resembled someone's loving grandmother than the ruler of all the Empire. Plump, with her crown resting over wispy white hair, she had gentle eyes that gazed at Violet expectantly. She had a large open fan that she waved at her face occasionally. Around her stood her various advisors, and some members of Parliament. And the duke, who had apparently been speaking the entire time that Violet had been staring at the Queen.

"Mr. Adams?" the duke prompted.

"Yes," Violet said. "Sorry. Your Majesty. Sorry, Your Majesty." Violet spoke in clunky bricks. A few of the nobles chuckled, but the Queen smiled reassuringly.

"Take your time, dear," she said, "and don't be nervous. We just want to see what your great contraption can do. It is lovely, isn't it?"

"Yes, Your Majesty," said one of the advisors. "It resembles Her Highness, if I may be so bold."

The Queen giggled and shot the advisor a look. "You ought not lie to the Queen."

"What does it do?" asked a rather gruff-looking man next to the Queen.

"Let him explain, Mr. Gladstone," the Queen said, and they all turned to Violet, who swallowed.

"I call her Pallas," Violet said, clearing her throat and speaking in as manly a voice as she could muster. "She is piloted by one person, and easy to learn. She can turn in any direction, move as fast as a horse at a steady trot, and is capable of lifting up to the weight of a large stallion in each hand. Furthermore, she runs on a spring engine of my own design, which recycles its own energy, so that just a few turns of the key can keep her running for several days. The material I used to build the engine was invented by Miss Cecily Worthing, and is extremely durable, so it does not wear down or lose its energy." Violet pointed at the sketch of the engine. "Here is the design, should Your Highness care to examine it." Violet bowed her head, unsure of the proper behavior. A few of the men in the group stepped forward to examine the engine. The Queen did not.

"Would Your Majesty care for a demonstration?" Violet asked after a minute.

"It would please us greatly," the Queen said.

Trembling, Violet opened Pallas—which caused a few gasps among the nobles—and climbed in, then she shut the door behind her, immediately took off her jacket, opened her shirt at the back, and began piloting Pallas. Timing was crucial. First, she demonstrated how Pallas could rotate full circle and move in any direction. When her window was facing away from the crowd, she took the opportunity to slip the dress on. While they could only see her face, they probably would have noticed her fussing about with a dress. Then, as she continued to pilot Pallas, she slipped her trousers off, tangling them for a moment in the pedals at her feet. She breathed in deeply, untangled her feet, and in one deft motion plunged them into her waiting shoes. Next, her hands free again, she lifted two large stone slabs she had had brought to the Crystal Palace, one in each hand, and had the hands move around in all possible directions. She bent her head down and quickly put her hair up in the bun Fiona had showed her, loose, with some hair still hanging from the front of her face. Suddenly, there was a deafening crash. Violet panicked. Had she just dropped one of the stones? Had she dropped it on the

Queen? She would be hanged. She pressed her face to the glass and looked out at the palace.

Everyone had turned to one of the walls, which had just been shattered by the small army of a skeletal automata that stormed the crowd. With vicious ease, they knocked people and tables to the ground, a wave of metal. People began to scream and flee from the army, but many were cut down, blood staining the glass walls of the palace in horrid violent streaks. And in the distance, Violet could see Volio, following his automata in, looking on proudly as the chaos grew and poured outward, taking over the entire palace. He looked around the room, and his eyes focused on something as a sneer crept onto his face. Then he hit a strange instrument around his neck, and the automata changed direction and headed for the other end of the palace. Quickly, the Queen's guard whisked her away from the battle. The duke ran through them, toward the automata, shouting, and the remaining soldiers from the Queen's entourage joined him, firing their rifles with quick sudden blasts of noise and smoke. Violet piloted Pallas forward into the fray.

✢❦◉❦✢

FROM the ground, it was more difficult to see what was going on. All Jack knew was that seemingly hundreds of automata, all clearly from the basement, had attacked the faire en masse, and his first thoughts were of Cecily.

Her booth was at the other end of the Crystal Palace. Around him, soldier and automaton fought, guns and swords and metal talons clanging together. Jack was unarmed and had no way of getting through the wall of war in front of him. He ran quickly from booth to booth, dodging claws and sabers. By the time he made it to Toby's booth, he had a gash in the back of his leg.

Toby's booth was overturned, and Toby was kneeling behind it, using it as a shield. Ashton knelt beside him.

"Exciting, isn't it?" Toby asked.

"Exciting is an excellent performance of a play, or a good book. This is merely life threatening," Ashton said.

"Have you seen Drew?" Toby asked.

"Last I saw, he had fainted at his own booth."

"Well, if you see him, tell him to come this way," Toby said. "I have an idea, but I could use his help."

There was a loud bang and a popping noise as a bullet flew through the wall of the booth, leaving a hole by Ashton's head.

"I'm heading to the other end of the faire," Jack said. "I've got to check on Cecily."

"Good luck, mate," Toby said, clapping Jack on the back. "And it's been fine knowing you, if we don't make it out of this one."

"Don't be morbid," Ashton said. "I'm going with you, Jack. I can't just sit here."

"Okay," Jack said, peeking out from around the corner of the booth. "Drew's booth is over there. I'm going to make a dash for it."

"I'll be right behind you," Ashton said. Jack took one more look to see that it was relatively clear, and ran for Drew's booth, the pain in his leg throbbing.

✦❀✦

ALL around Violet, automata fought with soldiers, metal talons fencing with dress sabers, but the soldiers seemed to be losing. Blood splattered on Pallas's window as a nearby soldier's heart was torn out and then crushed. Violet had never seen such violence, and she felt a little dizzy from it. The high-pitched scream of metal on metal vibrated through Pallas as another automata threw itself at her. She plucked it off and threw it across the Crystal Palace. But this barely made a dent in the oncoming mechanical forces. Nearby, she saw the duke leading a charge of soldiers against a cluster of automata that had surrounded some civilians. She wanted to go help them, and to make sure the duke was all right, but she turned her head away and piloted Pallas forward, deeper into the fight, determined to get to the heart of the attack, to Volio.

✦❀✦

HERBERT Bunburry knew that if his doctors realized he had left the hospital early for the Science Faire, they would probably disapprove, especially now that it had turned into a battlefield. He couldn't move very quickly, but he was doing his best to avoid the automata as he walked down the stairs from one of the upper levels. His concern was for Jess, his shopgirl, whom he had brought with him to see the faire, but who had gone to use one of the water closets in the retiring rooms moments before the attack started.

He made his way down the stairs and headed for the retiring rooms, but was set upon almost immediately by a skeletal automaton. It came at him with one outstretched arm and a vicious talon. Almost without thinking about it, Bunburry raised the metal part of his arm to meet the talon with a clang. He felt the vibrations from the impact, but no pain. The automaton stopped dead in its tracks a moment, giving Bunburry time to grab it around the neck and pull it to the ground, where he stomped on it with his metal foot before moving forward.

"Professor!" cried Merriman, running up to him from a corner. "It's horrible, Professor. I don't know where they came from!"

"Neither do I," Bunburry hacked out. "I'm trying to go to the retiring rooms. Will you help? Tell me if any of the things are coming at me from the sides—I think I can deal with them."

"Certainly," Merriman said, but he looked frightened, and his eyes were wet. Bunburry set his jaw and walked forward as fast as he could as the battle raged around him.

✥☙◉❧✥

VIOLET saw Volio's head look up at Pallas charging forward. He had captured Cecily somewhere along the line—Violet didn't know how, but she looked angry and terrified, and was trying to push him away. He made a gesture that caused a pack of the metal monsters to break off and throw themselves at Violet. She heard a horrible screech as their claws tore through Pallas's shell. A claw opened up Violet's inner sanctum to the smoke outside, and cut at the sleeve of her dress. She heard another screech and felt a sharp pain in her leg, and looked down to see another claw coming through the floor. There were too many of them, and they were all over Pallas, cutting her to shreds. Soon, Pallas would fall, and Violet would fall with her. She had come so far—was so close to completing her plan, to revealing herself, to claiming her place as a great mind—and now she would die, just seconds short of her goal. Her leg ached, and tears ran down her face. This is not how she had wanted to end the year, or her life.

❀

JACK and Ashton made it unscathed to Drew's booth, only to find him still passed out and in Fiona's lap, as she frantically fanned him with a paper fan. Her hair was a mess around her shoulders— the Saint Paul's Stand-on-End never held up under stressful circumstances—and her brow furrowed with concern. " 'E came to when the commotion started," she said, "but when 'e saw what was 'appenin' 'e fainted dead away again."

"Drew!" Jack shouted, taking his friend's face in his hands. Drew didn't stir. "Drew, wake up, we need your help!" he shouted, and then slapped Drew lightly on the face.

Drew opened his eyes. "The basement is attacking," he said, looking frightened.

"Toby is back by his booth, and he says he needs your help," Jack said.

"With what?" Drew asked.

"I think he's planning a counterattack," Ashton said. "He was organizing his chemicals."

"Yes," Drew said, nodding, "I can help."

"Aye," Fiona said. "Go help Toby, love. We'll make it outta this alive." She pulled Drew to her and kissed him passionately on the mouth. Ashton and Jack politely looked away.

"Yes!" Drew said, sitting up into a crouch. "I'll head over and help Toby. Fiona, will you be all right here?"

"I'm trying to get to Cecily's booth, so I can't stay," Jack said.

"I'm going with Jack," Ashton said.

Fiona bit her lower lip and looked around at the bottles of perfume oils that had fallen around her when she pulled the booth down to use as a shield.

"Drew, are these oils flammable?" she asked.

"Very," he said.

"Oh, aye, then" she said, removing a box of matches from her bosom. "I'll be fine, then."

✣◉✣

A LOUD explosion rattled the floor below Pallas, and Violet looked out to see Fiona throwing firebombs out into the crowd of automata. One of the creatures flew back, and its arm shattered with a loud clang. Smoke started to fill the air, along with the smell of burnt flowers.

Violet remembered Volio in the lab, working on the arms. She remembered the odd noise in the elbow joint, and how he had ignored her. She reached out Pallas's arms toward the nearest automaton, grabbed it by the elbow, and snapped it back. The elbow broke off like a twig, and the creature flailed with its now-impotent arm. Violet smiled. Her dress was ruined, her hair a mess, and her leg bleeding, but she knew the creatures' weakness now.

"Aim for the elbows!" she shouted, hoping someone could hear her, and began piloting Pallas to grab each of the creatures by their arms and snap their elbows back violently. A short distance away, Drew and Toby began throwing small vials, which caused the automata to fizz and melt when they hit them. Soldiers who heard Violet's cry repeated it, and began pushing back the creatures' elbows. Clawed talons began flying off all around; Volio's army began to shrink.

Violet set her jaw and headed toward Volio.

✣◉✣

JACK and Ashton had finally made it to Cecily's booth, but Cecily was nowhere to be found. Her booth showed no signs of struggle, and the various objects made with her clay—plates, wrenches, a birdcage—were still laid out for display. Professor Curio was crouched under the booth, hugging his knees to his chest.

"Professor!" Jack cried, and Curio looked up. His eyes had a strange appearance to them, the pupils tiny as pinheads, the color of both eyes having changed from one blue and one green to both orange.

"Can't talk," Curio said, as if forcing the words out. "Trying not to lose control."

"Where's Cecily?" Jack pleaded, but Curio didn't respond.

"Look out!" Ashton shouted as an automaton came charging toward them. Without thinking, Jack grabbed one of the plates from Cecily's display and raised it in front of him, like a shield. The creature's claw plunged toward the plate, and then bounced back, deflected. Jack and Ashton exchanged a look before Ashton rushed forward, grabbed the birdcage, and swung it at the automaton's head. The automaton stumbled, but didn't fall. Jack grabbed the wrench off the table and hit the automaton again in the head, as hard as he could. It collapsed to the ground.

"Seems we're armed, then," Jack said.

"I assure you, 'tis against my will," Ashton said.

"We have to find Cecily," Jack said.

"We'll cuff them soundly," Ashton said, gripping the birdcage, "and never draw a sword." Jack nodded, but looked back at Professor Curio, who was crouched and shaking under the table, like a powder keg ready to explode.

A CLUSTER of automata had formed a circle around Volio and Cecily, whom Volio held firmly at the waist. He had one hand on the odd device around his neck, the other holding a knife to Cecily's throat. Violet slowed Pallas as she approached them. Volio looked up at her machine and grinned. The duke and several soldiers were attempting to fight the automata, but they soon backed away or were knocked to the ground by the machines' claws. Volio seemed to be looking for something, but was distracted by Cecily's struggling to get away. Then his wall of mechanical men parted and he dragged something from the shadows. Violet felt a shiver as she saw Volio's smile.

FIONA's perfume bottles had made lovely, fragrant firebombs, but now she'd run out, and the horrible metal skeletons were still charging at her. Frantically, she looked in her purse: some more costume

jewelry, some money, hairpins, spare bloomers, and one of Mrs.
Wilks's oscillation therapy devices, which she kept on her because
she never knew when the opportunity to make a sale would arise.

If the metal skeletons had eyes, Fiona would be able to look right
into them. She swallowed. Her life was over, she thought. They
were nearly upon her. She'd never gotten to be a famous actress, but
at least she'd had some happiness with Drew at the end.

The first of the skeletons in the charge came at her, claws outstretched. Fiona tried to kick it away. It cut deep into her shin, a
sharp, cold pain, but stumbled backwards. She screamed and fell,
landing next to her bag again. The creature straightened itself and
charged forward again, hungry for more blood. Not knowing what
else to do, she pulled out Mrs. Wilks's oscillation therapy device
and thrust it at the creature, pushing the tip of it against its metal
chest. The skeleton stopped dead in its tracks, the sound of Mrs.
Wilks's device vibrating against it very loud in Fiona's ears.

"They work off vibrations," said a man with a metal neck who
was suddenly coming toward her.

"Are ye their leader?" Fiona asked, scared.

The man coughed. "What?"

A younger, short man appeared from behind him. "This is Professor Bunburry. I'm Humphrey," the younger man said.

"Don't take that device off the automaton," Bunburry said, "the
vibrations are what's stopping it from moving."

Fiona swallowed and tried to sit up, keeping the device pressed
against the skeleton, while also keeping an eye on the metal man,
a professor. All scientists were mad.

"Let me fix your leg," Humphrey said, tearing part of his sleeve
off and wrapping it tight around Fiona's shin.

"Thankee," she said. Her arm was growing tired from extending
Mrs. Wilks's device against the machine.

"You might be able to control the automaton with that thing,"
Bunburry said. "Depending on where you put it." Humphrey helped
her stand as she kept Mrs. Wilks's device on the automaton, and indeed, as her hand raised, moving the device, the automaton began
to behave differently. First one arm swung out, causing Humphrey to

duck out of the way—and then the other, and then the legs. After a few minutes, Fiona felt she could control it like a puppet.

"We're heading for the retiring rooms, my dear," Bunburry said, and then coughed. "Care to escort us?"

Fiona grinned, and piloted her new pet skeleton forward, using it like a weapon, slashing at other automata with jerky movements. She felt herself laughing a little. Was this what scientists felt? She had her puppet strike down another of its own kind with a quick movement. The metal man—whose name Fiona had already forgotten—took out another.

It didn't take long for them to get to the retiring rooms. The metal man nodded at her, took her puppet, and smashed it to the ground before they went inside. Fiona glanced around quickly. Where was Drew?

✦

WITH the sound of metal breaking wood, one of the automata rushed the table Drew and Toby had erected as a defense. Its claw splintered a hole in the table and reached out for Drew's throat. He stumbled back, knocking over several bottles of chemicals. And there weren't many left.

"We can't stay here anymore," Drew said, pouring some acid on the searching claw. It bubbled and hissed before melting away.

Toby glanced around. A short ways behind them were the retiring rooms, where it looked as though a group of soldiers had set up. They stood around them, rifles pointed outward, fending off any incoming automata.

"Let's see if they don't mind protecting a few loyal citizens," Toby said, pointing a thumb at the soldiers. Drew nodded and grabbed the remaining chemicals before heading toward the retiring rooms. They weren't really rooms—more like tents, with long draperies as doorways, and chairs and water closets within. The automata were coming on fiercely now, and Drew's shoulder was clawed by one as they ran forward. Toby managed to smash a vial on its head before it could do further damage. Someone had called for reinforcements, so more soldiers had filled the palace, firing into the wall of metal warriors. Drew tripped over a headless corpse of a civilian as they ran, and Toby helped him up, praying it wasn't anybody they knew.

Inside the retiring rooms, it was calmer. Many had sought refuge here, and there were sounds of sobbing and cries of pain. Valentine was tending to the wounded. Bracknell was hunched in a corner, covering his head, his trousers and face wet.

"Fiona!" Drew shouted. She was lying on the floor as Valentine sewed up a gash in her leg. He ran over to her and hugged her tightly, then kissed her on the mouth. Valentine looked up, then nodded approvingly.

"I'm all right, love," Fiona said with a weak smile. "The metal man saved me. An' fer a while, I got to pilot one of the skeletons."

"Metal man?" Drew asked, looking around. He caught sight of Bunburry in a tight embrace with a redheaded girl.

"Professors!" Toby shouted. He had been peeking his head out the curtain into the main pavilion. "I think we'd better blockade this entrance, if we can." Bunburry and Valentine nodded. There was a scramble as people began pulling up the chairs and piling them by the entrance.

"Is Miriam here?" Toby asked, looking around. No one answered.

�֍֎֍

VIOLET watched in horror as an automaton dragged a struggling Miriam out of the shadows and into Volio's circle. A few men tried to stop them, but were thrown aside. Cecily screamed again as they dragged Miriam toward Volio, but Volio slapped her, and she fell to her knees. Satisfied, Volio approached Miriam, who was struggling against the clutches of two automata. Volio said something to Miriam which Violet couldn't hear, and Miriam spit in his face.

Violet wasn't entirely sure what she was going to do, but she called out to clear the way in front of her, and the crowd parted. She faced the line of automata, narrowed her eyes, and, with Pallas's hand, began grabbing the automata, snapping their arms, and throwing them to the ground.

Volio looked up at the sound and drew his face into a sneer. Again he struck the device, and the automata stormed toward Pallas. In a wave they leapt at her, and knocked Pallas to the ground, toppling her like a turtle on its back. Violet felt the back of her head hit Pallas's wall with a crack, and her vision blurred, then faded to darkness.

※⊛※

JACK had just knocked another of the machines down with a solid swat from his wrench when Curio burst out from under the table, a changed man. He was somehow larger, his muscles bulged, and his eyes bugged out of his face. Jack swallowed, unsure of what was happening. Curio leapt forward, grabbed the heads of two of the mechanical men, and smashed them together with inhuman force.

"Is that a mate of yours?" Ashton asked, catching the outstretched claw of another automaton in the birdcage and then twisting it so the arm popped off.

"A professor," Jack said.

"An excellent example of why I don't feel a need to attend school," Ashton said. Jack raised the plate to block an incoming blow from another automaton, then smashed it on the head with the wrench. Curio bounded forward into the fray, clearing a path of fallen machines.

"Let's follow," Jack said. "Cecily must be nearby."

"You're mad," Ashton said with a sigh, and followed Jack forward.

Curio bounded like an animal before them, heading toward a great crowd at the middle of the palace, leaving a trail of oil and smashed metal in his wake. They were nearly at the crowd when Curio suddenly stopped charging, spun around, and fell to the ground, insensible.

"Damn," swore Ashton.

"Professor," Jack said, kneeling down to look at Curio, "are you all right?" Curio didn't respond. Jack checked his pulse. "He's alive, at least."

Ashton fended off a charging automaton with his birdcage. "Well, we can't just stand here," Ashton said. "Can you drag him?"

Curio had shrunk back down to regular size while they talked. Jack nodded. Spotting another overturned booth, Ashton led the way through battling soldiers and automata as Jack dragged Curio behind them.

"Good," Ashton said when they were kneeling behind the overturned booth, "I'll look after him. Go see to your girl. I'd head for that crowd if I were you."

"Thanks," Jack said with a nod, and clutched his wrench tightly. He ran out into the crowd, knocking down any machines that came near him with a sound blow. Just as he got to the crowd, there was a loud clanging, and he saw Violet's machine, Pallas, charge into a wall of automata. They toppled her, covering her like a swarm of wasps. Before he had time to worry for her, though, he spotted Cecily. Volio was clutching her around the waist, a knife to her throat.

⁂

VIOLET blinked open her eyes and shoved the pain away. The automata were weighing down Pallas like a sheet of lead, but she knew Pallas could handle it. Violet had built her, after all. She pulled on a lever and stomped down on both pedals with all her strength. Carefully, using her damaged arms, Pallas pushed back up from the ground. A few of the automata fell from her sides, and the others she plucked off her and smashed into one another. Then, with frightening speed, she drove herself toward Volio. Volio hissed at her and began to run, but he wasn't fast enough. Violet reached out with Pallas's arm and picked him up. He squirmed, but Pallas's giant hand held him tight. She brought him close to the bloodstained window.

"Call them off!" Violet screamed. "Call them off or I'll smash your head to the ground, Volio!" Volio hissed at her again, struggling in Pallas's grip, his eyes wide with madness. There was no reasoning with him. "Cecily!" Violet shouted. The automata had broken formation and were running throughout the palace and destroying everything in sight. The sound of shattering glass was everywhere, and chemicals from various exhibits had mixed on the floor and were smoking. People screamed, trying to get away, unsure of what was happening.

"Violet?" Cecily called. "Is that you?"

Violet didn't have time to worry about using the wrong voice, or being recognized. She kept a firm grip on Volio but lowered him within reach of Cecily. "There's something around his neck," Violet shouted. "It controls the automata. Take it and stop them."

Cecily nodded and grabbed the device, snapping it off Volio's neck. Volio hissed at her, and Cecily slapped him in return. Cecily stared a moment at the device before hitting it once. The automata stopped what they were doing and charged toward Cecily. Frightened, she hit it again, but they only came faster. She tried hitting it in a different place, and suddenly they slowed down and formed a line in front of her, as if awaiting instructions. Satisfied that the automata were under control, Cecily ran to Miriam, who lay on the ground faceup, a long bloody line down her cheek.

The rest of the palace was slowly coming under control. Violet could hear the duke shouting orders for cleanup and gathering the wounded, and a small circle had formed around Pallas, applauding. A group of soldiers ran forward and took Volio from Pallas's grasp. He was dazed and angry looking as they put the irons on him and led him out of the palace. Violet lay back in her chair. Tears were streaming down her face, and she didn't know why. She shook her head back and forth and wiped her face dry.

"Ashton!" the duke called. "Ashton, come out! You've quite saved the day."

Violet shivered, pulled her hair back, and then put it up again. She straightened out her dress and tightened it. The dress was torn, her leg bleeding, and she could only imagine what a fright she looked. She had wanted to be beautiful for Ernest. She let out a deep breath and opened Pallas, then limped down the steps into the crowd.

"Violet?" said the duke, confused.

"Yes," Violet said, looking down. She blinked and looked back up at him.

"Where's Ashton?"

"I am Ashton," Violet said. Everyone around them had gone quiet as they looked on. "The true Ashton, you've met as my cousin. The man whom you have called Ashton, and has been your student, has been me the entire time—disguised." Violet looked down as she declared this, and pushed a loose hair behind her ear. She raised her eyes back up to Ernest, who stared at her, openmouthed. He put his hand to his lips.

"I wanted so badly to go to Illyria," Violet said, her breath becoming ragged, "but you wouldn't accept me, wouldn't even have considered my application. . . ." The way he was looking at her was unbearable. Violet didn't know what to do or say, just wanted him to say something. Anything.

There was movement in the crowd. They stared at her, unsure of what to say or do, but then Cecily stepped forward, her hands clutching her skirts in tight bunches. Her face and eyes were red, and as she stared at Violet, tears started to run slowly down her face. "From the moment I first saw you I distrusted you," she said, her voice shaking. "I felt that you were false and deceitful." Cecily held her chin high, but she looked defeated.

"Cecily," Violet said softly, "I'm sorry." Cecily looked at her a moment longer, then walked away. Everyone else stared at Violet in silence.

"Has it been you, writing those letters to me?" the duke asked.

"Yes," Violet said.

The duke nodded, looking somewhere above and behind Violet. She tried to meet his eyes, but he wouldn't look at her. She tried to read his emotions in his body, but all she could see was shock. She opened her mouth to say something, maybe to apologize, or beg, but before she could think of what words to use, he turned away from her, as though he had just realized he was going the wrong direction on the street, and walked away.

"Well," said the Queen, who was watching from the side, her soldiers having escorted her out from wherever they had barricaded her, "this has been almost as exciting as the faire with the explosion that sent that irritating earl across the room." The Queen fanned herself idly and looked at Violet expectantly.

"I'm so sorry, Your Majesty," Violet said, "for everything I've done."

"My dear girl," the Queen said, "you've saved the day. Nothing to be sorry about. And your machine is quite remarkable, certainly proving you worthy of Illyria."

"Thank you, Your Majesty," Violet said. She felt her eyes begin to water.

"Oh dear," said the Queen. "You musn't cry, Violet. People will think you're just a girl."

Violet looked up at the Queen, who was smiling in a motherly way at her. She wiped the tears from her face, but they kept coming.

"Violet?" came a voice through the crowd. "Violet, my God, what's happened?" Her father emerged from the crowd, looking tan and panicked. "Violet!" he said when he saw her, and ran to hug her. Violet clung to his chest and cried there for a long while as he stroked her hair. When she looked up again, most of the people around her were gone. Her father looked down at her. "That was a very stupid thing you did," he said. "When I heard the fighting, I ran over, but you were fending off those things like a hero in armor. I knew it was you, because the face on that thing—" He motioned toward Pallas. "It looks just like your mother. But it was still a very stupid thing."

"I'm sorry," Violet said.

"We'll talk about it later. I'm just so happy you're safe," he said, his voice cracking with tears. "It's a good thing they liked me in America. We can move there."

"I thought there was something funny about you," came Toby's voice from behind them. Violet turned. Ashton walked alongside Toby, who supported a limping Miriam, and Drew and Fiona were a short ways behind them. Fiona's hair had come completely undone.

"Are you all right?" Violet asked Miriam.

"Fine," Miriam said, nodding. "A sprained ankle, a cut on my cheek, a few bruises. How are you?"

"I'm fine, too," Violet said, looking down at herself.

"I wasn't asking after cuts," Miriam said.

"I'm sorry I lied to all of you," Violet said.

"Eh," Toby said, waving her off. "You're still a mate in my book, right, Drew?"

"Fiona told me she was a woman ages ago," Drew said. "Doesn't matter to me."

"And you didn't tell me?" Toby asked, turning on him.

"She told me not to," Drew said.

"I can't believe it," Toby said. "Not telling me." He crossed his arms and frowned. Drew ran forward to embrace him in apology. Fiona sighed and rolled her eyes behind them.

"Where's Jack?" Violet asked.

"He ran off," Ashton said. "Said he had an errand to run."

"Oh," Violet said.

"There's something you should see," Ashton said, and took his sister's hand. Confused, Violet followed him to a wrecked table on one side of the room. There was a smashed bronze shape on top of it, and below that, a dented plaque that read

A MODEL OF A CRAFT BUILT FOR TRAVELING THE STARS,
PRESENTED BY THE DUKE OF ILLYRIA AND MISS VIOLET ADAMS

Violet gasped, and felt a sob pull its way out of her chest.

"You didn't need to dress as a man to prove anything, it turns out," Ashton said. "You proved it all just by writing to him."

Violet felt herself fall to her knees before the plaque, her brother still holding her hand.

"He must love you, Violet," Ashton said.

"Not anymore," Violet said, trembling. Not anymore. She fell into an ocean of her own tears, and then into darkness.

XLII.

CECILY felt a thousand things welling up inside her. She hated Violet, because she was Ashton, whom she had loved, but who didn't exist. But she had liked Violet so much when they had met. Surely, Cecily thought, she was no sapphist, for when she had thought of Ashton on their wedding night, she had imagined him with generous equipment of the sort he apparently did not possess, and with those loving green eyes looking down on her . . . No, Ashton didn't have green eyes. Who had green eyes? It didn't matter. She felt foolish and betrayed by Ashton—but not by Ashton, by Violet. There was only Violet. And Violet had saved her life. Surely she should be grateful for that.

She rolled over on her bed. She had come straight home by cab and flung herself into her room, her face wet with tears, and now her dress was wrapped around her from her tossing and turning. She had slept and cried and thought and she wasn't even sure what time it was anymore. Probably the next day. The light through her window was bright, but she knew it had been darker at one point, too. Her stomach felt tight and jumpy.

She felt guilty for not being more grateful to Violet, but surely it was understandable. She would write her a nice note, saying, Thank you for saving my life, and please never come near me again. That was the polite thing to do. Cecily sat up and wiped her face, which was sticky and felt disgusting to the touch. She wanted to take a bath. But she would write the note first. She sat down at her little desk and took out paper and quill, when there was a knock at the door.

"Yes?" Cecily called.

"Cecily, dear," said Ada, poking her head in. "Someone just came by and left this for you."

"Left what?" Cecily asked suspiciously. She didn't believe anything good could come to her any longer. Ada opened the door all the way and held out a cage. In it was a small, completely white rabbit, with ears sticking straight up from its head. The cage was golden, and had the name CONSTANCE carved on the bottom of it. "Oh," Cecily said, for the rabbit was wiggling its nose and staring up at her most adorably. "Who brought it?" she asked.

"A young man," Ada said. "A student here. I don't know his name."

Cecily furrowed her brow and knelt down to put the cage on the ground and open it. Constance hopped out and sniffed Cecily's knees. Cecily stroked her ears. Constance looked up at her, and then, as if by magic the room filled with the sound of a hundred birds, all singing sweetly and in perfect harmony. Cecily became lost in the sound of it, of the joy of it, and felt herself floating. She hadn't thought she would be happy ever again, and then, so suddenly, so easily, here it was again, the feeling of joy. It was as if all her cares were washed away by the birdsong. She looked down at the music-making rabbit, and suddenly realized who had sent it.

"Which door did he deliver it to?" Cecily asked, standing up.

"The one that leads to the bridge," Ada said. "Why?"

Cecily had no time to explain. She ran past Ada to the door to the bridge and flung it open. He was walking away, nearly at the end of the bridge, and she chased after him. When she was close enough, she called out his name. He turned around and smiled, his green eyes flashing.

"Jack!"

"Yes, Cecily?"

She grabbed his collar, pulled his mouth toward hers, and kissed him. It was her first kiss, and she felt as though the flower that had once bloomed inside her now exploded. Its petals flew up and everywhere, then floated down softly on the breeze. It was perfect.

"Cecily, marry me?" Jack asked.

Cecily grinned. After all, it had always been Jack. He made her laugh, he spoke to her of how he felt and understood how she felt as well, and she hadn't been able to see it. "No," she said. Jack's face fell. "Not yet, anyway. We haven't had a proper courtship. And besides, you must focus on your studies. I will marry you in two years' time, after you have graduated."

"You'll make me wait that long?"

"Am I not worth it?"

"No one is more worthy!" Jack said, and threw his hands around her waist and lifted her in the air. She shrieked with laughter.

"Come," she said when he had put her down again. She took his hand in hers. "We must go tell Ernest. He is my guardian."

"I don't know if he'll want to see me," Jack said. "After all, I am, or was, Violet's roommate. I was in on her scheme from the beginning."

"I know," Cecily said, "and you tried to keep me from falling in love with her, which was so sweet of you, dear boy. If I can forgive you, surely Ernest can as well. In fact, you should run and get Violet. I wish to apologize to her for my rudeness yesterday. She saved my life, and I was horrible to her."

"I'm sure she understands," Jack said. "She felt terrible for lying to you. She wanted you so badly to be her friend."

"And we will be friends," Cecily said after a moment. She understood why Violet had done what she had, and now that her own heart was no longer broken—was, in fact, feeling stronger and beating more furiously that it ever had—she forgave her. "Is she in the mechanical lab?"

"No," Jack said, "she's gone home. After yesterday, she felt she was no longer welcome here at Illyria. Especially after all she had been through with the duke."

"No longer welcome?" Cecily said, putting a hand on her hip. "Well, I'll see to that. Ernest loves her, and he would be a fool to ignore that, just because of . . . a little trick she played on all of us. Every time he received one of her letters, his face lit up as I had never seen it. He thought I didn't notice, but I did." Cecily smiled slyly. She had been leading Jack by the hand back across the bridge to the residence, but stopped now. "Is she still at her house in town?"

"Yes. She's going back to the country tonight."

"Then we haven't much time. Wait here. I will write her a letter. You must deliver it with all haste and see that she comes to meet me as I request."

"Oh?"

"Wait here," she said, pushing on his chest. It was a strong chest, firm, and she let her hand linger there. "I'll be back in a moment." She turned to go, then turned back again and kissed him briefly on the mouth before running inside. Jack waited with a grin on his face. All his plans had come to fruition, and he knew without a doubt that at that moment he was that happiest man in the world. He couldn't keep still; his happiness was pouring out of him. And so he danced back and forth on the bridge above the Great Hall until Cecily emerged again with a letter for Violet.

"Take it to her quickly," she said, and pressed the letter against his chest. He took it, kissed her, and ran back down the bridge to deliver the note. Cecily stared after him in wonder, and then turned around again to go back inside.

Ada was standing in the doorway, watching. "Feeling better?" she asked.

"Love is complex," Cecily said.

"Yes," Ada said, putting her arm around Cecily's shoulder, "it is." She and Cecily walked back inside.

"I'll need your help ironing out some of those complexities," Cecily said, "for Ernest."

"I'd be glad to."

"You knew the whole time, didn't you?" Cecily asked.

"I did."

"And you didn't say anything?"

"Violet had a point to make, and she made it. You are truly lucky, Cecily, to be a genius, and a woman, but to still be allowed in this place. Violet had to disguise herself as a man to take what your birth gave you. I supported that."

Cecily nodded. "I'm old enough to be a student here next year," Cecily said. "Perhaps I should apply."

"I think you should," Ada said. "I'll gladly write a recommendation for you." Ada went into the sitting room and lit a cigar.

"Where is Ernest?" Cecily asked.

"With the police, I believe. Volio is in prison, but things still needed explaining."

"He'll be back soon, though?"

"I would imagine."

"Good. And where is Miriam?"

"Resting in bed, with her leg up, on my orders. She seems quite put out about it, though. She's not the sort who rests well, it seems. I gave her pen and paper and some books. She was quite involved in *The Woman in White* when I left her. And she's had flowers sent. From one of the students."

"Oh?" said Cecily, raising her eyebrows.

"Yes," Ada said with a knowing look. "Apparently, Volio caught them together and threatened to tell the duke about it if Miriam didn't bring you his letters and make you love him in return—as though she could do that. So she wrote him false letters, and when he found out, he went quite mad. He's been raving about it from his prison cell."

"Oh," Cecily said. "That was my fault. He tried to speak to me and I laughed at him."

"It's not your fault, dear."

"I suppose. But I feel horrid anyway. She wouldn't have been hurt if not for me, if what you say is true."

"Go see her, then. I'm sure she'll forgive you. She's in her room."

Cecily nodded and went to Miriam's room. Miriam was on her bed, with her leg elevated on some pillows, reading.

"Miriam—," Cecily began.

"Did Jack deliver his gift?" Miriam asked.

"Yes," Cecily said, startled.

"And?"

"He asked me to marry him. I said yes, but in two years' time. He must focus on his studies."

"Oh, good," Miriam said. "He is a good young man. And he loves you wildly."

"And," Cecily said, smelling the large bouquet of flowers on the nightstand, "it seems you are loved wildly as well. By a student, Ada says."

"Yes," Miriam said, looking down. "Toby Belch."

"Has he asked you to marry him?"

"No," Miriam said, "and he never will. And if he did, I would say no. He is a baron. I am a dark-skinned Jewess."

"Oh," Cecily said, staring down at the flowers. They were red and in full bloom.

"It's all right," Miriam said. "I'm happy with the way things are. He's offered to buy me a house."

"But you live here."

"Not for much longer. Your cousin will fire me soon—he's been kind to let me come back at all. And besides, you don't need me anymore."

"Ernest won't fire you," Cecily said, aghast. "I won't let him."

Miriam laughed. "Then I shall quit," she said. "I can no longer be your governess, Cecily. You're a woman. You don't need one. I will always be your friend, though. *Une amie pendant la vie.*"

Cecily leaned down and hugged Miriam as tightly as she could, and Miriam squeezed her back.

"Now let me rest," Miriam said, "and read my book. It's very exciting."

Cecily smiled and left. She heard the front door to the residence slam shut downstairs, and Ernest mumbling as he came in. He was in a foul temper. Cecily ran back to Ada, who had gotten up and was heading toward him.

"Auntie Ada," Cecily said, "tell Ernest I wish to see him in the garden, in half an hour's time, and that I am quite upset. Promise?" Ada looked her up and down and nodded, and then walked off. Cecily ran to her room and quietly shut the door. She knew her plan would go smoothly in the end—it had to. She felt so full of love and happiness, and could not imagine a world in which others could not be filled with it, too.

❖

VIOLET read the letter Jack handed her, feeling relieved but sad that it was from Cecily, not the duke. Her father and Ashton were sitting near her, sipping tea.

====

Dearest Violet,

I hope you will excuse my behavior yesterday. I owe you many many thanks for saving my life and I will do all I can to repay you. I admit, I was upset, but I understand now why you had to deceive me, and that you were only trying to be my friend. I asked you once to call me sister, and I hope you still will. Please come and meet me at the garden outside Illyria, so that I may make amends.

Sincerely,
Cecily Worthing.

====

"I should go," Violet said. "I owe her an apology."

"I agree," Ashton said. "After all, lady geniuses such as yourself and Cecily ought to be friends, so as to make the rest of us quake in our boots with fear aroused by your combined potential."

"You should make amends," Mr. Adams said, "for all you've done. But come back here afterwards. We're going home tonight. You need some fresh country air to clear your head."

"Of course," Violet said. She had spent much of the night crying, and her eyes were tired, but by now she had resigned herself to her new life. No more Illyria, no more letters from the duke. Just back to her lab in the basement of their country home. Toby, Drew, Fiona, and Miriam promised they would visit her, so at least she had that. But it was not going to be the same. She stood, and everyone in the room saw how her shoulders had fallen and how she looked as though she had been defeated by a strong blow to the stomach.

"I'll go," she said. She took a silver hat to match her gray dress from the side table and put it on.

Jack walked out with her. "Cecily said she'd marry me," Jack said, "in two years."

Violet smiled. Jack glowed with joy. But it still wasn't enough to overpower her own sorrow. "I'm so happy for you, Jack. And for Cecily, too. I will tell her."

Jack had kept the cab waiting for her. They climbed into it and rode in silence to Illyria. Ashton had reported that the scandal Violet had expected wasn't as bad as anyone had feared. The Queen's forgiveness, and Violet's heroic actions, had retold the story, painting Violet a tragic heroine. She did not feel heroic, though. For the first time in her life, she felt lost. She knew that her gears and springs would never be enough to satisfy her ever again. She would spend the rest of her life empty and alone.

Illyria loomed up in front of them as they got out. Violet had to stop for a moment as she gasped with pain and nearly burst into tears at the thought of never being able to enter it again.

"Go wait in the garden," Jack said. "I need to get back inside." Violet nodded, but kept her eyes focused on Illyria awhile longer before heading into the garden. She looked at all the flowers, which were blooming and radiant. The dahlias in particular were stunning, she noted, and she observed the mathematics of their pattern and how the petals seemed to climb ever higher.

"Oh," said a voice behind her. She turned. It was the duke.

She bowed her head instantly. "Sir, I'm sorry. I know you probably don't want to see me, but Cecily wrote to me and asked me to meet her here, and I came because I wanted to apologize to her." Violet found she was speaking very quickly.

For a few moments, the only sound was of the river and the waterwheel. Violet stared at the ground.

"Volio has been sent to prison for the rest of his life," the duke said.

"That's good," Violet said, staring at her feet. The silence continued.

"I think Cecily arranged this. She asked me to meet her here as well."

Violet looked up at him. He looked tired, and his eyes were wet. "I should apologize to you as well, sir. I . . . I did not think we would become close. I only wanted to show you that you should let women into Illyria."

The duke laughed, a harsh sound. "And you have made your

point," he said. "I have already decided to begin accepting female applicants. Though I doubt any will be as brilliant as you."

Violet did not know what to say to this, so she just looked at him, tears welling up in her eyes.

"Why are you crying?" the duke asked, stepping forward. When he had walked away from her at the faire he had been stunned, but by the time he had reached Illyria he was angry. It had been a public humiliation. He, who supposedly cultivated intelligence in brilliant young minds, hadn't even noticed that one of his students and the woman he was falling in love with were the same person. Was she trying to make him look like a fool? Was that part of her plot—not only to gain entry to Illyria by subterfuge, but to seduce him? Why had she written to him like that? Why had she let him send her that ridiculous flower he had put so much work into? Did she write back to him just so he wouldn't notice she stood beside him in the classroom, at the river? Were the affections he thought he saw in her letters native to his own mind, or put there as part of her overall scheme? Didn't this vast lie just indicate a thousand more, tiny, supporting lies?

There was a lot to deal with those next few days, in the wake of Volio's madness. He spoke to the police, the students. And in the meantime, Violet had never returned to Illyria, he noted with a strange mix of feelings that made it impossible to eat. He put her out of his mind. He didn't speak of her. He couldn't stand to be around Cecily, seeing her cry over the same person Ernest himself wanted to cry over. Why had Violet done this to him, his family, his school?

And why couldn't he stop thinking about her? Whenever there was a lull, when he rode in a carriage or made himself eat something alone in his lab, she crept into his thoughts. He knew it was his father's damned foolish policy that had made her do it, but he planned to change it next year, anyway. Couldn't she have waited until then?

He would never see her again, he'd decided. He would put her, and all ideas of love, out of his mind forever, because it could not be worth going through all the betrayal, the feeling like a fool, ever again.

And because there would never be a more perfect woman.

But then, seeing her in the garden again, crying, he felt all his resolve melt. He loved her so completely, he suddenly couldn't help but forgive her her deceptions, forgive her her tricks. She had broken his heart, and he could forgive her that, too. He knew who she was, why she had enacted her scheme. She had been honest in every letter, had been honest when she spoke to him as Ashton, or as honest as she could be. He knew he loved her, still; knew the instant he saw her. It suddenly all made sense to him: his kiss with Ashton, who was really Violet; those moments they spent together on the river. Somehow knowing it was Violet made him love her even more.

"I wish we had met under different circumstances," Violet said. "Then we could be happy now."

"We?" the duke asked.

"I cannot expect you to love me, after what I have done," Violet said, "but your letters, even being with you when I was Ashton . . . they were my happiest moments. I fear, sir, that I am still in love with you."

"Oh, Violet," he said, stepping forward. She stepped back, her head down.

"But I know I have deceived you horribly."

"I don't care," the duke interrupted. "I admire you more for it. I was . . . unsettled by your revelation, and I admit I felt deceived, and hurt, and foolish for hours afterward. But I also could see why you did it. A mind such as yours . . . You deserve the best the world can offer you. Illyria is the best. Had I been you, I would have done whatever I could to get into Illyria as well. Nothing else would have satisfied me." He paused. "So, I forgave, I think. I do forgive you."

Violet looked up, smiling. Tears were pouring down her face. Ernest could stand it no longer. He took her and pressed his lips to hers. She kissed him back, their bodies fitting together like two parts of an engine. Ernest didn't care about her lies, her deception. He cared about only one thing: He loved her. They parted, and Violet looked up at him through long wet lashes.

"Ernest," she said, and his heart spun to hear her say his name.

"Will you marry me, Violet Adams?" he asked.

"Oh yes," she said. "Yes, Ernest." And they kissed again, while Cecily and Jack, who had been watching from the bushes, applauded.

XLIII.

THE wedding of Ernest, Duke of Illyria, and the noted lady scientist, Violet Adams, who had herself obtained a little fame and a little infamy at that year's Science Faire, was a grand spectacle. They chose not to be married in church, but in Illyria itself, with the Great Hall decorated and filled with chairs for the guests. Banners hung from the great gears on the wall in such a way that they rotated in time, so they kept flapping in the wind, giving the feeling that the wedding was taking place outside, and that a hundred white flags were waving in its honor.

The bride wore a long gown of white silk, and was accompanied by her matron of honor, Miriam Isaacs, who carried the train for her. Both her father and her brother escorted her down the aisle to give her away, and in the front row, the family's servant, Mrs. Wilks, could be seen blowing her nose most furiously, and crying. Violet's veil was long, but as transparent as possible, as she had felt that being veiled was not something she wanted to do much more of in her life.

The groom was done up in his ducal finery. In a most unorthodox move, he had chosen his lady cousin and ward, Cecily Worthing, to be his best man and ring bearer. She wore dark blue, and could be seen throwing glances to one of the groomsmen, Mr. Jack Feste, who would wink at her in return.

The ceremony was officiated by a great clergyman of some renown, who isn't particularly important to this story, and a powerful speech was given by the groom's godmother, Ada Byron, who toasted the wedding of love and science. In the crowd could be seen all the students and professors of Illyria, applauding the happy match.

Afterwards, the party, which was far too large for the garden, retired there anyway. Champagne was served and rice thrown as the now husband and wife clasped each other's hands in the breeze, surrounded by those they loved, and by those who loved them.

"I believe," Ada Byron said to Ernest, "that I have won my bet."

"Indeed you have," Ernest said with a laugh. "So you may choose a student for next year."

"Well, then, I choose Violet, Duchess of Illyria." Ada said, "You must promise to keep her in school, despite your nuptials."

Ernest laughed again. "No, dear Godmother, you cannot choose Violet, for I have already insisted on her continuing at Illyria next year. I would never dream of denying my school her brilliance," he said, and kissed her on the cheek. Violet laughed.

"Then I'll have to find someone else," Ada said, sipping her champagne. "And you, Violet? Do you plan to remain true to science and stay a student of Illyria?"

"Dear Godmother," Violet said with a smile, "I keep science for life. And now, I shall keep Ernest, too." Violet closed her hand tight around the duke's, their fingers interwoven like perfectly fitted gears.

They all raised their glasses in a toast to keeping earnest, and their laughter carried like song on the wind, overpowering even the noise from the gears of Illyria.

Special Thanks

ALTHOUGH it should be clear by now that I am talented and beautiful, I also endeavor to surround myself with talented, beautiful people. Without them, this book would not be what it is today, and I would most certainly be a puddle of crazy-beautiful-talent, oozing on the hardwood floors. These people are all amazing and they deserve as many thanks as I can give them, which alas, are limited to two pages:

My family, and in particular my parents, who have supported me above and beyond the call of any parents throughout this whole "I'm going to be a writer" fantasy. My mother has probably read more drafts of this book than I have, correcting and commenting late into the night.

And my agent, Joy, who is family as well at this point. No one fights harder with me, and no one fights harder for me, whether I made the changes or not. She is my paladin. No one looks out for me like she does.

My editor, Liz, who not only made my sentences clear and readable, but helped me craft the best version of the book I wanted, and didn't give up even when the Technical Difficulties began.

Leslie, not just for being amazing, but also for her feedback, and also for explaining to me, very slowly, every minute detail of the business and helping me through more than one crazy moment.

Robin, Paula, Laura, Holly, and Stella, who have pored over this manuscript countless times and given me constant feedback, support, and humor, not just in regards to writing this book, but in regards to writing in general.

Cassie, for all the amazing work getting my book out there, and also showing me how to dress.

Sam, Alexis, and Logan, not just for their excellent feedback, but for explaining how science works, and how I can best defeat it.

Jackie, Rebecca, Aire, Mary, Rora, Christina, Angela, and Barry, for their invaluable and brilliant feedback, finessing, and advice.

Barry and Desiree, for making me look way better than I do in real life, and Elyn and Macie, for the support and encouragement.

Dan, for doing what everyone above has done, and also telling me I should maybe, possibly be a writer to begin with (no taking it back now).

Larabell, Antonella, Allie, and everyone at David Black, for all the hard work they've put into this, and how universally awesome and funny they all are.

Bridget, Aubrey, Irene, Patti, Miriam, and everyone at Tor, for being so warm, welcoming, and dedicated.

Max, for being my go-to Latin Scholar, and for letting me flirt quite outrageously with him.

And Chris, for just being Chris.